It didn't matter that the hamburger joint was littered with uniformed police officers. Mia knew it was him the moment he walked in the door.

Officer Collin Grace sure stood out in a crowd. Brown eyes full of caution swept the room once, as if calculating escape routes, before coming to rest on her. She prided herself on being able to read people. Officer Collin Grace didn't trust a soul in the place.

Mia fixed her attention on the policeman. With spiked dark hair, slashing eyebrows and a five-o'clock shadow, he was good-looking in a hard, manly kind of way.

He came over and jacked up an eyebrow. "Miss Carano?"

A bewildering flutter tickled her stomach. "Yes, but I prefer Mia."

He slid into the booth and didn't ask her to use his given name. She wasn't surprised. He was every bit the cool, detached cop. This wasn't going to be easy.

Linda Goodnight, a *New York Times* bestselling author and winner of a RITA® Award in inspirational fiction, has appeared on the Christian bestseller list. Her novels have been translated into more than a dozen languages. Active in orphan ministry, Linda enjoys writing fiction that carries a message of hope in a sometimes dark world. She and her husband live in Oklahoma. Visit her website, lindagoodnight.com, for more information.

Margaret Daley, an award-winning author of ninety books (five million sold worldwide), has been married for over forty years and is a firm believer in romance and love. When she isn't traveling, she's writing love stories, often with a suspense thread, and corralling her three cats, who think they rule her household. To find out more about Margaret, visit her website at margaretdaley.com.

A Wish for the Season

New York Times Bestselling Author

Linda Goodnight

&

USA TODAY Bestselling Author

Margaret Daley

2 Uplifting Stories

A Season for Grace and *Heart of the Family*

LOVE INSPIRED
INSPIRATIONAL ROMANCE

LOVE INSPIRED®

INSPIRATIONAL ROMANCE

Recycling programs
for this product may
not exist in your area.

ISBN-13: 978-1-335-42996-4

A Wish for the Season

Copyright © 2022 by Harlequin Enterprises ULC

A Season for Grace
First published in 2006. This edition published in 2022.
Copyright © 2006 by Linda Goodnight

Heart of the Family
First published in 2007. This edition published in 2022.
Copyright © 2007 by Margaret Daley

For questions and comments about the quality of this book, please contact us at CustomerService@Harlequin.com.

Love Inspired
22 Adelaide St. West, 41st Floor
Toronto, Ontario M5H 4E3, Canada
www.LoveInspired.com

Printed in U.S.A.

CONTENTS

A SEASON FOR GRACE

Linda Goodnight

Special thanks to former DHS caseworker Tammy Potter for answering my social services questions, and to my buddy Maggie Price for helping me keep my cop in the realm of reality. Any mistakes or literary license are my own. I would also like to acknowledge the legion of foster and adoptive parents and children who have shared their insight into the painful world of social orphans.

A father to the fatherless, defender of widows,
is God in his holy dwelling.
God sets the lonely in families.
—*Psalms* 68:5–6

Prologue

The worst was happening again. And there was nothing he could do about it.

Collin Grace was only ten years old but he'd seen it all and then some. One thing he'd seen too much of was social workers. He hated them. The sweet-talking women with their briefcases and straight skirts and fancy fingernails. They always meant trouble.

Arms stiff, he stood in front of the school counselor's desk and stared at the office wall. His insides shook so hard he thought he might puke. But he wouldn't ask to be excused. No way he'd let them know how scared he was. Wouldn't do no good anyhow.

Betrayal, painful as a stick in the eye, settled low in his belly. He had thought Mr. James liked him, but the counselor had called the social worker.

Didn't matter. Collin wasn't going to cry. Not like his brother Drew. Stupid kid was fighting and kicking and screaming like he could stop what was happening.

"Now, Drew." The social worker tried to soothe the wild brother. Tried to brush his too-long, dark hair out of his furious blue eyes. Drew snarled like a wounded wolf. "Settle down. Everything will be all right."

That was a lie. And all three of the brothers knew it. Nothing was ever all right. They'd leave this school and go into foster care again. New people to live with, new school, new town, all of them strange and unfriendly. They'd be cleaned up and fattened up, but after a few months Mama would get them back. Then they'd be living under bridges or with some drugged-out old guy who liked to party with Mama. Then she'd disappear. Collin would take charge. Things would be better for a while. The whole mess would start all over again.

People should just leave them alone. He could take care of his brothers.

Drew howled again and slammed his seven-year-old fist into the social worker. "I hate you. Leave me alone!"

He broke for the door.

Collin bit the inside of his lip. Drew hadn't figured out yet that he couldn't escape.

A ruckus broke out. The athletic counselor grabbed Drew and held him down in a chair even though he bucked and spat and growled like a mad tomcat. Drew was a wiry little twerp; Collin gave him credit for that. And he had guts. For what good it would do him, he might as well save his energy. Grown-ups would win. They always did.

People passed the partially open office door and peered around the edge, curious about all the commotion. Collin tried to pretend he couldn't see them, couldn't hear them. But he could.

"Poor little things," one of the teachers murmured. "Living in a burned-out trailer all by themselves. No wonder they're filthy."

Collin swallowed the cry of humiliation rising up in his stomach like the bad oranges he'd eaten from the convenience-store trash. He did the best he could to keep Drew and Ian clean and fed. It wasn't easy without water or electricity. He'd tried washing them off in the restroom before school, but he guessed he hadn't done too good a job.

"Collin." The fancy-looking social worker had a hand on her stomach where Drew had punched her. "You've been through this before. You know it's for the best. Why don't you help me get your brothers in the car?"

Collin didn't look at her. Instead he focused on his brothers, sick that he couldn't help them. Sick with dread. Who knew what would happen this time? Somehow he had to find a way to keep them all together. That was the important thing. Together, they could survive.

Ian, only four, looked so little sitting in a big brown plastic chair against the wall. His scrawny legs stuck straight out and the oversize tennis shoes threatened to fall off. No shoestrings. They stunk, too. Collin could smell them clean over here.

Like Collin, baby Ian didn't say a word; he didn't fight. He just cried. Silent, broken tears streamed down his cheeks and left tracks like a bicycle through mud. Clad in a plaid flannel shirt with only two buttons and a pair of Drew's tattered jeans pulled together at the belt loops with a piece of electrical cord, his skinny body trembled. Collin could hardly stand that.

They shouldn't have come to school today; then none of this would have happened. But they were hungry and he was fresh out of places to look. School lunch was free, all you could eat.

Seething against an injustice he couldn't name or defend against, he crossed the room to his brother. He didn't say a word; just put his hand on Ian's head. The little one, quivering like a scared puppy, relaxed the tiniest bit. He looked up, eyes saying he trusted his big brother to take care of everything the way he always did.

Collin hoped he could.

The social worker knelt in front of Ian and took his hand. "I know you're scared, honey, but you're going to be fine. You'll have plenty to eat and a nice, safe place to sleep." She tapped his tennis shoes. "And a new pair of shoes, just your size. Things will be better, I promise."

Ian sniffed and dragged a buttonless sleeve across his nose. When he looked at her, he had hope in his eyes. Poor little kid.

Collin ignored the hype. He'd heard it all before and it was a lie. Things were never better. Different, but not better.

The tall counselor, still holding Drew in the chair, slid to his knees just like the social worker and said, "Boys, sometimes life throws us a curveball. But no matter what happens, I want you to remember one thing. Jesus cares about you. If you let him, He'll take care of you. No matter where you go from here, God will never walk off and leave you."

A funny thing happened then. Drew sort of quieted down and looked as if he was listening. Ian was still sniffin' and snubbin', but watching Mr. James, too. None of them could imagine *anybody* who wouldn't leave them at some point.

"Collin?" The counselor, who Collin used to like a lot, twisted around and stretched an open palm toward him. Collin wanted to take hold. But he couldn't.

After a minute, Mr. James dropped his hand, laid it on Collin's shoe. Something about that big, strong hand on his old tennis shoe bothered Collin. He didn't know if he liked it or hated it.

The room got real quiet then. Too quiet. Mr. James bowed his bald head and whispered something. A prayer, Collin thought, though he didn't know much about such things. He stared at the wall, trying hard not to listen. He didn't dare hope, but the counselor's words made him want to.

Then Mr. James reached into his pocket. Drew and Ian watched him, silent. Collin watched his brothers.

"I want you to have one of these," the counselor said as he placed something in each of the younger boys' hands. It looked like a fish on a tiny chain. "It's a reminder of what I said, that God will watch over you."

Collin's curiosity made his palm itch to reach out, but he didn't. Instead, Mr. James had to pry his fingers apart and slide the fish-shaped piece of metal into the hollow of his hand.

Much as he wanted to, Collin refused to look at it. Better to cut to the chase and quit all this hype. "Where are we going this time?"

His stupid voice shook. He clenched his fists to still the trembling. The metal fish, warm from Mr. James's skin, bit into his flesh.

The pretty social worker looked up, startled that he'd spoken. Collin wondered if she could see the fury, red and hot, that pushed against the back of his eyes.

"We already have foster placements for Drew and Ian."

But not for him. The anger turned to fear. "Together?"

As long as they were together, they'd be okay.

"No. I'm sorry. Not this time."

He knew what she meant. He knew the system probably better than she did. Only certain people would take boys like Drew who expressed their anger. And nobody would take him. He was too old. People liked little and cute like Ian, not fighters, not runaways, not big boys with an attitude.

Panic shot through him, made his heart pound wildly. "They have to stay with me. Ian gets scared."

The social worker rose and touched his shoulder. "He'll be fine, Collin."

Collin shrugged away to glare at the brown paneled wall behind the counselor's desk. Helpless fury seethed inside him.

The worst had finally happened.

He and Drew and Ian were about to be separated.

Chapter One

Twenty-three years later, Oklahoma City

Sweat burned his eyes, but Collin Grace didn't move. He couldn't. One wrong flinch and somebody died.

Totally focused on the life-and-death scenario playing out on the ground below, he hardly noticed the sun scalding the back of his neck or the sweat soaking through his protective vest.

The Tac-team leader's voice came through the earphone inside his Fritz helmet. "Hostage freed. Suspect in custody. Get down here for debrief."

Collin relaxed and lowered the .308 caliber marksman rifle, a SWAT sniper's best friend, and rose from his prone position on top of the River Street Savings and Loan. Below him, the rest of the team exited a training house and headed toward Sergeant Gerrara.

Frequent training was essential and Collin welcomed every drill. Theirs wasn't a full-time SWAT unit, so they had to stay sharp for those times when the callout would come and they'd have to act. Normally a patrol cop, he'd spent all morning on the firing range, requalifying with every weapon known to mankind. He was good. Real good, with the steadiest hands anyone on the force had ever seen. A fact that made him proud.

"You headed for the gym after this?" His buddy, fellow police officer and teammate Maurice Johnson shared his propensity for exercise. Stay in shape, stay alive. Most special tactics cops agreed.

Collin peeled his helmet off and swiped a hand over his sweating brow. "Yeah. You?"

"For a few reps. I told Shanita I'd be home early. Bible study at our place tonight." Maurice sliced a sneaky grin in Collin's direction. Sweat dripped from his high ebony cheeks and rolled down a neck the size of a linebacker's. "Wanna come?"

Collin returned the grin with a shake of his head. Maurice wouldn't give up. He extended the same invitation every Thursday.

Collin liked Maurice and his family, but he couldn't see a loner like himself spouting Bible verses and singing in a choir. It puzzled him, too, that a cop as tough and smart as Maurice would feel the need for God. To Collin's way of thinking there was only one person he trusted enough to lean on. And that was himself.

"Phone call for you, Grace," Sergeant Gerrara hollered. "Probably some cutie after your money."

The other cops hooted as Collin shot Maurice an exasperated look and took off in a trot. He received plenty of teasing about his single status. Some of the guys tried to fix him up, but when a woman started pushing him or trying to get inside his head, she was history. He didn't need the grief.

The heavy tactics gear rattled and bounced against

his body as he grabbed the cell phone from Sergeant Gerrara's oversize fist, trading it for his rifle.

"Grace."

"Sergeant Collin Grace?" A feminine voice, light and sweet, hummed against his ear.

"Yeah." He shoved his helmet under one arm and stepped away from the gaggle of cops who listened in unabashedly. "Who's this?"

"Mia Carano. I'm with the Cleveland County Department of Child Welfare."

A cord of tension stretched through Collin's chest. Adrenaline, just now receding from the training scenario, ratcheted up a notch. Child welfare, a department he both loathed and longed to hear from. Could it finally be news?

He struggled to keep his voice cool and detached. "Is this about my brothers?"

"Your brothers?"

Envisioning her puzzled frown, Collin realized she had no idea he'd spent years trying to find Ian and Drew. The spurt of energy drained out of him. "Never mind. What can I do for you, Ms. Carano?"

"Do you recall the young boy you picked up last week behind the pawn shop?"

"The runaway?" He could still picture the kid. "Angry, scared, but too proud to admit it?"

"Yes. Mitchell Perez. He's eleven. Going on thirty."

The kid hadn't looked a day over nine. Skinny. Black hair too long and hanging in his eyes. A pack of cigarettes crushed and crammed down in his jeans' pocket. He'd reminded Collin too much of Drew.

"You still got him? Or did he go home?"

"Home for now, but he's giving his mother fits."

From what the kid had told him, she deserved fits. "He'll run again."

"I know. That's why I'm calling you."

Around him the debrief was breaking up. He lifted a hand to the departing team.

"Nothing I can do until he runs."

He leaned an elbow against somebody's black pickup truck and watched cars pull up to a stop sign adjacent to the parking lot. Across the street, shoppers came and went in a strip mall. Normal, common occurrences in the city on a peaceful, sunny afternoon. Ever alert, he filed them away, only half listening to the caller.

"This isn't my first encounter with Mitch. He's a troubled boy, but his mother said you impressed him. He talks about you. Wants to be a cop."

Collin felt a con coming on. Social workers were good at that. He stayed quiet, let her ramble on in that sugary voice.

"He has no father. No male role model."

Big surprise. He switched the phone to the other ear.

"I thought you might be willing to spend some time with the boy. Perhaps through CAPS, our child advocate program. It's sort of like Big Brothers only through the court system."

He was already a big brother and he'd done a sorry job of that. Some of the other officers did that sort of outreach, but not him.

"I don't think so."

"At least give me a chance to talk with you about it. I have some other ideas if CAPS doesn't appeal."

He was sure she did. Her type always had ideas. "This isn't my kind of thing. Call the precinct. They might know somebody."

"Tell you what," she said as if he hadn't just turned her down. "Meet me at Chick's Place in fifteen minutes. I'll buy you a cup of coffee."

She didn't give up easy. She even knew the cops' favorite hamburger joint.

He didn't know why, but he said, "Make it forty-five minutes and a hamburger, onions fried."

She laughed and the sound was light, musical. He liked it. It was her occupation that turned him off.

"I'll even throw in some cheese fries," she added.

"Be still my heart." He couldn't believe he'd said that. Regardless of her sweet voice, he didn't know this woman and didn't particularly want to.

"I'll sit in the first booth so you'll recognize me."

"What if it's occupied?"

"I'll buy them a burger, too." She laughed again. The sound ran over him like fresh summer rain. "See you in forty-five minutes."

The phone went dead and Collin stared down at it, puzzled that a woman—a social worker, no less—had conned him into meeting her for what was, no doubt, even more of a con.

Well, he had news for Mia Carano with the sweet voice. Collin Grace didn't con easy. Regardless of what she wanted, the answer was already no.

Mia recognized him the minute he walked in the door. No matter that the hamburger café was littered with uniformed police officers hunched over burgers or mega-size soft drinks. Collin Grace stood out in a crowd. Brown eyes full of caution swept the room once, as if calculating escape routes, before coming to rest on her. She prided herself on being able to read people. Sergeant Grace didn't trust a soul in the place.

"There he is," the middle-aged officer across from her said, nodding toward the entrance. "That's Amazin' Grace."

Mia fixed her attention on the lean, buff policeman coming her way. With spiked dark hair, slashing eyebrows and a permanent five o'clock shadow, he was good-looking in a hard, manly kind of way. His fatigue pants and fitted brown T-shirt with a Tac-team emblem over the heart looked fresh and clean as though he'd recently changed.

Officer Jess Snow pushed out of the booth he'd kindly allowed her to share. In exchange, he had regaled her with stories about the force, his grandkids, and his plan to retire next year. He'd also told her that the other policemen referred to the officer coming her way as Amazin' Grace because of his uncanny cool and precision even under the most intense conditions. "Guess I'll get moving. Sure was nice talking to you."

She smiled up at the older man. "You, too, Jess."

Officer Snow gave her a wink and nodded to the newcomer as he left.

Collin returned a short, curt nod and then jacked an eyebrow at Mia. "Miss Carano?"

A bewildering flutter tickled her stomach. "Yes, but I prefer Mia."

As he slid into the booth across from her the equipment attached to his belt rattled and a faint stir of some warm, tangy aftershave pierced the scent of frying onions. She noted that he did not return the courtesy by asking her to use his given name.

She wasn't surprised. He was every bit the cool, de-

tached cop. Years of looking at the negative side of
life did that to some social workers, as well. Mia was
thankful she had the Lord and a very supportive family
to pour out all her frustrations and sadness upon. Her
work was her calling. She was right where God could
best use her, and she'd long ago made up her mind not
to let the dark side of life burn her out.

Sergeant Grace, on the other hand, might as well be
draped in strips of yellow police tape that screamed,
Caution: Restricted Area. Getting through his invisible
shield wouldn't be as easy as she'd hoped.

He propped his forearms on the tabletop like a barrier between them. His left T-shirt sleeve slid upward
to reveal the bottom curve of a tattoo emblazoned with
a set of initials she couldn't quite make out.

Though she didn't move or change expressions, a
part of her shrank back from him. She'd never understood a man's propensity to mutilate his arms with dye
and needles.

"So," he said, voice deep and smooth. "What can I
do for you, Mia?"

"Don't you want your hamburger first?"

The tight line of his mouth mocked her. "A spoonful of sugar doesn't really make the medicine go down
any easier."

So cynical. And he couldn't be that much older than
she was. Early thirties maybe. "You might actually
enjoy what I have in mind."

"I doubt it." He raised a hand to signal the waitress.
"What would you like?" he asked.

She motioned to her Coke. "This is fine. I'm not
hungry."

He studied her for a second before turning his attention to the waitress. "Bring me a Super Burger. Fry the onions, hold the tomatoes, and add a big order of cheese fries and a Mountain Dew."

The waitress poised with pen over pad and said in a droll voice, "What's the occasion? Shoot somebody today?"

One side of the policeman's mouth softened. He didn't smile, but he was close. "Only a smart-mouthed waitress. Nobody will miss her."

The waitress chuckled and said to Mia, "I never thought I'd see the day grease would cross his lips."

She sauntered away, hollering the order to a guy in the back.

"I thought all cops were junk-food junkies."

"It's the hours. Guys don't always have time to eat right."

"But you do?"

"Sometimes."

If he was a health food nut he wasn't going to talk to her about it. Curious the way he avoided small talk. Was he this way with everyone? Or just her?

Maybe it was her propensity for nosiness. Maybe it was her talkative Italian heritage. But Mia couldn't resist pushing a little to see what he would do. "So what *do* you eat? Bean sprouts and yogurt?"

"Is that why you're here? To talk about my diet?"

So cold. So empty. Had she made a mistake in thinking this ice man might help a troubled boy?

On the other hand, Grandma Carano said still waters run deep. Gran had been talking about Uncle Vitorio, the only quiet Carano in the giant, noisy family, and she'd been right. Uncle Vitorio was a thinker, an inventor. Granted he mostly invented useless gadgets to amuse himself, but the family considered him brilliant and deep.

Perhaps Collin was the same. Or maybe he just needed some encouragement to loosen up.

She pushed her Coke to one side and got down to business.

"For some reason, Mitchell Perez has developed a heavy case of hero worship for you."

The boy was one of those difficult cases who didn't respond well to any of the case workers, the counselors or anybody else for that matter, but something inside Mia wouldn't give up. Last night, when she'd prayed for the boy, this idea to contact Collin Grace had come into her mind. She'd believed it was God-sent, but now she wondered.

"More and more in the social system we're seeing boys like Mitchell who don't have a clue how to become responsible, caring men. They need real men to teach them and to believe in them. Men they can relate to and admire."

The waitress slid a soda and a paper-covered straw in front of Sergeant Grace.

"How do you know I'm that kind of man?"

"I checked you out."

He tilted his head. "Just because I'm a good cop doesn't mean I'd be a suitable role model to some street kid."

"I'm normally a good judge of character and I think you would be. The thing here is need. We have so many needy kids, and few men willing to spend a few hours a week to make a difference. Don't you see, Officer? In the long run, your job will be easier if someone intercedes on behalf of these kids now. Maybe they won't end up in trouble later on down the road."

"And maybe they will."

Frustration made her want to pound the table. "You know the statistics. Mentored kids are less likely to get into drugs and crime. They're more likely to go to college. More likely to hold jobs and be responsible citizens. Don't you get it, Officer? A few hours a week of your time can change a boy's life."

He pointed his straw at her. "You haven't been at this long, have you?"

She blinked, leaned back in the booth and tried to calm down. "Seven years."

"Longer than I thought."

"Why? Because I care? Because I'm not burned out?"

"It happens." The shrug in his voice annoyed her.

"Is that what's happened to you?"

A pained look came and went on his face, but he kept silent—again.

Mia leaned forward, her passionate Italian nature taking control. "Look, this may not make any sense to you. Or it may sound idealistic, but I believe what I do makes a difference in these kids' lives."

"Maybe they don't want you to make a difference. Maybe they want to be left alone."

"Left alone? To be abused?"

"Not all of them are mistreated."

"Or neglected. Or cold and hungry, eating out of garbage cans."

Collin's face closed up tighter than a miser's fist. Had the man no compassion?

"There are a lot of troubled kids out there. Why are you so focused on this particular one?"

"I'm concerned about all of them."

"But?"

So he'd heard the hesitation.

"There's something special about Mitch." Something about the boy pulled at her, kept her going back to check on him. Kept her trying. "He wants to make it, but he doesn't know how."

Collin's expression shifted ever so slightly. The change was subtle, but Mia felt him softening. His eyes flicked sideways and, as if glad for the interruption, he said, "Food's coming."

The waitress slid the steaming burger and fries onto the table. "There you go. A year's worth of fat and cholesterol."

"No wonder Chick keeps you around, Millie. You're such a great salesman."

"Saleslady, thank you."

He took a giant bite of the burger and sighed. "Perfect. Just like you."

Millie rolled her eyes and moved on. Collin turned his attention back to Mia. "You were saying?"

"Were you even listening?"

"To every word. The kid is special. Why?"

Mia experienced a twinge of pleasure. Collin Grace confused her, but there was something about him…

"Beneath Mitch's hard layer is a gentleness. A sweet little boy who doesn't know who to trust or where to turn."

"Imagine that. The world screws him over from birth and he stops trusting it. What a concept."

The man was cool to the point of frostbite and had a

shell harder than any of the street kids she dealt with. If she could crack this tough nut perhaps other cops would follow suit. She was already pursuing the idea of mentor groups through her church, but cops-as-mentors could make an impact like no other.

She took a big sip of Coke and then said, "At least talk to Mitch."

The pager at Collin's waist went off. He slipped the device from his belt, glanced at the display, and pushed out of the booth, leaving a half-eaten burger and a nearly full basket of cheese fries.

Mia looked up at the tall and dark and distant cop. "Is that your job?"

He nodded curtly. "Gotta go. Thanks for the dinner."

"Could I call you about this later?"

"No point. The answer will still be no." He whipped around with the precision of a marine and strode out of the café before Mia could argue further.

Disappointment curled in her belly. When she could close her surprised mouth, she did so with a huff.

The basket of leftover fries beckoned. She crammed a handful in her mouth. No use wasting perfectly good cheese fries. Even if they did end up on her hips.

Sergeant Collin Grace may have said no, but no didn't always mean absolutely no.

And Mia wasn't quite ready to give up on Mitchell Perez…or Collin Grace.

Chapter Two

"Hey, Grace, you spending the night here or something?"

Eyes glued to the computer screen, Collin lifted a finger to silence the other cop. "Gotta check one more thing."

His shift was long over, and the sun drifted toward the west, but at least once a week he checked and re-checked, just in case he'd missed something the other five thousand times he'd searched.

Somewhere out there he had two brothers, and with the explosion of information on the internet he would find them—eventually. After all this time, though, he wasn't expecting a miracle.

His cell phone played the University of Oklahoma fight song and he glanced down at the caller ID. Her again. Mia Carano. She'd left no less than ten messages over the past three days. He hadn't bothered to return her phone calls. Eventually she'd get the message.

The rollicking strains of "Boomer Sooner" faded away as his voice mail picked up. Collin kept his attention on the computer screen.

Over the years, he'd amassed quite a list of names and addresses. One by one, he'd checked them out and moved them to an inactive file. He typed several more names into the file on his computer and hit Save.

The welfare office suggested he should hire a private search agency, but Collin never planned to do that. The idea of letting someone else poke into his troubled background made him nervous. He'd done a good job of leaving that life behind and didn't want the bones of his childhood dug up by some stranger.

Part of the frustration in this search, though, lay with his own limited memory. Given what he knew of his mother, he wasn't even sure he and his brothers shared a last name. And even if they once had, either or both could have been changed through adoption.

Maurice Johnson, staying late to finish a report, bent over Collin's desk. "Any luck?"

He kept his voice low, and Collin appreciated his discretion. It was one of the reasons he'd confided in his coworker and friend about the missing brothers. It was also one of the reasons the man was one of his few close friends. Maurice knew how to keep his mouth shut.

"Same old thing. I added a few more men with the last names of Grace and Stotz, my mother's maiden name, to the list, but I'm convinced the boys were moved out of Oklahoma after we were separated."

Their home state had been a dead end from the get-go.

"Any luck in the Texas system?"

"Not yet. But it's huge. Finding the names is easy. Matching ages and plundering records isn't quite as simple."

"Even for a cop."

A lot of the old files were not even computerized

yet. And even if he could find them, there were plenty of records he couldn't access.

"Yeah. If only most adoption records weren't sealed. Or there was a centralized listing of some sort."

"Twenty years ago record-keeping wasn't the art it is today."

"Tell me about it."

He'd stuck his name and information on a number of legit sibling searches. He'd even placed a letter in his old welfare file in case one of the boys was also searching.

Apparently, his brothers weren't all that eager to make contact. Either that or something had happened to them. His gut clenched. Better not travel that line of thinking.

"Did you ever consider that you might have other family out there? A grandma, an aunt. Somebody."

He shook his head. "Hard as I've tried, I don't remember anyone. If we ever had any family, Mama had long since alienated them."

He'd had stepdads and "uncles" aplenty. He even remembered Ian's dad as a pretty good guy, but the only name he'd ever called the man was Rob.

A few years back he'd tracked his mother down in Seminole County—in jail for public intoxication. His lips twisted at the memory. She'd been too toasted to give false information and for once one of her real names, anyway a name Collin remembered, appeared on the police bulletin.

Their subsequent visit had not been a joyous reunion of mother and son. And, to his great disappointment, she knew less about his brothers' whereabouts than he did.

After that, she had disappeared off the radar screen again. Probably moved in with her latest party man and changed her name for the tenth or hundredth time. Not that Collin cared. It was his brothers he wanted to find. Karen Stotz-Grace-Whatever had given them birth, but if she'd ever been a mother he didn't remember it.

"Do you think they're together?"

"Ian and Drew? No." He remembered that last day too clearly. "They were headed to different foster homes. Chances are they weren't reunited, either."

His mother hadn't bothered to jump through the welfare hoops anymore after that. She'd let the state have custody of all three of them. Collin, who ended up in a group home, had failed in his promise to take care of his brothers. He hoped they had been adopted. He hoped they'd found decent, loving families to give them what he hadn't been able to. Even though they were grown men, he needed to know if they were all right.

And if they weren't…

He got that heavy, sick feeling in the pit of his stomach and logged out of the search engine.

Leaning back in the office chair, he scraped a hand over his face and said, "Think I'll call it a night."

Maurice clapped him on the shoulder. "Come by the house. Shanita will make you a fruit smoothie, and Thomas will harangue you for a game of catch."

"Thanks. But I can't. Gotta get out to the farm." He rose to his feet, stretching to relieve the ache across his midback. "The vet's coming by to check that new pup."

"How's he doing?" The other cops were suckers for animals just as he was. They just didn't take their concern quite as far.

"Still in the danger zone." Fury sizzled his blood every time he thought of the abused pup. "Even after what happened, he likes people."

"Animals are very forgiving," Maurice said.

Collin pushed the glass door open with one hand, holding it for his friend to pass through. Together they left the station and walked through the soft evening breeze to the parking garage.

"Unlike me. If I find out who tied that little fella's legs with wire and left him to die, I'll be tempted to return the favor."

Another police officer had found the collie mix, but not before one foot was amputated and another badly infected. And yet, the animal craved human attention and affection.

They entered the parking garage, footsteps echoing on the concrete, the shady interior cool and welcome. Exhaust fumes hovered in the dimness like smelly ghosts.

Maurice dug in his pocket, keys rattling. "Did your social worker call again today?"

Collin slowed, eyes narrowing. "How did you know?"

His buddy lifted a shoulder. "She has friends in high places."

Great. "The department can't force me to do something like that."

"You take in wounded animals. Why not wounded kids?"

"Not my thing."

"Because it hits too close to home?"

Collin stopped next to his Bronco, pushed the lock release, and listened for the snick.

"I don't need reminders." Enough memories plagued him without that. "You like kids. You do it."

"Someday you're going to have to forgive the past,

Collin. Lay it to rest. I know Someone who can help you with that."

Collin recognized the subtle reference to God and let it slide. Though he admired the steadfast faith he saw in Maurice, he wasn't sure what he believed when it came to religion. He fingered the small metal fish in his pocket, rubbing the ever-present scripture that was his one and only connection to God. And to his brothers.

"Nothing to forgive. I just don't like thinking about it."

Maurice looked doubtful but he didn't argue. The quiet acceptance was another part of the man's character Collin appreciated. He said his piece and then shut up.

"This social worker. Her name's Carano, right?"

Collin glanced up, surprised. His grip tightened on the metal door handle. "Yeah."

"She goes to my church."

Collin suppressed a groan. "Don't turn on me, man."

He'd had enough trouble getting Mia Carano out of his head without Maurice weighing in on the deal. The social worker was about the prettiest thing he'd seen in a long time. She emanated a sincere decency that left him unsettled about turning her down, but hearing her smooth, sweet voice on his voice mail a dozen times a day was starting to irritate him.

"Single. Nice family." White teeth flashed in Maurice's dark face. "Easy on the eyes."

Was she ever! Like an ad for an Italian restaurant. Heavy red-brown hair that swirled around her shoulders. Huge, almond-shaped gray-green eyes. A wide, happy mouth. Not too skinny, either. He never had gone for ultra-thin women. Made him think they were hungry.

"I didn't notice."

"You're cool, Grace, but you ain't dead."

"Don't start, Johnson. I'm not interested. A woman like that would talk a man to pieces." Wasn't she already doing as much?

Maurice chuckled and moseyed off toward his car. His deep voice echoed through the concrete dungeon. "Sooner or later, boy, one of them's gonna get you."

Collin waved him off, climbed into his SUV, and cranked the gas-guzzling engine to life. Nobody was going to "get" him. Way he figured, nobody wanted a hard case like him. And that was fine. The only people he really wanted in his life were his brothers. Wherever they were.

Pulling out of the dark underground, he headed west toward the waning sun. The acreage five miles out of the city was a refuge, both for the animals and for him.

His cell phone rang again. Sure enough, it was the social worker. He shook his head and kept driving.

The veterinarian's dually turned down the short dirt driveway directly behind Collin. The six-wheeled pickup, essential for the rugged places a vet had to traverse, churned up dust and gravel.

"Good timing," Collin muttered to the rearview mirror, glad not to be in back of Doc White's mini dust storm, but also glad to see the dependable animal doctor.

If Paige White said she'd be here, she was. With her busy practice, sometimes she didn't arrive until well after dark, but she always arrived. Collin figured the woman worked more hours than anyone he knew.

The vet followed Collin past the half-built house he called home to the bare patches of grass that served as parking spots in front of a weathered old barn.

A string of fenced pens, divided according to species, dotted the space behind the barn. In one, a pair of neglected and starved horses was slowly regaining strength. In another, a deer healed from an arrow wound.

To one side, a rabbit hutch held a raccoon. And inside the small barn were five dogs, three cats and ten kittens. He was near capacity. As usual. He needed to add on again, but he also needed to continue the work on his house. The bank wouldn't loan money on two rooms, a bathroom and a concrete slab framed in wood.

Booted feet first, the vet leaped from the high cab of her truck with a whoop for a greeting.

"Hey there, ornery. How's business?" she hollered as Collin came around the front of his SUV.

"Which one?"

"The only one that counts." She waved a gloved hand toward the barn, and Collin nearly smiled. Paige White, a fortysomething cowgirl with a heart as big and warm as the sun, joked that animals liked her faster, better and longer than humans ever had.

One thing Collin knew for sure, animals responded to her treatment. He fell in step with the short, sturdy blonde and headed inside the barn.

Without preliminary, he said, "The pup's leg smells funny."

"You been cleaning those wounds the way I showed you?"

"Every day." He remembered the first time he'd poured antiseptic cleaner on the pup's foot and listened to its pitiful cries.

Doc stopped, stared at him for a minute and then said, "We'll have a look at him first."

Paige White could always read his concern, though he had a poker face. Her uncanny sixth sense would have bothered him under other circumstances.

The scent of fresh straw and warm-blooded animals astir beneath their feet, they reached the stall where the collie was confined.

From a large, custom-cut cardboard box, the pup gazed at them with dark, moist, delighted eyes. His shaggy tail thumped madly at the side of the box.

As always, Collin marveled at the pup's adoring welcome. He'd been cruelly treated by humans and yet his love didn't falter.

Doc knelt down, crooning. "How's my pal today? Huh? How ya doin', boy?"

"I call him Happy."

"Well, Happy." The dog licked her extended hand, the tail thumping faster. "Let me see those legs of yours." She jerked her chin at Collin, who'd hunkered down beside her. "Make sure this guy over here's looking after you."

With exquisite tenderness, she inspected one limb and then the other. Her pale eyebrows slammed together as she examined the deep, ugly wound.

Collin watched, anxious, when she took a hypodermic from her long, leather bag and filled it with medication.

"What's that?"

"More antibiotic." She held the syringe at eye level and flicked the plastic several times. "I don't like the way this looks, Collin. There's not enough tissue left to debride."

"Meaning?"

"We may have to take this foot off, too."

"Ah, man." He scrubbed a hand over his face, heard his whiskers. He knew Paige would fight hard to avoid another amputation, so if she brought up the subject, she wasn't blowing smoke. "Any hope?"

"Where there's life, there's hope. But if he doesn't respond to treatment soon, we'll have to remove the foot to save him. Infection like this can spread to the entire body in a hurry."

"I know. But a dog with two amputated feet..."

He let the thought go. Doc knew the odds of the pup having any quality of life. Finding a home for him would be close to impossible, and Collin only kept the animals until they were healthy and adoptable or ready to return to the wild. He didn't keep pets. Just animals in need.

Doc dropped the empty syringe into a plastic container, then patted his shoulder. "Don't fret. I'll run out again tomorrow. Got Jenner's Feed Store to donate their broken bags of feed to you and I want to be here to see them delivered. Clovis Jenner owes me."

Warmth spread through Collin's chest. "So do I."

Doc was constantly on the look-out for feed, money, any kind of support she could round up for his farm. And she only charged him for supplies or medications, never for her expertise.

"Nonsense. If it wasn't for me and my soft heart, you wouldn't have all these critters. I just can't put them down without trying."

"I know." He felt the same way. Whenever she called with a stray animal in need of a place to heal, Collin took it if he had room. He was stretched to the limit on space and funds, but he had to keep going. "Let's go check on the others."

Together they made the rounds. She checked the cats and dogs first, redressing wounds, giving shots, poking pills down resistant throats, instructing Collin on the next phase of care.

At the horses' pen, she nodded her approval and pushed a tube of medication down each scrawny throat. "They're more alert. See how this one lifts her head now to watch us? That's a very good sign."

One of the mares, Daisy, leaned her velvety nose against Collin's shirtfront and snuffled. In return for her affection, he stroked her neck, relishing the warm, soft feel against his fingers.

The first few days after the horses had arrived, Collin had come out to the barn every four hours to follow the strict refeeding program Doc had put them on. Seeing the horses slowly come back from the brink of death made the sleepless nights and interrupted days worth the effort.

Sometimes the local Future Farmers of America kids helped out. The other cops occasionally did the same. Most of the time, Collin preferred to work alone.

At the raccoon's hutch, Paige declared the hissing creature fit and ready to release. And finally, she stood at the fence and watched the young buck limp listlessly around the pen.

"He's depressed."

"Deer get depressed?"

"Mmm. Trauma, pain, fear lead to depression in any species." She squinted into the gathering darkness, intelligent eyes studying every move the deer made. "The wound looks good though."

"You do good work."

Some bow hunter had shot the buck. He had escaped

with an arrow protruding from his hip, finally collapsing near enough to a house that dogs had alerted the owner. Paige had operated on the badly infected hip.

"I do, don't I?" The vet smiled smugly before sobering. "Only time will tell if enough muscle remains for him to survive in the wild, though."

She turned and started back around the barn to her truck. Collin took her bag and followed.

Headlights sliced the dusk and came steadily toward them, the hum of a motor loud against the quiet country evening.

Collin tensed. "Company," he said.

"Who is it?"

"My favorite neighbor," he said, sarcasm thicker than the cloud of dust billowing around the car. "Cecil Slokum."

Collin and his farm were located a half mile from the nearest house, but Slokum harassed him on a regular basis with some complaint about the animals.

The late-model brown sedan pulled to a stop. A man the size and shape of Danny DeVito put the engine in Park and rolled down a window. His face was red with anger.

"I'm not putting up with this anymore, Grace."

The sixth sense that made Collin a good cop kicked in. He made a quick survey of the car's interior, saw no weapons and relaxed a little.

"What's the problem, Mr. Slokum?" He sounded way more polite than he felt.

"One of them dogs of yours took down my daughter's prize ewe last night."

"Didn't happen." All his animals were sick and in pens.

"Just 'cause you're a big shot cop don't make you right. I know what I saw."

"Wasn't one of mine."

"Tell it to the judge." The man shoved a brown envelope out the window.

Collin took it, puzzled. "What is this?"

"See for yourself." With that, Slokum crammed the car into gear and backed out, disappearing down the gravel road much more quickly than he'd come.

Collin stared down at the envelope.

"Might as well open it," Doc said.

With a shrug, Collin tore the seal, pulled out a legal-looking sheet of vellum and read. When he finished, he slammed a fist against the offending form.

Just what he needed right now. Someone else besides the annoying social worker on his back.

"Collin?" Doc said.

Jaw rigid, he handed her the paper and said, "Nothing like good neighbors. The jerk is suing me for damages."

Chapter Three

Mia perched on a high kitchen stool, swiveling back and forth, her mind a million miles away from her mother's noisy kitchen as she sliced boiled zucchini for stuffing.

At the stove, Grandma Maria Celestina stirred her special marinara sauce while Mama prepared the sausages for baked ziti.

The rich scents of tomato and basil and sausages had the whole family prowling in and out of the kitchen.

"Church was good today, huh, Mia?"

"Good, Mama."

At fifty-six, Rosalie Carano was still a pretty woman. People said Mia favored her and she hoped so. She'd always thought Mama looked like Sophia Loren. Flowered apron around her generous hips, Rosalie sailed around the large family kitchen with the efficient energy that had successfully raised five kids.

The whole clan gathered every Sunday after church for a late-afternoon meal of Mama's traditional Italian cooking, which always included breads and pastries from the family bakery. In the living room, her dad,

Leo, argued basketball with her eldest brother, Gabe, and Grandpa Salvatore. Gabe's wife, Abby, had taken their two kids outside to swim in the above-ground pool accompanied by Mia's pregnant sister, Anna Maria. The other brothers, Adam and Nic, roamed in and out of the kitchen like starving ten-year-olds.

Mia was blessed with a good family. Not perfect by any means, but close and caring. She appreciated that, especially on days like today when she felt inexplicably down in the dumps. Even church service, which usually buoyed her spirits, had left her uncharacteristically quiet.

Collin Grace had not returned one of her phone calls in the past three days, and she'd practically promised Mitchell that he would. She disliked pulling in favors, tried not to use her eldest brother's influence as a city councilman, but Sergeant Grace was a tough nut to crack.

Nic, her baby brother, snitched a handful of grated mozzarella from the bowl at her elbow. Out of habit, she whacked his hand then listened to the expected howl of protest.

"Go away," she muttered.

His grin was unrepentant. At twenty, dark and athletic Nic was a chick magnet. He knew his charms, though they had never worked on either of his sisters.

"You're grumpy."

Brother Adam hooked an elbow around her neck and yanked back. She tilted her head to look up at him. Adam Carano, dark and tall, was eleven months older than Mia. From childhood, they'd been best friends, and he could read her like the Sunday comics.

"What's eating you, sis? You're too quiet. It scares me." He usually complained that she talked too much.

Gabe stuck his head around the edge of the door. "Last time she was quiet, Nic and Adam ended up with strange new haircuts."

Mia rolled her eyes. "I was eight."

"And we've not had a moment of peace and quiet from you since," Adam joked.

"And I," Nic put in, "was scarred for life at the ripe old age of one."

"I should have cut off your tongue."

"Mom," Nic called in a whiney little-boy voice. "Mia's picking on me."

Mia ignored him and set to work stuffing the zucchini boats.

"What is it, Mia?" Mama asked. "Adam's right. You are not yourself."

"It's a kid," Adam replied before she could. "It's always one of her kids."

Mia pulled a face. He knew her so well. "Smarty."

Mama shushed him. "Let her tell us. Maybe we can help."

It was Mama's way. If one of her chicks had a problem, the mother hen rushed in to fix it—bringing with her lasagna or cookies. So Mia told them about Mitch.

"He's salvageable, Mama. There is a lot of good in him, but he needs a man's influence and guidance. I tried getting him into the Big Brothers program but he refuses."

"One of the boys will talk to him. Won't you, boys?" Rosalie eyed her three sons with a look that brooked no argument.

"Sure. Of course we would." All three men nodded in unison like bobble toys in the back window of a car.

Heart filling with love for these overgrown macho

teddy bears she called brothers, Mia shook her head. "Thanks, guys. You're the best. But Mitch is distrustful of most people. He'd never agree. For some reason, he zeroed in on one of the street patrolmen and will only talk to him. The cop is perfect, but—"

"Whoo-oo, Mia found her a perfect man. Go, sis." The brothers started in with the catcalls and bad jokes.

When the noise subsided, she said, "Not that kind of perfect, unfortunately. I don't even like the guy."

But she couldn't get him out of her mind, either.

"Mia!"

"Oh, Mama." Mia plopped the last zucchini boat on a pan and sprinkled parmesan on top. "Our first meeting was disastrous. I bought the man a hamburger to soften him up a little, and he didn't even stick around long enough to eat it. And now he doesn't bother to return my phone calls."

"You've lost your charm, sis. Need some lessons?" Nic flexed both arms and preened around the kitchen, bumping into Grandma, who, in turn, shook a gnarled finger in his laughing face.

Rosalie whirled and flapped her apron at the men. "Out. Shoo. We'll never get dinner on."

Gabe and Nic disappeared, still laughing. Adam stayed behind, pulled a stool around the bar with one foot, and perched beside Mia.

The most Italian-looking of the Carano brothers, Adam was swarthy and handsome and a tad more serious than his siblings.

"Want me to beat him up?"

"Who? Mitch or the cop?"

He lifted a wide shoulder. "Either. Say the word."

"Maybe later."

They both grinned at the familiar joke. All through high school Adam had threatened to beat up any guy who made her unhappy. Though he'd never done it, the boys in her class had thought he would.

"If I could only convince Sergeant Grace to spend one day with Mitch, I think he'd be hooked. He comes off as cold and uncaring, but I don't think he is."

"Some people aren't kid-crazy like you are. Especially us men types."

"All I want is a few hours a week of his time to save a kid from an almost certain future of crime and drugs." Mama swished by and took the pan of zucchini boats. "The couple of times I managed to get him on the phone, he barely said three words."

Adam swiveled her stool so that her back was to him. Strong hands massaged her shoulders.

"The guy was short and to the point. *No.* The least he could do is explain *why* he refuses, but he clams up like Uncle Vitorio."

Adam chuckled. "And that drives you nuts in a hurry."

"Yes, it does. Human beings have the gift of language. They should use it." She let her head go lax. "That feels good."

"You're tight as a drum."

"I didn't sleep much last night. I couldn't get Mitch off my mind so I got up to pray. And then, the next thing I know I'm praying for Collin Grace, too."

"The cop?"

"Yes. There's something about him…sort of an aloneness, I guess, that bothers me. I can't figure him out."

Adam squeezed her shoulders hard. "There's your

trouble, sis. You always want to talk and analyze and dig until you know everything. Some people like to keep their books closed."

"You think so?" She swiveled back around to face him. "You think I'm too nosey? That I talk too much?"

"Yep. Pushy, too."

"Gabe thinks I'm too soft."

"That's because he's the pushiest lawyer in three states."

Didn't she know it? She'd lost her first job because of Gabe, and though he'd done everything in his power to make it up to her in the years since, Mia would never forget the humiliation of having her professional ethics compromised.

Nic stuck his head into the kitchen, then ducked when his mother threw a tea towel at him. "Mia, your purse is ringing. Should I get it?"

Mia slid off the stool and started toward the living room. She might be pushy, but she played fair.

A large masculine hand attached to a hairy arm— Nic's—appeared around the door, holding out the cell phone.

Taking it, Mia pushed the button and said, "Hello."

"Miss Carano, this is Monica Perez."

"Mrs. Perez, is something wrong?" Mia tensed. Today was Sunday. A strange time for calls from a client. "Is it Mitchell?"

The woman's voice sounded more weary than worried. "He's run away again. This time the worthless little creep stole money out of my purse."

Collin kicked back the roller chair and plopped down at his desk. He'd just returned from transporting a prisoner and had to complete the proper paperwork. Paperwork. Blah. Most Sundays he spent at the farm or crashed out on his couch watching ballgames. But this was his weekend to work.

"I need to see Sergeant Grace, please."

Collin recognized the cool, sweet voice immediately. Mia Carano, social worker to the world and nag of the first order, was in the outer office.

"Dandy," he muttered. "Make my day."

Tossing down the pen, he rose and strode toward the door just as she sailed through it. She looked fresh and young in tropical-print capris and an orange T-shirt, a far cry from the business suit and heels of their first meeting.

"Mitch has run away again," she blurted without preliminary.

"Nothing the police can do for twenty-four hours."

"We have to find him. I'm afraid he'll get into trouble again."

"Probably will."

Her gray-green eyes snapped with fire. "I want you to go with me to find him right now. I have some ideas where he might go, but he won't listen to me. He'll listen to you."

The woman was unbelievable. Like a bulldog, she never gave up.

"It's not police business."

"Can't you do something just because it's right? Because a kid out there needs you?"

Collin felt himself softening. Had any social worker ever worked this hard for him or his brothers?

"If I take a drive around, have a look in a couple places, will you leave me alone?"

"Probably not." Her pretty smile stretched wide beneath a pair of twinkling eyes.

She was a pest. An annoying, pretty, sweet, aggravating pest who would probably go right on driving him nuts until he gave in.

Against his better judgment, he reached into a file cabinet and yanked out a form. "Sign this."

"What is it?"

"Department policy. If you're riding in my car, you gotta sign."

The pretty smile grew wider—and warmer.

He was an idiot to do this. Her kind never stopped at one favor.

Without bothering to read the forms that released the police department of liability in case of injury, Mia scribbled her name on the line and then beat him out of the station house. At the curb, she stopped to look at him. He motioned toward his patrol car and she jumped into the passenger's seat. A gentle floral scent wafted on the breeze when she slammed the door. He never noticed things like that and it bugged him.

He also noticed that the inside of his black-and-white was a mess. A clipboard, ticket pad, a travel mug and various other junk littered the floorboards. Usually a neat freak, he wanted to apologize for the mess, but he kept stubbornly silent. Let her think what she liked. Let her think he was a slob. Why should he care what Mia Carano thought of him?

If she was bothered, she didn't say so. But she did talk. And talk. She filled him in on Mitch's likes and dislikes, his grades in school, the places he hung out. And then she started in on the child advocate thing. She told him how desperately the kid needed a strong male in his life. That he was a good kid, smart, funny and kind. A computer whiz at school.

This time there was no Delete button to silence her. Trapped inside the car, Collin had to listen.

He put on his signal, made a smooth turn onto Tenth Street and headed east toward the boy's neighborhood. "How do you know so much about this one kid?"

"His mom, his classmates, his teachers."

"Why?"

"It's my job."

"To come out on Sunday afternoon looking for a runaway?"

"His mother called me."

"Bleeding heart," he muttered.

"Better than being heartless."

He glanced sideways. "You think I'm heartless?"

She glared back. "Aren't you?"

No, he wasn't. But let her think what she would. He wasn't getting involved with anything to do with the social welfare system.

His radio crackled to life. A juvenile shoplifter.

Mia sucked in a distressed breath, the first moment of quiet they'd had.

Collin radioed his location and took the call.

"It's Mitchell," Mia said after hearing the details. "The description and area fit perfectly."

Heading toward the complainant's convenience store, Collin asked, "You got a picture of him?"

"Of course." She rummaged in a glittery silver handbag and stuck a photo under his nose.

Collin spotted the 7-Eleven up ahead. This woman surely did vex him.

He pulled into the concrete drive and parked in the fire lane.

"Stay here. I'll talk to the owner, get what information I can, and then we'll go from there."

The obstinate social worker pushed open her door and followed him inside the convenience store. She whipped out her picture of the Perez kid and showed it to the store owner.

"That's him. Comes in here all the time. I been suspicious of him. Got him on tape this time."

Collin filled out the mandatory paperwork, jotting down all the pertinent information. "What did he take?"

The owner got a funny look on his face. "He took weird stuff. Made me wonder."

Mia paced back and forth in front of the counter. "What kind of weird stuff?"

Collin silenced her with a stare. She widened rebellious eyes at him, but hushed—for the moment.

"Peroxide, cotton balls, a roll of bandage."

Mia's eyes widened even further. "Was he hurt?"

The owner shrugged. "What do I care? He stole from me."

"He's hurt. I just know it. We have to find him."

Collin shot her another look before saying to the clerk, "Anything else we should know?"

"Well, he did pay for the cat food." The man shifted uncomfortably and Collin suspected there was more to the story, but he wouldn't get it from this guy. He motioned to Mia and they left.

Once in the car, he said, "Any ideas?"

She crossed her arms. "You mean, I have permission to talk now?"

Collin stifled a grin. The annoying woman was also cute. "Be my guest."

"I know several places around here where kids hang out."

He knew a few himself. "I doubt he'll be in plain sight, but we can try."

He put the car in gear and drove east. They tried all the usual spots, the parks, the parking lots. They showed the kid's picture in video stores and to other kids on the streets, but soon ran out of places to look.

"We have to find him before he gets into more trouble."

"I doubt he'd come this far. We're nearly to the city dump."

As soon as he said the words, Collin knew. A garbage dump was exactly the kind of place he would have hidden when he was eleven.

With a spurt of adrenaline, he kicked the patrol car up and sped along the mostly deserted stretch of highway on the outskirts of the city.

When he turned onto the road leading to the landfill, Mia said incredulously, "You think he's here? In the city dump?"

He shot her an exasperated look. "Got a better idea?"

"No."

Collin slammed out of the car and climbed to the top of the enormous cavity. The stench rolled over him in waves.

"Ew." Beside him, Mia clapped a hand over her nose.

"Wait in the car. I'll look around."

Collin wasn't the least surprised when she ignored him.

"You go that way." She pointed left. "I'll take the right side."

Determination in her stride, she took off through the trash heap apparently unconcerned about her white shoes or clean clothes. Collin watched her go. A pinch of admiration tugged at him. He'd say one thing for Miss Social Worker, she wasn't a quitter.

His boots slid on loose dirt as he carefully picked his way down the incline. Some of the trash had been recently buried, but much more lay scattered about.

He watched his step, aware that among the discarded furniture and trash bags, danger and disease lurked. This was not a place for a boy. Unless that boy had no place else to turn.

His chest constricted. He'd been here and done this. Maybe not in this dump, but he understood what the kid was going through. He hated the memories. Hated the heavy pull of dread and hurt they brought.

This was why he didn't want to get involved with Mia's project. And now here he was, knee-deep in trash and recollections, moving toward what appeared to be a shelter of some sort.

Plastic trash bags that stretched across a pair of ragged-out couches were anchored in place by rocks, car parts, a busted TV set. An old refrigerator clogged one end and a cardboard box the other.

Mia was right. The kid had smarts. He'd built his hideout in an area unlikely to be buried for a while and had made the spot blend in with the rest of the junk.

As quietly as he could, Collin leaned down and slid the cardboard box away. What he saw inside made his chest ache.

The kid had tried to make a home inside the shelter. An old blanket and a sack of clothes were piled on one end of a ragged couch. A flashlight lay on an up-turned crate. Beneath the crate, the kid had stored the canned milk, a jar of water, cat food and a box of cereal.

In the dim confines Mitchell knelt over a cardboard box, cotton ball and peroxide in hand.

Collin had a pretty good idea what was inside the box.

At the sudden inflow of light, the kid's head whipped around. A mix of fear and resentment widened his dark eyes.

"Nice place you got here," Collin said, stooping to enter.

"I'm not doing anything wrong."

"Stealing from convenience stores isn't wrong?"

"I had to. Panda—" Mitchell glanced down at the box "—she's hurt."

Curiosity aroused, Collin moved to the boy's side. A mother cat with three tiny kittens mewed up at him. Mitchell stroked the top of her head and she began to purr.

Collin's heart slammed against his ribs.

Oh, man. Déjà vu all over again.

"Mind if I take a look?"

The kid scooted sideways but hovered protectively.

Collin frowned. The cat was speckled with round burns, several of them clearly infected. "What happened?"

"Some kids had her. Mean kids who like to hurt things. She was their cat, but I took her when they started—"

Collin held up a hand. He didn't need the ugly details to visualize what the kid had saved the cat from.

"You can't stay here, Mitchell. Your mother is worried."

"She's just worried about her ten bucks."

"You shouldn't have taken it."

The kid shrugged, didn't answer, but Collin's own eyes told him where the money had gone. And if his nose was an indicator, the kid had scavenged a pack of cigarettes somewhere too which would explain the store owner's guilty behavior. He'd probably sold cigarettes to a minor.

"I'm not going back to her house."

"You have to."

"I can't. Panda and her babies will die if I don't take care of her. Archie, too."

"Archie?"

The kid reached behind them to the other couch and gently lifted a turtle out of a shoe box. A piece of silver duct tape ran along a fracture in the green shell.

Emotions swamped Collin. He felt as if he was being sucked under a whirlpool. Memories flashed through his head so fast he thought he was going blind.

At that moment, little Miss Social Worker poked her head through the opening. "I thought I heard voices."

Mitchell shrank away from her, blocking the box of cats with his body.

"I won't leave her," he said belligerently. "You can't make me."

"Maybe your mother will let you keep them," Collin said, hoping Mitchell's mother was better than he suspected.

"I'm not going back there, I said. Never."

"Why not?"

The boy's face closed up tight, a look Collin recognized all too well. Something ugly needed to be said and the kid wasn't ready to deal with it.

As the inevitability of the situation descended upon him, Collin pulled a hand down his face.

After a minute of pulling himself together, he spoke. "Nothing's going to happen to your cat. You have my word."

Mitch's face lightened, though distrust continued to ooze out of him. "How can you be sure?"

"Because," Collin said, wishing there was a way he could avoid involvement and knowing he couldn't, "I'll take her home with me."

The boy's face crumpled, incredulous. The belligerent attitude fled, replaced by the awful yearning of hope. "You will?"

"I know a good vet. Panda will be okay."

Mia ducked under the black plastic and came inside. Her eyes glowed with pleasure. "That's really nice of you, Sergeant Grace."

"Yeah. That's me. Real nice." Stupid, too.

He was a cop. Tough. Hardened to the ugliness of humanity. He could resist about anything. Anything, that is, except looking at Mitch's face and seeing his own reflection.

Like it or not, he was about to become a big brother—again.

He only hoped he didn't mess it up this time around.

Chapter Four

Mitchell sat huddled in the backseat of the patrol car, tense and suspicious. The cardboard carton containing cat, kittens and turtle rested on the seat beside him. The rest of his property was in a battered paint bucket on the floor.

"I told you I'm not going back there."

Mia turned in her seat, antennae going up. "Why not? Is something wrong at home?"

The boy ignored her.

Ever the cop, Collin spoke up. "Juvie Hall is the other alternative."

"Better than home."

The adults exchanged glances.

Collin hadn't said two complete sentences since they'd left Mitch's lean-to. He'd simply gathered up the animals and the rag-tag assortment of supplies and led the way to the cruiser. Mitchell had followed along without a fuss, his only concern for the animals. For some reason that Mia could not fathom, the two silent males seemed to communicate without words.

Right now, though, Collin's words were not helping. Mia stifled the urge to shush him. Something was amiss with the child and he was either too scared or too proud to say so.

She pressed a little harder. "I wish you'd talk to me, Mitch. I can help. It's what I do. If there is a problem at home I can help get it resolved."

Dirt spewed up over the windshield as they bumped and jostled down the dusty road out of the landfill. Once on the highway, Collin flipped on the windshield washers.

"How do you and your mother get along? Any problems there?"

Mitch turned his profile toward her and stared at the spattering water.

Mia softened her voice. "Mitch, if there's abuse, you need to tell me."

His head whipped around, expression fierce. "Leave my mom out of this."

Whoa! "Okay. What about your stepdad?"

Collin gave her a sideways glance that said he wished she'd shut up. She didn't plan on doing that any time soon. Something was wrong in this boy's life. Otherwise, he wouldn't be running away. He wouldn't be shoplifting, and he wouldn't dread going home. She would be a lousy social worker and an even worse human being if she didn't investigate the very real possibility of abuse.

"Mitchell," she urged softly. "You can trust me. I want to help."

The cruiser slowed to a turn, pulled through a concrete drive and stopped. Mitchell jerked upright. His eyes widened in fright.

"Hey. What are we doing here?"

The green-and-red sign of the 7-Eleven convenience store loomed above the gas pumps. Mia recognized it as the store from which Mitch had shoplifted. Facing consequences was an important part of teaching a child right from wrong, but Mia still felt sorry for him. And she felt frustrated to be getting nowhere in their conversation.

Collin shifted into Park and got out of the car.

Mitchell shrank back against the seat. "I ain't going in there."

Mia braced for a strong-armed confrontation between the cop and the kid, prepared to intervene if necessary. But the cop surprised her.

He opened the back door, hunkered down beside the car and spoke quietly, almost gently, to the scared boy. "Everybody messes up sometime, Mitch. Part of being a man means facing up to your mistakes. Are you willing to be a man about it?"

Although Mia was dying to offer to go inside with the boy and talk to the owner, she knew Collin was right. For once, she had to bite her tongue and let the cop do the talking.

Several long seconds passed while Mia thought she would burst. The need to blurt out reassurances and promises swelled like yeast bread on a hot day. Would Mitchell go on his own? Would Sergeant Grace drag him inside if he didn't?

As if in answer to her unasked question, Collin placed one wide hand on the knee of the boy's dirty blue jeans and patiently waited.

The gesture brought a lump to Mia's throat. Her brothers would laugh at her if they knew, but she couldn't help it. There was something moving about the sight of a tough, taciturn cop conveying his trust-worthiness with a gentle touch.

The boy's shoulders were so tense, Mia thought his collarbone might snap. Finally, he drew in a shudder-ing breath and reached for his seat-belt clasp.

"Will you go with me?" Mouth tight and straight, he directed the question to Collin.

The policeman pushed to his feet. "Every step."

And then, as if the social worker in the front seat was invisible, the two males, one tall and buff and immacu-late, the other small and thin and tattered, crossed the concrete space and went inside.

The kittens in the backseat made mewing sounds as Panda shifted positions. Mia glanced around to be sure they were staying put. Yellow eyes blinked back.

"Hang tight, Mama," she said. "The abandonment is only temporary."

The poor, bedraggled cat seemed satisfied to stay with her babies and the hapless turtle. So, Mia tilted her forehead against the cool side glass and watched the people inside the store. There were a few custom-ers coming and going, an occasional car door slammed, though the area was reasonably quiet.

She could see Collin and Mitchell moving around inside, see the clerk. Although frustrated at being left behind, for once, she didn't charge into the situation. But she did use her time to pray that somehow the angry shop owner would give the child a break without let-ting him off scot-free.

Ten minutes later, Collin and Mitch emerged from the building. Collin wore his usual bland expression that gave nothing away. Mitch looked pale, but relieved as he slammed into the backseat.

Mia could hardly contain herself. "How did it go?"

"Okay." Collin started the cruiser and pulled into the lane of slow Sunday-afternoon traffic.

Mia rolled her eyes. That wasn't the answer she was asking for. But since the cop wasn't willing to elaborate, she asked Mitchell, "What was decided? Is he going to press charges?"

Mitch trailed a finger over one of the kittens. "I don't know yet. But he said he'd think about it."

The quiet, gentle boy she usually encountered had returned. The belligerence, most likely posturing brought on by fear, had dissipated. He looked young and small and lost.

Collin spoke up—finally. "We worked out a deal."

"And is this a secret all-male deal? Or can the nosy, female social worker be let in on it?"

Collin glanced her way, eyes sparkling. At least she'd badgered a smile out of him. Sort of.

"Didn't like being left in the car?"

The rat. He had already figured out that she needed to be in the middle of a situation. "This is the sort of thing I'm trained to do. I might have been useful in there."

He didn't argue the point. "We're asking for twenty hours of community service."

That was something she could help with.

"I'll talk to the DA if you'd like." She did that all the time, working deals for the juveniles she encountered. "He's a friend."

"Figures."

"Having friends is not a bad thing, Sergeant."

"It is when you use them to harass people."

Ah, the phone calls to the chief had not pleased him. "I did not harass you."

He lifted an eyebrow at her.

"Well, okay. Maybe I did. But just a little to get your attention."

"You got it."

"Was that a good thing or a bad thing?"

"Time will tell."

Was that a smile she saw? Or a grimace? He was the hardest man in the world to read.

The cruiser pulled to a stop in front of an older frame house in a rundown area of the city. Paint had peeled until the place was more gray than white, and the yard was overgrown. A rusted lawnmower with grass shooting up over the motor looked as though it hadn't been used all summer.

Mia knew the house. She'd been here more than once at the request of the school system, but never could find out anything that justified removing the boy from the home.

"I thought Mitch opted for Juvenile Hall?" she asked.

Collin shut off the engine and opened the car door. "He changed his mind."

A dark-haired woman who was far too thin came out into the yard and stood with her arms folded around her waist.

"Where's my ten bucks?" she asked as soon as Mitch was out of the car.

To Mia's surprise, Mitch reached in his jeans and withdrew a crumpled bill. She looked at Sergeant Grace, suspicious, but the man's poker face gave away nothing. The idea that the tough cop might have bailed the boy out with his mother touched her. Maybe he wasn't so heartless after all.

She listened without comment as Collin apprised

Mitchell's mother about the situation. Mrs. Perez didn't seem too pleased with her son, as expected, but her fidgety behavior raised Mia's suspicions. She didn't invite them into the house and seemed anxious to have them gone.

"What's going to happen to him?" she asked. "I don't have no money for lawyers and courts."

"He broke the law, Mrs. Perez. Miss Carano will talk to the DA for him, but at the least he'll do some community service to pay for the things he took from the store."

"He stole from me, too."

Collin's nostrils flared. "You want to press charges?"

Said aloud, the idea seemed harsh even to the fidgety mother. "I don't want him stealing from me anymore. That's all. He'll end up in jail like his old man."

Conversation halted as an old car, the chassis nearly dragging on the street, mufflers missing or altered, rumbled slowly past. Loud hip-hop music pulsed from the interior, overriding every other sound.

Collin turned and stared hard-eyed at the vehicle, garnering a rude gesture in return. Mia had a feeling the car's inhabitants hadn't seen the last of Sergeant Grace.

When the racket subsided, Mia picked up the conversation. "Have you considered counseling?"

Monica Perez rolled her eyes. "Mitchell don't need no shrink. He needs a new set of friends. Them Walters boys down the street get into everything. You oughta go arrest them."

"I could help him meet some new friends if you'd like," Mia said and received a sideways glance from Collin for her efforts.

"Fine with me."

"My church has a basketball league for kids. He could sign up to play."

"I wouldn't mind that, but I ain't got a car. Is it far from here?"

"I'll pick him up. Saturday morning at nine, if he wants to go." She looked at Mitch, stuck like a wood tick to Collin's side. "Mitch?"

"Sure. I guess so."

Collin dropped a hand on the boy's shoulder. "Miss Carano's going out on a limb for you."

Mitch gazed up at the tall cop, his expression a mix of frightened child and troubled youth. "I know."

Mia glimpsed his bewilderment, his failure to understand his own behavior. And as always, something about this kid got to her. A good person was inside there. With God's help, she'd find a way to bring him out.

"Someone will give you a call next week and let you know the DA's decision," Collin was telling Mrs. Perez.

And then with a curt nod, he turned and started back toward the police car. Mia, who preferred long goodbyes with lots of conversation and closure, felt off balance.

Mitch didn't seem to be finished either because he darted after the departing figure.

"Sergeant Grace."

Collin stopped, one hand on the car door.

Suddenly, every vestige of the tough street kid was gone. Mitch looked like what he was, a little boy with nothing and no one to cling to. "You'll take care of Panda?"

"I will."

"Can I come see her sometime?"

The hardened cop studied the small, intense face, his own face intense as if the answer would cost him too much. "She'd be sad if you didn't."

Mia said a quick goodbye to Mrs. Perez and hurried

across the overgrown lawn. Now was her chance. Now that Collin had softened just the tiniest bit.

"I could bring Mitch out to your place. Anytime that's convenient for you."

Collin looked from Mitchell to Mia and back again. Mia was certain she must be imagining things because the strong, hardened cop looked more helpless than the boy. Helpless…and scared.

Mia shoved away from the mile-high stack of file folders on her desk and scrounged in the bottom desk drawer for her stash of miniature Snickers. A day like today required chocolate and plenty of it. She took two.

Her case load grew exponentially every day to the point that she was overwhelmed at times. Looking out for the interests of kids was her calling, but on days like today, the calling was a tough one.

She'd made a school visit and six home visits. At the last one, she'd done what every social worker dreads. She'd pulled the two neglected babies and taken them to a foster home. Even now, though she knew she'd made the right choice, she could hear the youngest one crying for his mama. Poor little guy was too young to comprehend that he lived in a crack house.

She nipped the corner of Snickers number one and turned to the computer on her desk. All the reports from today had to be typed up and stored in the master files before she could go home.

"See ya tomorrow, Mia," one of the other workers called as she passed by the open office door.

Mia waved without lifting her eyes from the computer screen. "Have a good evening, Allie."

She reached for another bite of candy. Over the tick-

tick-tick of the keyboard, she heard another voice. This one wasn't her coworker.

"Mind if I interrupt for a minute?"

Her head snapped up.

"Collin?" she blurted before remembering he'd never given her permission to call him by his first name. But she had to face the fact. She thought about him, even prayed for him, by his first name.

During the three days since he'd helped her find Mitchell, she'd prayed about him and thought about him a lot. The fact that she didn't know him that well didn't get him out of her mind. She was intrigued. And attracted. More than once, she'd wondered if he was a Christian, but she was afraid she might already know the answer.

Now he stood before her in his blue uniform, patches on each sleeve, shiny metal pins on each collar point and above his name tag. He looked as crisp and clean as new money.

Great. And she looked like a worn-out, overworked social worker whose white blouse was wrinkled and pulling loose from her red skirt. She hoped like crazy there was no chocolate on her teeth.

"Can we talk?"

Collin Grace wanted to talk? Now there was a novel concept.

"Do you know how?" She softened the teasing jab with a smile.

Those brown eyes twinkled but he didn't return the smile. "I want to make a deal with you."

He scraped a client chair away from her desk a little. He might want to talk, but he was still keeping his distance.

Mia rolled back in her own chair to study his solemn face. Whatever was on his mind was serious business. "A deal?"

"In exchange for your help, I'll mentor the kid."

The wonderful thrill of victory shot much-needed energy into her bloodstream. After the day she'd had, this was great news.

"Mitchell Perez? Collin, that's marvelous. He told me on the phone last night that you stopped by after school yesterday. That was so nice of you, and it really made his day. He tried to act all tough about your visit, but he was thrilled. I could tell. And when I told him the DA agreed to community service, he asked if he could work for you. But I had no idea how to answer that without talking to you first and I've just been so busy today...."

Collin lifted one hand to slow her down. "The deal first."

Once she got on a roll, stopping was difficult. But that halted her in her tracks. "Am I going to like this deal?"

"This is confidential. Okay?"

Now her interest was piqued. Very. "Most of my work is confidential. Believe it or not, I can keep my mouth shut when necessary."

He made a huffing noise that sounded remarkably close to a laugh. She got up and moved around the desk past him to close the door even though the office was probably empty by now.

When she sat down again, she had to ask, "Do I have chocolate on my teeth?"

This time he *did* laugh.

"No. You look great."

"Such a smooth liar," she said, and then reached in

the file drawer and took out another candy bar. "Want one?"

"No, thanks."

"Oh, yeah. You're the health-food cop. Poor guy. You don't know what you're missing." She unwrapped a Snickers, nibbled the end and shifted into social-worker mode.

"You said you needed my help. What can I do for you, Officer?"

"Collin's okay."

Another thrill, this one as sweet as the caramel, and completely uncalled for, raced through her. Before she could wipe the smile off her face, he did it for her.

"I want you to help me find my brothers."

She blinked, uncomprehending. "Your brothers?"

"Yeah." Collin leaned forward, muscled forearms on his thighs as he clasped his hands in front of him. Steel intensity radiated from him as though the coming confidence was very difficult for him to share. "My little brothers, Drew and Ian, though neither of them are little now."

She got a sinking feeling in the pit of her stomach. "When did you last see them?"

His answer hurt her heart. "More than twenty years ago."

"Tell me," she said simply, knowing for once when to keep quiet and let the other person do the talking. Whatever he had to share, in confidence, about his brothers was important to him.

Over the next fifteen minutes, during which Mia went through three more Snickers bars, Collin told a story all too familiar to a seasoned social worker. Oh, he spoke in vague, simplistic terms about his childhood, but Mia had worked in social services long enough to fill in the blanks. Collin and his brothers had been separated by the social system because of major issues in his family.

"What happened after that day in the principal's office? Where did you go? Foster care?" she asked, hearing the compassion in her voice and wondering if he would resent it. But she had brothers she adored, too. She knew how devastated she would be if she couldn't find one of them.

"Foster care never worked out for me. I went into a group home," he said simply, and she heard the hurt through the cold retelling. "Ian was so little, not even five. Foster care, maybe even adoption, would be my best guess for him. He was small and sweet and cute. He could have made the adjustment, I think." His nostrils flared. "I hope."

"And your middle brother? Drew? What do you think happened to him?"

He shook his head. The skin over his high, handsome cheekbones drew tight, casting deep hollows in his face. Clearly, talking about the loss of his brothers distressed him. "Drew was a fighter. He would have had a harder time than I did. I remember the social worker that day saying he was headed to a special place or something like that."

"A therapeutic home?"

"Maybe. I don't remember." He pinched at his upper lip, frustrated. "See? That's the problem. I was a kid, too. My memories are more feelings than facts."

And those feelings still cut into him with the power of a chain saw.

"Did you ever see or hear anything at all about them?

Anything that could help us find them?" She didn't know why she'd said *us*. She hadn't agreed to do anything yet.

"The summer after we were separated, we both ended up at one of those summer-camp things they do for kids in the system. We immediately started making plans to run away together. But, like I said, Drew was a fighter. He got kicked out the second day. I didn't even know about the trouble until he was gone."

"And no one told you anything about him?"

"No more than I've told you. Twenty years of searching, of sticking my name in files and on search boards and registries hasn't found them." The skin on his knuckles alternated white and brown as he flexed and unflexed his clenched fists. "I've had leads, good ones, but they were always dead ends."

And it's killing you. All the things she'd wondered about him now made sense. His chilly reserve. The way he seemed isolated, a man alone.

Collin Grace *had* been alone most of his life. He'd been a child alone. Now he was a man alone.

To a woman surrounded by the warmth and noise and love of a big family, Collin's situation was not only sad, it was tragic.

"Somewhere out there I have two brothers. I want them back." And then as if the words came out without his permission, he murmured gruffly, "I need to know they're okay."

Of course he needed that. Mia's training clicked through her head. As the oldest of the three boys, he'd been responsible for the others. Or at least, he'd thought he was. Having them taken away without a word left him believing he'd failed them.

Now she understood why he'd been so reluctant to take Mitchell under his wing. He was afraid of failing him, too.

The sudden insight almost brought tears to her eyes.

Mia tilted back her chair and drew in a breath, studying the poster on the far wall. The slogan, Social Work Is Love Made Visible, reminded her why she did what she did. The love of Christ in her, and through her, ministered to people like Collin, to kids like Mitchell. If she could help, she would.

"Twenty years is forever in the social services system. Do you really think I can find them if you haven't had any success?"

"You know the system better than I do. You have access to records that I don't even know exist. Records that I'm not allowed to see."

Warning hackles rose on Mia's back. She tried not to let them show. "You aren't asking me to go into sealed records without permission, are you?"

"Would you?" Dark eyes studied her. He wasn't pressing, just asking.

"No." She'd done that once for her oldest brother, Gabe. The favor had cost her a job she loved and a certain amount of credibility with her peers. The bad decision had also cost her a great deal emotionally and spiritually. God had forgiven her, but she'd always felt as if she'd let Him down. "I will never compromise my professional or my Christian ethics."

Again.

"Okay, then. Do what you can. You still have access to a lot of records, even the unsealed ones. I've looked everywhere I know, but that's the problem. I don't know how to navigate the system the way you would. I can't seem to find much when it comes to child welfare records of twenty years ago."

"Records from back then aren't computerized."

"I finally figured that one out. But where are they?"

"If they exist, they're still in file cabinets somewhere or they could be piled in boxes in a storage warehouse."

"Like police records."

"Exactly." She crumpled the half-dozen Snickers wrappers into a wad, dismayed to have consumed so many.

"Are you willing to try?"

"Are you willing to be Mitchell's CAP? That's what we call adults who volunteer through our Child Advocate Partners Program." She would help Collin in his search no matter what, but Mitch might as well get a good mentor out of the deal.

"What do I have to do?"

"Some initial paperwork. Being a police officer simplifies the procedure since you already have clearances."

"How much is the welfare office involved?"

"You don't like us much, do you?"

He made a face that said he had good reason.

"Things are different now, Collin. We understand things about children today that we didn't know then."

He didn't buy a word of it. "Yeah. Well."

"If I help you and you become Mitch's CAP, you're going to be stuck with me probably more than you want to be."

"As long as it's you. And only you."

Now why did that make her feel so good? "But you think I talk too much."

The corner of his mouth hiked up. "You do."

"But you're willing to sacrifice?"

"Finding my brothers is worth anything."

Ouch. "Sorry. I was teasing, but maybe I shouldn't have. Finding your brothers *is* serious business."

"No apology necessary." He rose with athletic ease, bringing with him the vague scent of woodsy cologne and starched uniform. "I was teasing, too."

He was? Nice to know he could. "I'll need all the information you can give me about your brothers. Ages, names, dates you can remember, people you remember, places. Any little detail."

From his shirt pocket, he withdrew a small spiral notebook, the kind all cops seemed to carry. "The basics are in here. But I have more information on my computer."

"What kind of information?"

"The research I've done. Names and places I've already eliminated. Group homes, foster parents. I know a lot of places my brothers never were. I just can't find where they are."

He made the admission easily, but Mia read the hopelessness behind such a long and fruitless search. Twenty years was a long time to keep at it. But Collin Grace didn't seem the kind that would ever give up.

And that was exactly the type of person she was, too.

"Everything you've investigated will be useful. Knowing where *not* to look is just as important as knowing where *to* look. The files and the computer will be helpful, but we may have to do some legwork, as well." Now, why did the prospect of going somewhere with Collin sound so very, very appealing? "People are more comfortable with face-to-face questions about these kinds of things."

"Whatever it takes."

"I can't make promises, but I'll do what I can."

"Fair enough."

"Then I guess we have a deal. Will you go out and talk to Mitchell or do you want me to?"

Reluctance radiated from him in waves, but he'd made a deal and he was the kind of man who would keep it. Wasn't he still trying to keep a promise he'd made when he was ten years old? A man like that didn't back off from responsibility.

"I can contact him tomorrow," she offered.

"We could both tell him now. You know what's involved more than I do."

She shook her head, more disappointed than was wise, considering how little she knew about Collin as a person.

"I'm slammed with extra work tonight. I'll be here until seven at least." And Mitch was a lot more interested in Collin than he was in Mia.

"Too bad," he said. His expression was unreadable as usual so Mia didn't know what to make of his comment. Too bad she couldn't go with him? Or too bad she had so much work to do?

Either way, she watched him turn and stride out of her office and suffered a twinge of regret that she hadn't gone along anyway. She could be dishonest and say she wanted another look at Mitchell's living situation or that she needed to explain the program in more detail. But Mia was not dishonest. Even with herself. She had wanted to spend time with her enigmatic policeman.

And the notion was disturbing to say the least. She hadn't dated anyone in a while. To find her interest piqued by a man who didn't even seem to like her was a real puzzle.

He was a good cop, had a good reputation, and she'd had a sneak peek at the kindness he kept safely hidden. But he also carried a personal history that sometimes meant major emotional issues. Issues that might require counseling and work and, most importantly, healing from God.

And that was the big issue for Mia. Was Collin Grace a believer?

She reached for another Snickers.

Chapter Five

Sometimes Collin felt as if he spent his life inside a vehicle. He'd driven from Mia's office directly to Mitch's place, only to find the little twerp wasn't there. After driving through the neighborhood, he'd spotted him in a park shooting hoops with three other boys.

When Collin got out of the cruiser, Mitchell passed the ball off and headed toward him. The other boys quickly faded into the twilight and disappeared.

"Why are your friends in such a rush?" Collin leaned against the side of the car and folded his arms, watching the shadowy figures with a mixture of amusement and suspicion.

"You scared them off."

"They have reason to be scared of a cop?"

"Maybe."

Which meant yes in eleven-year-old talk.

"It's getting dark. Come on. I'll take you home."

"Am I in trouble?" Mitch asked, climbing readily into the front seat of the cruiser.

"No more than usual."

Streetlights had come on but made little dent in the

shadowy time between day and night. This part of town was a haven for the unsavory. Gang types, thugs, druggies, thieves all came sneaking out like cockroaches as soon as the sun went down. No place at all for a young boy.

Collin had to admit Mia was right about one thing. This kid needed a mentor before he fell into the cesspool that surrounded him. Though he still wasn't sure he wanted to be the one, Collin had begun to feel a certain responsibility toward Mitchell. He hated that, but he did. Who better than him to understand what this kid was going through? And that was all he planned to do. Understand and guide. He wasn't letting the kid get to him.

"Why're you here?" Mitch slouched down into the seat and stared out the window at the passing cars with studied disinterest.

"Miss Carano sent me."

Mitch sat up. "No kidding? You gonna be my CAP?"

So, she'd already prepared the kid for this. How had she known he would agree? He hadn't even known himself.

"What do you think about that?"

The kid hitched a shoulder. "I got plenty of other stuff to do."

"Yeah. Including a lot of community service. At least ten hours at the store where you jacked the stuff. The rest is up to you and me and Miss Carano."

"I guess I could come out to your place. Help with the animals. I'm good at that."

"Up to you." Mitch had to make the decision. Otherwise, he'd only resent Collin's interference.

"Panda probably misses me a lot. She doesn't trust many people."

"With good reason." A lot of people had let the cat—and the kid—down. The cruiser eased to a stop at the light. "You work for me, you'll have to lose the cigarettes."

The denial came fast. "I don't smoke."

One hand draped over the steering wheel, Collin just looked at him, long and steady. The boy's eyes shifted sideways. He swallowed and hitched a shoulder. "How'd you know?"

"I have a nose." The light changed. "Gonna lose them or not?"

"Whatever."

"Your choice."

"Why do you care?"

"The animals at my place depend on me."

"What's that got to do with anything?"

"You think about it and let me know which is more important. The animals or the smokes."

Collin slowed and turned into the drive-through of a Mickey D's. "Want a burger?"

He rolled down his window. The smell of hot vegetable oil surrounded the place.

"Miss Carano said you didn't eat junk food."

"She did?" The fact that she'd mentioned him to the boy in any way other than as a court-appointed advocate sent a warm feeling through him. Warm, like her sunny smile.

That warmth, that genuine caring both drew and repelled him. He didn't understand it. But he couldn't deny how good it had felt to dump his burden on her desk and to believe she would do exactly what she promised. Maybe she'd have no better luck than he'd had in finding Drew and Ian. But for the first time in years, he felt renewed hope.

Hanging out with a social worker might not be so bad after all.

Little more than a week later, Collin considered changing his mind.

He stood in the last stall of his barn showing Mitchell how to measure horse feed. The smell of hay and horses circled around his head.

The kid was all right most of the time. The social worker was a different matter.

He did okay on the days Mia dropped Mitch off as planned, said hello and goodbye and drove away in her power suit and speedy little yellow Mustang. The days she climbed out of that Mustang wearing blue jeans and a T-shirt gave him trouble. Regardless that she was here on business to assess the CAP arrangement, dressed like that, she was a woman, not a social worker. It was hard to dislike one and like the other, so he tried to keep his distance.

Trouble was, Mia didn't understand the concept of personal space. She was in his, talking a mile a minute, smile warm, attitude sweet. The more he retreated, the more she advanced.

Over the clatter of horse pellets hitting metal, he could hear her talking in soft, soothing tones to Happy, the pup with the lousy luck and the cheerful outlook.

"How much feed does Smokey get?" Mitch's question pulled Collin back to the horse feed.

"None of the pellets. Just some of this alfalfa."

Mitch frowned, dubious. "He's awful skinny."

"Too much at first can kill him."

"How come somebody let him get like that? I can see his ribs."

The buckskin colt stood quivering in the stall, head down, so depressed Collin wondered if he'd survive.

"Some people don't care."

It was a cold, hard fact that both he and the boy knew all too well. "Yeah."

In the few days Mitch had been here, Collin had ferreted out a few unsavory facts about his home life. The stepdad wasn't exactly father-of-the-year material. And mom wouldn't win any prizes, either, although the kid was loyal to her anyway. Collin didn't press him about his mother. He'd been the same once, until the woman who'd birthed him walked away and never looked back. He hoped that never happened to Mitchell.

Hand full of green, scented hay, the kid knelt in front of the little horse. "Come on, Smokey. It's okay."

The colt nuzzled the outstretched fingers, then nibbled a bit of grass.

Mitch had a way with all the creatures on the farm. Even Doc had commented on that. Like a magnet, he was drawn to the sickest ones, the most wounded, the near-hopeless. Street-kid wariness melted into incredible tenderness when he approached the animals. Not one of them shied away from the boy's tenacious determination to make them all well.

"I promised Happy I'd soak his foot later. Is that okay?" Mitchell was on a mission to save the crippled little collie. Every day, he went to Happy's stall first and last with some extra time in between.

"What did Doc say?"

"She said extra soaks can't hurt nothing."

She was right about that. Happy's foot had reached

the point when hope was all but gone. Soaking couldn't make the wound any worse, and any action at all made them feel as if they were doing something. "All right, then."

Collin moved down the corridor, taking care of the menial tasks so necessary for the survival of these wounded creatures who depended on him. Cleaning pens, scooping waste, lining stalls and boxes with fresh straw.

Mia was inside the cat pen.

He frowned at her. "I thought you left." He hadn't really, but he didn't know what else to say.

"You wish." With a laugh, she lifted one of Panda's kittens from the box and draped the fur ball over her shoulder. "What's wrong? Rough day?"

Yeah, he'd had a lousy day, but how did she know? He didn't like having some woman, a social worker at that, inside his head.

"I'm all right." He ducked into Happy's stall to escape her. She followed, but didn't press him about his gray mood.

"Mitch seems to be doing a good job for you, don't you agree?"

"Yeah." The dog wobbled up from his straw bed, tail wagging. The smell of antiseptic and dying flesh was hard to ignore.

"Has he opened up at all about why he runs away so much?"

"A little."

"But you're not going to tell me."

"Confidential."

She rolled her big eyes at him. She had interesting eyes. Huge and almond-shaped, soft and sparkly. He didn't know how a person made her eyes sparkly, but she did.

Mia knelt to stroke the pup while still holding the kitten against her shoulder. Happy, tail thumping a mile a minute, didn't seem to mind having a cat invade his territory. Dumb dog didn't seem to mind much of anything.

"What's going to happen to him?"

"Happy? Or Mitch?"

She gave him another of her wide-eyed looks. He wanted to laugh. "The dog."

"If things don't improve this week, Doc's going to amputate the other foot on Monday."

"Oh, Collin." Her face was stricken. She glanced toward the stall door. "Does Mitch know?"

"No."

"No wonder you're in a bad mood tonight. I thought maybe you'd had to shoot somebody today."

"That would have made me feel better."

She looked up. "Not funny."

"Sorry. Bad cop joke." Using force was the last thing he ever wanted.

"How do you cops do that, anyway? Shoot somebody, I mean."

"We pretend they're lawyers." He shook kibble into Happy's bowl. "Or social workers."

"Ha-ha. I'm laughing." But she did giggle. "When are you going to tell him?"

He crumpled an empty feed sack into an oversize ball. "I don't know."

"Want me to do it?"

"My responsibility." He tossed the sack into a trash

bin and knelt beside the pup. "I wish I knew who did this to him."

The little dog licked his outstretched hand, liquid brown eyes delighted by the attention. Anger and help-lessness pushed inside Collin's chest. He hated feeling helpless.

"I ran a computer search of the system today on you and your brothers."

His pulse quickened though he told himself to expect nothing. "And came up empty?"

"Mostly."

"Figures." Refusing to be disappointed, he stood and took the kitten from her. The soft, warm body wiggled in protest. As many years as he'd searched he couldn't expect miracles from Mia in a week.

"There's some information about you, but the facts on Drew and Ian seem to be the same that you already have. A couple of foster placements. Some medical re-cords."

He wanted to ask what she'd found on him, but didn't bother. She'd probably tell him anyway. Mia already knew too much about him and she was likely to learn more. Opening his sordid background to anyone always made him feel vulnerable, and nothing scared him like vulnerability.

He led the way out of Happy's stall to take the kit-ten back to Panda. A glance toward the horses told him Mitch was busy mucking out stalls. A perverse part of him figured that particular job was adequate punish-ment for shoplifting.

"Collin."

He lowered the tiny tabby to her mother. Panda's burns were healing, but she didn't let anyone except

Mitch touch her. Even Doc had had to sedate the cat before treating the wounds, an unusual turn of events.

"Collin," she said again, this time from beneath his elbow.

With a sigh, he turned. "What?"

She wrinkled her nose at him, fully aware her chatter bothered him. She looked cute, and he didn't like it. Social workers weren't supposed to be cute.

"I brought the file of information with me. Do you want to see it?"

"Might as well."

Nothing like cold, hard welfare facts to make a man stop thinking about a pretty woman.

Inside Collin's house for the first time, Mia thought the interior of the unfinished, basically unfurnished house was exactly what she expected of him. Neat and tidy to a fault, one long room served as kitchen, living room, and dining room. The furniture consisted of an easy chair, a TV and a small dining-room set. There were no pictures on the walls, no curtains on the shaded windows, no plants or other decorating touches. Collin lived a neatly Spartan lifestyle.

To Mia, who lived in a veritable jungle of plants, terra-cotta pots and pieces of Tuscan decor jammed into a tiny apartment, the house was sadly bare but filled with potential. A pot here. A plant there.

"I live simply," he said when he caught her looking.

"The place has great potential."

"It's not even finished."

"That's why it has great potential."

He shook his head and pulled out two chairs. "Sit. I'll move the laptop."

She eyed the animated screen saver. "Did Mitchell do that?"

"Yeah. He loves the thing."

Mia knew the boy didn't have a computer at home. "His teacher says he's a regular whiz kid."

"He knows keystroke shortcuts I didn't know existed and can navigate sites I can't get into. I'm afraid to ask if he's ever tried hacking."

"The answer is probably yes."

"I know." With a self-deprecating laugh that surprised her, Collin admitted, "He even offered to teach me keyboarding."

"You should let him. Teaching you would be good for his self-esteem."

"It wouldn't be too good for mine." He wiggled his two index fingers. "Old habits die hard."

A large brown envelope lay on the table beside the computer. She reached for it. "Is that more information about your brothers?"

"No. Just another problem I'm working on."

"Anything I can help with?"

"Not unless you're a lawyer. My neighbor," he said, his lips twisted, "is suing me."

"What for?" She couldn't imagine Collin Grace ever being intrusive enough for any neighbor even to know him, much less be at cross-purposes.

"He claims one of my animals has attacked his prize sheep on more than one occasion."

"They couldn't." All the animals here were both too sick and too well-confined to bother anything.

"Cecil Slokum has found something to complain about ever since I bought this place."

"Why?"

"Don't know. This time though—" he waved the envelope in the air "—I ran a background check on him."

"Oooh, suspicious. Remind me never to tick you off."

"Too late."

There was that wicked sense of humor again, coming out of nowhere.

"Have you hired an attorney?"

"No."

"You should."

"And I suppose you just happen to know one. Or two. Maybe you even know the judge."

"Well…" She cupped her hands under her chin and leaned toward him. "As a matter of fact, one of my brothers is an attorney. He's also a city councilman."

Collin leaned back his chair. "So he's the one."

"Don't look like that. If my brother hadn't spoken to the chief, you might never have agreed to mentor Mitch. And you like having him out here. You know you do."

"The kid's all right. He's good for the animals."

She laughed. If Collin wanted to pretend he cared nothing about the boy, fine. But he did.

"You've made more progress with Mitchell in a week than anyone else has made in a year."

The boy basked in the policeman's attention, eager to please him, ready to listen to his few, terse words. According to his fifth-grade teacher, Mitch had even turned in all his homework this week, a first.

Collin set the laptop and the brown envelope on an empty chair. "So, you gonna show me that file you brought or talk me to death?"

"Both." She handed over the manila folder.

His eyes twinkled. "Figures."

"You won't die from a little conversation, Collin. Talking things out might do you some good."

She liked listening to his quiet, manly voice as much as she enjoyed looking at him. He was an attractive man. Mia squelched a stomach flutter. Very attractive.

Less intimidating in street attire, tonight he wore a Tac-team T-shirt neatly tucked into well-worn blue jeans. Muscular biceps, fine-cut by exercise and work, stretched the sleeves snug.

"I keep noticing your tattoo." Among other things. "What is it?"

He looked up from studying the file. For a moment, she thought he wouldn't tell her, but then he pushed the sleeve higher and rotated toward her.

Her heart stutter-stepped. Each leaf of a small sham-rock bore, not initials as she'd thought, but a name. "Drew, Ian, Collin," she read.

"I didn't want to forget," he said simply. "Not even for a day."

All her preconceived ideas about tattoos went flying out the door. Without forethought, Mia placed her fingers on his arm just beneath the clover. His dark skin was warm and firm and strong with leashed power.

"What an incredibly loving thing to do."

He slid away from her and stood, closing the file. "Mitch should be up here by now. He has homework."

Helping Mitchell with his homework hadn't been part of the court order but Collin didn't let that deter him.

He crossed the few steps to the door and stood gazing out, his back to her. She felt the uncertainty in him, the discomfort that she'd generated with her comment. Or maybe with her touch. One thing was clear. Collin had a hard time expressing emotions. He might feel them. He just couldn't let them show.

She held back a smile. To an Italian, Collin Grace was a red flag waved in front of a bull. Expression was what she and her family did best. She would either drive Collin crazy or help him heal. She hoped it was the latter. Collin had a lot to offer people if he would only open up and trust a little more.

"Collin?"

He tensed but didn't turn around. "What?"

"My family's having a birthday party on Saturday for Nic, my youngest brother. He's turning twenty-one. If you'll come, I'll introduce you to Adam. He might be able to help with the lawsuit."

He looked at her over one shoulder. "How many brothers do you have?"

"Three bros, one sister and a lot of cousins, aunts and uncles."

"You're lucky."

"Yes. Incredibly blessed. You'll like them, Collin. They're great people."

He turned all the way around, tilting his head so she would know he teased. "Do they all talk as much as you?"

She grinned. "All but Uncle Vitorio. Come on, Collin. Say you'll be there."

"I wouldn't want to intrude." Which meant he wanted to come.

"No such thing at a Carano gathering. We have a motto. The more the merrier."

"Not too original."

She shrugged. "Who cares? It fits. So what do you say?" She really, really wanted him to come. For professional reasons, of course.

Cocoa-colored eyes holding hers, he considered the invitation for a minute but finally said, "Better not."

Disappointment seeped into her, but disappeared as quickly as the next thought arrived. "You could bring Mitch. He needs to interact with a strong family unit, and even if I do say so myself, mine fits the bill."

Hanging out with the Caranos would be good for Collin, too, but she couldn't say that.

"Proud of them, are you?"

"They're a little crazy, and none of us is perfect by any stretch of the imagination, but yeah, I have a great family."

"Taking Mitch is a good idea, but you don't need me along."

"He won't go without you." And she was glad. Collin needed the warm circle of family around him as much as the child did. A man who'd grown up in the system wouldn't have had too many opportunities to witness healthy family relationships. Besides, the Caranos were a lot of fun and if anyone could melt the ice shield from Collin and Mitchell, her family could.

"Here he comes now," she said at the sound of feet tromping on the porch. "Why don't we ask him?"

Collin held the door open as Mitch, Archie the turtle in hand, came inside. To everyone's astonishment, the turtle with the cracked shell was thriving.

"Ask me what?" The little turtle's claws scratched at the air and found purchase when Mitchell placed him on the table.

"You want to go to a party at my house on Saturday?"

Mitch squinted at Mia and then up at Collin. "You going?"

Mia giggled. Collin slanted his eyes at her in silent warning. She laughed out loud.

"It'll be a great party. Lots of food and games and craziness. My folks have a swimming pool." She let that little bit of enticement dangle.

Scooping Archie against his chest, Mitch plopped into a chair. "A real pool? Or one of them kiddie things?"

"Above-ground, but it's big. Has a slide and everything."

"Are your parents rich?"

Mia laughed. "No. They've run a little family bakery forever, but they know how to save money for the things that matter."

Mitch eyeballed Collin, who had gone to the fridge for boxes of juice. Mia knew avoidance behaviors when she saw them.

"They probably wouldn't want me to come." The boy's voice held a longing that neither adult could miss. "I don't have any trunks."

Collin slammed a straw through the top of a juice box with such force the plastic bent.

"We'll get some," he said gruffly.

"You're going too?" Mitch sat up straight and punched the air. "All right. This will be awesome!"

Collin sent Mia a look that would have quelled anyone but a determined social worker.

And she knew she'd won.

Chapter Six

By the time Saturday afternoon rolled around, the knot in Collin's stomach had grown from the size of a pea to that of a watermelon. Mitchell wasn't in any better shape. The kid, usually mouthy as Mia, had barely said two words on the drive to the Carano place.

Collin knew how the kid felt. Out of place. A misfit. The uncertainty was one of the reasons he avoided hanging out with his police buddy, Maurice. How did a person fit into a family when they didn't know what a family should be?

But Collin had learned about and yearned for the kind of relationships Mia bragged about. Even if he might never have them for himself, he wanted them for Mitch. The kid needed to know there was better out there than a stepdad who knocked your mom around and hung out with thugs. Mitchell needed this, which was exactly why Collin had swallowed his reluctance and put on a show about wanting to meet the Caranos.

When they pulled up in front of the sprawling home in a nice older neighborhood in northwest Oklahoma City, a half-dozen other cars already lined the street out front. Collin did his usual scan of the premises, committing the vehicle descriptions and the entrances and exits to memory, the police officer in him never off duty.

Mitch fidgeted with his seat belt. "You think they'll like me?"

The question bothered Collin but he didn't let his feelings show. The kid already knew that people would judge him by his rough clothes and poor grammar. He might as well have White Trash tattooed on his forehead.

"If Mia likes you, they will, too."

"She likes me because she has to. It's her job."

Collin squeezed the back of Mitch's neck. "You know better."

"Yeah." The boy pumped his eyebrows in silliness. "She likes me 'cause I'm cute."

Collin made a rude noise. Mitch's laughter relaxed them both.

As they started up the hedge-lined walkway, squeals and laughter echoed from the backyard. A football came flying over a wooden privacy fence and landed at Collin's feet. He picked it up just as the gate opened. He expected a kid to come charging after the ball. Instead, a grown man, probably near his age, trotted toward him. His maroon T-shirt was sweat-plastered to his upper body.

Collin held up the ball. "This belong to you?"

"Coulda had a touchdown if I'd been taller." The man stopped in front of them and bent forward, hands on knees to catch his breath. "You must be Collin and Mitch. Glad you're here. Mia's wearing a hole in the carpet."

She was?

"I'm Adam, Mia's favorite brother." He laughed, smile bright in a dark face, and extended his hand to Mitch and then to Collin. "You must be the cop Mia's been telling us about."

She talked about him? "I hope it's good."

"So far."

The man was friendly enough, but Collin knew when he was being checked out. He didn't miss the subtle warning. Mess with a Carano and you have to answer to the whole clan. He admired that. He had been that way with his own brothers, though he was surprised that Adam would feel the need to warn him about anything. He'd come here to help a troubled kid, not because of Mia.

Adam tossed the ball back and forth from one hand to the other. "You play football?" he said to Mitchell.

"I stink at it."

"Awesome." Adam gently shoved the ball into the boy's midsection. "You can be on my team. We all stink at it, too. How about you, Collin?"

"Yeah. I stink at it, too."

Adam laughed and slapped him on the back. "Come on. I'll take you inside to find Mia. We'll get a game going later."

Adam's friendly greeting took some of the tension out of Collin's jaw. Maybe he could get through this afternoon with a minimum amount of stress.

Collin's first impression of the Carano house was the noise, good noise that came from talk and laughter and activity. Several conversations bounced around the large, crowded living room in competition with a big-screen TV blasting a game between the Texas Longhorns and the Oklahoma State Cowboys. There were kitchen noises too, of pots and pans and cabinets opening and closing.

Through patio doors at the opposite end, the pool was visible, along with the remnants of the touch football game they'd interrupted. He glanced down at Mitch, saw the boy scanning the backyard with typical kid radar. He figured Mitch would be fine as soon as he worked his way outside.

The incredible smell of home-cooked food issued from the enormous area to his left. The kitchen was exactly the kind he had envisioned for Mia, though she no longer lived here. Washed warm with sunlight and the rich earthy colors of brick-red flooring, the room was dappled with overflowing fruit baskets, clear jars of colorful pasta, and copper pots dangling above a center island. He located Mia at the island arranging cheese and fruit on a platter.

The knot in his stomach reacted oddly. He was glad to see her, whether because she was the only familiar face in the crowd or otherwise, he didn't know. And he wasn't bothering to go there. Two weeks ago, she was a pain in his neck.

She looked so natural here, so much more real than she did in her office and business suits. Home was her element.

She said something to a pretty older woman who could only be her mother. They both had the same large, almond eyes and full mouths. And like her mother, Mia tended to be more rounded and womanly than was currently the trend—a look Collin appreciated.

Today her long hair was down, flowing in soft red-brown waves around her shoulders. Her red T-shirt fitted her to perfection and topped off a pair of white, loose-fitting cropped pants and sandals.

She was talking—no big surprise—as she popped a piece of cheese in her mouth. Suddenly she laughed, clapping one hand over her lips.

"Hey, Mia," Adam hollered over the noise. "You got company."

When she caught sight of him, her face brightened. Hurriedly, she said something over her shoulder, wiped her hands on a towel and rushed in their direction.

"You're here!" For a minute, Collin thought she might hug him. Instead, she grabbed his elbow with one hand, dropped the other arm over Mitch's shoulder, and drew them into the melee.

"I see you've already met Adam, so follow me and we'll try to forge a path to the others."

Adam disappeared into the mix as Mia introduced the newcomers to her sister, parents, grandparents and a number of other people whose connection escaped him.

"I don't expect you to remember everyone the first time," Mia said.

The first time? Collin wasn't sure he could survive a second go-round. Though everyone was as friendly as Mia, he felt like a bug under a microscope.

"This is my baby brother, Nic," Mia was saying. "The birthday boy."

"That's birthday *man* to you, big sister." Across Nic's T-shirt were the words, *What if the Hokey Pokey really is what it's all about?*

Mia laughed and rolled her eyes. "He's twenty-one today and I suspect he will be impossible to live with now that he thinks he's become one of the grown-ups."

Collin shook the younger man's hand. "Good to meet you, Nic. Happy birthday."

"Thanks," Nic answered, his grin wide as he looked from Collin to Mia. Speculation, totally unwarranted, was rife. Just what exactly had Mia told them about him anyway? "You want to hear some secrets about my evil big sister?"

Mia poked a teasing finger in Nic's chest. "No, he doesn't. Not if you want to live to be twenty-two."

Speculation or not, Collin enjoyed the joking exchange between brother and sister.

He leaned toward Nic and spoke in a low voice. "Maybe we should talk later. When Mia isn't around."

Mia pretended horror. "Don't you dare. Nic tells lies about how mean I was to him when he was small."

"They're not lies. Just ask Adam." Nic whipped around. "Hey, Adam. Come help me out."

Adam, the football player in the maroon shirt, popped up from the couch, where he was surrounded by kids who fell away like brushed-off dust. Collin was startled to see Mitchell in the mix. At some point the kid had wandered off toward the big-screen TV, and Collin hadn't even noticed. Chalk up one demerit for the Big Brother.

"What's up?" Adam asked, his sweaty T-shirt still damp and dark. "The birthday boy already showing off?"

"Of course," Mia said. "I'm leaving Collin in your mature company so I can help Mom and Grandma get dinner on the table. Do not allow Nic to tell horror stories."

Nic guffawed and Adam struggled to keep a straight face. "Sure, sis. Whatever you say."

"I mean it," she warned with a wagging finger. "Collin, I'll be back to rescue you in five minutes."

Then she returned to the oregano-scented kitchen, leaving Collin with Adam again. The feeling of abandonment came with startling swiftness, that emptiness he despised. Collin bit down on his back teeth, annoyed. He was a grown-up. He didn't need a babysitter. In fact, he didn't need to be here. He didn't fit.

He shifted uncomfortably and wished for a quiet corner where he could watch and listen without being noticed. Mitchell was probably miserable, too. But one look in the living room told him he was wrong. Mitch was deep in conversation with Mr. Carano and they were both fiddling with a laptop chess game. Give the kid a computer and he was at home anywhere. Collin envied that ease and wondered if he'd ever had it as a kid. If he had, it had been very early in his life. He sure didn't remember.

"You have that shell-shocked look that says Mia didn't warn you about us." Adam's voice broke into his thoughts.

"What? Sorry, my mind strayed."

"No wonder. The noise level in here could rival a landing strip."

"No problem." The noise wasn't what bothered him, though it *was* loud. Loud and enthusiastic. He could see where Mia got her positive energy and upbeat attitude.

"From the look on your face, I'd say your family isn't as big or rowdy as the Carano bunch."

"You'd be right about that." If he had a family.

Adam grabbed a bowl of chips from the coffee table. "Come on, let's head out to the backyard, where there's some relative peace. There could be a football game in your future. How about you, Nic? Ready to rumble?"

"Not now. Dana Rozier just pulled up out front with a carload of babes." He cranked his eyebrows up and down a few times. "Can't disappoint the ladies."

Nic rubbed his hands together and then bounded for the front door.

"Ask them if they want to play football," Adam called and was rewarded with a hyena laugh from the birthday boy. "Oh, well, it was worth a try." He shook his head. "Nic and his girls. I don't see the attraction, do you?"

The Carano brothers were fun. He'd say that for them.

Adam shrugged, hollered at Gabe to organize a team, and then led the way through the sea of people and at least one large dog. The backyard was filled with kids, some swimming, two shooting hoops, and a couple of little ones just running in circles squealing for the joy of it.

Adam set the bowl of chips on the ground and collapsed into a lawn chair. "Grab a chair."

Collin did.

"Man, is this a gorgeous day or what?"

"Yeah." He thought of all the work he could be doing on his house on a day like this. Winter would come soon and he wouldn't be any closer to finishing than he'd been at the beginning of summer.

"Mia says you run a rescue ranch for hurt animals."

"That's right."

"She told me about your problem."

Collin stiffened. Mia had promised to keep his search for Drew and Ian confidential. "Why would she do that?"

"Mia doesn't keep much from her family. But in this case she thought I could help."

He should have known he couldn't trust a social worker. "I can handle it."

"Sometimes lawsuits, even frivolous ones, can be tricky."

A truckload of tension rushed out of Collin. The lawsuit.

"Mia told me her brother was a lawyer. I didn't realize she meant you."

"I hope you didn't think she meant Nic."

They both chuckled. "Seeing him in a courtroom might be entertaining."

"What about in the operating room?"

"Excuse me?"

"He's applying for medical school. There really is a brain beneath that happy-go-lucky personality."

"I'm impressed."

"Don't be. He hasn't been accepted yet." Adam reached for another handful of tortilla chips and offered the bowl to Collin. "So how can I help you with this lawsuit?"

"I don't want to impose."

"No imposition. A friend of Mia's is a friend of mine."

Were they friends? He hadn't wanted to be, hadn't really thought about it until now. "She's a nice girl."

"A very nice girl." Adam shifted around in the lawn chair so they were face-to-face.

"Sometimes she pushes too hard, comes on too strong, but don't hold that against her. Gabe and I call her a coconut. Tough on the outside, a little nutty when she gets on one of her crusades to change the world, but soft and sweet on the inside."

Collin had seen the sweet side at the ranch. He'd also wrestled with her talkative, pushy side.

"She hounded me for days until I agreed to mentor Mitchell."

"See what I mean? She's so sure she can change the world with love and faith that she never gives up. Sometimes she gets hurt in the process. I wouldn't want to see that happen again."

Mia had been hurt? How? Why? And, most importantly, by whom? Collin, who seldom ate chips, took a handful.

"She's in a tough profession," was all he could think of. "The ugliness burns out a lot of strong people."

"Not Mia. She'll never let that happen. There's too much of God in her. She'll always stay tender and vulnerable to hurt. That's just the way she's made." Adam tossed a chip into the air, caught it in his mouth and crunched. "You know why she's not married?"

He'd wondered. Mia was smart, pretty, personable… though he wondered more that Adam would bring up the subject with a stranger like him. "I figure she's had her chances."

"She has. But Mia is waiting for the right guy. Not just any guy, but the one God sends."

Well, that left him out for sure. Not that it mattered. He wasn't in the market for a woman. Especially a nosey social worker who talked too much and made him think about things and feel things he'd kept buried most of his life.

Adam could relax. Neither he nor his sister had anything to fear from Collin Grace.

Chapter Seven

"He's out in the backyard." Adam jerked a thumb in that direction. "The guy looked like he could use a breather from all of us."

Mia took a fresh glass of tea, sugarless the way she'd seen Collin take it during the meal, and pushed open the patio doors.

The glorious blue sky hung over a perfect early-autumn afternoon. She breathed in a happy breath of fresh air. What a great day this had been. Collin and Mitchell had seemed to have a good time. And her family had risen to the occasion as they always did, wrapping the two newcomers in a welcome of genuine friendliness. Nic had been his usual wild and crazy self, celebrating his twenty-first birthday by shooting videos of all the attendees wearing the Groucho glasses he'd bought for party favors.

This kind of gathering was good for Mitchell. He could learn here, interact with real men and motherly women, learn how to have fun in a clean and healthy way. Though she knew Collin would argue the fact, he needed this kind of thing, too. The protective shell around him kept away hurt, but it also kept away the good emotions.

When he'd walked in the door this afternoon, she'd been almost giddy with pleasure. Later, she'd have to examine that reaction.

In the shady overhang of the house, he leaned against the sun-warmed siding to watch Mitchell splash around in the pool. Was it her imagination or did Collin look isolated, maybe even lonely, standing there apart from the bustle of people? She'd thought a lot about him lately, about his upbringing, about how awful he must feel to be alone in the world, not knowing where his family was, or even if they were alive.

Yes, he was on her mind a great deal.

"You look like you could use this." Ice tinkled against the glass as she held the tea out to him.

"Thanks."

Mia wiped her hand, damp from condensation, down her pant leg. "Overwhelmed?"

He sipped at the tea and swallowed before answering. "A little."

"If a person survives their first dose of Caranos, they're a shoo-in for navy SEALs training or a trip to the funny farm."

He smiled his appreciation of the joke. A day with her family showed him where she derived her great sense of humor.

"My experience with family gatherings is pretty limited."

"Well, you're a hit. You officially passed inspection by the Carano brothers."

"Carano brothers." He held up his Groucho glasses. "Sounds like a family of mobsters."

"Shh. Don't say that too loud. We are Italian, re-member."

They grinned into each other's eyes. From inside the house came a shout of "Touchdown."

The Cowboys must have scored. Here in the yard, the sounds were quieter, the splash of kids sliding into the pool, the occasional yip of the dog.

Though he'd felt out of place all afternoon, Collin liked Mia and her family. A couple of times he'd seen Mrs. Carano, who insisted on being called Rosalie, pat Mitchell's back and ply him with goodies from the family bakery. The kid must be ready to explode, but he'd soaked up the attention like Happy did, as though starved for positive reinforcement.

Had he been like that? He couldn't recall. He'd spent so much time keeping Drew out of trouble and Ian fed and safe that he really didn't remember ever being a child.

Mia swirled the melting ice round and round in her own glass, then pressed the coldness to the side of her neck. Collin's belly reacted to the feminine sight. Mia, with her nice family, her chatterbox ways and her honest concern for people was putting holes in his arguments against social workers. Except for the title and the business suits, she didn't fit the stereotype. Adam hadn't helped any with his innuendoes.

"You won Gabe over when your phone played 'Boomer Sooner.'" A soft smile lifted her pretty mouth, setting a single tiny dimple into relief. He'd never noticed that dimple before.

"I saw the Oklahoma Sooner tag on a couple of cars out there." He didn't bother to say Adam had grilled him about his intentions. No point in embarrassing Mia about a simple misunderstanding. Adam was a good guy. He'd meant well. Even if he was badly misguided.

"We all attended OU. Adam played a little baseball, so we're pretty hard-core Sooner fans. Gabe even has season tickets to the football games."

Collin had never made it to college. "I'm a big football fan myself." Which had made conversation with the Caranos a little easier.

"But not of the Dallas Cowboys. Nic is a little miffed about that, though he thinks he can convert you."

"Want me to lie to him since it's his birthday?"

She punched his arm. "Silly."

"Bully." He rubbed the spot just over his shamrock. A lot of people had asked him about the tattoo before and he'd told them nothing. But Mia was different. She had a way of slipping under his guard, catching him unawares, and the next thing he knew he was telling her way too much.

"I never liked tattoos before. But I like yours," she said as if reading his mind. "When did you have it done?"

"When I was seventeen." He wasn't about to tell her the shape he'd been in when he'd gone to the tattoo parlor.

"Isn't it illegal to get one at that age?"

"I wasn't a cop then."

He'd made the remark to encourage a smile. She didn't disappoint him.

"Well, even if it was illegal, you were very insightful to choose a tattoo that represents so much."

"Yeah. Real insightful." To him the tattoo represented a man, a cop at that, who couldn't find the brothers he'd promised to look after. It represented years of failure. He made a wry face. "I chose a shamrock because I needed space for three words and I like the color green."

Undaunted by his dry tone, she studied the figure. "Three leaves, three brothers. Your names are Irish. And green means everlasting, like the evergreen trees. Everlasting devotion."

He blinked down at the tattoo. Then at her.

She came to his shoulders and he could see the top of her hair. In the bright sunlight, the soft waves gleamed more red than brown. He defeated the sudden and unusual urge to touch her hair.

The tattoo had come about on what would have been Ian's twelfth birthday. Collin had been fighting a terrible depression, and the tattoo seemed like a grown-up, proactive thing to do at the time. Now he looked back on the day with a sense of chagrin and failure.

That had been a tough time for him. His days of being cared for in the foster system had been coming to an end, and he was scared out of his mind. He had no place to go, no training, no family, no money. Only a dim memory of two brothers to cling to and the fish keychain that somehow bound the three of them together. Then as now, every time he smoothed his fingers over the darkening metal, he felt closer to Drew and Ian.

"I can't say I was all that deep and symbolic about a tattoo, Mia. I think I was just hoping for a little good luck." He'd needed all the help he could get in the days following his eighteenth birthday.

"Did it work?"

She tilted her head back against the white siding and stared out at the pool, where Mitch splashed with Gabe's ten-year-old son. Abby, Gabe's wife, watched from a lawn chair.

"Nah. Mostly, I think we make our own luck. What about you? Got a rabbit's foot in your purse?"

She smiled, but her eyes remained serious.

"I don't put much stock in luck, either. God, on the other hand, is a different matter. I truly believe He, not luck or coincidence, controls my destiny."

"Like a robot?"

She laughed and shook her head. The reddish waves danced back from her pretty face. "Not like that. People have free will. But if we let Him, God will guide our lives and work everything out for our good."

"You really think that?"

"Yes. I really do."

Well, he didn't. He thought you had to claw and fight and struggle uphill, hoping like mad that some crumb of good would fall in your lap.

"I always figured God was out there somewhere, but He was probably too busy to bother with one person."

"God's not like that, Collin. He's very personal. He cares about the smallest, simplest things in our lives."

"If that's so, why is there so much trouble in the world? Why do kids go hungry and parents mistreat and abandon them?" And why couldn't he find his brothers?

The seed of bitterness he tried to hide rose up like a sickness in his throat.

Mia placed a hand on his arm, a gentle, reassuring touch much like the ones he'd seen Rosalie give to Mitchell. He wanted her to stop. "I hear what you're not saying."

Of course she would. She dealt with people in his shoes all the time. She was trained to read behind the mask, a scary prospect if ever there was one. He didn't want anybody messing around inside his mind.

While his insides churned and he wondered what he was doing here, Collin tossed the remaining ice cubes onto a small bush growing beside the house. When the movement dislodged Mia's hand from his arm, he suffered a pang of loss. Talk about messed up. One minute he wanted her to stop touching him, and the next he was disappointed because she did.

"God can help you find your brothers," she said. "Or at least find out what happened to them."

He kept quiet. Mia had a right to her faith even if he had never witnessed anything much from God.

He rolled the empty glass back and forth between his palms. "Like I said, I don't know much about religion."

"That's okay. Faith's not about religion anyway."

She was losing him again.

"Faith is about having a relationship with the most perfect friend you could ever have. Jesus is a friend who promises to stick closer than a brother."

"Closer than a brother," he murmured softly. And then for some reason, he slid a hand into his pocket, found the tiny fish. The metal was warm from his body heat. "For me that wouldn't be too close."

"Then why can't you stop looking for them? And why is your arm tattooed with their names?"

She had a point there. "I guess I'm trying to keep them close even though they're lost." He pulled the tiny ichthus from his pocket. "See this?"

Her expressive face couldn't hide her surprise. "A Jesus fish?"

"I suppose you want to know why I carry it if I'm not a believer?"

"Yes."

He started to tease and say he carried the fish for luck.

But that wasn't true. His feelings were deeper than that though he wasn't sure he had the words to express them.

"The day my brothers and I were separated the school counselor gave us each one of these." He turned the fish over. The bright sunlight caught the faded engraving, *Jesus will never leave you nor forsake you.* He'd thought of that scripture often and hoped it was true. He hoped there was somebody in this world looking after Ian and Drew.

"I wonder if they still have theirs," she murmured quietly.

"Why would they keep a cheap little keychain?" But he hoped they had.

"You kept yours."

He rubbed a finger over the darkened engraving as he'd done dozens of times. This was his link, his connection to Drew and Ian. That link, religion aside, gave him comfort. And if he'd tried to pray a few times as a boy, asking the distant God for help, well, he'd been a kid who just didn't understand the facts of life.

He wished that God could do something about his lost brothers, but he didn't know how to believe in anything but himself. His own strength and determination had gotten him where he was today. He knew better than to rely on anyone or anything else.

Before he could say more, Nic came sprinting around from the opposite side of the house, an orange plastic water pistol in one hand.

Gabe was right behind him, squirting his own water pistol like mad.

"You're gonna pay, birthday boy," he roared. And from the looks of Gabe's soaked shirtfront, Nic had started the trouble.

With a wild hyena laugh, Nic turned and fired, squirting Gabe as well as the two innocent bystanders. Mia jumped aside with a squeal of laughter.

Oddly disappointed to have his strange conversation with Mia interrupted, Collin brushed a water droplet from his arm.

"And you said your family was functional."

They both laughed as Adam came running past, wearing the Groucho glasses and carrying two squirt guns with another stuck in his shirt pocket.

"Defend yourself," he yelled and tossed a purple plastic pistol in their general direction.

With quick reflexes, Collin caught the squirt gun. As soon as the toy hit his hand, a sudden flashback hit Collin square in the heart.

Drew and Ian armed with water guns they'd gotten somewhere chased him around the trailer. He'd hidden under the house, behind the dangling insulation, and unloaded on them when they'd discovered his whereabouts.

They had all squirted and yelled and chased until the night grew too dark to see each other. As they often did, they'd spent that night without adults, but for once they'd gone to bed smiling.

"Collin?" Mia said, touching the hand that held the water pistol. "What's wrong?"

Even the good memories hurt. All those years he'd missed. All the good times he and his brothers had deserved to have. Though he recognized the irrationality of his emotions, he envied the Caranos. They had what he wanted and would never have. The missing years could not ever be recaptured.

"I gotta go." He handed her the squirt gun and abruptly strode to the pool. "Time to roll, Mitchell."

He felt Mia's gaze on his back.

Mitchell was instantly protesting. "I don't wanna leave yet."

"Sorry. I have to work tomorrow." He did have to work. On his house.

Water sluicing off his hair and shoulders, body language screaming in protest, Mitchell pulled himself slowly out of the pool. He grumbled, "It's not fair."

"Yeah, well, life isn't fair, kid. Get used to it."

Mitch stopped and tilted his head back to look into Collin's face. "Are you mad at me?"

Collin relented the slightest bit. The kid had behaved himself today. No use making Mitch pay for his lousy mood. He hooked an elbow around the boy's wet head.

"I'm not mad."

Trailed by an unusually quiet Mia, they went into the house to bid a civil goodbye to all the Carano clan. Mitchell dragged through the house like a man condemned, gathered his clothes and shoes for departure. Rosalie bustled into the kitchen and came back with two foil-wrapped plates.

"Leftovers. You two could use a little meat on your bones."

A funny lump formed inside Collin's chest. Was this what a mother did? Just like on television? Did normal mothers fret over the children and make huge family dinners and nag everyone to eat more?

"Take them, Collin," Mia murmured. "Make her happy." She'd protested their departure with all the usual niceties, but his mind was made up. He couldn't be here among this family any longer. It was killing him.

"I hope you'll come back soon, Collin," Rosalie was

saying. "And bring this boy." She patted Mitchell's head. "You come anytime you want to, Mitchell. A friend of Mia's is our friend, too."

Finally, when he could bear no more of their kindness, he worked his way out to the sidewalk.

Mia stood in the doorway. She looked uncertain, worried. "Thank you for coming, Collin."

"Our pleasure, huh, Mitch?"

"Yeah." Mitch's bottom lip was dragging the ground. He looped a towel around his neck and sawed the rough terry cloth back and forth.

Collin didn't want to answer the questions in Mia's eyes, so he turned and started toward his truck. The door behind him didn't close for several more seconds.

He'd gotten himself into this mess with Mia. He'd known from the beginning that a social worker only brought trouble. Now he was knee-deep in this big-brother thing with Mitch and stuck with the constant reminders of everything he and his brothers had missed out on. He knew that sounded selfish and envious. Maybe he was.

Long ago, he'd made peace with who he was as well as who he wasn't. He'd made a decent life for himself and, except for his fruitless search for Drew and Ian, he was happy most of the time.

There was an old adage that said you don't miss what you've never had. He'd always thought it was a lie. Today confirmed his suspicion.

He wished he'd never come here.

Halfway down the sidewalk, Mitch asked, "Can I have Miss Carano bring me out to your house tomorrow afternoon?"

"Miss Carano goes to church. She's not your personal chauffeur."

"I can walk, then. No big deal."

"Five miles?"

"I could borrow a bike."

When Collin didn't answer, Mitchell said, "I guess you don't want me to. That's cool. It's okay. I got plenty of stuff to do."

They walked in silence, Collin feeling like a major jerk. He didn't want the kid around right now. He wanted to be alone, to sort out whatever was eating a hole in him.

One hand on the truck door, Mitchell said, "Will you soak Happy's foot for me? I promised him, ya know."

That clinched it. The little dog *was* making progress with Mitch's tender, relentless care. "Be ready at one. I'll pick you up."

He was in over his head. He had agreed to mentor Mitchell indefinitely, and he wasn't a man to go back on his word. But Mia's brothers with their camaraderie and craziness stirred up a nest of hornets inside him. The reminders were there, too strong to ignore.

He'd have to set up some ground rules if he was to keep his sanity. Working with Mia was part of the deal but mentoring didn't have to include her family. If she wanted Mitch to experience family relationships she could bring him here herself. He was never coming back to this place again.

Mia sat on the floor of her office surrounded by bent, bedraggled cardboard boxes filled with old files dating back more than twenty years. Three weeks ago she'd hauled these files over from the storage room and had been going through them a few at a time whenever she could break away from her caseload.

So far, dust and an occasional spider were the only things she'd found. The task was, after all, a daunting one that could take years to turn up something. If it ever did.

With the back of her hand she scratched her nose, itchy from the stale smell and dust mites. The Lord had sent Collin Grace her way, and she wouldn't let a little thing like twenty years and a mountain of dusty files stop her from trying to show him that God cared enough to help him find his brothers.

"You busy?"

She looked up to find Adam standing in the doorway. He held out a tall paper cup. "Could you use a break?"

"I hope that's a cherry icy." She took the cup, peeked under the lid and said, "You are the best brother on the planet."

"Does that mean you'll help me clean my apartment this weekend?"

"I knew there was a catch." She sipped the cold drink, let the cool, clean sweetness wash away some of the dust. "New girlfriend coming over?"

He grinned sheepishly. "How did you know?"

Mia chuckled. Every time Adam started dating someone new he went into a cleaning frenzy. Only he wanted Mia to do the cleaning. And the redecorating. And the cooking.

"As long as I don't have to repaint this time."

"We only repainted last time because Mandy isn't a big sports fan."

And Adam's living room had been painted in red and white with a Red Sox insignia emblazoned on the ceiling. "I knew she wouldn't last long."

"If only I were as wise...." He toasted her with his

fountain drink. "Which reminds me, I brought some information by for you to take to your new guy."

She eyed him from beneath a piece of floppy hair. "Excuse me? I haven't had a date in four months. There is no new guy."

"Collin. The cop." He made himself comfortable on the floor beside her. From inside his jacket he extracted an envelope, handing it to her.

"He's a friend, Adam." She read Collin's name on the front of the envelope. "Is this about that lawsuit?"

Adam nodded, but wouldn't be deterred from his original intent of matchmaking. "A few weeks ago you didn't even like the guy. The relationship is progressing pretty fast if you ask me."

"There is no relationship." Even if she wanted there to be, Collin had an invisible shield around him that held others at arm's length. "Ever since the birthday party he's been different. Cooler than usual." And for someone like Collin, that was as cool as this slush.

"He left soon after we started the water fight. Do you think we scared him off somehow?"

She'd wondered the same thing, though she couldn't imagine anything scaring a tough cop like Collin. "I don't know. Collin's hard to read sometimes. He holds a lot of himself in reserve."

From the bare-bones information Collin had shared about his childhood, he had every reason to distrust other human beings. But Mia didn't like the idea that he distrusted her, which accounted for her redoubled efforts to find some bit of information for him in these files. Trust had to be earned. And she wanted his.

"I keep wondering if we offended him somehow." He'd been fine while they were talking.

"Anyone who listens to Grandpa tell that story about the nanny goat and doesn't run at the first opportunity is not easily offended. Did he mention anything about why they left so early?"

She'd been out to his farm on a regular basis since the party, but their conversations had mostly been about Mitchell's latest truancy from school and the rescued animals. Once they'd talked about his search and another time he'd shocked her to no end by asking a question about God. She'd been frustrated to have no answer, but thrilled to know he was thinking about spiritual matters.

She rifled through another file, saw nothing related to Collin or his brothers and reached for another.

"Only that he appreciated our hospitality, thought we were a great family. You know, the usual polite stuff. And he thought the afternoon had been good for Mitchell."

Adam took the file folder from her hand and stuck it back in the box. "The boy needs a lot of attention. Did you see Mama plying him with cookies and questions?"

"Mama thinks food is the answer to everyone's problems."

"Isn't it?"

"My hips seem to think so." Every time Mia decided to do something about her few extra pounds, Mama invited her over for pasta and bread or asked her to work a few hours at the bakery. Or she went through a mini-crisis and baked some marvelous creation for herself. Having a family in the bakery business was both a blessing and a terrible temptation.

"So, do you like him?"

"Mitchell? Sure. He's basically a good boy, but he needs a firm hand and a strong role model. He went to Sunday School with me last week."

Adam gave her a look reserved for thick-headed sisters. "I'm talking about Collin."

"And I'm not." Every time a new man appeared on the horizon, her brothers zeroed in like stealth missiles. "I can hope, can't I?"

"Not in this case." Though there was something about Collin that kept him on her mind all the time, she knew better than to let her feelings take over. She wanted God to choose the right man for her.

"Want me to beat him up? Get things moving?"

She laughed. "You know how I feel about the whole husband-hunting thing. God's timing is always perfect."

"If God is going to send you a husband, He needs to hurry."

"Adam," she admonished. But she had to admit to a certain restlessness lately. Though her job and her community and church activities kept her life more than busy, she had always planned to be married with a big house filled with kids by now. "You're a fine one to talk. When are you going to find Miss Right and settle down?"

He shrugged a pair of shoulders that had plenty of women interested. "I want what Mom and Dad have. I'm willing to wait as long as it takes to get it."

And she was willing to wait, as well. She only hoped she didn't have to wait forever.

Chapter Eight

An excited Mia jumped out of her Mustang, leaving her jacket behind and hurrying through the cool, windy evening to Collin's front door. In the west the sun was setting, a testament to the shorter days of late autumn.

The hollow sound of a hammer rang through the otherwise quiet countryside. Not once in the months since meeting him had she come to this house and found Collin idle. He was either working on the house, with the animals or helping Mitchell do something. Didn't the man ever lie around on the couch like a slob the way her brothers did?

She waited for a pause in the hammering and then pounded hard on the door. She'd finally found something and she couldn't wait to share the news with Collin.

"Collin, hello."

The hammering ceased. After a minute, she saw movement from the corner of her eye and heard Collin's voice. She spotted him near the side of the house, the area still mostly in skeleton form.

In the fading light, Collin raised the hammer in

greeting, a smile lifting the corners of his mouth. Dressed in jeans and a denim shirt, he wore a tool belt slung low on his hips.

"Hey," he said.

She started toward him, her heart doing a weird ker-thumping action. Okay, so she was glad to see him. And yes, he was good-looking enough to make any woman's heart beat a little faster. But she was excited because of the news she had, not because Collin had smiled as if he was glad to see her, too. Mostly.

Adam and his insinuations were getting to her.

"Watch your step." Collin gestured at the pile of tools strewn about on the concrete pad, and then reached out to put a hand under her elbow.

His was a simple act of courtesy, but her silly heart did that ker-thump thing again. Come to think of it, this was the first time Collin had ever intentionally touched her.

A naked lightbulb dangled from an extension cord in one corner to illuminate the work space. The smell and fog of sawdust hung cloudlike above a pile of pale new boards propped beside a table saw.

"I finally have the decking on top," he said with some satisfaction, unmindful of her sudden awareness of him as a man. "Even if the room won't be completely in the dry before the really cold weather sets in, I'll be able to work out here."

Usually Mitchell was under foot, pounding and saw-ing under Collin's close supervision. She looked around, saw no sign of the boy. "Where's Mitchell?"

Collin placed the hammer on a makeshift table, his welcoming expression going dark. "I caught him smok-ing in the barn. Took him home early."

"Oh, no. I thought you'd made him see the senseless-ness of cigarettes."

"Yeah, well that was a big failure, I guess." He sighed, a heavy sound, and ran both hands up the back of his head. "He's been acting up again. Mouthy. Moody. Maybe I'm not doing him any good after all."

"Don't think that, Collin. All kids mess up, regress. But he's come a long way in a short time. The school says he's only missed two days since you spoke to his class on careers in law enforcement. His discipline referrals for fighting are down, too."

He squinted at her. "You know what he's been fight-ing about?"

"No. Do you?"

"I've got a clue." He turned to the closed door leading into the living area. "Come on in. You're getting cold."

Pleasure bloomed. He'd noticed.

Inside the kitchen, he motioned toward a half-full Mr. Coffee. "Coffee?"

"Sure." She took the offered cup, wrapping her hands around the warmth. "Are you going to share your in-sights with me?"

Collin leaned a hip against the clean white counter. If she was a betting woman, she'd bet he'd laid the tile himself. "I think Mitch is under a lot of pressure from some of the other boys."

"What kind of pressure?"

"I haven't figured that part out. There's something though. I have a feeling it has to do with his stepdad. That's a very sore subject lately."

Her caseworker antennae went up. "Anything I need to investigate on a professional basis?"

Over the rim of his coffee cup, Collin gave her the

strangest look, a look she'd come to recognize each time she mentioned her job. He took a long time in answering such a simple question.

"I guess it wouldn't hurt to keep your eyes and ears open."

She was already doing that.

"How's Happy?"

"Still happy." He grinned at his own joke and pulled a chair around from the table to straddle the seat. "Doc says the foot is still in danger. It'll kill Mitchell if she has to amputate."

She could tell Collin wouldn't be too happy either, but he wasn't about to say so.

"He's attached."

"Very." Arms folded over the back of the chair, the coffee mug dangled from his fingers.

"You are, too."

He made a face. "Yeah."

And she was glad to know he could form bonds this way, even though they saddened him. Some kids who grew up in the system were never able to love and bond.

"I have a bit of news for you." She laid her purse on the table and pulled out a slip of paper.

"I could use some today. Shoot."

"This may turn out to be nothing, but—" she handed him the note "—this is the address of foster parents who took care of one of your brothers shortly after you were separated. They're not on your list."

The expression on his face went from mildly interested to intense. "Seriously?"

"The address hasn't been updated and there was no telephone, so we may not find anything."

He shoved out of the chair and grabbed a jacket. "Let's go see."

"Collin, wait."

He paused, face impassive.

Suddenly, she regretted her impulsive action to come here first before checking out the address herself.

"I haven't made contact. We don't know if anything will come from this. Don't get your hopes up, okay?"

"It's worth a shot." He shrugged the rest of the way into his jacket. "We'll take my truck."

She had known he'd react this way, pretending not to hope, but grasping at anything. If the foster parents were still around, they might not remember one little boy who passed through their lives so long ago. And if they did, they probably wouldn't remember where the child had gone from there.

"This is the first new piece of the puzzle I've had in a long time," Collin admitted as he smoothly guided the truck around the orange barrels and flashing lights of the ever-present road construction that plagued Oklahoma City. "Dartmouth Drive is back in one of these additions. I've been out here on calls. Not the best part of town."

A bad feeling came over her. She felt the need to say one more time, "Remember, now. This address comes from a very old file."

"I heard you." But she could tell that he didn't want to think that the trip might be futile.

Night had fallen and the wind picked up even more. An enormous harvest moon rose in the east. Mia had a sense of trepidation about approaching a strange house at night.

"Maybe we should have waited until tomorrow."

"I've waited twenty years." The lights of his vehicle swept over a wind-wobbled sign proclaiming Dartmouth Drive. He turned onto a residential street. "Should be right down here on the left."

She could feel the tension emanating from him like heat from a stove. He wanted to find out something new about his brothers so badly. And now that they were nearing the place, Mia was scared. If the trip proved futile, would he be devastated?

"Here's the address." He pulled the truck to a stop along the curb.

She squinted into the darkness. "I don't think anyone is at home, Collin."

"Maybe they watch TV with the lights off."

They made their way up the cracked sidewalk. In the moonlight Mia observed that the grass was overgrown, a possibility only if no one had been here for a long time. Growing season had been over for more than a month.

She shouldn't have let him come here and be disappointed. But she'd been so excited that she hadn't thought everything through in advance. She'd only wanted to give him hope. Now, Collin could be hurt again because of her.

He banged on the front door.

"Collin," she said softly, wanting to touch him, to comfort him.

He ignored her and banged again, harder. "Hello. Anybody home?"

"Collin." This time she did touch him. His arm was like granite.

He stared at the empty, long-abandoned house. In the moonlight, his jaw worked. She heard him swallow and knew he swallowed a load of disappointment.

Abruptly, he did an about-face. "Dry run."

Inside the truck, Mia said, "This was my fault. I'm so sorry."

He gripped the steering wheel and stared at the empty house. "I should be used to it by now."

That small admission, that no matter how many times he came up empty he still hurt, broke Mia's heart. She couldn't imagine the pain and loneliness he'd suffered in his life. She couldn't imagine the pain of being separated from her loved ones the way Collin had been.

When they'd first met, she'd thought him cold and heartless. Now she realized what a foolish judgment she'd made.

Because she didn't know what else to do, Mia closed her eyes and prayed. Prayed for God to help them find Drew and Ian. Prayed that Collin could someday release all his heartache to the only One who could heal him. Prayed that she would somehow find the words to compensate for her bad judgment.

In silence they drove out of the residential area and headed toward Collin's place and her vehicle. Mia was glad she'd left her car at the farm. Collin didn't need to be alone even if he thought he did.

"Are you okay?" she finally asked.

In the dim dash lights he glanced her way, his cop face expressionless. "Sure. You hungry?"

The question had her turning in her seat. "Hungry?"

"As in food. I haven't had dinner."

"Neither have I." She felt out of balance. He had shoved aside what had to be, at least, a disappointment. Was this the way he handled his emotions? By ignoring them?

They parked behind a popular steak house and went inside.

They passed a buffet loaded with steaming vegetables and a variety of meats that had her mouth watering.

"You look confused," Collin said as he held a chair for her.

She was. In more ways than one. "I was expecting a tofu bar with bean sprouts and seaweed."

"I eat what I like."

There went another assumption she shouldn't have made about him.

They filled their plates from the hot bar and found a table. Collin had ordered a steak, as well.

"Comfort food?" she asked gently after the waitress brought their drinks and departed.

He shrugged. "Just hungry. This place makes great steaks."

She squeezed the lemon slice into her tea.

"Want mine?" Collin said, removing the slice from the edge of his glass.

"You're giving up vitamin C?" She teased, but took the offered fruit. "Do you eat out like this all the time?"

"Not that much. Mostly I cook for myself."

She should have figured as much. He'd been self-reliant of necessity all of his life, a notion that made her heart hurt. But that strength had made him good at about anything he set his mind to. She wondered if he knew that about himself and decided that he didn't.

"What's your specialty?" she asked.

"Meat loaf and mashed potatoes. How about you? You live alone, too. Do you eat at your folks' or cook for yourself?"

"For myself most of the time. Although I sneak over to the bakery a little more often than I should."

"You any good?"

"Look at this body." With a self-deprecating twist of her mouth, she held her hands out to the side. "What do you think?"

"I think you look great." His brown eyes sparkled with appreciation.

"That wasn't what I meant." A rush of heat flooded her neck. "I meant—"

He laughed and let her off the hook. "I know what you meant." He pointed a fork at her. "But you still look good."

"Well." She wasn't sure what to say. She got her share of compliments, but she'd never expected one from Collin. He was full of surprises tonight. "Thank you."

The waitress brought his steak and they settled in to eat, making comments now and then about the food. After a bit the conversation lagged and all she could think about was the night's failed trip. Collin might want to ignore the subject, but Mia would explode if she didn't get her feelings out in the open.

"Will you let me apologize for not checking out that address before telling you about it?"

"No use talking the subject to death."

"We haven't talked about it at all." Which was driving her nuts.

"Just as well." He laid aside his fork and took a man-size drink of tea.

"Not really. Talking helps you sort out your feelings, weigh your options." And made her feel a whole lot better.

Collin looked at her, steady and silent. If anyone was going to talk, she would have to be the one.

"I'll keep looking. The information has to be there somewhere. We'll find them."

"You could check the adoption files. See if either of my brothers was adopted."

"I'm checking those."

Attention riveted to his plate, he casually asked, "The sealed ones?"

Her breath froze in her throat. "I won't do that."

He looked up. The naked emotion in his eyes stunned her. "Why not?"

Shoulders instantly tense, she had to remind him, "I told you from the beginning I wouldn't go into sealed files."

"That was before you knew me. Before we were friends."

Friends? "Is that what the compliment was about? To soften me up?"

His jaw tightened. "Is that what you think?"

She leaned back in her chair, miserable to be at odds with him over this. "No. Not really, but I can't believe you'd ask me to do such a thing."

Anger flared in the normally composed face. His fork clattered against his plate. "Wanting to find my brothers is not a crime. I'm not some do-wrong trying to ferret out information for evil purposes. This is my life we're talking about."

"I know that, Collin. But the files are closed for a reason. Parents requested and were given sealed records because they wanted the promise of privacy. And until those people request a change, those files have to stay sealed."

He crammed a frustrated hand over his head, spiking the hair up in front. "Nearly twenty-five years of my life is down the drain, Mia. I need to find them. They're men now. Opening those files won't hurt them or anybody else."

She shook her head, sick at heart. "I can't. It's wrong. Please understand."

Back rigid, he pushed away from the table and stood. The cold mask she'd encountered the first time they'd met was back in place.

Chapter Nine

Collin was not having a good day. In fact, the last two had been lousy.

He pushed the barn door open, stopping in the entrance to breathe in the warm scents of animals, feed and the ever-present smell of disinfectant. He went through gallons of the stuff trying to protect the sick animals from each other.

Since the night he'd let himself hope, only to be slapped down again, he'd battled a growing sense of emptiness.

After work tonight he'd gone to the gym with Maurice and true to form, his buddy had invited him home for dinner and Bible study. For the first time, he'd wanted to go. But he always felt so out of place in a crowd. And a Bible study was a whole different universe.

Not that he hadn't given God a lot of thought lately. Every time he showered or changed shirts and noticed his shamrock, Mia's words rang in his memory. She had something in her life that he didn't. And that something was more than a big, noisy family. Maurice had the same thing, so Collin figured the difference must be God.

One of the horses nickered as Collin moved down the dirt-packed corridor. These animals depended on him, regardless of the kind of day he'd had. He could take care of himself. They couldn't.

As was his habit, he headed to Happy's pen first. The little dog's attitude could lighten him up no matter what.

Mitchell, whom he hadn't seen since the smoking incident, was already inside the stall.

Irritation flared. The little twerp had some nerve coming back around the animals without permission.

Collin was all prepared to give him a tongue-lashing and send him home when the boy looked up.

What he saw punched him in the gut.

The kid's face was bruised from the eyebrow to below the cheekbone. A sliver of bloodshot eye showed through the swelling.

"What happened?" He heard his own voice, hard and angry.

Mitchell dropped his head, fidgeting with the dog brush in his hands. "I won't smoke anymore, Collin."

"Not what I asked."

Mitchell jerked one narrow shoulder. "Nothing."

With effort, Collin forced a calm he didn't feel. "Home or school?"

The boy was silent for a minute. Then he blew out a gust of air as if he'd been holding his breath, afraid Collin would send him away. "Not my mom."

The stepdad, then. Collin had run a check on Teddy Shipley. He had a rap sheet longer than the road from here to California, where he'd spent a year in the pen for assault with a deadly weapon and manufacturing an illegal substance. A real honey of a guy.

Collin hunkered down beside the boy, rested one hand lightly on the skinny back. "You can tell me anything."

Mitchell developed a sudden fascination with the bristles of Happy's brush. He flicked them back and forth against his palm. "I can't."

And then he dropped the brush and buried his face in Happy's thick fur. Happy, true to his name, moaned in ecstatic joy and licked at the air.

The kid was either scared or he knew something that would incriminate someone he cared about. And the cop in Collin suspected who.

He sighed wearily. Life could be so stinking ugly.

"If he hits you again, I'm all over him."

Mitch's head jerked up. His one good eye widened. "I never told you that. Don't be saying I did."

Compassion, mixed with frustration, pushed at the back of Collin's throat. He clamped down on his back teeth, hating the feelings.

"Did you go to school like this?"

Mitch shook his head. "No."

So that's why he'd shown up here this evening. Things were out of hand at home.

"Does he hit your mom, too?"

Tears welled in the boy's eyes. "She'd be real mad if she knew I told."

"Why?"

"She just would."

What Mitch wasn't saying spoke volumes. Collin had seen this scenario before. He'd also lived it.

Violence. Codependence. Drugs. A mother who preferred the drugs and a violent man to the safety and well-being of herself and her child. He wouldn't be a bit surprised if Teddy was cooking meth again, a suspicion that deserved checking into.

The sound of a car engine had Mitchell scrubbing frantically at his face. Collin turned toward the interruption. He'd know that Mustang purr anywhere. Mia. Just who he did not want to see. A social worker who'd stick her nose into something she couldn't fix. He was a cop. He could handle the situation far better than she could.

Mitch leaped up, recognizing the car, as well. His one good eye widened in panic. "Don't say anything, huh, Collin?"

Like she wouldn't notice an eye swollen shut.

"Go brush down the colt and give him a block of hay," he said, giving the kid an out. If Mia didn't see him, she wouldn't ask questions, and no one would have to lie.

Mitch shot out of the pen, disappearing into the far stall.

Collin picked up an empty feed sack and crushed it into a ball.

His world had been orderly and uneventful until Mia had come barging into it, hounding him, talking until he'd said yes to shut her up. And then her family had gotten in on the deal. First the birthday party. Then Adam's help with the lawsuit. And now Leo, Mia's father, found daily reasons why Collin had to stop by the bakery. Try as he might, Collin couldn't seem to say no.

Man. What had he gotten himself into?

The colt whickered. One of the dogs started barking. And the whole menagerie began moving restlessly.

Collin didn't rush out to greet his visitor. He needed

some time to think. Still baffled by Mia's stubbornness over something as simple as looking into a file, he wasn't sure what to say to her.

They didn't share the same sense of justice. He believed in obeying the law, but there was a difference in the spirit of the law and the letter of the law. To him, opening his own brothers' adoption files, if they existed, would fall under the spirit of the law. It was the right and just thing to do.

But he had to be fair to Mia, too. She'd gone above and beyond the call of duty in searching those moldy old files in the first place. And even if she was a pain in the backside sometimes, having her around lightened him somehow, as if the goodness in her could rub off.

After a minute's struggle, Collin decided to wait her out. Mia knew where he was if she had something to say. He'd known from the start he didn't want the grief of some woman trying to get inside his head. He had enough trouble inside there himself.

He went to work scrubbing down a newly emptied pen. The last stray, hit by a car, hadn't made it. He'd been hungry too long to have the strength to fight.

Fifteen minutes later, when Mia hadn't come storming inside the barn, smiling and rattling off at the mouth, Collin began to wonder if he'd heard her car at all. He dumped the last of the bleach water over the metal security cage and went to find out.

Sure enough, Mia's yellow Mustang sat in his driveway but she was nowhere to be seen.

Mitch came to stand beside him, one of Panda's adolescent kittens against his chest. "Where is she?"

"Beats me."

At that very moment, she flounced around the side of the house, her sweater flapping open in the stiff wind. She wasn't wearing her usual smile. Almond eyes shooting sparks, she marched right up to Collin.

"I don't stop being a friend because of a disagreement."

That didn't surprise him. The sudden lift in his mood did. Renewed energy shot through his tired muscles. He hid a smile. Mia was pretty cute when she got all wound up.

She slapped a wooden spoon against his chest.

"I brought food. Home-cooked." She tilted her head in a smug look. "And you are going to love it."

He fought the temptation to laugh. Normally, when a woman pushed too hard, she was history, but with Mia he couldn't stay upset. That fact troubled him, but there it was.

Unmindful of the sparks flying between the adults, Mitch stepped between them. "Food. Cool."

Mia started to say something then stopped. Her mouth dropped open. She stared at Mitchell's bruised face, expression horrified. "What happened to you?"

Mitchell shot Collin a silent plea and then hung his head, averting his battered face.

"I got in a fight."

"Oh, Mitch." And then her fingers gently grazed the boy's cheekbone in a motherly gesture. The tension in Mitch's shoulders visibly relaxed, but his eyes never met Mia's.

Collin let the lie pass for now. Whether Mitch liked the idea or not, a cop was mandated by law to share his suspicions with the proper authorities, and that was Mia. If there was any possibility that a child was in danger, welfare had a right to know. The policeman in him accepted that regardless of his personal aversion.

"I'm starved," he said, knowing his statement would be an effective diversion. Mia's respondent smile washed through him warm and sweet, like a spring wind through a field of flowers. "Cleaning pens can wait until after dinner."

"Not mad at me anymore?" she asked.

Quirking one brow, he started toward the house and left her to figure that out for herself. He wasn't sure he knew the answer anyway.

The early sunsets of November were upon them and the wind blew from the north promising a change in weather. Leaves loosened their tree-grip and tumbled like tiny, colorful gymnasts across the neatly fenced lots housing the grazers. The deer with the bad hip had healed and now roamed restlessly up and down the fence line longing to run free. Collin and Doc had decided to wait until after hunting season ended to give the young buck a fighting chance.

When they reached the house, Collin opened the door and let Mia and Mitchell enter first. The smell of Italian seasoning rushed out and swirled around his nose.

"Smells great. What is it?" Not that he cared—a home-cooked Italian dinner was too good to pass up. Especially one cooked by Mia.

"Lasagna. Wash your hands. Both of you." She shooed them toward the sink. "Food's still hot."

Along with Mitchell, he meekly did as he was told, scrubbing at the kitchen sink. If anyone else came into his house issuing orders and rummaging in his cabinets, he would be furious. Weird that he wasn't bothered much at all.

While Mia rattled forks and thumped plates onto his tiny table, he murmured to Mitch, "A lie will always come back to bite you. Better tell her."

Mitchell darted a quick glance at Mia and gave his head a slight shake, his too-long hair flopping forward to hide his expression. Collin let the subject drop. For now.

Moments later, they dug into the meal. Collin could barely contain a moan of pleasure.

Lifting a forkful of steaming noodles and melted mozzarella, he said, "If this is your idea of a peace offering, I'll get mad at you more often."

Mia sliced a loaf of bread and pushed the platter toward him. Steam curled upward, bringing the scent of garlic and yeast.

"There are still things I can do to help, Collin. Unlike foster-care files, many of the adoption files have been computerized. I started searching the open ones today."

He took a chunk of the bread and slathered on a pat of real butter. "Are the sealed files on computer, too?"

There was a beat of silence, and then, "It doesn't matter."

She wasn't budging from her hard-nosed stand.

"After all the years I've searched and come up empty, I think the adoption files are the answer. They have to be."

Mitchell was already digging in for seconds. "Why are you trying to get into adoption files?"

Collin started. He never spoke openly about his brothers or his past. He'd never before said a word about them in front of Mitchell. Was this what hanging around with a chatterbox did for a guy? He started to lie to the boy, and then remembered his words only moments before. A lie would always come back to haunt you.

"I'm looking for my brothers," he said honestly. "We were separated in foster care as kids."

Saying the words aloud didn't seem so hard this time.

"No kidding?" Mitch backhanded a string of cheese from his mouth. "You were a foster kid?"

"Yeah. I was." He held his breath. Would the knowledge lessen him in Mitchell's eyes?

Mitch's one unblemished eye, brown and serious, studied him in awe. "But you became a cop. How'd you do that?"

And just that simply, Collin experienced a frisson of pride instead of shame. Mia had been right all along. Mitch needed to know that the two of them shared some commonalities.

"A lousy childhood doesn't have to hold you back."

By now, the boy's mouth was jammed full again, so he just nodded and chewed. He chased the food with a gulp of iced tea and then said, "So where are your brothers? Can Miss Carano find them? Can't the police find them? I'll help you look for them. How many do you have?"

His words tumbled out, eager and naive.

Collin filled him in on the bare facts. "And Miss Carano's helping me search, too. Even though I've been a pain about it."

He gave her his version of an apologetic look. He wasn't sorry for asking her to bend the rules a little, but he was glad to be back on comfortable footing with her. The last couple of days had been lousy without her.

"I've started a hand search of the old records in the storage room of the municipal building," Mia told him. "That's where I found that address the other day."

The police records were warehoused the same way,

and he knew from experience that hand searches were tedious and time-consuming. And often fruitless.

"I appreciate all you're doing, Mia. Honestly. But you can't blame me for wanting to investigate every available option."

"I don't blame you." She pushed her plate aside and said, "Anyone for dessert?"

"Dessert?" Both males moaned at the same time.

"You should have warned us." Collin put a hand over his full belly. He looked around the tiny kitchen, spotted a covered container on the bar. "What is it?"

Mia laughed. "My own made-from-scratch cherry chocolate bundt cake. But we can save dessert for later."

"You made it yourself?"

"Yep. The bread and lasagna, too."

The sweet Italian bread *must* have come from her parents' bakery. "No way."

"Way. I didn't grow up a baker's daughter for nothing. All of us kids cut our teeth on the old butcher-block table in the back of the bakery where Mom and Dad hand-mixed the dough for all kinds of cakes and breads and cookies."

She got up and started clearing the table. Collin grabbed the glasses.

"Let me help with this."

"I can get the dishes. Didn't you say you still have work in the barn?"

"Work can wait."

Mitchell, who looked as if he'd rather be anywhere but in a kitchen with unwashed dishes, piped up. "I'll do the rest of the chores outside. I don't mind."

With a knowing chuckle, Collin gave him instructions and let him go.

"Did you see the look on his face?"

"And to think he prefers mucking out stalls to our esteemed company." Mia feigned hurt.

In the tiny kitchen area, they bumped elbows at the sink. Collin didn't usually enjoy company that much, but over the weeks and months he'd known Mia, she'd become a part of his life. Sometimes an annoying part, but if he was honest, even when they disagreed he depended upon her to see through his anger to the frustration and still be his friend.

He'd never expected to call a social worker "friend."

At times, he could be brooding and moody, and admittedly, he wore a protective armor around his heart. Trouble was, Miss Mia had slipped beneath it at some point and discovered the softer side of him. The idea unhinged him.

"Thanksgiving's coming soon," she said, her voice coming from above a sink of soapy hot water. "We always have a big to-do at Mama's. Turkey, dressing, pecan pie. The works. The Macy's Thanksgiving Day parade on TV and then a veritable marathon of football games afterward."

He knew what was coming and didn't know what to do. Nic's birthday party had stirred up something inside him, a hunger for the things missing in his own life, and he wasn't sure he could go there again.

Mia rinsed a plate under the hot tap. As he reached to take the dish, she held on, forcing him to look down at her.

Green eyes, honey-sweet and honest, held his. "We'd love for you to come. Please say you will."

Steam rose up between them, moist and warm. Her eyes, her tone indicated more than an invitation of kindness to a man who had nowhere else to go. She really wanted him there.

Like most holidays, Thanksgiving was a family occasion. The time or two he'd accepted an invitation, he'd felt like an intruder. "I usually volunteer to work so the officers with families can be off that day."

"Then I'd say you're due a day off this year. Wouldn't you?"

"I'd better not."

Disappointment flashed across her face. Unlike him, she could never hide her feelings. They were there for the whole world to see. And what he saw both troubled and pleased him. Mia liked him. As more than a friend.

She let go of the plate and went back to washing. The air in the kitchen hung heavy with his refusal and her reaction. He didn't want to hurt her. In fact, he couldn't believe she was disappointed. Couldn't believe she'd be interested in him. He didn't belong with her all-American perfect family.

Mia, true to form, rushed in to the fill the quiet, and if he hadn't known better, her chatter would have convinced him that she didn't really care one way or the other. But now he knew her chatter sometimes covered her unease.

Then she mentioned some guy she'd met during the 10-K charity walk last weekend, and his mood turned from thoughtful to sour. If she was attracted to him, why was she having Starbucks with some runner?

He interrupted. "Wonder what's keeping Mitchell?"

Mia stopped in midsentence and gave him a funny look. "He hasn't been gone that long."

"Long enough." He tossed his dish towel over the back of a chair that served as a towel rack, coat rack, whatever.

The water gurgled out of the sink. Mia dried her hands. "If you'll stop scowling, I'll go check. I need to get something out of my car anyway."

"I can go. He's my responsibility."

"Mine, too. You stay here and slice the cake. I have a book in the car for you."

"A Bible?" he asked suspiciously.

Tossing on her sweater, she laughed and opened the door. "You'll see."

Halfway out, she stopped and looked over her shoulder. "I want coffee with my cake."

The door banged shut and Collin found himself grinning into the empty space. Tonight Mia had made this half-finished, scantily furnished, poor excuse for a house feel like a home.

He turned that thought over in his head and went to make the lady's coffee.

Four scoops into the pot, a scream shattered the quiet. Coffee grounds went everywhere. His heart stopped.

"Mia."

He was out the door, running toward the barn before he realized the previously dark sky was lit with bright light. Fire light.

"Mitchell!"

He heard Mia's cry once more and this time he spotted her, running toward the burning barn. Before he could yell for her to stop, to turn back, she disappeared inside.

Collin thought he would die on the spot. Adrenaline ripped through his veins with enough force to knock him down. He broke into a run, pounding over the hard, dry ground.

Flames licked the sky. Sparks shot fifty feet up, fueled by the still wind. The horses screamed in terror. Dogs barked and howled. Several had managed to escape somehow and now scrambled toward him. A kitten streaked past, her fur smoking.

A horrible sense of doom slammed into him, overwhelming. Mia and Mitchell were inside a burning barn along with more than a dozen helpless, trapped, sick and injured animals.

He darted toward the outside water faucet, thankful for the burlap feed sack wrapped around the pipes to prevent freezing. Yanking the sack free, he dipped the rough cloth into the freshly filled trough then rushed into the barn just as Mitchell came stumbling out.

Collin caught him by the shoulders. "Where's Mia?"

Mitchell shook his head, coughing. "I don't know."

With no time to waste, he shoved Mitchell out into the fresh air. "Call 911."

He could only hope the boy obeyed.

And then he charged into the burning building.

Smoke, thick and blinding, wrapped him in a terrifying embrace.

"Mia!" he yelled as he slung the wet sack around his face and head.

Eyes streaming, lungs screaming, he traversed the interior by instinct, throwing open stalls and pens as he called out, over and over again. The animals would at least have a chance this way. Locked in, they would surely die.

He stumbled over something soft and pitched forward, slamming his elbow painfully into a wall. A familiar whine greeted him. When he reached down, the dog licked his hand. Happy.

With more joy than he had time to feel, he scooped

the little dog up and headed him in the direction of the open doorway. Even a crippled dog would instinctively move toward the fresh air.

A timber above his head cracked. Honed reflexes moved him to one side as the flaming board thundered to the barn floor. If he stayed too long, he'd never make it out.

Another board fell behind him and then another. Common sense said for him to escape now. His heart wouldn't let him.

"Mia." His voice, hoarse and raspy, made barely a sound against the roaring, crackling fire. Heat seared the back of his hands. His head swam.

If something happened to her. If something happened to Mia.

Suddenly, he heard her coughing. And praying.

Renewed energy propelled him forward.

"I'm coming."

Keep praying, Mia, so I can find you.

With his free hand, he felt along the corridor wall. No longer could he hear animal sounds, but Mia's prayers grew louder.

In the dense darkness he never saw her, but he heard her and reached out, made contact. She frantically clawed at his arm.

"I've got you."

"Thank God. Thank God." A fit of harsh coughing wracked her. "Mitch," she managed.

"He's safe."

Without a thought, Collin stripped the covering from his face and pressed the rough fabric against Mia's mouth and nose. Her breath puffed hot and dry against his fingers.

"This way."

With his knowledge of the barn, he guided them away from the falling center toward the feed room. There, a small window would provide escape.

Though the seconds seemed to drag, Collin knew by the size of the fire that they'd been inside only a few minutes. Thankfully, the flames had not reached this section of the barn yet, but they were fast approaching.

"Hurry," he said needlessly, pushing and pulling her stumbling form.

Inside the feed room, he felt for the window, shoved the sash upward, then easily lifted Mia over the threshold and to safety on the ground.

A roar erupted behind him. The flames, as if enraged by Mia's escape, chased him. Licking along the wall, they found the empty paper sacks and swooshed into the room.

Collin scrambled up and out the window, falling to the ground below. What little air he had left was knocked out in the fall.

Mia grabbed his hand and tugged. "Get up. We have to get away."

Hands clasped, they stumbled around the side of the barn to an area several yards out from the flames. Mia fell to her knees, noisily sucking in the fresh air.

Collin went down beside her, filling his lungs with the sweet, precious oxygen.

"You okay?" he asked when he could breathe again.

"Fine."

But he couldn't take her word for it. By the flickering light of the fire that had nearly stolen her, he searched her face for signs of injury and found none.

"If anything had happened to you—"

And then before his reasonable side could stop him, he pulled her into his arms and kissed her.

She tasted smoky and sweet and wonderful. Emotion as foreign as an elephant and every bit as powerful coursed through him. His world tilted, spun, shimmered with warning.

He pulled back, suddenly afraid of what was happening to him. It was only a kiss, wasn't it? Given out of fear and relief. That was all. Only a kiss.

But he knew better. He'd kissed other women before, but not like this. The others he'd kept at a distance, outside of the armor. Mia was different. Way different.

And the truth of that scared him more than the barn fire.

Chapter Ten

"Here Mitch, take this end down to Adam."

Mia stood in the yard of her parents' home surrounded by large plastic containers filled with Christmas lights and decorations. Twined around her shoulders and across her arms was a tangled strand of frosty icicle lights. Adam worked at the opposite end of the fence attaching the strands as she unraveled them.

The other Caranos were scattered about in the yard and over the exterior of the house in similar activity. Each year on a given Saturday, Rosalie commandeered all available family members to set up outside Christmas decorations while the weather was decent. Today was the day.

Mitch, eager for a promised turkey hunt with Mia's dad, was trying to hurry the process.

"Why are you putting up Christmas lights so early? We haven't even had Thanksgiving yet."

He took the proffered end of the lights and trudged toward Adam.

Mia squinted at him, the November sun bright, the wind light but sharp. "That's the whole point. At the

Caranos, turning the lights on for the first time on Thanksgiving night is a big deal. You *are* still coming, aren't you?"

One narrow shoulder jerked. "I guess. Nothing else to do."

Mia recognized Mitch's unique method of saving face. Holidays at his house, from what he'd told her and from what she'd seen, were not festive occasions. And from the latest information Collin had shared, Mia was more concerned than ever. Life at the Perez house grew more troubled with each passing week, and Mitchell spent most of his time on the streets, or with her or her mother and dad to avoid going home. His was a worrisome situation indeed, especially with the added tension between Collin and Mitch since the fire.

"Sure he's coming," Adam hollered. "We're going to finish that computer chess tournament, and I'm going to beat the socks off him."

Mitch handed him the light cord and grinned. "Wanna bet?"

"If I win, you have to wash my car inside and out."

"When *I* win, I get to wear your OU jersey to school."

"No betting around here, boys," Rosalie called from her spot on the front porch. She was winding greenery around the columns.

"Yes, ma'am," Adam replied, his swarthy face wreathed in ornery laughter. He loved to get Mama riled up.

"Yes, ma'am," Mitchell echoed, grinning at Adam.

Mia's dad came around the corner of the house, carrying the last of the nativity pieces that would grace their front yard. "As soon as I put this with the others, I'm going out to Collin's place."

Mia looked up in surprise, her pulse doing the usual flip-flop at Collin's name. "What for?"

Leo, like the other Caranos, had worked overtime to draw Collin into the fold. Though they'd yet to get him back to a large family gathering, he'd started hanging out with regularity at the Carano Bakery—at Leo's insistent invitation.

"Cops and doughnuts. They're a natural," her dad had said, but she knew he liked the quiet cop.

So did she.

"We need a couple of bales of hay to make the stable scene look authentic," Leo said. "I figured Collin might have some extra."

"Dad," Mia said, stricken at the memory. "Collin won't have any hay."

"Sure he will…" He stopped and set the manger down with a thud. "What was I thinking? All his hay went up with the barn."

"Yeah." Mitch scuffed a toe against the brown grass.

After their escape, while the firefighters drenched the glowing remains of the animal refuge, Collin had asked Mitch if he'd been smoking in the barn again. The question had devastated the boy. He hadn't been to the farm in the days since.

"He doesn't want me out there anymore."

"That's not true. He's upset right now because of the lost animals, but he's not upset with you."

"I could hear the puppies crying."

A heaviness tugged at Mia. They'd discussed this before, but the dying animals haunted him. "I know."

"I tried to find them, but the smoke was so bad."

She slid the lights from her shoulder and signaled Adam with a glance. He touched a finger to his eyebrow in silent agreement, understanding her need to counsel with Mitch. "Let's go sit on the porch and talk."

He followed her, slumping onto the step of the long concrete porch. Rosalie had moved down to the end post to add a red bow to the greenery.

"The investigators are still checking into the fire, but if you say you weren't smoking, I believe you."

"But Collin doesn't."

"I think he does, Mitchell, and he's sorry he hurt your feelings. He just has a hard time saying so."

"He's mad because of the puppies."

"No. He's sad. The same way you and I are."

The young boy stared morosely across the street where two squirrels gathered nuts beneath a pecan tree. "Do you think God cares about animals? Strays, I mean?"

She'd wondered when he'd ask something like that. Her faith was an open topic with anyone who knew her and the two of them had had more than one deep discussion.

"Sparrows aren't worth much in our eyes, but the Bible says God feeds them and watches over them." She pointed toward the squirrels. "And just look at those guys. God provided all the nuts they could ever want in that one tree. And they don't even have to buy them!"

Her attempt at humor fell flat. Mitchell wasn't in a joking mood.

"I'm going to miss them. Rascal and Slick and Milly and her kittens." Mitchell had named them all, something that had bothered Collin at first.

He gathered a handful of dead grass and tossed the blades one at a time.

"There would be something wrong with us if we

didn't grieve over what we care about. But remember this one good thing—God allowed us to love them and give them a nice home in their last days. They hadn't had that before."

"Yeah. That's true." He tossed the remaining grass and wiped a hand down his jeans' leg. "I guess God is okay."

Mia draped an arm across Mitch's shoulders. "God is the best friend you could ever have, Mitchell."

"Is Collin a Christian?"

Something sharp pinched at her heart. "You'll have to ask him about that."

She wanted to believe that Collin would eventually accept Christ. Especially now. And not just because of Mitch's adoration, though that certainly loomed large. Mitch admired her Christian dad and brothers, too, but he shared a bond with Collin.

"You miss him, don't you?"

"Yeah."

"He misses you, too."

Mitch looked at her, hope as rich as the coffee-colored eyes. "You think?"

"I know. He told me on the phone last night." A phone call she'd instigated. Since the fire, he'd drawn back somewhat, as though he couldn't deal with all the emotions that had come pouring out that night. She was still puzzled and exhilarated by that unexpected kiss. Puzzled even more at how he had seemed to develop amnesia afterward.

"He needs your help out there to get things going again. Let's call him later, huh?"

She would keep on calling until he opened up again.

"I guess so."

"Hey, Mitchell," Mia's dad called. "Are you going to sit around on the porch and suntan or are we going to that turkey shoot?"

"I'm ready." Mitchell leaped up, then caught himself and looked back at Mia. "Okay, Mia?"

After the fire she'd become Mia instead of Miss Carano. That kind of familiarity had never happened before with one of her clients, and she prayed she wouldn't lose perspective. Somehow Mitchell had wound his scruffy self around her heart and that of her family.

"Have fun."

Mitch was gone in a flash.

"You can depend on Dad to interrupt an important conversation," Rosalie murmured, coming to join Mia in Mitch's now-abandoned spot.

"Mitch needs the distraction. He's been pretty down since the fire."

"So have you. Maybe not down so much as too quiet. Want to talk about it?"

"I have a lot on my mind, Mama. That's all. Work, Mitch." She shrugged.

"Collin," Mama concluded.

"Yes. Him, too." She picked at a thread on her knit jacket. "He kissed me the night of the fire."

"Who could blame him? You're beautiful."

Mia laughed. "Oh, Mama, no wonder I love you so."

"You like him?"

"Maybe more than I should. I don't date guys who aren't Christians, Mom. You know that. You taught me that."

"But you're falling for him anyway."

Mia stared morosely at the crystal lights Adam and Nic were tacking in place along the board fence. The brothers argued happily as they worked, the sound of frequent laughs punctuating the air. Two big ol' macho men with marshmallow hearts. How she loved them.

No wonder Collin Grace appealed to her. For all his outward toughness, he was a softie on the inside just like her brothers.

Two nights ago, he'd lost his hard facade, both with her and then later when he'd found the first of several dead animals. Happy, the little survivor, had saved himself. Mitchell had freed Panda and her remaining kittens, and the large animals were safe in outside pens. But one litter of new kittens and an old sickly dog and her pup hadn't made it out alive. Mia couldn't forget the look on Collin's face: stricken, haunted, guilty.

He'd looked the same in those seconds before he had kissed her. She couldn't get that look or that kiss off her mind.

A kiss shouldn't be such a big deal. She wasn't a teenager. But she had already been fighting her growing emotions and when he'd looked at her, fear and firelight in his eyes, and wrapped her in a hard, protective hug, she'd faced the hard truth. Christian or not, she had strong feelings for Collin Grace. And even if he never admitted it, Collin felt something for her, too. Maybe that's why he was running scared. Collin didn't like to feel.

The wind blew a lock of hair across her face. She pushed the curl behind one ear.

"At first, I thought I was helping Collin. You know, doing the Christian thing, being a witness, going the extra mile, trying to draw him out to a place where he can heal. Collin's a good man, Mama. But he's had so much heartache that he's afraid to trust anybody. Even God."

Mama took Mia's chilled hands in her warm ones. "Then our job is to show him that he can. That God is trustworthy. And so are we. Dad's trying to do that at the bakery."

"I know. After the fire I gave him a book to read, the one about finding your purpose through Christ. We talked about the Lord a little then, but I felt so inadequate in the face of what had happened. I'm not sure I said the right things. I wanted him to know that God cared about him and his animals and his losses."

She yearned to tell Mama about Collin's lost brothers and lean on her wisdom. But she'd promised confidentiality even though telling her mother would help both of them. Rosalie was a prayer warrior who never stopped praying for something until the answer came. Mia wasn't having much success on her own, but God knew where Ian and Drew were.

"How is he handling the fire?"

"The usual way—by pretending he isn't bothered." The fact that he'd retreated into his shell again told her the tough cop with the marshmallow center was mourning the animals and the uninsured barn.

If only she could find some trace of his brothers to cheer him. Some bit of good news. She gripped her mother's hands tighter, giving them a quick bounce.

"Mama. I need you to help me pray about something."

Rosalie's eyes lit up. "Of course. What is it?"

"Well, that's the trouble. I need you to pray. But I can't tell you why."

Her mama looked at her for one beat of time, then smiled a mother's knowing smile. And Mia felt better than she'd felt since the night of the barn fire.

* * *

"Thank you, Lord," Mia said as she hung up the telephone. After going through dozens of boxes and hundreds of old records, she'd hit pay dirt two days after the conversation with her mama.

This time, she'd tempered her excitement long enough to make some phone calls and verify that a foster mother named Maxine Fielding not only still lived in Oklahoma City, but also remembered caring for a rowdy eleven-year-old named Drew Grace.

She glanced at the clock. Another two hours before she could head for Collin's place with her news. She thought about calling his cell, but found that unsatisfactory. She wanted to see his face, to watch him smile again. The past week had been a rough one.

A desk laden with paperwork needed her attention anyway, so she went to work there, weeding through files, making calls, setting up appointments. She phoned Mitchell's school to check on his attendance and discipline referrals and to inquire about any further indication of abuse.

Even with the barn fire setback, the boy had held his ground. And after the turkey shoot last Saturday, he'd let her take him out to Collin's, where the three of them had spent hours putting together makeshift pens for the remaining animals.

The problems with the stepfather were accumulating though, and all her praying hadn't changed that one bit. The man had been furious when she'd interviewed him about Mitch's black eye, and Mitch hadn't helped by claiming he'd gotten into a fight at school. She wanted to get Mitch out of that house, though she couldn't without substantiated evidence. But now, both she and Collin were watching. Collin had even alerted the drug unit to be aware of possible illegal activities, though nothing had surfaced yet.

At ten after five she rotated her head from side to side, stretching tired muscles. Time to go. She tossed three Snickers wrappers into the trash and then dialed Collin's cell number.

"Grace."

She smiled at the short bark he substituted for a simple hello. And she couldn't deny that her heart jumped at the sound of that strong, masculine voice.

"Your name always makes me think of a song."

"Oh. Hi, Mia," he said. "I didn't recognize the number."

"My office."

"How does my name remind you of a song?"

She'd known he wouldn't let that one pass. With a smile in her voice, she said, "'*Amazing grace, how sweet the sound, that saved a wretch like me.*' It's a song about God's incredible love for us."

"The guys call me Amazing Grace sometimes. I never quite got that."

"Do you know what grace actually means?"

"I'm sure you're going to tell me." She heard the humor behind the gentle jab.

"Unmerited favor. God chooses to love and accept us, not because of what we do or don't do, but all because of His amazing grace."

A moment of silence hummed through the line. Though she hadn't planned to talk about her faith just now, she wanted Collin to understand how much Jesus loved him. She prayed that the truth of amazing grace would soak into his spirit and draw him to the Lord.

She also hoped she hadn't just turned him ice-cold to the whole idea.

Finally, his voice soft, Collin said, "I'll never let the guys call me that again."

"Oh, Collin." He'd understood.

"So what's up?" he asked, sidestepping the emotion they both heard in her voice.

"I'm about to leave the office. Are you home?"

"Not yet. Why?"

"I want to talk to you in person."

"News?"

"Maybe." She didn't want to get his hopes up again and have them shattered.

"I'm off duty. Meet me at Braums on Penn. I'll buy you a grilled chicken salad."

"Throw in a hot chocolate and you've got yourself a date."

A soft masculine laugh flowed through the wires and straight into her heart. The memory of their kiss flared to life, unspoken but most definitely not forgotten. Oh, dear.

Mia bit down on the inside of her lip. Why couldn't she ever keep her big mouth shut?

Maxine Fielding had a great memory. The silver-haired woman regaled Collin with the good, the bad and the ugly about his brother's behavior. And the pleasure in Collin's face served as a reward for the lunch hours Mia had spent in the spooky, smelly basement of the municipal building.

"You don't by any chance have some pictures from that time, do you?" she asked the older woman. "Any-

thing that could lead us to some of the boys who might
have known Drew?"

"Sorry, hon," Maxine said, her fleshy face sorrow-
ful. "I used to have a lot of pictures of my kids. That's
what I always called them. Every one of them that came
through here was mine for a while." She gestured with
one hand. The knuckles were twisted with arthritis.
"Anyways, while I was in the hospital a while back,
my daughters decided to clean my house. Threw out all
my mementos." She shook her head. "I'm still peeved
about that."

Mia wished she hadn't asked, though Collin, sitting
on an old velvet couch with his elbows on his knees,
showed no emotion. His uniform was still neat after a
day's work. And even with a five-o'clock shadow on his
normally clean-shaven face, he looked good. A woman
could get distracted with him around.

In fact, she *was* distracted. She let Collin do most of
the talking, a strange turn of events. She was falling for
him, all right, and didn't quite know what to do about it.

In the end, the foster mother recalled two other families that had cared for troubled boys during the same
time period as well as a couple of group homes no longer in operation. That information alone gave Mia more
names to plug into the computer, some specific files to
dig through, and more chances to come up with something solid.

"So what do you think?" she asked when she and
Collin were back inside his truck. He cranked the engine and pushed the heat lever to high. As night had
fallen, so had the temperatures, and now a light rain
spat at the windshield.

"Nice lady. I'm glad Drew was here for a while."

She could hear the unspoken wish that he'd been here, too. "Doesn't that give you hope that your brothers did okay in the system? That maybe they even found a family?"

"Wanna look into those locked files and find out?" A ghost of a smile reflected in the dashboard lights.

"No."

"I knew you'd say that." But his reply held humor instead of animosity, and she hoped he finally understood. There were some things she wouldn't do, even for him.

"Mrs. Fielding liked Drew."

"I've worried about him for so long, thought the worst." He shifted into Reverse and backed the truck onto the street. "Hearing that someone cared about him, even temporarily, felt good."

She was glad. More than glad, she was thankful. Collin had needed this news. He'd needed to leave the tragedy of the barn fire behind for a while. He'd needed to believe something positive had happened to his brothers. As he'd talked with Mrs. Fielding, he'd smiled, even laughed at her fond memories.

Collin's love for his lost brothers was fierce and steadfast, a powerful testament to the way he might someday love a woman. Mia refused to dwell on the lovely thought.

"We're going to find them, Collin."

He reached across the seat and touched her hand. "After tonight, I'm starting to believe you."

Three days before Thanksgiving the weather turned sunny and mild. Collin felt pretty sunny himself as he left the gym with his partner, Maurice, along with

Adam Carano. The other two men argued amiably over which sit-ups worked best, straight knee or bent.

Adam had first come to the gym to discuss the lawsuit, but now he'd become a permanent member along with the two cops. Collin liked the guy. And he also admired the way Adam was handling the lawsuit. When he took on a case, he was a real bulldog. Like his sister.

Collin's smile widened. Thinking about Mia did that to him lately.

"What are you grinning about, Grace?" Adam slapped him on the back. Collin's sweat-damp sweatshirt stuck to his shoulder.

"You talk as much as your sister."

"That's a terrible thing to say to your lawyer."

"When are you going to quit torturing me and get that problem solved?"

"I'm getting close. Did you know your neighbor has a real problem with cops? Especially you?"

Collin sawed a towel back and forth behind his neck. "Tell me something I don't already know."

"Okay, I will." Adam looked pleased with himself. "You remember busting a kid named Joey Stapleton a few years back for breaking and entering?"

"No, but the fire inspector suspects my barn was arson. Not B and E." His good mood evaporated at the memory of the animals Mia, Mitch and he had buried beneath the harvest moon.

Adam held up a hand. "Collin, my man. Lesson one about attorney-client privileges. Never interrupt your lawyer when he's on a roll. You disappoint me. You didn't even ask how Stapleton was connected."

"Okay, I'll bite. Who is he?"

"First of all, Stapleton didn't burn down your barn.

He's still serving time. However, his half-brother, who mortgaged his land to defend Stapleton, lives down the road from you. His name is Cecil Slokum."

Now that *was* interesting. But there were plenty of do-wrongs out there with a grudge against him. "You think Slokum could be responsible?" Collin asked.

"Maybe. If Slokum can force you to pay damages for his daughter's ewe and destroy your barn at the same time, he not only gets revenge, he gets back some of the money he spent on his so-called innocent brother."

Collin had entertained the thought before, but a man didn't accuse his neighbor of arson without some kind of evidence. He'd also suspected Mitch of the fire and had lived to regret that mistake. Though his young friend was hanging around the farm once more, Collin could feel a hesitancy in the relationship, as though Mitch feared Collin would turn on him again.

"You got evidence?"

"Circumstantial, but enough to strongly suspect."

Collin's jaw tightened. Though he wanted to grab Cecil Slokum by the neck and shake the truth out of him, he wouldn't. He wasn't that kind of cop.

"Where do we go from here? Anything we can bust him on?"

"I've turned my findings over to the fire marshal and the DA. If I'm right—" Adam's grin was cocky "—and I usually am, an arrest could come at any time."

"I appreciate it." Although sincere, Collin heard the gruffness in the thanks. He wasn't a lawyer and couldn't do the job Adam could, but he didn't like needing anyone's help either. More and more lately, Adam and Mia and the whole Carano clan made him feel needy. Inside and out. It kept him off balance, edgy, vulnerable.

"I can't believe I didn't figure out Cecil's grudge my-self." In fact, he was annoyed that he hadn't dug deeper when the suspicion first sprouted. But work and Mitch-ell and rebuilding, not to mention Mia and his search, had kept him too busy to think straight.

"That's what friends are for, Collin. To lighten the load."

The words *unmerited favor* flitted through his mind. Was that what Mia meant? He'd thought a lot about that conversation, and the idea that anyone would do something for him without expecting anything in re-turn never would jibe.

"How much do I owe you?" he asked.

Adam looked at him, an odd smile on his face. "My sister would hurt me if I took your money."

A cord of tension wound around inside him. Cool from drying sweat and November air, he shrugged into his hoodie. "I pay my debts."

"There are some debts you can't pay, Collin. The sooner you learn that the better off you'll be. The bet-ter off my sister will be, too."

Collin had no clue what Adam meant. And he didn't think he wanted to ask. Especially about the reference to Mia.

They were nearing his truck, and he needed this set-tled now. "How much, Carano?"

Adam rubbed a hand over his chin as if in deep thought. "Tell you what, Grace. If you really want to repay me, you can do me a favor."

"Name it."

Too late, Collin saw the ornery twinkle.

"Come to Mama's house for Thanksgiving dinner."

Maurice started to laugh. His partner knew his aversion to large family gatherings. He'd also been on Collin's case about Mia.

"I think he blindsided you, partner."

Adam shrugged his wide shoulders and didn't look the least bit sorry. "What do you expect? Lawyers are supposed to be sneaky." He pointed a finger at Collin. "You're going to show up, aren't you?"

"Do I have a choice?"

"Actually, no." Then, with a laugh and a wave, Adam hopped into a sleek SUV and left him standing in the parking lot. To make matters worse, Maurice was still laughing.

Chapter Eleven

Anticipation, sweeter than Christmas morning, filled Mia. She'd had so many failures, but today she felt sure something new would turn up in this stack of records.

With Mrs. Fielding's information, she had located the placement files of the family that had taken Drew after he'd run away from the Fielding home. Surely some mention of Collin's brother would be inside this folder.

She rummaged in her desk for a Snickers, but after a glance at her dusty hands, changed her mind. With the holidays coming up, she'd be fighting more than five pounds if she wasn't careful.

She flipped through page after page, eyes straining at the faded typewritten print until some of her excitement began to fade. The records seemed jumbled, bits and pieces of several files that might or might not relate to Collin's brothers. Then, as if lit by a neon sign, Drew's name leaped out at her.

"Yes!" she whispered, barely able to contain her excitement.

Collin knew she and Mama were praying for a breakthrough, and he'd been politely receptive, but Mia was ready for God to show off a little and prove to Collin that prayer really worked.

She quickly perused the document, found nothing of significance and decided to put the sheet aside while she searched for others. If there was one page about him, perhaps there would be more.

But when she reached the bottom of a rather thick file, two yellowing forms was all she had found. Disappointed, but not disheartened, she settled back to read, hoping for any tidbit to share with Collin.

One was a general report concerning the reasons Drew continued to live in foster care. There was a chronicle of his psycho-social problems, his habit of skipping school, and numerous reports for fighting. He'd been removed from any number of places because of the chip on his shoulder and his propensity for running away.

The other was a social worker's report indicating a placement in a therapeutic group home with six other teenage boys. Her heart fell into her high heels. Drew was fifteen at that point and had been in foster care since age seven. Gone was any hope that he had found a forever family.

She stopped to rub her tired eyes. Thirty was creeping closer and she'd always heard the eyes were the first to go. She needed to schedule a checkup with her optometrist—soon.

After jotting down names and addresses that might prove useful she started to replace the folder in the appropriate box when a newspaper clipping slipped out and filtered to the floor.

The word *fire* caught her attention. Her heart thumped once, hard. The reaction was silly, she told herself. A newspaper article about a fire wasn't necessarily about Drew.

But the clipping *had* been in the same file.

Unable to shake the foreboding, Mia picked up the two-inch column and read. A fire had broken out in a foster home claiming the lives of several teens, though no names were mentioned.

Dread, heavy as a grand piano, came over her. The address matched one of the homes that had cared for Drew. And the timing was perfect.

She rifled through the box, hoping to find something more about the tragedy but came up empty. Finally, she rested her chin in her hand and stared at the clipping, unsure of what to do with this new information. Should she tell Collin right away? Or keep the clipping to herself until she could verify whether Drew had been in that fire?

She rubbed at her eyes again. This time they were moist.

Collin stood in the doorway watching Mia. Deeply focused on her work, she hadn't heard him come in.

Her dark auburn hair swung forward, brushing her cheek, grazing the top of her desk. He studied her, remembering the silkiness of that hair, the softness of her skin.

He couldn't escape the memory of that night. Especially that insane moment when he'd kissed her and she'd kissed him back. More than once, he'd been tempted to repeat the performance, but caution won out. She pretended nothing incredible had happened. So would he. But that didn't stop him thinking about it.

Her mouth was turned down tonight, unusual for

Mia. She rubbed at the corner of one eye and sighed. She was tired.

Her regular workload was always heavy and she was involved in church and the community, but for the past few months, she had been committed to helping him and Mitch. In her spare time, if there was such a thing, she searched the records for his brothers. In the evenings, she was now an active participant, along with Mitch, in rebuilding the barn. He'd asked too much of her.

He was suddenly overcome with a fierce need to take the load off her shoulders. To cheer her up. To make her laugh. Mia had a great laugh.

"Got a minute?"

Mia jumped and slapped one hand over her heart. Her red-rimmed eyes widened. "Collin."

"Didn't mean to scare you." He stepped inside the small office.

"What's wrong?" She didn't smile her usual wide, happy welcome.

"Why does anything have to be wrong?" Man, she was pretty, even with her hair mussed and her eyes red and every bit of makeup rubbed away.

"Because you hate this place. You never come here." She didn't look all that happy to see him.

He frowned. What was going on with her tonight? "Want me to leave?"

She rotated her head from side to side, stretching tight muscles. Collin thought about offering a neck rub, but decided against it. Last time he'd touched her, he'd gone nuts and kissed her, too.

"Don't be silly."

Which was no answer at all. He shifted from one foot to the other and checked out the messy office. Boxes, bent and aging, lined one wall and stacks of manila folders with glaring white typewritten labels were spread here and there.

"Are these the old records you've been searching for me?"

A funny expression flitted across her face. For a second, he wondered if she'd found something. But if she had, wouldn't she be shouting from the rooftops and talking a mile a minute? Instead, she was abnormally quiet tonight.

"These are only a few of the hundreds and hundreds of boxes in that basement," she said.

"Maybe I could help." His offer should have come long before now, but he suspected the files were confidential.

Mia shook her head, long hair swishing over the shoulders of a bright-blue sweater. Blue was definitely her color.

"I was about to stop for the night anyway." She slid some papers into a folder and looked up at him. "So are you going to tell me why you're here or can I assume I'm under arrest?"

This time she offered a smile.

This was the Mia he knew and...appreciated.

"I came with some news." He scraped a straight-backed chair up closer to her desk and sat down. "Unless Adam beat me to it."

Her smile disappeared and she tensed again. "What kind of news? Did something happen?"

Collin waved away her concern. "Nothing bad. At least, I hope you don't think so. Adam invited me to your Mom's for Thanksgiving."

She studied him for two beats. "So did I, but you said no."

That wasn't the reaction he'd anticipated.

"I'm coming now."

"What changed your mind?"

"Your brother is a devious man."

He expected her to laugh and agree. She didn't. She seemed distracted, not really into the conversation. Earlier he'd felt unwanted, but now he saw what he hadn't before. Something was wrong.

He leaned across the desk to tug at her hand. The bones felt small and fine, and her skin was smoother and softer than Happy's fur. "Let's get out of here. You're exhausted."

"It's not that, Collin. Oh, I am tired, but I'm also upset about something I found in an old file. I need to tell you and I'm not sure how."

That got his attention. The desire to tease her about Thanksgiving dinner disappeared. "Whose old files are we talking about?"

"Drew's. Or at least files associated with Drew. There's some confusion in them. Several files seem to be jumbled together with parts missing. Maybe a box was spilled somehow and hastily repacked. I don't know. But I did find some information that may or may not involve Drew."

He saw the pinched skin around her mouth, the worry around her eyes. And he knew beyond a shadow of a doubt, the news was not going to make him happy.

The day before Thanksgiving Collin unearthed an ancient police report which identified the cause of the Carter Home fire as an electrical short. Better yet, the report listed several witnesses, one of whom turned out to be another former foster kid, Billy Johnson. Collin needed less than thirty minutes to track down the man's name, address and place of employment.

"I'm going with you," Mia said, when he called to tell her of the discovery.

"This is your day off. I thought you and your mom were cooking."

"We are. We still can. But I'm going with you. Don't argue. Come pick me up."

Collin hid a smile. Deep down, he was glad that the bulldog in Mia insisted on going along. Something in him worried that the interview might produce bad news. And though Mia couldn't stop bad news, she was a dandy with moral support and comforting prayers. He'd come to respect that about her. He'd even tried praying a few times himself lately.

Someone had died in that house fire. That's when he'd started praying in earnest. Praying that Drew wasn't the one. He'd even taken to bargaining with God. If Drew was alive, he would believe. If Drew was okay, God must care. He knew such prayers were selfish and unfruitful, but he was a desperate man.

Billy Johnson met them in the grease bay of an auto repair shop on the east side of town, a rag in hand. His blue service uniform was streaked with oil and grease and his fingernails would never see clean, but when he offered his hand, Collin shook it gratefully. This man had known Drew at age fifteen.

"Kinda cold out here," Billy said. "Y'all come inside the office. My boss won't care. I told him you were coming."

They followed the mechanic inside the tiny office

stacked with tools and papers and red rags and reeking of grease. A small space heater kept the room pleasantly warm.

"Y'all have a seat." He shoved a car-repair manual off one chair and swiped the red rag over the seat for Mia. Collin settled onto a canvas camp stool. No one sat around this place much.

"I remember Drew." Billy rolled a stool from beneath the desk and balanced on it, pushing himself back and forth with one extended foot. "He was a wiry rascal. Liked to fight."

Collin shot Mia a wry glance. "Sounds like my brother."

"He was okay, though. Me and him, we only punched each other once. After that, we was kinda buddies, ya might say." He grinned. "Foster kids, ya know. We sneaked smokes together. Raided the kitchen. Tormented the house parents. The usual."

"What do you remember about the night of the fire?" Mia asked, and Collin was grateful. His shoulder muscles were as tight as security at the White House. He wanted to get this over with.

"More than I want to," Billy said, scratching at the back of his head. The metal rollers on his stool made an annoying screech against the cement floor. "The house was full, seven or eight boys, I think, so I was asleep in the living room on the couch when the fire broke out."

"But you woke in time to escape?"

"Yes, ma'am. Me and this one other kid." He rolled the stool in and out, in and out, oblivious to the screech.

"Was it Drew?"

"No, ma'am." *Screech. Screech.* "A kid named Jerry. I think he's in the pen now."

Blood pulsing against his temples, Collin leaned forward. "What about Drew?"

Billy hesitated. Collin got a real bad feeling, worse than the time he'd walked into a dark alley and come face to face with a double-barrelled shotgun.

The screeching stopped. "Drew slept in the attic. I'm sorry, officer. Your brother never made it out."

Mia wanted Collin to get angry. She wanted him to cry. She wanted him to react in some way, to show some emotion. But he didn't.

With his cop face on, he thanked Billy Johnson and quietly led the way to the car. The drive back to Mia's apartment was unbearable. She talked, muttered maddeningly useless platitudes, said she was sorry a million times, reminded him that Ian was still out there somewhere, but Collin said nothing in response.

"Why don't you come inside for a while?" she asked when he stopped outside her apartment. "I'll make us something to eat. Better yet, my tiramisu brownies are already baked for tomorrow's dinner. We can sneak one with some fresh coffee. I know brownies and coffee won't change things, but comfort food always makes me feel better."

"I don't think so."

Her heart broke for him. Lord, hasn't he had enough sorrow in his life? Why this?

She pushed the door open, hesitant to leave him alone. "Will you call me later if you need to talk?"

For a minute, she thought he might respond, might even smile. He'd teased her so many times about her tendency to rattle on, but this time he was hurting too much even to tease.

"I'll come out to your place later if you want me to. Or you can come back here. You really shouldn't be alone."

He looked at her and what she read there was clearer than words and so terribly sad she wanted to cry. He'd always been alone.

"I'm here for you, Collin. If you need anything at all, please call me. Let me help. I don't know what to do, either, but I want to do something."

Feeling helpless, she slid out of the truck and stood with one hand holding the door open. Wind swirled around her legs, chilling her. Someone slammed an apartment door and pounded down the metal stairs outside her complex.

"I'm praying for you, Collin. God cares. I care. My family cares. Please know that."

This time he answered, his voice low, and Mia thought she saw a crack in the hard veneer. "I do know."

She couldn't help herself. She reached back inside the cab and touched his cheek. Her heart was full of sorrow and love and the desire to help him heal, but this time she was the one with no words.

Collin reached up and took her hand from his whisker-rough face, gave it a squeeze and let go. "Better get inside. You'll freeze."

She backed away, reluctant to let him leave, but having no other choice.

"We'll see you tomorrow at Mama's, won't we?"

"I don't know, Mia," he said. "I probably wouldn't be very good company."

And then he drove away.

Chapter Twelve

*D*ead.

The word clattered round and round in Collin's head like a rock in an empty pop can.

Drew, his full-of-energy-and-orneriness brother, was dead. Long dead.

All the years of searching, hoping, gone up in smoke in a house where the kids were throwaways that nobody wanted anyway. Nobody missed them. Nobody mourned them.

He lay on his bed in the darkness, staring up at the shadows cast by the wind-tossed maple outside his window. He had used all the energy in him to drive home and care for the animals. By the time he'd dragged his heavy heart inside, he hadn't had the energy to undress except for his boots.

He'd been alone for years, but tonight he felt empty as if part of him had disappeared. In a way, he supposed it had. The search for his brothers had sustained him since he was ten years old. The hope of reunion had kept him moving forward, kept him fighting upstream when he'd been ready to give up on life in general. The search had given him purpose, made him a cop. Now, half of that hope was gone forever. And with it, half of himself.

He heard the soft shuffle of animal feet on wood floors. The familiar limp and thump that could only belong to Happy.

After the fire, Collin hadn't had the heart to leave the little guy outside with the others. So Happy had moved into a box in the living room, quietly filling Collin's evenings with his sweet presence.

But now, he whined at the bedside, an unusual turn of events.

"What do you want, boy?" Collin said to the dark ceiling.

Happy whined again.

Though his body weighed a thousand pounds and moving took effort he didn't have, Collin rolled to his side and peered down at the shadowy form. The collie lifted one footless leg and pawed at him. When Collin didn't pick him up, Happy tried to jump, a pitiful sight that sent the dog tumbling backward.

Collin swooped him up onto the bed. "Here now."

With a contented sigh, Happy buried his nose under his master's arm and settled down. Collin had never had a dog. Not as a pet. But Happy was getting real close. Both his legs had finally healed after the second amputation, but a dog with two missing feet wasn't likely ever to be adopted.

He smoothed his hand over the shaggy fur, glad for the company of another creature, especially one that didn't talk.

No, that wasn't fair. He liked Mia to talk. He loved her soothing, sweet voice. He loved her enthusiasm for life, her positive take on everything, her belief in the ultimate goodness. She was a light in a dark place.

Mia had been so upset for him. He'd wanted to talk to her, wanted to let her help, but he couldn't. He didn't know how.

Burrowing one hand deep into Happy's thick fur, Collin drew comfort from the warm, loving dog.

A lot of good prayer had done. Not that he expected God to pay any attention to him. But Mia had prayed. And if God was going to listen to anybody, wouldn't He hear someone like her?

With his free hand, Collin dug down into his pants' pocket, felt the metal fish. All this time he'd carried the keychain as a reminder of his brothers. Of that last day together. Of the counselor who'd prayed for them and shown them kindness, given them hope. Had Drew still carried his that fateful night?

A fire. Another fire. He squeezed his eyes shut, but quickly opened them when flames shot up behind his imagination. Drew in a fire. Helpless. Just like the animals in his barn.

All night, he lay there, unable to sleep, unable to stop picturing the burned animals he'd had to bury. Unable to stop his imagination from making the terrible comparison.

When at last the sun broke above the horizon, heralding the new day, Collin rolled onto his belly and pulled the pillow over his head.

Today was Thanksgiving.

And he wasn't feeling too thankful.

At noon Collin awakened, cold and depressed, to a very urgent demand from Happy to be let outside.

Amazed to have slept at all, he stumbled to the front door, bleary-eyed and heavy-headed. The house was cold and the wood floors chilled his bare feet. He'd forgotten to turn on the heat last night.

After cranking the thermostat, he stood at the door to watch the collie hobble around the front yard, tail in motion, sniffing the scent of the resident squirrel as if he had the legs to catch it. Collin had to admit, the little dog's attitude had a positive effect on his own.

When Happy made the choice to stay outside and play, Collin closed the door and went to make coffee.

He felt bad about backing out of dinner at the Caranos'. He didn't like disappointing Mia—or any of the others for that matter. They were a great family. The best. The kind he would have loved to have grown up in. But he didn't belong, especially not today when negative energy was all he had to share.

He hoped Mitch was there, though, instead of at home. The boy needed the Caranos.

While the coffee brewed, the kitchen grew warmer, but Collin's feet didn't. He headed for the bedroom in search of clean socks.

As he opened the dresser drawer, his attention fell to the book Mia had given to him the night of the barn fire. She'd said the contents would encourage him, help him understand his purpose. Until yesterday he'd believed his purpose was to find his brothers. Now he wondered if there had to be more to life than a single-minded effort to accomplish only one thing. He'd found Drew, for whatever good that had done him. What would he do after he found Ian? Once his only purpose was fulfilled, then what? Would his life be over?

Without giving the decision too much thought, he

grabbed the book along with a pair of socks and headed for the kitchen and that much-needed cup of coffee. The smell alone was waking him up.

He poured a cup and sat down at the table, flipped the book to a random page, and began to read.

Late that afternoon Happy's excited yip warned Collin that he was not alone. He jammed his hammer into the loop on his tool belt and walked around to the front of the house. For the last few hours, he'd sweated out his depression on the house-in-progress while mulling over the things he'd read in Mia's book.

As he stood in the front yard, chilled by winter wind on sweat, a caravan of familiar-looking vehicles wound down his driveway, stirred dry leaves and dust and elicited a cacophony of barking from the penned dogs. Happy danced on two feet and a pair of stubs, furry tail in overdrive, mouth stretched into a wide smile.

One fist propped on his hip, Collin blinked in bewilderment at the incoming traffic. Mia's yellow Mustang led the pack, an entire invasion of Caranos.

"Hi, Collin." Mitch jumped out of Mia's barely stopped car, wearing new jeans and an oversize OU jersey. Happy was all over him like honey glaze on ham, wiggling and whining, eyes aglow with love. Mitch laughed in delight and fell to the ground, pulling the dog onto his chest.

Adam bolted out of his red SUV and came charging across the yard, a mock scowl on his face. "Hey, squirt. Don't be desecrating my OU jersey like that."

Mitch leaped up, brushing away the dust. "Sorry, Adam."

Mitchell had come a long way from the defiant kid Collin had picked up for shoplifting.

Adam ruffled his head. "Joking. The jersey is yours. I told you that." He stuck a hand out toward Collin, his dark eyes sparking with the Carano humor. "As your lawyer, I have an obligation to tell you something." He jerked his head toward the rest of the laughing, jabbering group who came toward the house loaded with boxes and dishes. "These women cooked a mega meal. And any invited man who doesn't show up to eat it could be in serious danger."

"What is all this?"

"You know the old saying. If Mohammed won't come to the mountain, the mountain will come to him. So, the Caranos have moved Thanksgiving to your place."

"You're kidding." Collin stared in amazement as the whole group trouped inside his house. A waft of incredibly delicious smells trailed them.

Adam clapped him on the back. "Caranos take their food seriously. Especially Thanksgiving food."

The old feelings of inadequacy crowded in with the unexpected company. His house was tiny and his table impossibly small. How would they have a dinner inside there? How would they all even get inside?

But the undaunted Carano clan had thought of everything. From the back of a pickup came folding tables and chairs. He watched, unmoving for several long, bewildered minutes while all around him people laughed and joked and juggled boxes and covered dishes. Why had they done this? Why would Mia and her family go to so much trouble to bring Thanksgiving to a guy who was accustomed to having no holidays at all? Why did they care?

"Close your mouth, Collin," Mia said as she swished past him smelling like sunshine and banana nut bread. "And take this into the house."

Her smile warmed a cold place inside him.

He accepted the foil-wrapped package, still warm from the oven. "You didn't have to do this."

She pointed a finger at him. "Don't say that to Mama."

He didn't understand this kind of family bond. He didn't understand these people. They scared him and nurtured him and made him long to be someone he wasn't. He didn't know whether to run away from them or to them.

For today, he figured he didn't have much say in the matter either way. If this was a game of tag, you're it, he was it. Might as well make the best of the situation.

The twenty-odd people were a tight fit inside Collin's home-in-progress, requiring some creative arrangement, but in no time at all his house smelled of the huge Thanksgiving dinner spread out before them on folding tables. Someone, Mia, he figured, had even thought of brown-and-orange tablecloths and a perky tissue-turkey centerpiece.

Around him, conversation ebbed and flowed. Nic, wearing a sweatshirt that proclaimed *I'm going to graduate on time no matter how long it takes,* wielded a carving knife and fork with a maniacal laugh that had the girls squealing.

As he watched the interaction of people who loved each other, some of the heavy sorrow lifted from Collin. Every time he hung out with the Caranos, he was overwhelmed with both yearning and fear. Yearning to be a part. Fear that he didn't have what it took.

He removed a stack of plates from Mia's hands and began to set them out in long rows.

"I hope you aren't upset with our invasion," Mia said, her sweet eyes seriously concerned that he was angry with her. "I couldn't stand to think of you out here alone on Thanksgiving."

He'd figured Mia was the instigator. She had wanted to be here—with him—and the idea gave him a happy little buzz. Maybe he had it in him after all.

Dinner was over, but the pleasant zing of having Mia and her family in his house didn't go away. The television blared a game between the Lions and the Cowboys which brought occasional shouts of victory from Adam and Nic. Gabe and his wife were deep into a game of Go Fish with their oldest child while the youngest was fast asleep in Collin's bedroom. Mitchell was sprawled with his back against Leo's knees, Happy in his lap. They all looked as full and drowsy and content as Collin felt.

Contentment was not a word he used very often. But something had happened to him today when Mia's family had come onto his turf to draw him into their midst with food and love. If he dwelled on the idea, he'd probably get nervous and back off, so he chose to enjoy. His mind needed their exuberant distraction.

"I'm on KP," he said, gently nudging Rosalie out from in front of his shiny stainless-steel sink. "Cleaning up is the least I can do."

A chorus of groans issued from the Carano men.

"Traitor," Nic grumbled.

"You're starting a terrible precedent," Adam called. "Next year, they'll expect us to cook."

This time the women hooted.

"Anna and I will help Collin, Mama. There's really

not room for more than three, anyway. You go sit down.
You've cooked for three days."

"Sounds good. I wanted to watch this game anyway."
Rosalie untied her apron and hung the starched poplin
over the back of a chair. "When these tables are cleared,
you boys get them folded and put out in the truck so we
have room to play charades or something."

"Will do, Mama."

Rosalie bustled around the tables and squeezed a
chair into a tiny space between the wall and Leo. Collin leaned toward Mia and murmured, "Your mom likes
football?"

Mia looked up from scraping leftover yams into a
container and grinned. He loved the way she always had
a smile ready to share. "Mama doesn't know a touchdown from a field goal, but she treasures the time with
her boys."

"Your family's lucky to have her."

Mia studied him, expression soft and understanding.
"We're very blessed."

Blessed. Yeah, he could see that. But they worked at
being a family, too. At this whole togetherness thing.
They were a clear picture of how functional families
made it happen. Sacrifice, commitment, overlooking
each other's quirks. He understood that now in a way
he hadn't before.

"I'll wash. You dry. Dish towels in that top drawer."
He took a heavy ceramic dish from her and dumped
the empty bowl into the soapy water. "You Caranos
are great cooks. I can't believe I ate two pieces of pie."

Mia reached for a rinsed glass and their arms
brushed. Suddenly, he was remembering that discon-
certing kiss.

"There's more for later."

He'd like that a lot. And he didn't mean pie.

They made short work of the kitchen, Anna and Mia whisking dishes and leftovers from the tables while he scrubbed away. While the women carried on most of the conversation Collin listened, comfortable with their chatter.

"I think that's the last one," Mia said, taking a huge stainless pot from his drippy hands.

Collin looked around, saw the tables cleared, and pulled the plug. "Good. The animals are probably thinking I've abandoned them. Can you take over from here?"

"I can," Anna said, her smile a mirror of Mia's. "You two go on. I'll finish up and make some fresh coffee, too."

"I'm not arguing with a deal like that," Mia said.

Nic popped up from his folding chair as Collin and Mia donned their coats. "Need any help?"

"We've got it. Thanks, anyway." As much as he liked Nic and the other Caranos, he was ready to be alone. Well, almost alone.

Collin pushed the storm door open and waited for Mia to pass through. Her companionship no longer felt like an intrusion. He figured he should worry about that. Later.

Once outside he was tempted, if only for a split second, to take her hand. He settled for a hand under her elbow instead. A man had to form some kind of boundaries with a woman like Mia.

As they fell into step toward the lean-to that now served as shelter for the remaining animals, she glanced over at him. "You didn't get much sleep last night."

"Perceptive." Beneath a narrow slice of silver moon,

the air had grown frosty. Collin's breath puffed out beneath the bright yard light. Last night had been one of the worst nights of his life.

"The bags under your eyes gave you away." She slowed her steps to rest one hand on his upper arm. Whether imagined or real, Mia's warmth penetrated the sleeve of his thick coat. "How are you? Really."

"Better now." That surprised him. To know that family not his own could lift his spirits this much.

"I'm so sorry. Deeply, truly sorry. You have every right to be angry and hurt and grief-stricken. I wish I knew what to do to make things better."

She already had. She and her rambunctious family with their big hearts and their open arms.

"Every holiday for more than twenty years, I've wondered about my brothers. I know what happened to Drew now, but what about Ian? Does he have a family to go home to? A wife and kids? Is he having turkey and dressing and pumpkin pie right this minute with a loving family?"

Or is he as lonely and messed up as me?

"We're going to keep on believing and praying that he's okay and that we are going to locate him. If we found information about Drew, we can find Ian."

"I hope you're right." Maybe then the hole inside him would heal a little.

As they approached the pens, the animals moved restlessly, eager for their own Thanksgiving dinner. The colt whinnied a greeting. A cat meowed, followed by a chorus of kitten mews.

Even after losing six animals to the fire and making the decision to take no more until the barn was rebuilt, he still had too many animals. Caged up this way was no life for them and he hated the arrangement, though there was no other place for the strays to go. He'd ruled out the animal shelter knowing that sick animals wouldn't be adopted and the alternative was euthanasia. Better with him than there. Some were well enough to move around inside a stall but not well enough to be safe from coyotes and other predators if he left them loose. The puppies and kittens were in borrowed cages that opened out to short, makeshift runs. The larger dogs were on chains next to borrowed dog houses. The grazing animals were the lucky ones, unaffected by the fire except for the loss of stall space.

He went to the row of barrels that contained a variety of animal feed. "I have to find a way to get this barn up faster."

At the rate he was going, the barn wouldn't be finished for a year. He had only one stall completed to house the sickest, and a chain-link run for the dogs.

Mia began to distribute dry dog food, stopping to give each animal an ear rub. "I'll feed everyone while you take care of the medications."

He gave her a grateful look. "Good idea."

Panda, who had survived the fire and recovered sufficiently to be adopted, had yet to find a home, though her kittens had. Collin figured he'd never find a place for her. The mama cat allowed Collin or Mia to feed her, but otherwise she feared humans except for Mitchell.

"I thought this was Mitchell's job," Mia said, coming around the shadowy side of the lean-to.

Collin knelt on the ground dabbing antibiotic cream onto a pup's stitches. "He's through serving his time."

"I know. But the responsibility has been good for him."

"He's changed a lot."

"Thanks to you." She handed him a roll of adhesive tape.

"And your family. Sometimes I wonder what will happen to him."

"His stepdad scares me."

Collin looked at her sharply. She'd shoved her hands into her pockets. "Do you mean personally or professionally?"

Even in the halflight, he saw her frown. "Both. Since you told me of your suspicions, I want Mitch out of there, but…"

"But Mitch won't tell you the truth." He put the finishing touches on the bandage and stood. He was as frustrated as Mia over Mitch's reluctance to give them a reason to move him to safety. And for all his watchfulness, Collin couldn't find reasonable cause to pay Teddy Shipley an unexpected official visit.

"I think Mitch won't talk because his mother is using, too. He's afraid of what will happen to her."

In his entire life, including twelve years on the force, Collin had seen nothing but horror come from drugs. He was lucky. Mia would say blessed. And maybe he was. Whichever, he'd somehow escaped the trap of drugs. Too many of the boys he'd known in the group homes were dead, in jail, or living lives of unspeakable despair because of drugs.

"If a meth lab is operating in that house, it's only a matter of time until something bad goes down."

Her voice was stunned. "Do you think that's the case?"

"Maybe." Probably. They were gathering more evidence daily.

A chill of fear trickled down his backbone. "Stay out of there, Mia. You hear me?"

"I'm afraid for him, Collin."

"Me, too," he admitted grimly. Collin knew the reality of Mitchell's situation. Mia was an experienced professional, but she hadn't lived the life. He had.

In silence, his thoughts churning, he put the medical supply box away and doubled-checked the cage latches for security. He couldn't keep the whole world safe, but he could take care of these animals. And Mitchell, too, if the kid would only let him.

Mia tugged on the front of his coat. Her hair blew softly back from her face as she looked up at him. "Stop fretting. You can't always be with him. But Jesus is."

"'He'll never leave you nor forsake you,'" he quoted softly, the words of his keychain making more sense at that moment than they ever had.

"Exactly."

If he was indeed blessed to have avoided the curse of drugs, was Jesus the reason? Had God been with him through everything? "Do you think it's true?"

"I know it is." She pulled her hood up and shivered against a sudden gust of wind.

Collin draped an arm around her shoulders and drew her against his side. She fitted beneath his arm as if curved in exactly the right places for that purpose.

They started back toward the house. Collin reined in his long stride to accommodate her shorter one.

"Mind if I ask you something?" His words were deep and thoughtful.

"Anything." And she meant it.

"I can't believe how much I've laughed tonight."

She bumped him with her hip. "That's not a question."

"After hearing about Drew—" He stopped. Talking about his brother's death was still too fresh and cut too deep.

Mia slipped an arm around his waist and squeezed. She prayed he could feel her compassion and somehow gain comfort. From the time she and Adam had come up with the idea to bring Thanksgiving to him, she'd prayed. Thankfully, he'd responded well to their invasion and had even seemed to enjoy himself in spite of the awful sorrow in his heart.

"I want to ask you something," he said, stopping in a wind break next to the front porch. From inside the house Mia could hear one of the first Christmas commercials of the season.

"Sounds serious."

"It is. I've spent most of my adult life coming to terms with my crazy life, but I'll never understand Drew's death. That's where I'm confused about God. I want to believe He cares but the evidence isn't too strong. I don't mean I'm angry at Him or that I blame Him. But He doesn't seem too involved in my life so far."

His words were not bitter. Instead, they held a yearning, a seeking to understand. Somehow in all the past rejections, Collin had come to see himself as unlovable.

Mia looked up at him, at the strong, manly profile illuminated by the moon. She admired so much about Collin Grace that he didn't even recognize as good. He'd overcome some incredible odds to become a man with so much depth of character, so much rich emotion that he didn't know how to express all that was inside him.

She shifted against the wall and gazed off into the darkness, praying for wisdom. She'd been a Christian since she was twelve years old. She had a strong, healthy family and many friends. Though she'd had hurts and struggles, nothing in her experience could compare to what this good and decent man had lived through. How could she make him understand that God was here, caring? How could she make him understand that he was loved and loveable?

Her heart filled with realization. Tonight was the night he needed to know.

"I don't have any easy answers. I wish I did. But there's something I want to share with you. Actually, three somethings."

Collin peered down at her, his expression sincere and curious. She saw a trust there that gave her courage.

"First of all, I don't pretend to understand why terrible things happen to innocent people, especially kids. But I do know that God cares. So much that He sent His son to give us hope of a better place than this. A perfect place called Heaven.

"Secondly, He knew Drew's death would devastate you. He kept the news from you until you were ready to handle it. Until you had met a crazy bunch of Caranos who would try their best to help you through the grief."

"Why didn't he just give me back my brother? That's the only thing I've ever wanted."

"I don't know, Collin. I wish He had. But God has a plan for you. And even if Drew isn't a part of your future, he'll always be a part of who you are and what you've become—a good cop, a caring man, a dear and trusted friend."

A gust of wind whipped her hood back. Collin caught

each side and tugged the hood up around her face. When she thanked him with a half smile, he moved a fraction closer.

Mia's skin tingled from his nearness. As hard as this was going to be, she had to tell him the truth—all of it.

In the narrow space between them, her breath mingled with his, moist and warm. They really should go inside.

She could see he wanted to kiss her again. And she wanted that too, but she wouldn't follow through. The first time had been unplanned reflex, completely understandable and forgivable. This time would be premeditated.

"Wasn't there a third thing you wanted to tell me?" he murmured, wonderfully, painfully near.

She wasn't scared of the truth, but she didn't know how to predict Collin's reaction. Was she doing the right thing by telling him? She fidgeted with the string on her hood but held Collin's gaze with hers. His expression might not change, but his eyes would tell her what he wouldn't.

"Yes. There is. Something very important. Something that I hope will make you realize how special and valuable you are. At least to me."

Inside the house, Nic's voice shouted "Touchdown!" Neither she nor Collin reacted.

She had his full attention now.

Throat thick with emotion, Mia bracketed Collin's face in her gloved hands. And then, her voice sure, she said, "The third thing is this—I'm in love with you, Collin."

Chapter Thirteen

Collin blinked into her eyes, stunned. She loved him?

A thousand responses thundered through him as wild as mustangs. He didn't know what she expected him to say. He had feelings for her, wanted to kiss her, to be with her, but love? He wasn't even sure what that was.

"You don't have to respond to that." She gave his jaws a final caress and dropped her hands. "I just wanted you to know."

She started to slip under his arm and move away, but he caught her. "No, you don't. You don't drop a bomb like that and walk off."

She stopped and looked up at him, her gaze as clear and honest as a baby's. Something dangerous turned over inside Collin's chest. She was serious. She loved him.

Oh, man. How did he deal with that? And why had she chosen to tell him now in the midst of a conversation about God and Drew?

If her intention was to distract him, she'd succeeded. The idea of kissing her had been on his mind since she'd bopped out of that yellow Mustang and sashayed across his front yard with her family in tow.

Ah, what was he talking about? He'd wanted to kiss her a lot longer than that.

Now that he knew she loved him, he wasn't quite so hesitant to follow through.

Drawing her closer, he lowered his face to hers.

She shrank back against the house and placed a hand on his chest. "I'm sorry, Collin. As much as I'd like to kiss you, I won't."

He frowned. "You love me? But you won't let me kiss you?"

Her eyes filled with tears, confusing him more. He'd made her cry, though he had no idea what he'd done. "I'm sorry. Let me explain."

Reluctantly, he dropped his hands and backed off. Everything in him wanted to hold her more than ever now.

The wind circled in between them. Mia shivered and hugged herself, and he had to fight to keep from taking her in his arms again.

"I could do that for you," he said with a half smile.

But they both knew he wouldn't push the issue.

She rubbed her hands up and down her arms, eyes focused on some distant point in the darkness. "Tonight, I understood something about you, Collin."

"Yeah?" He wished she'd tell him because right now he didn't understand much of anything.

"I realized that you don't know how to receive love. From God or anybody else. You've been hurt and rejected so much in your life that you think you're unlovable."

He didn't much like the idea of anyone poking

around inside his head, and he liked it even less when someone thought they knew what made him tick. But he had to admit, there was validity to her words. Normally, he didn't listen to psychobabble, but from Mia— well, Mia was different.

"Love is a gift, Collin, and unless a gift is given away, it has no value. You're valuable to me. I wanted you to understand that. I wanted to give that to you."

"Then why—?" He left the question hanging. She loved him, but she wouldn't kiss him?

He shoved his hands into his jacket pockets.

Her logic didn't make sense.

"Because as much as I love you, I love God more. And I trust Him to know what's best and right for me even when His rules hurt."

Her words were a splash of cold water in the face. One minute she declared her love and the next she shut him out. "And God says I'm not good enough for you?"

"That's not what I mean."

She closed the distance between them and rested her head against his chest. He didn't yield. He'd never let a woman get this close. And now she was telling him she loved him but he wasn't good enough?

But in his heart, he knew she was right. A foster kid from questionable bloodlines could never be good enough for a woman like Mia.

"Will you hear me out?" she asked softly. "This has nothing to do with being good enough."

He relented then, letting her tug one hand from his pocket. He couldn't seem to say no to Mia.

"You have a lot of baggage from the past to deal with, Collin. None of that scares me off. God can heal anything. But that's the key. You have to let Him."

"What does any of that have to do with me kissing you? Does God have rules against a man kissing a woman he cares about?"

Okay, so he cared about her. Maybe a lot, though love wasn't a word in his vocabulary.

Mia's full mouth widened in a characteristic smile. "God's all for kissing. He probably invented it. But he has rules about Christians kissing non-Christians. That's hard for me to accept, but I have to. I'll be your friend. And I won't stop loving you even for a second, but that's as far as we go."

"You mean if I was a Christian, I could kiss you?"

"Yes." She tilted her head to one side and gave him a lopsided smile. "But don't be thinking I go around kissing just anybody, Christian or not."

He already knew that about her.

"Okay, then. Friends. I can do that." Friendship was all he'd ever expected anyway. Just knowing she was in love with him was burden enough.

Yes, friendship was far better anyway.

Mia dropped the last gaily wrapped gift into her shopping bag and headed out of the mall. The Christmas crowd was thicker than Grandma Carano's spaghetti sauce.

She had met her best girlfriend for a late lunch and they'd talked about Collin. Sharing her concerns with a praying friend had helped. She was thinking about her cop far too much lately and though convinced she'd done the right thing by admitting her love for him, holding to the friendship rule was harder than she'd imagined.

Collin had the uncanny ability to move right on as

if nothing had happened. But with a subtle difference. Last night, he'd come to her apartment, bearing a glorious red poinsettia and asked her out to dinner. When she'd refused, he'd wanted to stay and talk about the book she'd loaned him.

Not knowing if she was playing with fire or trying to be a good witness for the Lord, she'd made microwave popcorn and spent the next two hours in an interesting discussion about her faith. Collin was a bright man with a lot of questions and misconceptions about God. He was stuck on the idea that God had abandoned him along with everyone else in his childhood, and nothing she said seemed to help.

But he was seeking the truth, and that alone was a big step.

Upon leaving the crowded mall, Mia picked Mitchell up from school and took him back to her office. They had some things to discuss that couldn't be said at his home. Later, she had his mother's permission to take him Christmas shopping with the money Collin had paid him for working with the animals. No matter that she'd already spent two hours at the mall, shopping was something Mia could always do.

Mitchell looked scruffy and smelled worse. She hoped the odor was normal boy sweat and not cigarette smoke. He'd come too far these six months to regress now.

Once inside her small office, she handed him a stick of beef jerky and motioned to a chair. "Sit down. We need to talk."

He ripped into the jerky. "About Collin?"

That surprised her. "Why do you think this is about Collin?"

One shoulder hitched. He flopped into the chair. "Since we didn't go out to his place, I figure something's up. He said I don't have to come anymore."

"You don't."

"I guess he's tired of me hanging around."

Mia rounded her desk and sat down. "You know that's not true. Your official community service time is completed so nobody will force you to work on the farm anymore. Now the decision to go or not is yours to make."

"Did he and Adam find the guy who started the fire?"

"They think so."

He chewed thoughtfully, then spoke around a wad of jerky. "I don't."

Mia frowned. "What do you mean?"

Mitchell took a sudden interest in the tip of his beef stick. "Nothing."

"Is there something you want to tell me?"

He slouched a little lower in the chair. "No."

Which meant there was.

She sighed and let the subject drop. Mitchell shared confidences according to his timetable, not hers. "Collin needs your help now more than ever."

"It really stinks about his brother. I wish I could do something."

"You already do. You help with the animals. Keep him company. Cheer him up. He depends on you." The boy *was* good for Collin, and the cop was finally at a place where he could realize as much.

Mitchell sat up straighter. "Yeah. I guess he does. He hates mucking out stalls." One tennis-shoed foot banged the front of her desk. "But I meant about his brother."

"We can't do anything about Drew's death, Mitch."

"I meant the other one."

She smiled. "Sooner or later, we'll find Ian."

She let a couple of seconds pass. The subject she needed to broach wasn't a good one. Muffled voices came and went outside her closed door.

"You want a Coke?" she asked to soften him up.

"Nah."

"Later, then. We'll go to that Mexican place you like."

"Cool." His toe tapped the front of her metal desk over and over again.

Mia picked up a pen. Put it down. Took it up again. "We need to discuss your stepdad."

Mitchell stiffened. The thudding against her desk ceased. He didn't look up.

"I know you're scared of him."

No answer.

"I talked to your mother about going to a women's shelter, but she refuses. She says there's nothing wrong. Frankly, I don't believe her, and I'm worried about both of you." When he didn't respond, she dropped the pen and leaned toward him. She was getting nowhere with this one-sided conversation.

"Mitch, if something should happen, anything at all, if you should ever be afraid, will you call me? Or Collin?"

He thought about her question for several seconds while a telephone rang in another office and a door down the hall slammed shut. Finally, he nodded. "Yeah."

That was the best she was going to get. She rubbed the back of her neck and stretched. "I'll trust you on that."

Her office door opened and another social worker peeked inside. "Mia, could I see you for a minute?"

"Of course." She stood and said to Mitch, "Stay put, okay?" She glanced at the clock. "When I get back we'll head for the mall."

"Can I play on your computer?"

"Sure. And have another beef jerky. I'll be back in a few minutes."

Three days later, Collin bounded up the stairs to the second floor of the Department of Human Services. Mia had said she loved him, but he'd never believed she'd do this.

She looked up from a stack of paperwork, the kind of overwhelming mountain he understood too well. Jammed into one corner of her office, a miniature Christmas tree blinked multicolored lights. A whimsical Santa waved from the wall behind her desk, and Christmas carols issued from her computer speakers.

"Oh, hi, Collin." Mia's face lit up. "I got your note."

"Sorry I missed you." More than sorry. Every day since she'd said those shocking words he'd found an excuse to talk to her, either in person or on the phone. The last couple of days she'd been out of contact and he'd missed her. He'd wanted to surprise her with a special offer that was sure to make her happy. Instead, she'd surprised him.

Somehow the knowledge that she loved him had changed him. He wasn't sure what was happening inside him, but he liked the difference. He felt lighter, happier, freer, which made no sense at all considering the news of Drew's death.

But then today in his mailbox... He slapped the

brown envelope down onto her desk. He could never repay her for this.

"This is the best news I've had in a long time."

She grinned at his unusual enthusiasm. "You could use some good news."

He didn't want to think she'd done this out of pity, but if he told the truth, he didn't really care why she'd done it.

"I think this is Ian, don't you?"

She blinked, puzzled. "Excuse me?"

He slid a sheet of paper from the envelope and laid the all-important document in front of her. "I think this is my Ian. I think this is the agency that handled his adoption."

And he hadn't even known Ian was adopted. Part of him rejoiced. At least one brother had found a family.

"Collin, I don't know what you're talking about—" She froze in midsentence as her eyes moved across the confidential document.

All the color drained from her face. Disbelief mixed with hurt, she shot to her feet. Rollers clattered as her chair thunked against the wall behind her. "I can't believe this, Collin. How could you?"

Now he was confused. "How could I what?"

"Break into these confidential files. Compromise me this way. I thought we were at least friends."

They were friends. A lot more than friends. "What are you talking about?"

"You were here in my office while I was gone."

He rocked back, stunned at the unspoken accusation. "You think I broke into your files?"

"What else can I think? This document is from a sealed adoption file. No one, not even me, is supposed to look at those files without express permission or a court order."

He knew how important her professional integrity was. He'd never even considered such a thing. "I wouldn't do that."

"Somebody did."

His jaw grew hard enough to bite through concrete as her accusation hit home. "And you think it was me."

She stared at the twinkling Christmas tree. He sensed a battle going on behind those warm gray-green eyes, but her silence was an affirmation. Finally she said, "Who else would want to?"

He had an idea but if she couldn't figure that one out on her own, he wasn't about to toss out accusations. Not like she'd done. "You'll have to trust me on this, Mia."

She pushed the sheet of paper back into the envelope and handed the packet across the desk. Her hands trembled. "I hope you find him."

"Will you help me?" He needed her. And he wanted her there beside him when Ian was found.

She shook her head, expression bleak. "I'm sorry, Collin. I can't."

She didn't believe him.

All his joy shriveled into a dusty wad. He'd finally let a woman into his heart and she couldn't even give him her trust. Some love that was.

Fine. Dandy. He should have known.

He yanked the envelope from the desk and stalked out.

Mia locked the door of her office and cried. From her computer radio, Karen Carpenter's lush voice sang "Merry Christmas, Darling." She clicked Mute.

How could Collin have done such a thing? He'd been in here two days ago, at her desk while she was at lunch. He'd even left a note. She'd wanted to believe he wouldn't do this to her, but how could she? Hadn't he pressured her more than once to open those files?

Over and over she remembered when Gabe had badgered confidential information from her. Just like Collin he'd said, "Trust me, Mia. You know I wouldn't do anything that could hurt you."

But in the end, her actions on his behalf had hurt her plenty. She'd lost her job and her credibility. And though Gabe had worked hard to make the loss up to her, she couldn't forget the awful sense of betrayal and shame.

Her own flesh-and-blood brother had compromised her for his own gain. How could she believe that Collin wouldn't do the same for a much more worthwhile reason?

Not that she wasn't glad he had the information about Ian. She only wished he'd come by it more honestly.

Collin stewed for two days, hammering away his anger on the barn that didn't seem to be getting any larger.

He hadn't broken into Mia's computer, but even if he had, he wouldn't lie about it. Why couldn't she see that? He'd considered questioning Mitch, but why bother? The deed was done and Mia blamed him.

If he'd known falling for a Christian was this much trouble, he would have run even harder the day she'd bought him a hamburger.

His cell phone rang and he slapped the device from his belt loop. "Grace."

"Mr. Grace, this is the Loving Homes Adoption

Agency in Baton Rouge. I think I may have some in-formation for you."

His heart slammed against his rib cage. His ham-mer dropped to the ground. Happy gazed up at him, puzzled as he grappled in his shirt pocket for a pencil. With shaking fingers, he scribbled the information on a piece of plywood.

His brother's name might be Ian Carpenter.

Everything in him wanted to call Mia, to share the excitement of finally having a concrete lead.

But he wouldn't. She wouldn't want him to.

Chapter Fourteen

The call came in at ten minutes to nine in the morning. A hostage situation. The suspect a convicted felon, armed and dangerous. And probably high on drugs.

Collin donned his gear along with the rest of the Tac-team members as the captain drilled them on the situation. During the serving of a warrant, the suspect had gone ballistic and taken a woman hostage, probably the common-law wife.

Collin exchanged glances with Maurice. He knew his buddy was already praying and he was glad. In situations like this, they needed all the help they could get. The Christmas holidays were high-stress periods. If anyone was going off the deep end, this time of year seemed to bring it on.

As the van approached the neighborhood, Collin grew uneasy. He knew this area.

"This is the Perez house," he said.

Captain Gonzales nodded. "Isn't that the name of the kid you've been mentoring?"

"Yeah. Is he in there?"

"Not anymore. We just got a call from Shipley on

somebody's cell phone. There's a social worker inside with him. Not the wife."

Collin's blood ran cold. "Who's the social worker?"

He already knew before the captain spoke. "Adam Carano's sister, Mia. You know her?"

He and Maurice exchanged quick glances.

"We've met." What was Mia doing in there? Hadn't he told her to stay away?

The captain gave him a strange look. He'd told no one except Maurice about his friendship with Mia. If the captain knew he was personally involved he'd send him back to the station. No way Collin was going to leave Mia at the mercy of some doped-up maniac whose last address was the state penitentiary.

Keeping his face passive, he readied his equipment, mind racing with the possibilities. Anything could go down in a situation like this. Anything.

"Why's the social worker involved? Was she there to grab the kid?"

"Bad timing, I think. She was inside when an arrest warrant was served. Shipley flipped out when he saw the cops approaching, and took her hostage."

Dandy.

"Anyone else in the house?"

"We don't know that yet, either. Jeff is working on getting the floor plans from the rental company that owns the house. Gomez is talking to neighbors to see what they know."

They set up a command post in the parking lot of an apartment complex across the street. Team members quietly dispersed around the property while uniformed officers blocked off the streets and cleared the surrounding area of bystanders.

Collin climbed to the second floor of the apartment building, seeking an advantageous position from which to view the Perez place. Adrenaline raced through his bloodstream at a far greater rate than usual in a call-out. He'd practiced this scenario a thousand times. Had even executed it. But no one he loved had ever been inside the premises.

He squeezed his eyes shut and rubbed a hand over his forehead. Of all the times to realize he was in love, he'd sure picked a doozy.

Through the earpiece in his helmet he heard the captain. They'd made contact with Teddy Shipley. The guy was spewing all kinds of irrationalities, blaming the cops for harassing him, for his inability to get a job, asking for money, a car, amnesty from prosecution.

For the next hour and a half, the negotiator tried to soothe the frenzied suspect. Collin wished like crazy he could hear the conversation but all his information was filtered through the commander. He could hear the other officers, and from his vantage point above the scene he watched the stealth movement of Tac members maneuvering closer to the house, hoping for a chance.

After a while, the suspect moved the hostage into the living room, though even through his scope, Collin could see only their shadowy forms. One of those shadows belonged to Mia. The other much larger form definitely brandished a weapon. And as much as Collin wanted to charge the place and take the guy out with his own hands, right now all he could do was wait.

By noon, the tension hung as thick as L.A. fog. Shipley grew angrier and more demanding by the minute.

Collin, jaw tight, spoke into his mouthpiece. "Has anyone talked to the hostage?"

The answer crackled back. "Yes. She sounded okay. Scared, but pretty calm under the circumstances. We gathered from her subtle answers that Shipley is popping pills on top of meth. He's seriously messed up."

No big surprise there. Collin ground his teeth. No surprise but a really big problem.

At one o'clock, food was brought in. No one bothered to eat it.

At two o'clock, the negotiator still had not established a rapport. The suspect was spewing vitriol with the frequency and strength of a geyser. He was sick of being harassed. He wasn't taking it anymore. He wasn't going back to the pen. And scariest of all, they'd never take him alive.

By three in the afternoon, hope for a peaceful resolution was fading. Shipley came to the dirty window, dragging Mia with him, a nine millimeter at her temple. Collin saw her expression through his scope. Saw the fear in her eyes, the bruises on her face. Hot fury ripped through him.

Collin knew the minute Shipley spotted an officer outside the house. Wild-eyed and crazed, he fired one shot through the picture window. Glass shattered. Shipley shoved Mia toward the opening, screaming threats.

They had an active shooter with a hostage. Things could go south fast. Real fast.

The question came through his earpiece, terse but strong. "Have you got a visual?"

"Yeah." For a man whose knees had turned to water, his voice sounded eerily calm.

He slid down onto his belly, the rough shingles scraping against his vest. He had a visual, but Mia was in the way.

"If you have the shot, take it."

The surge of adrenaline prickled his scalp. His mouth went dry. To his horror, his hands, renowned for their steadiness, began to shake.

In twelve years on the force, he'd never missed, never been scared, not even when he took down a cop killer. But Mia had never been the hostage. Her bright red Christmas sweater and frightened eyes were imprinted in his brain.

What if he hit the woman he loved more than his own life? What if the ice-water-in-his-veins sniper they called Amazing Grace missed?

The December temperature was in the thirties, but sweat broke out all over Collin.

He was the only person standing between Mia and the maniac, and he was terrified.

He couldn't do this. But there was no one else. The other sniper had no shot. Mia's life was in his hands—hands that wouldn't stop shaking.

He needed help. And there was only one place to get it.

Intent on the house, he was afraid to blink and too focused to move. Under the circumstances, he figured God would understand if his prayers weren't too formal. There was no time to close his eyes and bow his head.

"Help me, Lord. I can't handle this one. Steady me. Give me the perfect shot. For Mia."

Then as if God had actually heard him, the strangest thing happened. His hands and guts stopped trembling. The usual cool detachment settled over him. Only the feeling wasn't cool. It was warm, comforting. Something incredible had just happened to him, but he had no time to dwell on it.

"Thanks," he whispered. Later, he'd do a lot better.

His gaze flicked from the felon to Mia. Eyes wide, she stared outward toward the invisible cops. As if in slow motion, Collin saw her mouth move. For a second, he thought she was praying, too, but then through his scope, he read her lips.

"Do it."

She knew he was out here. She knew he was the sniper on duty. And she trusted him to take care of her. Mia trusted him.

And he wasn't about to let her down.

With exacting skill, he trained the sights on the suspect and waited for the precise moment. No muscle quivered. Not an eyelash blinked.

Suddenly, Mia slumped in a faint.

Collin pulled the trigger. The crack ripped the air, and the suspect crumpled.

In the next few milliseconds that seemed like hours, the Tac-team swarmed the house. Voices screamed in his earpiece.

"Suspect down. Suspect down."

Collin pushed up from the roof. A minute ago, he'd been deadly calm. Now his legs wobbled with such force he wasn't sure he could walk. Rifle in hand, he started down. He made it to the first-floor stairwell and collapsed, sliding down with his back against the hard, block wall.

He could have killed her. He could have hit Mia.

"I will never leave you nor forsake you."

The words entered his head unbidden and he knew they didn't come from him. He shoved one hand into his pocket and withdrew the little keychain.

"Thank you," he muttered. Keychain in his fisted

hand, he pressed the little fish to his mouth, dropped his head to his elevated knees, and did something he hadn't done since he was ten years old.

He wept.

"I don't need an ambulance. I'm okay. Really." Mia struggled against the strong arms of too many paramedics and police officers who wanted her to get into the ambulance. There was only one cop she wanted to see and he was nowhere around.

"Humor us, Mia." Maurice Johnson's familiar face materialized from the crowd. "You're in shock."

Maybe she was in shock. Except for an overriding sense of relief, she felt numb.

A paramedic wrapped a blood pressure cuff around her arm. As she started to resist, her knees buckled. Maurice grabbed her slumping form and helped the paramedic lift her into the back of the ambulance.

"Where's Collin?" she asked. The bruise on her cheekbone started to throb and her head swam.

"Right here."

A tall, lean officer in SWAT uniform pushed through the crowd. His handsome face exhausted, he was the most wonderful thing she'd ever seen.

"Collin," she said, and heard the wobble in her voice, felt the tears in her eyes. She dove out of the ambulance into the strongest arms imaginable. Collin wouldn't let her fall.

"I'm sorry. I was so wrong. I do trust you. I do." The tears came in earnest then.

"I know." His lips brushed her ear. "It's okay. Everything is okay now."

She searched his face and saw something new. A peace she hadn't seen before.

He was still strong and solid and every bit the confident police officer, but something about him had changed.

Later, she'd have to ask. Yes, later, she thought, as she snuggled against his chest and the world went dark.

Collin didn't bother to clean up. Still in uniform, he made one stop before heading to the hospital.

When he walked into the room, Mia was sitting in a hospital bed, chattering at mach speed to convince a young doctor to let her go home.

"Might as well say yes," Collin said.

The blond resident gave him a weary smile. "Persistent, is she?"

"Like a terrier. She'll yap until you give in."

"You sound like a man of experience."

Collin looked at the smiling Mia and his heart wrenched. Her pretty face was swollen and bruised from eye to chin. But that didn't keep her from talking.

"Just trust me on this." He winked at Mia. "And let her go. She'll be well taken care of. I can promise you that."

The doctor scribbled something on the chart and dropped the clipboard into a slot at the foot of the bed. "I'll see what I can do."

As he left, Collin scraped a heavy green chair up to the bedside. "How ya doin'?"

"Better. How are you?"

No one had ever asked him that before except the force psychologist.

"It's part of the job."

"I didn't ask you that." She took the single red rose from him and pressed the bud to her nose. "I knew you were out there today. And I knew you and God would take care of me."

"How?"

She tapped her heart. "I felt you. In here. Just the way I felt God's presence. You saved my life."

Just thinking about what could have happened made Collin want to crush her to him and never let her go. "I've never been that scared."

"You?"

"Terrified," he admitted. "I prayed, Mia. And the strangest thing happened. My hands were shaking and I couldn't do my job. One prayer later, I'm a changed man."

"Oh, Collin." Hope flared in her sweet eyes.

He smiled, the tenderness inside him a scary thing. He had to tell her. He had to say the words no matter how difficult. With Mia, he could be vulnerable.

"I realized that I need God in my life even more than I need you. And I need you more than my next breath. I love you, Mia. Please say you haven't given up on me."

Collin had never seen an angel, but he couldn't imagine anything more beautiful than the expression on Mia's face.

"I don't ever give up, Collin. Don't you know that by now?" She shifted on the bed, grimaced at the IV in her arm. "Mitchell came by with another social worker. He wanted to tell me not to be mad at you anymore."

"He broke into your confidential files?"

"How did you guess?"

"I figured as much all along."

"And said nothing."

"Now don't get your back up. I wanted him to be man enough to own up to mistakes on his own."

"He told us something else, too. Shipley set your barn on fire. Revenge for messing in his business, as he put it. He's just a mean man."

Now that was a stunner. "I guess I owe my neighbor an apology on that at least."

"What about the lawsuit?"

"You brother convinced Mr. Slokum to play nice. He dropped the case when Adam brought up the half brother."

"Adam's a good lawyer."

"What's going to happen to Mitch now?" He hated to ask the obvious. "Foster care?"

She offered a smug smile. "Yes, but I have a plan."

"Which means someone is about to be hit by a bulldozer named Mia."

"The people I have in mind are used to it."

"If you're thinking who I'm thinking, I approve."

"Mom and Dad love him. He's crazy about them. They're starting the paperwork and foster-care classes, but I think I can pull a few strings so he can live with them now while his mom is in treatment."

"Miss Carano, I love you. Even if you are a social worker."

With a relieved and happy heart, he leaned across the metal rail and kissed her. When she didn't protest, he kissed her again. This time she kissed him back.

Epilogue

The halls were decked with tinsel and garland and rows and rows of white lights. Christmas carols played softly, and the stockings really were hung by the chimney with care.

The Carano Christmas was in full swing. Mia had managed to spirit Collin away from the prying eyes and teasing brothers to give him her gift in private.

"Open your present."

"I don't need presents. I have you, your awesome family and an even more awesome relationship with Christ. What more could a man want?"

He was different since accepting the Lord into his life. Not that his quiet personality had changed, but he was less tense, warmer, freer.

She pressed a small box, wrapped in shiny blue paper and topped with silver ribbon, into his hands. "Don't argue with me, mister. You know I'll win."

Mia watched him, her heart in her throat. He took his time sliding the ribbon over the corners. Turning the box over and over, he slowly caressed the slick, smooth foil with his fingertips.

Mia bubbled with impatience, but she didn't inter-
fere. He grinned up at her. "I haven't done this many
times. Let me enjoy the moment."

The notion that his Christmases weren't filled with
good memories stabbed at her. She was determined
to make up for lost time, and her family felt the same.
They'd finally managed to draw him into the fold and
he had begun giving back the banter, though his was
still far more reserved than Nic's or Adam's.

Finally, when Mia thought she'd have to rip the gift
from his hands and open the box herself, he pulled away
the last bit of tape. Tissue paper crinkled as he lifted
out the blue-and-white Christmas ornament.

The fragile bulb, held gently in his palm, glimmered
beneath the bright light. The old black-and-white photo
of three small boys was perfectly centered amidst a
snowy Christmas scene. Collin, Drew and Ian in a photo
she'd found stuck in a file.

"How did you—?"

The expression on his face was one she would never
forget. The cop who hid his feelings couldn't hide them
now.

Awe. Yearning. Joy.

With exquisite care, he replaced the bulb and set the
box aside to wrap his arms around Mia.

She knew him. Knew he would struggle with the
right words to express his feelings. His heart thundered
against her ear. She heard him swallow once. Twice.

"I knew you'd love it."

"Yeah." His chest rose and fell as he continued to
press back a tide of emotion. This was one of the things
she'd learned to love the most about him. He was so

deeply emotional. He felt things so intensely, but all his life he'd stuffed them deeper to avoid hurt.

Finally, he sighed and then with the same sweet tenderness kissed the top of her head. "It's the best present I've ever had."

"Want to hang it on the tree?"

He cast a sideways glance toward the noisy living room. "Dare we go back in there?"

"Actually, I'd rather stay right here with you forever."

"But your brothers would never allow that to happen."

As if on cue, Adam's voice yelled down the hallway. "What's taking you two so long? We got a party going on in here."

"Yeah," Nic hollered. "And I wanna open my presents."

Mia giggled and took Collin's hand. "Be brave."

Such a silly thing to say to a man who had never been anything else in his entire life.

As they entered the living room, everyone quieted. Mitchell stood by the enormous Christmas tree with Nic, Adam and Gabe. Each male wore a Cheshire grin.

"Now you've corrupted Mitchell," she said to them. "What are you up to?"

They all looked at Collin. He, in turn, flicked at glance at her dad who gave a slight nod. Her mother and grandmother, each holding one of Gabe's kids, beamed from the couch. Her very pregnant sister, Anna Maria, waddled across the room and handed Collin a beautiful maroon velvet box topped with a gold plaid bow.

He cleared his throat. "Your present," he said.

Mia got a fluttery feeling in the pit of her stomach. Her gaze ran around the room, saw the intense, excited faces of all the people who loved her best. Gabe aimed the video camera in her direction.

They knew something she didn't.

She lifted the lid and frowned in puzzlement. Lavender rose petals sprang out of the box and fluttered to the floor. She plunged her hands into the velvety petals, releasing the rich spicy scent as she pulled out yet another box. A velvet jeweler's box.

She gasped and looked up at Collin, her mouth open in surprise.

"Look, guys," Nic muttered. "Mia's speechless."

She was too stunned and thrilled to react to the titter of amusement circling the warm, festive room.

"Mia." Collin took the final box from her shaking fingers and went down on one knee in front of her. "I'm not too good with words." He cleared his throat again.

One of the brothers guffawed. Collin slanted him a look. "Give me a break, Nic."

"Want me to ask her for you?"

"Shut up, Adam," Mia said good-naturedly. She touched a trembling palm to Collin's cheek. "You were saying?"

"I love you."

"I love you, too."

"All my life I've distrusted other people. I've kept them on the outside. But you wouldn't let me do that. You forced me to open up, to feel. And I'm so glad you did. To love and know that I'm loved back is an awesome thing."

Mia's heart was about to burst with love. She knew how hard this was for him. For a man of few words, he'd just said a mouthful.

In the background came the soft strains of "I'll Be Home for Christmas."

"Mia." A quiver ran from Collin's hand into hers. He bent his head and placed a whisper of a kiss upon her hand, then slid the ring onto her finger. "Will you marry me?"

Tears sprang into her eyes.

"Yes, I will," was all she could manage as she collapsed against him. Sure and strong, he absorbed the impact and rocked her back and forth, laughing and laughing while she sobbed into his shoulder.

Much later, after Mia's brothers and dad had pounded his back in congratulations and the ladies had kissed his cheek declaring this the most romantic proposal they'd ever witnessed, Collin finally stopped shaking. He'd known how important Mia's family was to her and proposing this way would make her happy. He just hadn't known how nervous he'd be.

Then as if to overwhelm him to the point of no return, Mia's brothers had pledged their time and talents along with that of their church—now his church, too—to help rebuild and expand his animal rehab facility. Their Christmas gift to him and the animals, they'd said. And he was too moved to speak.

"Spiced cider, anyone?" Rosalie manned the large urn that emitted the rich scents of cinnamon and apple.

Standing with his back against the cold patio doors, his new fiancée leaning into him, the fragrance of her perfume embracing him, Collin felt more content than he could remember. He didn't need or want anything else.

Well, perhaps one other thing. "Could I tell you something?" he murmured against Mia's hair.

"Anything." She twisted around to smile at him and he couldn't resist another kiss.

"I followed up on that information Mitchell found."

She was quiet for a moment and he hoped he hadn't rekindled her anger over the unfortunate incident. "I'm glad."

"You are?"

"God turned Mitchell's mistake into something good. How could I be upset about that?"

He should have known she'd say that. "I have a phone number and a name. Someone who may be Ian."

She whirled around, sliding her arms around his waist, her expression joyous. "Collin, that's wonderful! Have you called? What did he say? When are you going to meet him?"

He swallowed a laugh. "Whoa, Miss Bulldog. I have the name and number but I haven't called yet."

"Why not?" But being Mia, she answered her own question. "You're nervous."

"Scared spitless. What if it isn't him?"

"What if it is?" She grabbed his arms and shook him a little. "Collin, you may have found Ian. Come on. Let's call right now. Where is that number?"

He took the slip of paper from his shirt pocket and shared the bits of information. "Ian Carpenter. The dates match. The age matches. I think it's him, but I've had hope before."

"This time, my love, you have something else. You have a family who will always love you and stand with you no matter what. And best of all you have the Lord. He'll—"

"Never leave me nor forsake me," Collin finished with a smile, feeling the truth of her words. He was full to the brim with the kind of love he'd craved all his life. Finding Ian would be icing on his very sweet cake.

He reached into his pocket and took out the small fish keychain, now polished to a pewter gleam.

Mia smiled gently, her face full of love, and stretched out a palm. Instead of handing her the keychain, he took her hand. "I love you, Mia."

"I love you, Collin."

"Good." He drew in a breath, feeling the strength of his faith urging him on. "Let's go make that call."

* * * * *

HEART OF THE FAMILY

Margaret Daley

To my family: my husband, mother-in-law, son,
daughter-in-law and granddaughters

To all the foster parents who have done
such a great job helping out in a difficult situation

Then said Jesus, Father, forgive them;
for they know not what they do.
And they parted his raiment, and cast lots.
—*Luke* 23:34

Chapter One

The child's name on the chart held Jacob Hartman's gaze riveted. Andy Morgan. The eight-year-old from Stone's Refuge had possibly another broken bone. Flashes of the last time the boy had been in his office, only a few weeks before, paraded across his mind.

With a sigh, Jacob entered the room to find the boy perched on the edge of the exam table, his face contorted in pain as he held his left arm, in a makeshift sling, close to his body. A woman Jacob wasn't familiar with stood to the side murmuring soothing words to Andy. She turned toward Jacob, worry etched into her face—and something else he couldn't decipher. Her mouth pinched into a frown that quickly evolved into an unreadable expression.

Jacob shook off the coolness emanating from the young woman. "Hi, Andy. Remember me? I'm Dr. Jacob," he said, using the name the children at the refuge knew him by. "How did you hurt your arm?" He gently removed the sling made from an old T-shirt and took the injured, swollen limb into his hands.

When he probed the forearm, Andy winced and tried

to draw it back. "I fell." The child's lower lip trembled, and he dug his teeth into it.

"He was climbing the elm tree next to the barn and fell out of it." When Jacob glanced toward her, taking in the concern in the woman's dark blue gaze, she continued in a tense voice that had a soft Southern lilt. "I'm the new manager at Stone's Refuge. Hannah Smith. I was told when there was a medical problem to bring the children to you. This is only my second day, and no one else was around. The other kids are at school. Andy was supposed to be there, too. I—" she offered him a brief smile that didn't reach her eyes "—I talk too much when I'm upset."

No doubt the tension he felt coming from the refuge's new manager was due to Andy's accident. "I take care of the children's medical needs." Jacob buzzed for his nurse. "Andy, can you do this for me?" He demonstrated flexing and extending his wrist and fingers.

With his forehead scrunched, the boy did, but pain flitted across his features. He tried to mask it, but Jacob knew what the child was going through. He'd experienced a few broken bones in his own childhood and remembered trying to put up a brave front. He learned to do that well. Jacob unlocked a cabinet and removed a bottle of ibuprofen.

He handed the boy the pain pills and a glass of water. "Why weren't you at school?" Children like Andy were the reason he had become a pediatrician, but he hadn't quite conquered the feelings generated when he was confronted with child abuse.

The boy dropped his head, cradling his arm against his chest. "I told the other kids I was going back to the cottage because I didn't feel good. I hid instead. I don't like school. I want to go home."

"Just as soon as I get a picture of your arm and we get it fixed up, you can go home."

Andy's head snapped up, his eyes bright. "I can? Really?"

Hannah Smith stepped closer and placed a hand on the child's shoulder. Apprehension marked her stiff actions. "Back home to the refuge."

"No! I want to go *home*." Tears welled up in Andy's brown eyes, and one slid down his thin face.

"Andy, you can't. I'm sorry." Calmness underscored her words as tiny creases lined her forehead. Her concern and caring attitude accentuated her beauty.

Having realized his mistake, Jacob started to respond when the door opened and the nurse appeared. "Teresa, Andy's visiting us again. We need an X-ray of his left arm."

"Hello, Andy. What did you do to your arm?" Teresa, a petite older woman with a huge, reassuring smile, helped the child down from the table. "I bet you remember where our prize box is. Once we get the X-ray done, I'll let you check it out."

"I can?"

"Sure. If I remember correctly, you were also eyeing that red car the last time. It's still there."

"It is?" Andy hurried out of the room, still holding his arm across his chest.

The refuge's manager started to follow the pair. Jacob blocked her path and closed the door. Frowning, she immediately backed up against the exam table.

"I'd like a word with you, Ms. Smith. Teresa will

take care of Andy. He knows her. She spent quite a bit of time with him several weeks ago."

Her dark blue gaze fixed on him, narrowing slightly. "I haven't had a chance to read all the children's files yet. What happened the last time he was here?"

Obviously she was upset that something like this occurred on her watch. But beneath her professional demeanor, tension vibrated that Jacob suddenly sensed went beyond what had occurred to Andy. "His mother brought him in with a nasty head wound, and I called social services. Her story didn't check out. Thankfully he was placed quickly at Stone's Refuge."

"I was in the middle of reading the children's files when the school called to find out why he wasn't there. I found Andy lying on the ground hugging his arm and trying his best not to cry, but his face had dry tear marks on it." She pushed her long blond hair behind her ears and blew a breath of air out that lifted her bangs. "When I approached him, he tried to act like nothing was wrong."

"Sadly, Andy is used to holding his pain in. I took several X-rays last time because he was limping and discovered he'd broken his ankle and it was never set properly. He probably will always limp because of the way his bone healed without medical attention."

"His mother didn't seek care for him?"

He shook his head. "I think the only reason she came in last time was because there was so much blood involved. She thought he was dying. He'd passed out briefly. She flew into a rage when he was taken from her." Jacob didn't know if he would ever forget the scene Andy's mother created at the clinic that afternoon. If looks could kill, he would be dead, but then he should be accustomed to that from an angry mother.

"Is there a father?"

"No. I don't think there ever was one in the picture. His mother clammed up and hasn't said anything about the new or old injuries." Jacob picked up the child's chart. "I want you to know what you're dealing with since you haven't been on the job long. The only time Andy cried was when he found out he wasn't going with his mother when he left the hospital. He kept screaming he needed to go home. When he settled down, he whimpered that his mother needed him, but I could never get him to tell me why he thought that." He jotted his preliminary findings down on the chart. "Have you been a social worker for long?"

A gleam glittered in her eyes. "No, I got my degree recently."

A newbie. No wonder she'd wanted to know if Andy's mother had sought help. He would hate to see that light in her eyes dim when the reality of the system sank in. But having dealt with the Department of Human Services and the lack of funding that so often tied its hands when it came to neglected or abused children, he knew the reality of the situation, first as a boy who had gone through the system and now as a pediatrician.

"I've been impressed by the setup at Stone's Refuge, especially since it hasn't been around for long. We could use more places like that." Hannah hiked the straps of her brown leather purse up onto her shoulder. "I'm glad they've started building another house at the ranch. Mr. Stone has quite a vision."

Jacob laughed. "That's Peter. When he came up with using the students from the Cimarron Technology Center to help with the construction of the house, it was a blessing. They're learning a trade, and we're getting another place for kids to stay at a cheaper rate."

"I heard some of his ideas, as well as his wife's when I interviewed with them. It's quite an ambitious project." She started forward. "I'd better check and see—"

The door opened, and Andy came into the room with Teresa and a red car clutched in his hand. "It was there, Dr. Jacob. No one took it."

The child's words, *no one took it,* stirred a memory from Jacob's past. He'd been in his fourth foster home, all of his possessions easily contained in a small backpack. Slowly his treasures had disappeared. The first item had been stolen at the shelter after he'd been removed from his mother's care. By the age of twelve he hadn't expected any of his belongings to stay long, so when he had received a radio for Christmas from a church toy drive, he hadn't thought he would keep it more than a day or so. But when he had moved to his fifth foster home seven months later, he still had the radio in his backpack. No one had taken it. His body had begun to fill out by then, and he'd learned to defend himself with the older children.

"Here's the X-ray, Dr. Hartman."

Teresa handed it to him, drawing him back to the present.

After studying the X-ray, Jacob pointed to an area on Andy's forearm. "That's where it's fractured. Teresa will set you up with Dr. Filmore, an orthopedic surgeon here in the clinic, to take care of your arm."

Andy's eyes grew round. "What will he do?"

"He'll probably put a cast on your arm."

"Can people sign it?" Andy stared at the place where Jacob had pointed on the X-ray.

"Yep, but you won't be able to get it wet. You'll have it on for a few months."

Andy grinned. "You mean, I don't have to take a bath for months?"

Jacob chuckled, ruffling the boy's hair. "I'm afraid a few people might have something to say about that."

"But—"

"We'll rig something up to keep your arm with the cast dry while you take a bath." Hannah moved next to Andy, her nurturing side leaking through her professional facade. "And I'm thinking when we get home, we'll have a cast signing and invite everyone. I've got some neat markers we can use. We can use different colors or just one."

"My favorite color is green."

"Then green it is." Hannah glanced toward Jacob. "Where do we go to see Dr. Filmore?"

Jacob nodded toward Teresa who slipped out of the room. "He's on the third floor. He owes me a favor. If he isn't in surgery, he should be able to see Andy quickly. Teresa will arrange it."

Hannah smiled, her glance straying to Andy. "Great."

It lit her whole face, transforming her plain features into a pretty countenance. It reached deep into her eyes, inviting others to join her in grinning. Jacob responded with his own smile, but when her attention came back to him, her grin died. An invisible but palpable barrier fell into place. Was she still worried about the accident on her second day on the job? Or something else?

As Teresa showed Hannah and Andy out of the room, Jacob watched them leave. He couldn't shake the feeling he'd done something wrong in Hannah's eyes, that her emotional reaction went beyond Andy's accident. Jacob was out at the refuge all the time, since he was the resident doctor for the foster homes and on the board of the foundation that ran Stone's Refuge. But the ice beneath her professional facade didn't bode well for their working relationship. As he headed into the hall, he decided he needed to pay Peter a visit and find out what he could about Hannah Smith.

The sun began its descent toward the line of trees along the side of the road leading to Stone's Refuge. Tension gripped Hannah's neck and shoulders from the hours sitting in the doctor's office, waiting for Andy's arm to be taken care of. No, that wasn't the whole reason. The second she'd seen Dr. Jacob Hartman she'd remembered the time her family had been torn apart because of him. After the death of her older brother, Kevin, everything had changed in her life, and Jacob Hartman had been at the center of the tragedy.

But looking at him, no one could tell what he had done. His bearing gave the impression of a proficient, caring doctor. Concern had lined his face while interacting with Andy. Even now she could picture that look in his chocolate-brown eyes that had warmed when he'd smiled. The two dimples in his cheeks had mocked her when he had turned that grin on her. And for just a second his expression had taunted her to let go of her anger. But she couldn't.

The small boy next to her in the van had been a trouper the whole time, but now he squirmed, his bottled-up energy barely contained. "Mrs. Smith, ya ain't mad at me, are ya?" Andy stared down at his cast, thumping his finger against it over and over.

The rhythmic sound grated on Hannah's raw nerves, but she suppressed her irritation. Andy wasn't the source of her conflicting emotions. "Mad? No. Disappointed, yes. I want you to feel you can come talk to me if something is bothering you rather than playing hooky from school."

Andy dropped his head and mumbled, "Yes, ma'am."

"Please call me Hannah. You and I are the new kids on the block. Actually, you could probably show me the ropes. How long have you been at the house? Two, three weeks?"

He lifted his head and nodded.

"See? This is only my second day. You've got tons more experience at how things are done around here." *Why had she accepted this job? How was she going to work with Dr. Hartman?* The questions screamed for answers she couldn't give.

"Sure. But I don't know too much. The other kids…"

When he didn't continue his sentence, Hannah slanted a look toward him, his chin again resting on his chest, his shoulders curled forward as though trying to draw inward. "What about the other kids?"

"Nothin'."

She slowed the van as she turned onto the gravel road that led to the group of houses for the foster children at Stone's Refuge. "Is anyone bothering you?"

His head came up, and he twisted toward her. "No. It's not that."

In the short time she'd been around the boy, she felt as though she was talking to a child two or three years older, especially now after the half a day spent at the clinic and his staunch, brave face. But after reading part of his file and hearing what the doctor had said, she understood where the boy was coming from. He'd seen the ugly side of life and experienced more than most kids his age. "Then what's wrong?"

"I don't fit in."

Those words, whispered in a raw voice, poked a dagger into old wounds. She had always been the new kid in school. After her family had fallen apart with Kevin's death and her parents divorced, she and her mother had moved around a lot. "Why do you say that?" she managed to get out, although her throat tightened with buried pain she'd thought she had left behind her. But coming back to her hometown where she had lived for the first nine years of her life had been a mistake. How had she thought she wouldn't have to confront what had happened to Kevin? Of course, she hadn't discovered Dr. Jacob Hartman's involvement with the refuge until yesterday.

Andy averted his gaze, hanging his head again. "I just don't. I never have."

The pain produced from his declaration intensified, threatening her next breath. She slowly drew in a lungful of rich oxygen and some of the tension eased. "Then maybe we could work on it together. The staff at the refuge has been there since it opened last year. In fact, I just moved here last week." Cimarron City had been the only place that had resembled a home to her in her wayfaring life. She'd spent much more time here than any other place. Even while attending college, she'd moved several times. She wanted stability and had chosen the familiar town to be where she would put down roots. Maybe that was a mistake.

"You did?"

"Yep." She parked between the two houses she managed—still wanted to manage. This job had been a dream come true—until she realized that Jacob Hartman was involved. "Up until recently, I'd been in school."

"Aren't you too old for that?"

Hannah grinned. "In your eyes, probably. I had to work my way through college as a waitress, which took longer than normal."

Andy tilted his head. "How old are you?"

"Don't you know you aren't supposed to ask a woman how old she is?" she said with a laugh, then immediately added when she saw the distress on his thin face, "But I'll tell you how old if you promise not to tell anyone. I'm twenty-nine."

"Oh," he murmured, as though that age really was ancient.

She almost expected him to say, "I'm sorry," but thankfully he didn't. Instead, he shoved open the door, slowly climbed from the van, and walked toward the house. Seeing him limp renewed her determination to do well in her first professional job, to help these children have a better life.

But she couldn't help thinking: her second day at work and a child in her care had broken a bone. Not good. She would make sure that Andy went to school if she had to escort him every day. She needed to let Laura and Peter Stone, the couple who ran the Henderson Foundation that funded the refuge, know that they were back and what happened with Andy. Hannah looked toward the main house off in the distance, on the other side of the freshly painted red barn.

The refuge was perfect for children who needed someone to care about them. At the moment there were two cottages but the foundation for a third had been poured last week. The best part of the place was the fact it was on a ranch, not far from town. The barn housed abandoned animals that the children helped take care of. The wounded helping the wounded. She liked that idea.

Before she went in search of the couple, she needed to check on Andy and the other seven children in the house where she lived. Meg, her assistant at the cottage and the cook, should be inside since the kids had come home from school an hour ago.

Ten minutes later, after satisfying herself that everything was fine, Hannah trekked across the pasture toward the Stones' place. When she passed in front of the large red double doors thrown open to reveal the stalls inside, she heard a woman's light laugh followed by a deeper one. She changed her direction and entered the coolness of the barn. In the dimness, she saw both Laura and Peter kneeling inside a pen with several puppies roughhousing on the ground in front of them.

"We're going to have a hard time not keeping these." Peter gestured toward the animals that had to be a mix of at least three different breeds.

Laura angled her head toward him. "What's another puppy or two or three when we have so many? They're adorable."

"Are you going blind, woman?"

"Okay, they're so ugly they're cute." Laura caught sight of Hannah and waved her to them. "Don't you think they're cute?"

Hannah inspected the black, brown and white puppies with the elongated squat body of a dachshund, the thick, wiry coat of a poodle and the curly tail and wrinkled forehead of a pug. *Ugly* was an understatement. "I can see their attraction."

Peter's laughter reverberated through the cavernous barn. "I meant that we would have a hard time finding homes for them since they are so— unattractive."

"But that's their appeal. They're different, and you and I love different." Laura stood, dusting off her jean-clad knees.

He swept his arm in a wide arc, indicating the array of animals that had found a refuge at the ranch along with the children. "That's for sure."

Laura stepped over the low pen and approached Hannah. "I heard about Andy. Is he okay?"

"Yes. Broken left forearm. He told me he'd wanted to climb to the very top of that elm tree you have outside the barn."

Laura chuckled "I've found my twins up there more than once." She glanced back at Peter. "Maybe we should cut it down."

"And rob the kids of a great tree to scale? No way! We'll just have to teach Andy the art of climbing."

"There's an art to climbing trees?" Hannah watched as Peter came up to Laura's side, draped his arm over her shoulder and cradled her against him. Wistfulness blanketed Hannah—a desire to have her own husband and family. She'd almost had that once when she'd married Todd. Would she ever have that kind of love again? A home she would stay in for more than a year?

"Of course. The first rule is to make sure you have good footing before you reach up. I'll talk with Andy."

"He's gonna be in a cast for a few months."

"When he's ready, I'll show him how to do it properly." Peter nuzzled closer to Laura.

"I'm sorry I didn't realize he wasn't on the school bus. If I had, he would—"

Laura shook her head. "Don't, Hannah. Boys will be boys. I have three, and believe me, I know firsthand there's little we can do when they set their minds to do something. I gather you took him to see Jacob."

The name stiffened Hannah's spine. "Yes. He got Andy in to see Dr. Filmore, who put the cast on him."

"We don't know what we would do without Jacob to take care of the children for free." Laura looked up at her husband, love in her eyes. "We've taken up more and more of his time as the refuge has grown."

"Wait until we open the third home. Before we know it, there'll be eight more children for Jacob to take care of." Peter shifted his attention to Hannah. "That should be after the first of the year. Are you going to be ready for the expansion?"

"I'm looking forward to it. The more the merrier." By that time she would know how to deal with Jacob without her stomach tensing into a knot. And hopefully she would become good at masking her aversion because she could do nothing to harm the refuge.

"I knew there was a reason we hired you to run the place. I like that enthusiasm. I've got to check on a mare." Peter kissed his wife's cheek, then headed toward the back door.

"Don't blame yourself for Andy's accident." Laura pinned her with a sharp, assessing regard.

"I'm that obvious?"

"Yep." Laura began walking toward the front of the barn. "Kids do things. They get hurt. Believe me, I know with four children. The twins get into more trouble than five kids. I'm always bandaging a knee, cleaning out a cut."

Outside Hannah saw an old black car coming down the road toward them, dust billowing behind the vehicle. As it neared her, Hannah glimpsed Jacob Hartman driving. Even with him wearing sunglasses, she knew that face. Would never forget that face. She readied herself mentally as the car came to a grinding stop and Jacob climbed from it.

In her last year in college she had discovered the Lord, but she didn't think her budding faith had prepared her to confront the man responsible for her brother's death.

Chapter Two

Jacob's long strides chewed up the distance between him and Hannah. Her heartbeat kicked up a notch. Even inhaling more deep breaths didn't alleviate the constriction in her chest.

A huge grin appeared on his face. He nodded toward Laura, then his warm brown gaze homed in on Hannah. "It's good to see you again. How's Andy doing?"

Lord, help! When she had decided to come back to the town and settle down, she'd discovered Jacob Hartman still lived in Cimarron City and was a doctor, one of nine pediatricians, but why did he have to be involved with *her* children?

"Hannah, are you all right?"

His rich, deep-toned voice penetrated her thoughts. She blinked and focused on his face, his features arranged in a pleasing countenance that made him extra attractive—if she were interested, which she wasn't. His casual air gave the impression of not having a care in the world. Did he even comprehend the pain his actions caused?

"I'm fine." Hannah stuffed her hands into her pants

pockets. "Andy's doing okay. He's going around, having everyone sign his cast. If any good has come out of the accident, I would say it has been an icebreaker for him with the others." When she realized she was beginning to ramble, she clamped her lips together, determined not to show how nervous and agitated she was.

Jacob's smile faded as he continued to stare at her. "I'm glad something good came out of it."

Tension invaded his voice, mirroring hers. She curled her hands in her pockets into fists and forced a grin to her lips as she turned toward Laura. "I'd better get back to the house. I just wanted to let you know about Andy. Good day, Dr. Hartman." If she kept things strictly formal and professional, she would be all right.

Hannah started across the pasture toward the refuge, the crisp fall air cooling her heated checks. Keep walking. Don't look back. She thought of her Bible in her room at the house and knew she needed to do some reading this evening when the children were settled in their beds. Somehow she had to make enough peace with the situation to allow her to do her job. She wanted what was best for the children and if that meant tolerating Dr. Hartman occasionally, then she could do it. The needs of the children came first.

"Do you get the feeling that Hannah Smith doesn't like me?" Jacob followed the woman's progress across the field.

Laura peered in the same direction. "There was a certain amount of tension. I just thought it was because of Andy's accident. I think she blames herself."

"I think it's something else." Jacob kneaded the nape

of his neck, his muscles coiled in a knot. "Tell me about our new Stone's Refuge's manager."

"She just completed her bachelor's degree in social work from a college in Mississippi."

"What brought her to Oklahoma? The job?"

Laura laughed. "In our short existence we are garnering a good reputation but not that good so we can attract job candidates from out of state. She used to live here once and wanted to come back. She heard about the job from a classmate, who lives in Tulsa, and applied. Personally I think the Lord brought her to us. She's perfect for the job and beat every other candidate hands down."

"High praise coming from you."

"When the third house is finished, we're going to need someone highly organized and capable. We'll have almost thirty children, ranging in ages from five to eighteen. I'm hoping to bring in another couple like Cathy and Roman for the third home and eventually have one in the second cottage, too."

"What happens to Hannah Smith then? I understand she's living in the second cottage right now." He had heard and sensed Hannah's passion for her job earlier and agreed with Laura she would be good as the refuge's manager.

"We'll need someone to oversee all three homes. I can't do it and run the foundation, too. Raising money is a full-time job. If she wants to continue living on-site, we'll come up with something, but I'd like a man and woman in each cottage in the long run, sort of like a surrogate mother and father for the children."

He had pledged himself and his resources to the Henderson Foundation because he knew how lacking good care was for children without a home and family. "I'll do whatever you need."

"I want you to find out what's going on with Hannah. If there's something concerning you, take care of it. She's perfect for the job, and I don't want to lose her. You can charm the spots off a leopard."

"I think you've got me confused with Noah." He peered toward the group homes. "Are you sure there isn't something else I could do?" He wished he had the ease with women that Noah did. His foster brother rarely dated the same lady for more than a month while lately he had no time to date even one woman.

"Yeah, while you're over there, check and see how Andy is faring. I worry about him."

"You worry about all of them."

"Hey, I thought I heard your car." Peter emerged from the barn, a smile of greeting on his face. "What brings you out this way? Is someone sick?"

"Do I have to have a reason to pay good friends a visit?"

Peter slipped his arms around Laura's waist, and she leaned back against him. "No, but I know how busy you've been, and it isn't even flu season yet."

Watching Peter and Laura together produced an ache deep in Jacob's heart. He wanted that with a woman, but Peter was right. His work and church took up so much of his life that he hadn't dated much since setting up his practice two years ago. And you have to date to become involved with a woman, he thought with a wry grin. Maybe Noah could give him lessons after all.

Laura's gaze fastened on him. "Jacob's just leaving. He's going over to check on Andy."

A scowl descended over Peter's features. "Andy's

situation is a tough one. His mother is fighting the state. She wants him back."

"To use as a punching bag." Jacob clenched his jaw. He couldn't rid himself of the feeling Andy and his situation were too similar to his own experiences growing up, as though he had to relive his past through the child. He'd been blessed finally to find someone like Paul and Alice Henderson to set him on the right path. "If at all possible, I won't let that happen." He needed to return the gift the Hendersons had given him.

"Stop by and have dinner with us when you're through. I want to discuss the plans for a fourth house."

"Peter, I love your ambition, but the third one isn't even half-finished." Jacob dug into his pocket for his keys.

"But maybe it will be by the holidays. What a wonderful way to celebrate Christ's birthday with a grand opening!"

"I can't argue with you on that one, but the weather would have to cooperate for that to happen and you know Oklahoma. When has the weather cooperated?" Jacob headed toward his car. He twice attempted to start it before he managed to succeed and pull away from the barn. He had a woman to charm, he thought with a chuckle.

Andy held up his cast. "See all the names I've gotten. All in green."

Hannah inspected it as though it were a work of art. "You even went to the other cottage."

"Yep, I didn't want to leave anyone out."

Because he knew what it was like to be left out, Hannah thought and took the green marker from Andy to pen her own name on the cast. "There's hardly any room left."

He flipped his arm over. "I had them leave a spot for you here."

Hannah wrote her name over the area above his wrist where a person felt for a pulse.

"I've saved a place for Dr. Jacob, too."

Andy's declaration jolted Hannah. She nearly messed up her last letter but managed to save it by drawing a line under her name. "You aren't going back to see Dr. Jacob. Dr. Filmore will be seeing you about your arm." She realized Jacob Hartman was at the barn talking with Peter and Laura, but hopefully he would leave without coming over here. She needed more time to shore up her defenses. The walk across the pasture hadn't been nearly long enough.

"He told me he would come see me. He'll be here. The others said he never breaks a promise."

That was just great! She was considering retreating to her office off her bedroom when the front door opened and the very man she wanted to avoid entered the cottage. His dark gaze immediately sought hers. A trapped sensation held her immobile next to Andy in the middle of the living area off the entrance.

"Dr. Jacob. You came! I knew you would." With his hand cradled next to his chest, Andy hurried across the room and came to an abrupt halt inches from the doctor. The boy grinned from ear to ear. "See all the names I have!" He held up the green marker. "Will you sign it?"

"Where?"

"Right under Hannah's."

"I'd be honored to sign your cast." Jacob again looked at her and said, "I'm in good company," then scribbled his signature on the plaster, a few of his letters touching hers.

The adoring expression on Andy's face galled her. If the boy only knew—Hannah shook that thought from her mind. She would never say anything. She couldn't dwell on the past or she would never be able to deal with Jacob in a civil way. She had to rise above her own anger if she was going to continue to work at Stone's Refuge and put the children's needs before her own.

Was she being tested by God?

She didn't have time to contemplate an answer. Kids flooded into the living room to see Dr. Jacob. In less than five minutes, every child in the house surrounded him, asking him questions, telling him about their day at school.

How had he fooled so many people? Maybe she was here to keep an eye on him. But in her heart she knew that wasn't the reason, because she couldn't see Peter and Laura having anyone but the best taking care of the foster children.

Jacob tousled Gabe's hair. "I see you've got your baseball. How's that throwing arm?"

"Great. You should see me." Gabe grasped Jacob's hand and tugged him toward the front door. "I'll show you."

Jacob allowed himself to be dragged outside, all the kids following. Hannah stepped out onto the porch and observed the impromptu practice in the yard. Laughter floated on the cooling air while the good doctor took turns throwing the ball to various children. They adored Dr. Jacob. She should be cheered by that thought, but Hannah couldn't help the conflicting emotions warring inside her.

If God had put her here to forgive Jacob, she had a long way to go.

"I thought I saw Jacob's car." Cathy, the other cottage mom, came up next to her at the wooden railing. "It's the ugliest—thing. I can't even call it a car. I sometimes wonder how he even makes it out here in that rolling death trap."

Hannah's fingernails dug into the railing. She hadn't even been able to see Kevin for one last time at his funeral because of how messed up he had been after the car wreck. Although seven of the children were running around and throwing the ball, all she could see was Jacob standing in the middle, smiling, so full of energy and life. Not a care in the world.

Before long several of the boys ganged up on him, and they began wrestling on the ground even though Jacob had on nice khaki pants and a long-sleeved blue cotton shirt. The gleeful sounds emphasized the fun the kids were having. But the scene was tainted by Hannah's perception of Jacob Hartman.

"He's so wonderful with them. If he ever decided to take time for himself, he might find a nice woman to marry and have a boatload of children. He'd make a great dad. Too bad I'm already spoken for."

Seizing the opportunity to turn her back on Jacob, Hannah swung her attention to Cathy. "To a very nice young man."

Her assistant smiled. "I know. Roman is the best husband."

"Where is he?"

"He went over to help Peter at the barn with one of the animals."

"It's nice he works at a veterinarian clinic."

"One day he hopes to go back to school to become a vet even if he's the oldest student in the class."

Hannah relaxed back against the railing, allowing some of the tension to flow from her body. The sounds of continual laughter peppered the air. "I was beginning to think that would be the case with me. It's hard working and going to college at the same time, but it's worth it when you do finally graduate."

"I almost forgot the reason I came out here. I passed through the kitchen and Meg said dinner will be ready in fifteen minutes." Cathy left, walking back to the other cottage next door.

Good. That should put an end to the doctor's visit. Hannah wheeled around and called out to the nearest two girls who were standing off to the side, watching the melee with the boys. "Let's get everyone inside to wash their hands for dinner."

Shortly the group on the ground untangled their limbs and leaped to their feet. They raced toward the door while Jacob moved slowly to rise, his shirttail pulled from his pants, his brown hair lying at odd angles. He tucked in his top and finger combed his short strands.

Andy, who had been standing off to the side watching the fun, shuffled toward Jacob, taking his hand. "Why don't you eat with us, Dr. Jacob?"

The too-handsome man glanced toward her. The child followed the direction of his gaze and asked, "Can he, Hannah?" When she didn't immediately answer, he quickly added, "He'd better check me out before bedtime to make sure I'm okay."

Having stayed behind, too, Gabe took Jacob's other hand. "Yeah. Don't forget you promised me the last time you were here that you'd read a story to me before I went to bed."

That trapped feeling gripped Hannah again. She really didn't have a reason to tell the man no, and yet to spend the whole evening with him wasn't her idea of fun.

Hannah shifted from one foot to the other, realizing everyone was staring at her, waiting for an answer she didn't want to give. She pasted a full-fledged smile on her face that she fought to maintain. "Sure, he can if he doesn't mind hamburgers, coleslaw and baked beans."

He returned her grin. "Sounds wonderful to a man who doesn't cook. Meg can make anything taste great, even cabbage."

His warm expression, directed totally at her, tempted her cold heart to thaw. "Cabbage is good for you," was all she could think of to say.

"Yeah, I know, but that doesn't mean it tastes good."

"Yuck. I don't like it, either." Gabe puffed out his chest as though he was proud of the fact he and Dr. Jacob were alike in their food preferences.

"Me, neither." Andy followed suit, straightening his thin frame.

Jacob peered down at both boys. "But Meg makes it taste great, and Hannah is right. It's good for you. I'll play a board game with you guys if you finish all your coleslaw. Okay?"

"Yes," the two shouted, then rushed toward the door.

Oh, great. The evening was going to be a long drawn-out affair with games and reading. Maybe she could gracefully escape to her room after dinner while he entertained the children. Hannah waited until he had mounted the porch steps before saying, "Nice recovery."

He gave her another heart-melting grin. "I keep forgetting how impressionable these children can be. They're so hungry for attention and love. I wish I had more time to spend with them."

No! Please don't! She pressed her lips together to keep from saying those words aloud. But she couldn't keep from asking, "Just how involved are you with the refuge?"

He chuckled. "Worried you'll have to be around me a lot?"

Heat scored her cheeks. Obviously she wasn't a very good actress, a fact she already knew. She forced a semi-smile to her lips. "I was curious. I just thought you were the refuge's doctor and that's all."

He planted himself in front of her. "I'm more than that. Peter, Noah and I were the ones who started this. Peter is the one in charge because he lives on the property, but I keep very involved. I'm on the foundation board. This project is important to me."

His words and expression laid down a challenge to her. "It's important to me, too." She took one step back. *He's on the foundation board. It's worse than I thought.* "Why?"

Although the space between them was a few feet, Hannah suddenly had a hard time thinking clearly. A good half a minute passed before she replied, "I went into social work because I want to make a difference, especially with children who need someone to be their champion. Stone's Refuge gives me a wonderful opportunity to do my heart's desire." *If I can manage my feelings concerning you.*

"Then we have something in common, because that's why I'm involved with the refuge."

The idea they had anything in common stunned Hannah into silence.

The front door opened, and Gabe stuck his head out. "Dr. Jacob, are you coming?"

"Sure. I'll be there in a sec." When the door closed, he turned back to her, intensity in his brown gaze. "I sense we've gotten off on the wrong foot. Somehow we'll have to manage to work together. I won't have the children put in the middle."

She tilted up her chin. "They won't be."

"Good. Then we understand each other."

He left her alone on the porch to gather her frazzled composure. He was absolutely right about never letting the children know how she really felt about their "Dr. Jacob." She had two choices. She could quit the perfect job or she could stay and deal with her feelings about him, come to some kind of resolution concerning Jacob Hartman. Maybe even manage to forgive him.

There really is only one choice.

Trembling with the magnitude of her decision, Hannah sank back against the railing and folded her arms across her chest. She'd never run from a problem in the past, and she wasn't going to now. She didn't quit, either. But most of all, these children needed her. She had so much love to give them. A lifetime of emotions that she'd kept bottled up inside of her while she had been observing life go by her—always an outsider yearning to be included.

So there's no choice. Lord, I need Your help more now than ever before. I want this to work and I can't do it without You. How do I forgive the man who killed my brother because I can't expose his past to the others? The children adore him, and I won't hurt them.

Jacob finished the last bite of his hamburger and wiped his mouth with his napkin. "So next week is fall break. What kind of plans do you all have for the extra two days off from school?"

Several of the children launched into a description of their plans at the same time.

He held up his hand. "One at a time. I think you were first, Gabe."

"Peter wants us to help him when he takes some of the animals to several nursing homes on Thursday."

"And there's a lot of work to be done on the barn expansion." Susie, the oldest child in this cottage, which housed the younger kids, piped up the second Gabe stopped talking.

"He's getting new animals all the time." Terry, a boy with bright red-orange hair, stuffed the last of his burger into his mouth.

Jacob laughed. "True. Word has gotten around about this place."

Nancy nodded. "Yep. I found a kitten the other day in the trash can outside."

Jacob caught Hannah's attention at the other end of the long table. "Do you have any activities planned that you need a chaperone for next week? Maybe I—"

"I think I've got it covered." She looked down at her plate, using her fork to stir the baked beans around in a circle as if it were the most important thing to do.

"I'm sorry, Hannah, I didn't get a chance to tell you I won't be able to go to the zoo with you on Friday." Meg, the cook and helper, stood and removed some of the dishes from the center of the table. "That was the only time I could get in to see the doctor about the arthritis in my knees."

Nancy's blond pigtails bounced as she clapped her hands. "Then Dr. Jacob can go with us!"

Hannah lifted her head and glanced from Meg to Nancy before her regard lit upon him. For a few seconds anxiety clouded her gaze. He started to tell her he didn't have to go when a smile slowly curved her lips, although it never quite touched her eyes.

"You're welcome to come with us to the zoo. It'll be an all-day trip. We leave at ten and probably won't get home until four." Her stare stayed fixed upon him.

The intensity in her look almost made Jacob squirm like Andy, who had a hard time keeping still. She might not have meant it, but deep in her eyes he saw a challenge. Determined to break down the barrier she'd erected between them, he nodded. "I'll be here bright and early next Friday, and I even know how to drive the minibus."

"That's great, since I don't think Hannah's had a chance to learn yet. If you aren't used to it, it can be a bit awkward." Meg stacked several more plates, then headed for the kitchen.

"You can take that kind of time off just like that?" Hannah snapped her fingers.

"I always leave some time during a break or the holidays for the kids."

"Yep." Terry, the child who had been at the cottage the longest, stood to help Meg take the dishes into the kitchen.

"Well, then it's settled. I appreciate the help, especially with the minibus." Hannah rose. "Who has homework still to do tonight?" She scanned the faces of the eight children at the dining-room table.

Several of them confessed to having to do more homework and left to get their books.

Gabe, short for his nine years, held up his empty plate. "I ate all my coleslaw."

"Me, too." Andy gestured toward his as Susie took it.

"You two aren't part of the cleanup crew?" Jacob gave the girl his dishes.

Both boys shook their heads.

"Then get a game out, and I'll be in there in a minute."

"Can I play, too?" Nancy leaped to her feet. "I don't have to clean up."

Gabe frowned and started to say something, but Jacob cut him off with, "Sure you can."

Nancy, being in kindergarten, was the youngest in the house. Jacob suspected that and the fact she was a girl didn't set well with Gabe, and judging by Andy's pout, him, either. But Jacob knew the importance of bonding as a family and that meant every child, regardless of sex or age, should have an opportunity to play.

Gabe and Andy stomped off with Nancy right behind them, her pigtails swinging as she hurried to keep up. Jacob turned toward Hannah and noticed the dining-room table had been cleared and they were totally alone now. That fact registered on her face at the same time. Her eyes flared for a second, then an indecipherable expression descended as though a door had been shut on him.

"I'm glad we have a few minutes alone." The look of surprise that flashed into her eyes made him smile. "I forgot to tell you earlier that Andy's mother is fighting to get him back. Peter just found out today."

"She is?"

"And I'm not going to let that happen. I've seen his injuries." *I've been there. I know the horror.* "He's better off without her."

"If she cleans up her act and stops taking drugs, he might be all right going back home. In the short time I've been around him, I've seen how determined he is to get back there."

"He isn't better off if he returns to her. Believe me."

A puzzled look creased her forehead. "Then why does he want to go home?"

He shook his head slowly. "You're new at this. Take my word in this situation—he shouldn't go back to his mother. He's the caretaker in that family of two and he feels responsibility as a parent would. Certainly his mother doesn't."

Hannah's face reddened. She came around the side of the table within a few feet of him. "How do you know this for a fact? Has Andy said anything to you?"

"No, I just know. I was in foster care for many years. I've seen and heard many things you've never dreamed of. Give yourself a year. Your attitude that the birth parent is best will change."

"I believe if it's possible a family should be together. Tearing one apart can be devastating to a child."

The ardent tone in her voice prodded his anger. His past dangled before him in all its pain and anguish. His heartbeat thundered in his ears, momentarily drowning out the sounds of the children in the other room. "Keeping a family together sometimes can be just as devastating." He balled his hands at his sides. "Why did you really go into social work?" he asked as though her earlier reason wasn't enough.

Her own temper blazed, if the narrowing of her eyes was any indication. "As I told you earlier, to help repair damaged families. But if that isn't possible, to make sure the children involved are put in the best situation possible."

His anger, fed by his memories, sizzled. Before he said anything else to make their relationship even rockier, he spun around and left her standing in the dining room.

The children's laughter, coming from the common living area, drew him. He needed that. For years he'd dealt successfully with the wounds of his childhood by suppressing them. Why were they coming to the surface now?

Lord, what are You trying to tell me? Aren't I doing enough to make up for what I did? What do You want of me?

Jacob stepped into the room and immediately Gabe and Andy surrounded him and pulled him toward the table in front of the bay window where the game was set up. Nancy sat primly, toying with a yellow game piece. Her huge grin wiped the past few minutes from his mind as he took his chair between the boys.

He lost himself in the fun and laughter as the three kids came gunning for him. He kept being sent back to the start and loving every second of it. Until he felt someone watching him. Jacob glanced up and found Hannah in the doorway, a question in her eyes—as though she couldn't believe a grown man was having so much fun playing a kid's game. He certainly hadn't done much of this as a child.

Across the expanse of the living room that challenge he had sensed earlier reared up. If she was staying at the refuge as its manager, then he would have to find a way for this situation to work. He didn't want the kids to feel any animosity between him and Hannah. They'd had enough of that in their short lives. Before he left tonight, he would find out exactly why she was wary of him.

Chapter Three

Hannah stood in the entrance into the living room and observed the children interacting with Jacob. She hadn't intended to stay and watch them play, but for some reason she couldn't walk away. Jacob had a way with the kids, as if he knew exactly where they were coming from and could relate to them on a level she didn't know she would ever reach.

The bottom line: he was good with them. Very good.

When the trip to the zoo had come up at dinner, she hadn't wanted Jacob to come. Now though, she saw the value in him being a part of the outing.

A fact: if she stayed, Jacob would be in her life whether she wanted him to or not. She was a realist, if nothing else, and she would come to terms with her feelings concerning him for the children's sake.

Andy yawned and tried to cover it up with his palm over his mouth. When he dropped his hand away, however, his face radiated with a smile as Jacob directed a comment to him.

"Gotcha! Sorry but you've got to go back to the start,

buddy." Jacob triumphantly removed Andy's peg from its slot and put it at the beginning.

Gabe took his turn and brought one of his pieces home. He pumped the air and shouted his glee. "I've only got one more out. I'm gonna win!"

Hannah needed to check to see if the others were doing their homework. But she found she couldn't leave. There was something about Jacob that kept her watching—after years of hating the man for what he'd done to her family.

At Gabe's next turn he jumped up and pranced about in a victory dance as if he'd crossed the goal line. "I finally won!"

Andy tried to grin but couldn't manage it. Instead he blinked his eyes open wide and yawned again and again.

Hannah entered the room. "Gabe, please put the game up. It's time for bed."

"But we haven't played enough." Gabe stopped, a pout pushing his lips out.

Jacob began removing the pegs from the board. "You'd better do as she says or I might not get to read you a story. If there's not enough—"

Gabe leaped toward the table and scrambled to put up the game. Andy's head nodded forward. Nancy stifled her own yawn.

Hannah made her way to Andy's side and knelt next to him. "Time for bed."

His head snapped up, his eyes round as saucers. "No. No, another game. I haven't won yet."

"Sorry. You'll have to wait for another day." Hannah straightened.

"Andy, I'll make you a promise, and you know I

don't go back on them. The next time I'm here, we'll play any game you want." Jacob stood and moved to the boy, saying to Hannah, "Here, I'll take him to his room," then to Andy, "I think everything has finally caught up with you, buddy. You've been great! I can't believe you went this long. Most kids would have been asleep hours ago after the day you had."

As Jacob scooped up the eight-year-old into his arms and headed to the boys' side of the house, Andy beamed up at him, then rested his head on Jacob's shoulder.

After hurriedly putting the game away, Gabe raced to catch up with them. "We share a room."

Nancy looked sleepily up at Hannah. "I want a story, too."

"How about if I read one to you? You get ready for bed while I check on the others finishing their homework."

Nancy plodded toward the girls' side while Hannah went back into the dining room where Terry and Susie were the only ones still doing their work. "How's it coming?"

Susie looked up, a seriousness in her green eyes. "We're almost done."

"Need any help?"

"Nope." After scratching his fingers through his red hair, Terry erased an answer to a math problem on his paper. "Susie had this last year in school. She's been helping me."

Leaving the two oldest children, Hannah walked to Nancy's room and found the little girl in her pajamas, stretched out asleep on her twin bed's pink coverlet. Her clothes were in a pile on the floor beside her. Her roommate was tucked under her sheets, sleeping, too.

Hannah gently pulled the comforter from under Nancy and covered her, then picked up the child's clothes and placed them on a chair nearby.

With the youngest girls in bed, Hannah made her way to the boys' side to see how Gabe and Andy were doing. The evening before, her first night in the cottage, both of them had been a handful to get to bed. Even with Andy half asleep, Jacob could be having trouble.

Sure, Hannah, she asked herself, *is that the real reason you're checking on them?*

At the doorway she came to a halt, her mouth nearly dropping open at the scene before her. Andy was in bed, lying on his side, desperately trying to keep his eyes open as he listened to the story Jacob was reading. The doctor lounged back against Gabe's headboard with the boy beside him, holding the book on his lap and flipping the pages when Jacob was ready to go on to the next one. Neither child was bouncing off the walls. Neither child was whining about going to bed. Jacob's voice was calm and soothing, capable of lulling them to sleep with just the sound of it.

Cathy is right. Jacob would make a good father.

That thought sent a shock wave through her. She took a step back at the same time Jacob peered up at her, the warmth in his gaze holding her frozen in place. For several seconds she stared at him, then whirled and fled the room. She didn't stop until she was out on the porch. The night air cooled her face, but it did nothing for the raging emotions churning her stomach.

How could she think something like that? For years she had hated Jacob Hartman. In her mind he wasn't capable of anything good. Now in one day her feelings were shifting, changing into something she didn't want. She felt as though she had betrayed her family, the memory of her brother.

Her legs trembling, she plopped down on the front steps and rubbed her hands over her face. *Lord, I'm a fish out of water. I need the water. I need the familiar. Too much is changing. Too fast.*

She leaned back, her elbows on the wooden planks of the porch, and stared up at the half-moon. Stars studded the blackness. No clouds hid the beauty of a clear night sky. The scent of rich earth laced the breeze. Everything exuded tranquility—except for her tightly coiled muscles and nerves shredded into hundreds of pieces.

She'd lived a good part of her life dealing with one change after another—one move after another, the accidental death of her husband after only one year of marriage. She had come to Cimarron City finally to put down roots and hopefully to have some permanence in her life. *Instead I'm discovering more change, more disruption.*

"Hannah, are you all right?"

She gasped and rotated toward Jacob who stood behind her. So lost in thought, she hadn't even heard him come out onto the porch. She didn't like what the man was doing to her. She wanted stability—finally.

"I'm fine," she answered in a voice full of tension.

He folded his long length onto the step next to her. She scooted to the far side to give him room and her some space. His nearness threatened her composure. Leaning forward, he placed his elbows on his thighs and loosely clasped his hands together while he studied the same night sky as she had only a moment before. His nonchalant poise grated along her nerves, while inside she was wound so tightly she felt she'd break any second.

She didn't realize she was holding her breath until her lungs burned. She drew in deep gulps of air, suffused with the smells of fall, while grasping the post next to her, all the strain she was experiencing directed toward her fingers clutching the poor piece of wood.

He was no fool. He would want to know what was behind her cool reception of him. And she intended to keep her past private. After today she knew now more than ever the secret could harm innocent people—children. She couldn't do that for a moment of revenge. Their shared past would remain a secret.

"Have we met before this morning?" he asked, finally breaking the uncomfortable silence.

She sighed. This was a question she could answer without lying. "No." She was relieved that her last name was no longer the same as her brother's.

"I thought maybe we had, and I'd done something you didn't like."

"I've never met you before this morning." Which was true. Kevin and Jacob hadn't been friends long when the car wreck occurred. She felt as though she were running across a field strewn with land mines and any second she would step in the wrong spot.

"I get the feeling you don't care for…my involvement in the refuge."

Thank You, Lord. His choice of words made it possible for her not to reveal anything she didn't want to. "I've seen how you interact with the kids this evening. They care very much for you. How could I not want that for them? They don't have enough people in their lives who do."

Jacob faced her. "Good. Because I intend to continue being involved with them, and I didn't want there to be bad feelings between us. The children can sense that. Gabe already said something right before he went to sleep."

"He did? What?"

Although light shone from the two front windows, shadows concealed his expression. "He wanted to know what we had fought about. He thought I might have gotten mad at you because Andy got hurt. I assured him that accidents happen, and I wasn't upset with you."

Hannah shoved to her feet. "I should go say something to him."

"What?"

"Well…" She let her voice trail off into the silence while she frantically searched for something ambiguous. "I need to assure him, too, that we haven't fought."

"By the time I left him he was sound asleep. I've never seen a kid go to sleep so fast. I wish I had that ability."

Had he ever lost sleep over what he did, as she had? "You have a lot of restless nights?" slipped out before she could censor her words.

He surged to his feet, and his face came into view. "I have my share."

The expression in his eyes—intense, assessing—bored into her. She looked away. "It's been a long second day. I need to make sure the rest of the children go to bed since they have school tomorrow. Good night."

She'd reached the front door when she heard him say in a husky voice, "I look forward to getting to know you. Good night, Hannah."

Inside she collapsed back against the wooden door,

her body shaking from the promise in his words. Against everything she had felt over twenty-one years, there was a small part of her that wanted to get to know him. His natural ability to connect with these children was a gift. She could learn from him.

On the grounds at the Cimarron City Zoo Hannah spread the blanket out under the cool shade of an oak tree, its leaves still clinging to its branches. Not a cloud in the sky and the unusually hot autumn day made it necessary to seek shelter from the sun's rays. She'd already noticed some red-tinged cheeks, in spite of using sunscreen on the children. Susie, the last one in Hannah's group to get her food from the concession stand, plopped down on the girls' blanket a few feet from Hannah's.

Where were the boys and Jacob? She craned her neck to see over the ridge and glimpsed them trudging toward her. Jacob waved and smiled.

Terry hurried forward. "I got to see a baby giraffe! Giraffes are my favorite animal."

"I'm not sure I can pick just one favorite." Out of the corner of her eye she followed Jacob's progress toward her. He spoke to the guys around him, and they all headed toward the concession stand. "You'd better go get what you want for lunch." Hannah nodded toward the departing boys and Jacob.

Terry whirled around and raced after them. Ten minutes later everyone was settled on the blankets and stuffing hamburgers or hot dogs into their mouths.

Nibbling on a French fry, Hannah thought of the trip this morning to the zoo on the other side of Cimarron City with Jacob driving. Not too bad. She'd managed to get a lively discussion going about what animals they were looking forward to seeing.

Quite a few of the children had never been to a zoo and were so excited they had hardly been able to sit still in the minibus. Andy literally bounced around as though trying to break the restraints of the seat belt about him. Since his accident he had gone to school every day and the minute he returned to the cottage he would head to the barn to help with the animals. Last night he had declared to her at dinner that he wanted to be a vet and that he was going to help Peter and Roman with "his pets."

"May I join you?"

Jacob's question again took her by surprise. She swung her attention to him standing at her side. She glanced toward the other two blankets and saw they were filled with the children. "Sure." She scooted to the far edge, giving the man as much room as possible on the suddenly small piece of material.

"How are things going so far?" Jacob sat, stretching one long leg out in front of him and tearing open his bag of food, then using his sack as a large platter.

"Good. The girls especially liked the penguins and the flamingos."

"Want to guess where we stayed the longest?" Jacob unwrapped his burger and took a bite.

"The elephants?"

"Haven't gone there yet."

"We haven't, either."

"Why don't we go together after lunch? They have a show at one."

"Fine." Her acceptance came easier to her lips than she expected. He'd been great on the ride to the zoo.

He'd gotten the kids singing songs and playing games when the discussion about animals had died down. Before she had realized it, they had arrived, and she had been amazed that the thirty-minute trip she had dreaded had actually been quite fun. "So where did y'all stay the longest?"

"At the polar bear and alligator exhibits. Do you think that means something? The girls like birds and the boys like ferocious beasts?"

Her stomach flip-flopped at the wink he gave her. Shock jarred her. Where had that reaction come from? "I had a girl or two who liked the polar bears. One wanted a polar bear stuffed animal."

"Let me guess. Susie?"

She shook her head. "Nancy."

He chuckled. "I'm surprised. She's always so meek and shy."

"She's starting to settle in better." Nancy had only been at the refuge two weeks longer than Andy, and being the youngest at the age of five had made her adjustment to her new situation doubly hard on her.

"That's good to hear," he said in a low voice. "Her previous life had been much like Andy's, except that her mother doesn't want her back. I heard from Peter this morning that she left town."

Hannah's heart twisted into a knot. How could a mother abandon her child? Even with all that had happened in her life, she and her mother had stuck together. "I always have hope that the parents and children can get back together."

Jacob's jaw clamped into a hard line. He remained quiet and ate some of his hamburger. Waves of tension flowed off him and aroused her curiosity. Remembering back to her second night at the cottage, she thought about his comments concerning Andy and his mother fighting to get him back. What happened to Jacob to make him feel so fervent about that issue? Was it simply him being involved with the refuge or something more personal? *And why do I care?*

For some strange reason the silence between her and Jacob caused her to want to defend her position. She lowered her voice so the children around them wouldn't overhear and said, "I was up a good part of the night with Nancy. I ended up in the living room, rocking her while she cried for her mother. It tore my heart to listen to her sorrow, and I couldn't do anything about it."

"Yes, you did. You comforted her. Her mother wouldn't have. She left her alone for days to fend for herself."

"But her mother was who she wanted."

"Because she didn't know anyone else better."

The fierce quiet of his words emphasized what wasn't being spoken. That this conversation wasn't just about Nancy. "But if we could work with parents, give them the necessary skills they need to cope, teach them to be better parents—"

"Some things can't be taught to people who don't want to learn."

"Children like Nancy and Andy, who are so young and want their mothers… I think we have to try at least."

"Andy wants to go home. He never said he wanted his mother. There's a difference."

Hannah clutched her drink, relishing the coldness of the liquid while inside she felt the fervor of her temper rising. "Maybe not in Andy's mind. Just because he doesn't say he wants his mother doesn't mean he doesn't. The biological bond is a strong one."

"Hannah, can we play over there?" Susie pointed to a playground nearby with a place to climb on as though a large spider had spun a web of rope.

All the children had finished eating while she and Jacob had been arguing and hadn't eaten a bite. A couple of the boys gathered the trash and took it to the garbage can while Terry and Nancy folded the blankets. "Sure. We'll be done in a few minutes."

"Take your time." Susie raced toward the play area with several of the girls hurrying after her.

When the kids had cleared out, Hannah turned back to Jacob to end their conversation, since she didn't think they would ever see eye to eye on the subject, and found him staring at her. All words fled her mind.

One corner of his mouth quirked. "Do you think she heard?"

Granted their words had been heated, but Hannah had made sure to keep her voice down. "No, but I'm glad they're playing over there." She gestured toward the area where all the children were now climbing on the spiderweb, leaping from post to post or running around. "While in college I helped out at a place that worked to find foster homes for children in the neighborhood where their parents lived."

"I'm sure that was a complete success." Sarcasm dripped over every word.

"Actually they had some successes and some failures, but those successes were wonderful. They went beyond just placing the children near their parents. They counseled the parents and tried to get help for them. While I was there, several made it through drug rehab and were becoming involved in their child's life again. The children still stayed in their foster home while the problems were dealt with, but the kids didn't feel abandoned by their parents. That went a long way with building up their self-esteem."

"What about the child's safety and welfare when that parent backslides and starts taking drugs or abusing alcohol again?" Jacob pushed to his feet and hovered over her.

His towering presence sent her heart hammering. She rose. "You can't dismiss the importance of family ties."

He glared at her. "I've seen too many cases where family ties meant nothing."

She swung her attention to the children playing five yards away, but she sensed his gaze on her, drilling into her. "Family is everything."

"I'm not saying family isn't important—when it is the right one. When it isn't, it destroys and harms a child."

She noticed Andy say something to a woman. "I can understand where you're coming—"

"Don't!"

Out of the corner of her eye she saw Jacob pick up the blanket they'd been on and begin folding it. When she looked back to the children, she counted each one to make sure everyone was there. Shoulders hunched, Andy, now alone, sat on a post and watched the others running around and climbing on the ropes.

Jacob came up to her side. "I was in foster care. I got over it and moved on."

"So these children will, too?"

"With our help."

Andy walked a few feet toward her and stopped. "Hannah, I'm going to the restroom."

"Sure, it's right inside the concession stand." She started toward the boy.

Andy tensed. "I can go by myself. I'm eight!"

"I'll just be out here on the porch waiting for you, then we're going to the elephant exhibit."

He grinned. "Great."

Five minutes later Jacob rounded up the children on the playground when Andy came out of the concession stand.

"I can't wait to see the elephants." The boy limped toward the large group heading toward the other side of the zoo.

Hannah took up the rear as they made their way to the elephant building. Inside, the kids dispersed to several different areas. Andy and Gabe crowded around the skeleton with another group. People packed the Elephant Enclosure with a few youngsters running around, shouting.

Jacob stared toward the entrance, a frown descending.

"What's wrong?"

He shook his head as though to clear it. "I thought I saw someone—" he scanned the area "—but I guess I didn't."

"Who?"

"Andy's mother."

Alarm slammed Hannah's heartbeat against her rib cage. "Let's get our children together." She began gathering the girls into the center of the exhibit.

One pair of boys joined the four girls. Hannah counted six. She searched for Jacob, Gabe and Andy.

She found Jacob with Gabe off to the side of the skeleton. The fear and concern in the man's expression told Hannah something was wrong—very wrong. She corralled the kids near her and hurried toward the two.

"Where's Andy?"

Tears streaked down Gabe's face. "Andy told me to be quiet. Then he left with a lady."

Jacob leaned close to her and whispered, "It *was* his mother I saw. She has him."

Chapter Four

The fury in Jacob's words scorched Hannah. She stepped back and scanned the throng at the zoo, checking the exits. All the children were watching her. She schooled her expression into a calm one. When she faced Jacob again, his jaw clenched into an impenetrable line.

"I'll notify security. Keep the kids together." He didn't give Hannah a chance to say anything. He strode toward a man wearing a zoo uniform.

"Hannah, will Andy be all right?" Terry stood in front of the children as if he were their spokesman.

"He isn't with a stranger. He's with his mother. He'll be fine." She prayed she was right. "There's nothing to worry about. Let's go outside where it's less crowded." She took Nancy's and Gabe's hand and headed for the door nearest them.

As she left the building, she caught Jacob's attention and pointed toward the exit. The grim look on his face didn't bode well. *Lord, please bring Andy back to us safe and sound.*

Hannah sought a shaded area where she could keep

an eye on the door into the Elephant Enclosure. The children circled her with Gabe off to the side. Tears ran down his cheeks. She drew him to her and draped her arm over his shoulder.

"I didn't...mean—" Gabe released a long sob "—to do anything wrong."

"Sometimes keeping a secret isn't a good thing."

Gabe looked up at her, fear invading his blurry gaze. "Am I in trouble?"

Hannah gave the boy a smile. "No." Then she surveyed the other six children and added, "But this is a good time to talk about what y'all should do if someone approaches you and wants you to go with them. Don't go without first checking with one of the staff at the refuge. Even if you know that person." She made eye contact with each child.

Susie broke from the circle and hurried past Hannah. "Dr. Jacob, did you find Andy?"

Hannah pivoted and saw relief in Jacob's expression as he nodded. The tautness in her stomach uncoiled. "Where is he?"

"Security has him and his mother at the front gate. I told them we'd be right there."

Hannah gathered the children into a tight group, then they headed toward the zoo entrance. A member of security waited in front of a building. The young man indicated a door for them to go through. Inside Andy sat in a chair with another security guard at a desk.

Hannah hurried to Andy and sat in the vacant seat beside him while the other children milled about the room, trying not to look at them. "Are you all right?"

Swinging his legs, Andy stared at his hands entwined together in his lap and mumbled, "Where's my mom?"

Hannah scanned the area and noticed Jacob talking with a man who appeared to be in charge. "I don't know."

He lifted his tear-streaked face. "They took her away."

"Who?"

Andy pointed toward the guard nearest him, his hand shaking. "One of them."

Hannah patted his knee. "Let me find out what's going on. Stay right here."

His head and shoulders sagged forward. "I want to see my mom." He sniffed. "She came to see me."

The quaver in the child's voice rattled Hannah's composure. All she wanted to do was draw him into her arms and hold him until the hurt went away. Instead she rose and crossed the room to Jacob and the security guard by the desk.

Susie approached. "Is Andy all right? Can we help?"

"He'll be fine. And if you can keep the others quiet and together over there—" she waved her hand toward an area off to the side "—that would be great."

"Sure. I'll get Terry to help me." The young girl hurried to her friend and whispered into his ear.

As Susie and Terry gathered the children into a group and lined them up along the wall, Hannah stopped near Jacob by the desk. "Where's Andy's mother?"

"Security has called the police for me. They're on their way. She violated a court order. She can't see Andy unless it's a supervised visit arranged ahead of time."

Hannah glanced over her shoulder to make sure Andy—for that matter, the other children, too—hadn't heard what Jacob said. Thankfully he'd kept his voice low. The boy continued to look down at his hands. "Andy wants to see her."

"No!"

Although whispered, the force behind that one word underscored Jacob's anger. From the few comments he'd made, Hannah wondered what was really behind his fury. She moved nearer in order to keep their conversation private, aware of so many eyes on them. "She's still his mother. We could be in the room with them to make sure everything is all right."

He thrust his face close. "I won't have that woman disrupt his life any more than she already has by pulling this stunt."

She met his glare with her own. "I am the manager at the refuge, and I do have a say in what is done with the children."

Jacob started to speak but instead snapped his jaw closed.

"I'll talk with Andy's mother first and see what prompted this action today."

"It won't do any good. She doesn't deserve a child like Andy."

There were so many things she wanted to retort, but she bit the inside of her mouth to keep her thoughts quiet. It was important that Andy not realize they were arguing over him. "Beyond that day in your office, have you had any contact with the woman?"

His eyes narrowed. "No."

"Then let me assess the situation." Again she sent a quick glance toward Andy then the other seven kids to make sure they weren't hearing what was said. "If I don't think her intentions are honorable, I won't let her see Andy. Deal?" She presented her hand to seal the agreement.

Jacob looked at it then up into her face. His fingers

closed around hers, warm, strong. "Deal. But I want you to know I don't think this is a good idea."

She wasn't sure it was, either, but for Andy's sake, she needed to try. Maybe there was a way to salvage their family if the mother was trying this hard to see her son.

"Where's Andy's mother?" she asked the head of security, not sure that Jacob would have told her.

The man pointed toward a door at the end of the hall where another guard stood. She made her way down the short corridor, stopping for a moment in front of Andy to give him a reassuring smile. His tear-filled eyes reinforced her resolve to try and make this work for him.

At the door she paused and peered back. Jacob's sharp gaze and the tightening about his mouth emphasized his displeasure at what she was attempting. Then she swung her attention to Andy, and the hopefulness she saw in his expression prodded her forward.

Lord, let this work. Help me to reach Andy's mother somehow.

When Hannah entered the room, she found Andy's mom sitting at a table, her head down on it as though she was taking a nap. The sound of the door closing brought the woman up, her gaze stabbing Hannah with fury.

"You don't have no right to take my son away. I wanna see Andy."

Calmness flowed through Hannah. She moved to the table and took the chair across from Andy's mother. "I'm Hannah Smith, the manager at Stone's Refuge where your son is staying." She held her hand out.

The young woman glared at it, then angled sideways to stare at the wall.

"Mrs. Morgan, Andy wants to see you, but I want to be assured that you won't upset him and cause a scene."

Again her angry gaze sliced to Hannah. "He should be with me. This ain't none of your business. He's my son!"

Hannah assessed the woman, focusing on her eyes to try and discern if she was on any drugs. Other than anger, she didn't see anything that indicated she was high. "The court has taken Andy away from you and is reviewing your parental rights. You may see Andy when you make prior arrangements with his case manager. You can't see him alone."

Some of the anger leaked from her expression. "I just wanna see my baby. I shouldn't have to ask for permission. I haven't taken no drugs in days."

"That's good. Would you consider going into a rehab facility?"

Her teeth chewed on her lower lip. "Yes. Anything. Will I get Andy back then?"

"That isn't my decision. It will have to be the court's. But it will be a step in the right direction." Hannah folded her hands on the table, lacing her fingers together. "How did Andy get hurt the last time you were with him?"

Tears sprang into the young woman's eyes. "It was an accident. He fell and hit his head." Her gaze slid away from Hannah.

"Why did he fall?"

Silence. Andy's mother bit down hard on her lip.

"If I'm going to help you, I need to know everything. I need the truth."

The young woman opened her mouth to speak, but clamped it closed without saying anything. The indentation in her lower lip riveted Hannah's attention. When she finally peered into Andy's mother's eyes, a tear rolled down her cheek.

"If you're serious about being in Andy's life, you have to trust me."

The lip with the teeth marks quivered. "My boyfriend pushed him away." More tears welled into Andy's mother's eyes and fell onto the table.

"Why did he do that?"

Mrs. Morgan dropped her head, much as Andy often did. "Because he was hitting me and Andy wanted to stop him."

"I see."

Her head jerked up. "No, ya don't! He didn't want me to take him to the doctor. Andy was throwing up. When my boyfriend passed out, I brought my baby to see Dr. Hartman. That's when everything went bad. They took Andy from me. I went home and my boyfriend had left me. He's—he's— I'm all alone." She swiped her trembling hands across her cheeks. "I don't—" she sucked in a shuddering breath "—wanna be alone."

"So all Andy's injuries were caused by this boyfriend?"

"Yes, yes, I'd never hurt my baby. Never!" Tears continued to flow from her eyes.

"But staying with your boyfriend did hurt your child."

"I know, but I don't have no money. I'm—" Andy's mother sagged forward and cried. "I love Andy. I…" The rest of the words were lost in the woman's sobs.

Hannah came around the table and touched her shaking shoulder. "Let's start with you talking to Andy.

If that goes well, we can discuss the next step, Mrs. Morgan."

The woman lifted her head, rubbing her hands down her face. "My name is Lisa Morgan. I ain't never been married."

"How old are you?" Hannah went back to her chair.

"Twenty-three. I can't pay for rehab. I don't have no money." She dashed her hands across her cheeks then through her hair.

"Let me worry about that. When you think you're ready, I'll go get Andy."

Lisa straightened, smoothing her shirt. "I'm ready to see my baby."

Hannah pushed to her feet and headed for the door. She hoped she was doing the right thing, that Jacob was wrong. Lisa had been a child when she'd had Andy. Maybe she'd never had a break.

Out in the hall she motioned for Andy to come to her. She caught Jacob's regard over the heads of all the kids who had surrounded him in the security office. "We won't be long. Maybe the children would like to ride the train."

"Yeah!" several of them shouted.

"Can we?" Terry asked Jacob.

"Sure."

His gaze intent on her, Jacob crossed to her while she opened the door into the small room where Lisa was. Andy slipped inside. Out of the corner of her eyes, she saw the boy throw himself into his mother's outstretched arms and plaster himself against her. His cries mingling with his mother's could be heard in the hallway.

"This is a mistake," Jacob whispered while he peered inside at Andy and his mom.

"What if it isn't?" Hannah lifted her chin a notch. "I'm going to have security call the police back and tell them they don't have to come."

"She should be held accountable for breaking the court order." A steel thread weaved through each word.

"That will only happen if, as a member of the foundation board, you overrule me." She directed a piercing look at him. "Are you?"

He met her glare for glare while a war of emotions flitted across his face. Finally resignation won. "No, I'm not going to. But don't leave them alone together." He pivoted and strode to the group of children hovering around the head of security's desk, asking him tons of questions.

Hannah paused in the entrance into the room and said to the guard nearby, "Please call the police and tell them it isn't necessary to come." Then she went in and closed the door.

"Mom, when can I come home?" Andy pulled back from his mother. "I miss ya."

Lisa shifted in the chair until she faced her son, clasping his hands. "And I missed ya, too. I have some things to work out, but once I do, you'll be able to come home with me."

"When?"

Lisa shook her head. "I ain't sure." She slid her gaze to Hannah, then back to her son. "I'm gonna do everything I can, but it'll be up to the judge when."

Andy puffed out his chest. "I'll tell him I want to come home. He'll listen to me."

"Baby, I'm sure he will, but I hafta do a couple of

things before we go in front of the judge. Then ya can tell him what ya want. Okay?"

Andy frowned. "I guess so."

"Good. I know I can count on ya, baby." Lisa drew her son to her and held him tightly.

Emotions clogged Hannah's throat. She swallowed several times before she said, "Andy, I'm sure we'll be able to arrange for your mother to come see you at the refuge. You can show her your room. She can meet your friends."

Hope flared in the boy's expression. "Yes. How about tomorrow?"

Hannah rose. "Let me see what I can arrange, Andy. It may have to be some time next week."

The light in his eyes dimmed. "Promise?"

"I can promise you I'll do everything I can to make it happen." *Please, Lord, help me to keep that promise.*

Jacob leaned into the railing on the porch of the cottage and stared up at the crystal clear night sky, littered with hundreds of stars. The cool fall air soothed his frustration some as he waited to speak with Hannah after the children were in bed. He didn't want to have this conversation where the kids might overhear.

Not only didn't Lisa Morgan get hauled down to the police station for defying a court order, but now Hannah was making arrangements for the woman to see Andy here at the refuge. Dinner, no less, in two nights! And worse, she'd persuaded Laura and Peter to go along with this crazy plan of hers.

The sound of the front door opening and closing drew Jacob up straight, but he didn't look at Hannah. He kept his gaze glued on the stars.

Lord, give me the right words to convince Hannah of the folly of getting Andy and his mother together except in a courtroom.

"You wanted to talk to me." Hannah moved to the other side of the steps and leaned against the post. "I'm tired so can we make this quick."

He clenched the wooden railing. Patience. He faced her, a couple of yards between them, her expression hidden in the shadows of evening, although Jacob didn't need to see her to imagine her glower. "We need to talk about Andy and his mother."

"No, we don't. You may be on the board, but I was hired to be the manager." She pushed away from the post, her posture stiff. "That means I run the refuge. I have Peter and Laura's support."

Which he intended to change the first opportunity he got a chance to speak with them. "And what happens when Lisa Morgan takes Andy again and harms him. Or comes to the cottage on drugs. Or lets her son down by not showing up when she's supposed to."

"She isn't the one who hurt Andy. It was her boyfriend who isn't around anymore."

"She allowed it to happen. That's the same thing in my book."

"One of the calls I placed this afternoon was to a drug-rehab facility. I got her in. She can start the program next week."

Jacob snorted. "So she goes through the motions of getting clean, and the second she gets Andy back she's taking drugs again and hooking up with that boyfriend or some other who is equally abusive to Andy." As much as he tried to keep visions of his past from flashing across his mind, he couldn't. The first time his mother had come out of drug rehab, he'd had such hope that she would stay clean. She'd lasted one whole day. He could still remember as if it were yesterday finding her passed out on the floor in the living room. "Then where does that leave Andy?"

"I have to try."

"Why?"

"Andy loves his mother. He wants to be with her. He told me he called her to come to the zoo." She could never share the pain she had gone through when her family had fallen apart. Even though it was under different circumstances and she had continued to live with her mom, she'd essentially lost her that day her older brother was killed. And the person responsible stood in front of her. She tamped down on the words of anger she suddenly wanted to shout at him. They would do no good. She needed to learn to work with this man—somehow.

"He'll get over it."

Hannah drew in a sharp breath. "How can you say something like that?"

"Because I did."

His whispered words hung in the air between them. Did she hear him right? She stepped closer. "What did you say?"

He pivoted away from her, gripping the railing. "My mother was like Lisa Morgan. On drugs. Nothing else was important to her. Certainly not me. Or where the rent and food money was going to come from. And when she didn't have enough money for her drugs, she took her frustration out on me with a fist or a belt."

Her anger disintegrated at the anguish in his voice. She wasn't even sure he was aware of it lacing each word. A strong impulse to comfort inundated her. She held her ground for a few seconds before she covered the distance between them to stand next to Jacob.

"I'm sorry," she whispered, meaning it. She caught a glimpse of his expression in the moonlight. Painful memories etched deep lines into his face as though he was reliving his past.

Finally as if he realized he had an audience to witness his agony, he blinked and shook his head. "I don't need your pity. All I want from you is to put a stop to getting Andy together with his mother."

As though she had no control over her actions, she lay her hand on his arm. "I can't. Andy is so excited about his mother coming to dinner."

He jerked away. "What you mean is, you won't! You want to try some little social experiment to see if it works." He thrust his face close to hers. "You're experimenting with a young boy's life."

Hannah stepped back. "And you're not? What happened to you was a tragedy, but that doesn't mean it will happen to everyone in the same situation. What if Lisa can successfully kick the habit? Wouldn't Andy be better off with his mother rather than in the foster-care system, possibly never adopted? We owe it to him to try."

"We owe him protection and a quality life."

"I'm not going into this with my eyes closed. I know what can happen and I plan to be there every step of the way."

"And I plan on being here, too. Plan to have another person at dinner on Sunday night."

"Fine. You're welcome to come here anytime." The second she said it she wanted to take it back. That meant she would see him more than an occasional call to the doctor's office or a social visit from him to see the children every once and a while.

"Good, because I'll be here a lot."

Her earlier exhaustion assailed her. Her legs weak, she sank down onto the steps. Her emotions had taken a beating today, and it looked as if it wouldn't be over with for a long time. Again she thought about walking away from the job, but then she remembered Andy's huge smile at bedtime because his mother was coming to visit him in a few days. He'd already started cleaning his room so it would be perfect for her.

"You know, I'm not going into this lightly. I told you about my involvement in a program where the children lived in the same neighborhood as their parents and saw them frequently in supervised situations. The program also worked with the parents, helping them address whatever forced the state to take their children, whether it was anger management, drug or alcohol abuse."

He sat next to her. "And what was the success rate?"

"Thirty to forty percent."

"What happened to the sixty or seventy percent it didn't work with?"

"Other arrangements were made for them. No one was left in a bad situation."

"That you know of."

"The program had long-term follow-up built into it. When I interviewed with Laura and Peter, they knew my desire to try something like that here."

His expression displayed surprise. "They did?"

"We need to explore all opportunities for the children. One is trying to get them back with their parents. Do you feel every child in the foster-care system should never go back home?"

"No."

"Then why are you against this?"

He closed his eyes for a few seconds. "Because Andy could be me."

"But he isn't."

"That remains to be seen." Jacob shot to his feet and dug into his pocket for his keys. "I'll be here Sunday." He stalked toward his old car in front of the cottage.

She sat on the porch step watching him drive away, stunned by what she had discovered about the person she had grown up hating. He had been abused. It didn't change what he had done to her brother, but it did alter her feelings. It was hard to look at him and not see what he must have gone through as a child.

She thought about a sermon she'd heard a few months ago about being careful not to judge another. How could we know what that person had gone through unless we walked in his shoes? Until this moment she hadn't really contemplated its true meaning.

Chapter Five

"You're early for dinner." Hannah glanced up from reading the paperwork needed for Lisa's rehab facility.

Jacob fit his long length into the small chair to the side of her desk. "I promised some of the kids I'd play touch football. The day has turned out to be great so here I am." He spread his arms wide.

Indeed, he was, looking ruggedly handsome with tousled hair and warm brown eyes. "Who?"

"Some of the older boys in the other cottage, but Gabe and Terry want to play, too."

"Is that safe?" She stacked the papers to the side to give to Lisa later.

He grinned, his two dimples appearing. "I'll protect them. They've always watched before, but both boys love football so I said yes."

"Still…aren't they a little young to play?"

He pushed to his feet, giving her a wink. "I promise they will be fine, and you know I don't break a promise."

"You can't control everything."

The merriment in his eyes died. "I, more than most,

realize that. Your life can change instantly and take you in a completely opposite direction than you ever imagined." He headed for the door. "I'm going to have a few words with the older guys about making sure Gabe and Terry have fun but aren't hurt." He peered back at her. "Okay?"

"Yes," she said as he disappeared out into the hall.

She had a report to read, but maybe she should go watch the game just in case something unforeseen happened. *Yeah, right. Is that the only reason?*

She had to admit to herself that since Friday night, when Jacob had told her something about his childhood, she hadn't been able to get the man out of her mind. And only a moment before he'd referred to life changing so quickly. Perhaps he hadn't walked away from the wreck unscathed.

She left her office and went in search of the touch-football game. She found a group of kids in the area between the two cottages and among them was Jacob giving instructions on the rules. Gabe and Terry, smaller than the other boys, flanked Jacob. How good he was with the children was reconfirmed as she watched.

"Will Terry and Gabe be all right?" Susie asked, coming to Hannah's side with Nancy.

"Dr. Jacob told me they would be."

"Then they will. Good. I wouldn't want anything to happen to them. Terry wants to try out for the basketball team at school and tryouts are next week."

"He didn't say anything to me. When?" She shouldn't be surprised Susie knew before her. The young girl was a mother hen to the kids in the cottage.

Susie shrugged. "He probably forgot. It isn't until Thursday after school.

Nancy tugged on Hannah's hand. "I'm gonna be a cheerleader. Susie taught me some cheers."

Hannah scanned the children assembled. "Where's Andy? I thought he would be out here in the thick of things, even if he can't play."

"He's cleaning his room—again." Susie clapped as the two teams lined up, with Nancy mimicking the older girl's action.

"I'll go check on him and get him to come out here." Hannah hurried toward the house. She didn't want to miss the game—in case there was a problem. *Yeah, sure. You're fooling yourself again. Jacob Hartman is the reason you're out here and not inside reading that report you need to go through.*

In the cottage she discovered Andy folding his clothes in his drawer and having a hard time with only one hand. "Hey, there's a big game being played outside. Dr. Jacob is here and in the middle of it."

"I know. But my room isn't clean enough." Andy attempted to refold the T-shirt.

Hannah surveyed the spotless area. She walked to Andy and took the piece of clothing. "You want to talk?"

"Nope. I've got to get this done." He averted his gaze.

"This looks great."

"It isn't good enough yet."

She thought about leaving him alone, but the quaver in his voice demanded her full attention. She drew him around to face her. "Andy, I won't lie to you. You can't do anything else to this room to make it better. I wish all the children's bedrooms were this clean."

"But—but it's got to be perfect for Mom."

"Why, hon?"

"Mom needs to know I can keep our place clean."

Hannah tugged Andy to the bed and sat with him next to her. "Then she will know. Why do you feel that way?"

"'Cause—" he sniffled "—'cause her boyfriend got mad at me for leaving the cereal out. He started to hit me when she came in between us. He hurt her instead."

She settled her arm along his shoulders. "He moved out so you won't have to worry about him."

Sniffing, Andy wiped his sleeve across his face. "But he could come back. He's left before and come back."

Hannah hugged the boy to her. "Let's not worry about that right now. I want you to have a good time showing your mother around and introducing her to your friends." She stood. "C'mon, let's see what everyone else is doing."

Andy remained seated. "Can I tell ya a secret?"

"Sure."

"He gave Mom money to live on. She's tried some jobs, but they never last long. Do you think if I get a job it'll help? 'Course, I can't quit school. Mom didn't finish, and she told me how important it is I do."

Staring down at Andy, Hannah felt she was talking to a little adult. Her heart broke at the worry and seriousness she saw in the boy's eyes. "Tell you what. If you promise me you won't worry about finding a job, I'll help your mother find one after she gets out of drug rehab. Okay?"

"You will?" Joy flooded his face as he leaped to his feet. "That would be so good!"

She held out her hand. "Let's go see what's going on outside."

As they strolled toward the yard between the cottages, Hannah mulled over what Andy had told her. She knew Lisa wasn't well educated from the way she talked. Getting her help with her drug problem was only the beginning of what Lisa and Andy would need if reuniting the family were going to work. She hadn't really thought beyond getting Lisa through a drug-rehab program. Maybe she was naive. Jacob certainly thought so.

I'm just going to have to prove him wrong.

Outside Hannah positioned herself on the sidelines of the makeshift football field with Andy on one side and Nancy on the other. Watching Jacob playing with the children, Hannah decided he was a big kid at heart. The laughter and ribbing filled the cool fall air. Before she knew it the sun began to slip down the sky toward the western horizon.

"Shouldn't Mom be here by now?" Andy asked as the losing team shook hands with the winners.

Hannah checked her watch. "She's only a few minutes late." *Please, Lord, let Lisa show up. If she doesn't...* Hannah didn't have any words to express her regret if the woman didn't come.

Jacob jogged toward her, his shirttail hanging out of his jeans, some dirt smudges on his face, his hair tousled even more than usual where some of the children tackled him to the ground at the end. Gabe and Terry had hung back until all the bigger kids were on the pile then they joined the others on top.

Jacob peered toward the road that led to the cottages and mouthed the words, "Not here?" so that Andy, who was staring at the same road, wouldn't hear.

She shook her head. "Everyone needs to clean up.

Dinner is in an hour." She eyed Jacob and his smudges. "Including you."

"I brought an extra shirt in case something like this happened, which it does every time." With a wink, he loped toward his car.

"What if something happened to Mom?"

Hannah put her hands on Andy's shoulders and pulled his attention away from the road by blocking his view. "We have an hour until we eat. Don't you know women are notorious for being late to important events. We have to make our grand entrance."

"Ya think that's it?"

I hope so. "Yes," she said, and sent up another prayer.

She and the children walked toward the cottage as Jacob joined them, carrying his clean shirt. He slipped into the house ahead of them and made his way to the bathroom off the kitchen. The kids dispersed to their bedrooms to clean up. Hannah stood in the foyer with Andy, Nancy and Susie.

The boy glanced back at the front door. "I'm gonna wait out on the porch."

After Andy left, Hannah said to Susie, "Will you make sure everyone really cleans up? I'll be outside with Andy."

"Sure. I hope his mother comes. He's been so excited." Susie took Nancy's hand to lead her back to the bedrooms.

Nancy stuck her thumb into her mouth and began to suck it. Hannah watched them disappear down the hall, wondering why the five-year-old was sucking her thumb. She hadn't seen that before, and it now worried Hannah.

Out on the porch Hannah eased down next to Andy

on the front steps. He cradled his chin in his palm and stared at the road. Her heart contracted at the forlorn look on the boy's face. *Maybe Jacob is right. I should have left well enough alone.*

She searched her mind for something to make the situation better when she heard the door open and close. She glanced back at Jacob, who came to sit on the other side of Andy. She saw no reproach in Jacob's expression, which surprised her. Lisa was a half an hour late, and a lot of people would now be gloating about how she had been wrong.

"You know, I want a rematch tonight. I can't let Gabe's win stand. Want to join us in the game, Andy?" Jacob lounged back, propping himself up with his elbows and appearing as though he had not care in the world.

Until you looked into his eyes, Hannah thought, *and glimpsed the worry deep in their depths.*

"Can Mom play, too?"

It took Jacob several heartbeats to answer, "Sure." But again nothing was betrayed in his expression or tone of voice.

Andy jumped to his feet. "Look! She's coming." He pointed toward a woman walking down the road toward the cottage.

Before Hannah could say anything, the boy leaped off the steps and raced toward his mother. Relief trembled through Hannah at the sight of the woman. Lisa scooped up Andy into a bear hug, then looped her arm around him.

"She came," Hannah murmured, tears smarting her eyes.

The silence from Jacob electrified the air. She resisted the urge to look at him and instead relished this step forward in Andy and his mother's relationship. *Maybe my plan will work after all. Thank You, Lord.*

"I'm glad she's here," Jacob finally said, straightening.

When Hannah peered at him, relief replaced the worry in his gaze as he observed the pair make their way toward him. She realized in that moment that he wanted what was best for Andy, even if he was wrong. They didn't agree what was best, but they had a common goal: Andy's safety and happiness. There was a part of her that was unnerved that she would have another thing in common with Jacob, but she couldn't deny it. In that moment she felt close to him, and that sensation surprised her even more than his earlier lack of reproach.

Hannah brushed her hand across her cheek and rose as mother and child approached. "It's so good to see you, Lisa, but how did you get here?"

Lisa stopped at the bottom of the steps with Andy cradled against her side. "I walked from the bus stop."

"That's two miles away." She couldn't believe she hadn't thought about the fact that Lisa might not have transportation out to the farm.

Andy's mother grinned. "I need to get in shape. It took me a bit longer than I thought." She splayed her hand across her chest. "I had to rest about halfway. But I'm here now."

Hannah stepped to the side. "Welcome to Stone's Refuge. The children are waiting inside to meet you."

Andy took his mother's hand and led her into the house. Jacob nodded his head and indicated Hannah go through the entrance before him. She did and felt his gaze burning a hole into her back. She paused in the foyer to watch the children greet Andy's mother in the living room. The only one who didn't was Nancy. She hung back with her thumb in her mouth and her gaze trained on the floor by her feet.

"What's wrong with Nancy?" Jacob whispered into her ear.

Nearly jumping, Hannah gasped and spun around. She'd been so focused on Andy and his mother that Hannah hadn't heard Jacob approach from behind her. "Give a gal some warning."

"Sorry. I haven't seen Nancy sucking her thumb before. When did it start?"

"I think this afternoon. At least that's the first time I've seen it since I've been here."

Jacob frowned and peered at the little girl, still off to the side while everyone else was crowded around Andy and Lisa, all trying to talk at the same time. A dazed look appeared in Lisa's eyes.

Hannah moved forward. "Andy, why don't you give your mother a tour of the house and show her your bedroom? Dinner will be in half an hour."

En masse the group started for the back of the house. Except for Nancy. She stayed in the living room, continuing to stare at the floor. Hannah covered the distance between her and the little girl and knelt in front of Nancy.

"What's wrong?"

With thumb still in her mouth, Nancy shook her head.

"Are you sure I can't help you with something?"

She nodded, hugging her arms to her, her eyes still downcast.

"Well, I sure could use someone to help me set the table. Will you, Nancy?"

"Yes," the child mumbled around her thumb.

"I'll help, too." Jacob came up to join them.

"Great. We'll get it done in no time." Hannah held out her hand for Nancy to take. She did.

Jacob flanked the little girl on the other side and extended his palm to her. She stared at it for a long second before removing her thumb from her mouth and grasping him. "Are you looking forward to going back to kindergarten tomorrow after your fall break?"

"My teacher's so nice. I'm gonna tell her about the zoo and the pla—mingos."

Hannah left Nancy and Jacob in the dining room while she went into the kitchen to get the place mats and dishes. Arms loaded, she backed through the swinging door and nearly collided with Jacob. Nancy giggled. He took the plates, set them on the table, then passed the mats to the girl.

"I'll do these while you put those down." Jacob gestured toward the mats held in Nancy's hands.

Hannah hurried back for the rest of the dishes. In ten minutes the dining-room table was set. She stood back with Jacob on one side and Nancy on the other. "We're a good team. Next time I need some help, I'll have to ask you, Nancy."

She peered up at Hannah, a question in her eyes. "How about Dr. Jacob? He helped."

"Yeah, a team has to stick together," Jacob said with a laugh.

"Him, too." The heat rose in Hannah's cheeks. The idea of them being a team wasn't as disturbing as she would have once thought.

* * *

Hannah examined the piece of paper Nancy held up. "I like your flamingo. Are you going to share it with your class tomorrow?"

The little girl nodded. "Just in case they don't know what one looks like."

"Well, they will now with this picture." Hannah tilted her head, tapping her chin with her finger. "You know, it seems I remember someone has a birthday coming up."

"Me!" Nancy pointed to herself. "I'll be six in four days."

"We'll have to think of something special to celebrate such an important birthday."

Shouts of victory permeated the living room. Hannah glanced toward the game table by the bay window.

Andy stood by his chair, pumping his good arm into the air and dancing around in a circle. "I won finally!"

"Why don't you take this back to your room and start getting ready for bed." Hannah handed the paper to Nancy.

"But I'm not tired."

"Tomorrow will be here soon enough."

As Nancy trudged from the room, Hannah rose and walked to the table where Jacob sat with Andy, Gabe and Lisa playing a board game. Gabe began to set up the pieces again for another game.

"Sorry, guys. It's time for bed."

Moans greeted Hannah's announcement.

"But Dr. Jacob hasn't won yet," Gabe said, continuing to put the pieces on the board.

"Too bad. He'll have to win some other day."

Gabe pouted. "But—"

"Gabe, Hannah is right. This just means we'll have to play again at a later date." Jacob picked up the game box.

Andy jumped to his feet. "Mom, can you put me to bed?"

Lisa peered at Hannah. "If it's okay?"

"That's great. I'll help Jacob clean up while you two boys get into your pajamas." Hannah surveyed the other children in the room. "That goes for everyone." As the kids filed into the hallway, Hannah stopped Lisa. "May I have a word with you?"

"Andy, I'll be there in a sec." Lisa waved her son on.

"How are you getting home?" Hannah asked when the room emptied of children.

"Walking to the bus stop. The last one is at ten."

"I'll drive you home. I don't want you walking at night on the highway."

"I don't want ya to go—"

"I'll take you home. I have to go that way." Jacob boxed up the last piece of the game and put it in the cabinet.

Appreciation shone in Lisa's expression. "I won't be long. I'll go say good-night to Andy."

"I'll go with you." Jacob started after Andy's mother.

Hannah halted him. She waited until Lisa had disappeared from the room before asking, "Are you sure? I don't mind taking her. Meg is still here to watch the children. I won't be gone long."

"No, I need to get to know her better. This will be a good opportunity to see what her intentions are toward Andy."

"Maybe I'd better take her after all."

He chuckled. "Afraid I'll scare her away?"

"No."

"Good, because if I can then she shouldn't be involved with Andy and finding out now would be better than later."

Hannah's eyes widened. "You're going to interrogate her?"

He saw the concern in her gaze that quickly evolved into a frown. "No, I'll be on my best behavior. I offered because there really is no reason for you to drive her into town." Shrugging, he flashed her a grin. "I'm going that way."

"Just so you'll know, tomorrow I'm taking her to the rehab facility to begin the program. Don't frighten her away."

"Who, me?" He thumped his chest. "I'm wounded. I want it to work out for Andy. I just don't think it will." He held up a hand to ward off her protest. "But I'm willing to go along so long as Andy isn't hurt. The second he is—"

Hannah walked toward the entrance, cutting off his words with a wave. "I have the child's best interest at heart, so you don't have to threaten me."

"Excuse me?"

She wheeled around at the door. "What are you going to do? Come riding in on your white steed and save the day?"

"Why, Ms. Smith, I do believe that's sarcasm I hear in your voice."

She put her hand on her waist. "I think we can agree on disagreeing about how to handle Lisa and Andy."

"Hey, I'm willing to give it a try. I behaved at dinner."

Her other hand went to her waist. "If you call behaving, giving the poor woman the third degree, then, yes, you behaved like a perfect gentleman."

"Ouch! I do believe your barb found its mark." He flattened his palm over his heart. "I wanted to know how she was going to support Andy."

"I could have told you she doesn't have a job. I intend to find her one."

"You do?"

"Well, yes, when she's completed the drug-rehab program. Do you know of anyone who might hire her?"

"Not off the top of my head. But let's wait and see what happens in a few weeks before you go out pounding the pavement looking for a job for Andy's mom." He strode to her, gave her a wink and headed down the hallway. "You may not have to worry about it."

Jacob heard Hannah's gasp and chuckled. He enjoyed ruffling her feathers, so to speak. He expected Hannah to follow him to Andy's room, but when he stopped at the boy's door, she still hadn't come down the corridor. Disappointment fluttered through him.

Cradled against his mother, Andy sat on his bed in his pajamas, listening to her read a story. When she closed the book, Andy said, "Again."

Lisa glanced toward Jacob. "I have to go, but I'll be back."

"Promise."

"If it was just me, I would, but the judge makes the decisions now. I hope so." Emotions thickened her voice.

"I love you, Mommy." Andy threw his arms around her.

She kissed the top of his head, then stood. "I'm gonna get help, Andy. This time it'll work."

This time? As Jacob had thought, Lisa had gone through rehab before and it hadn't been successful. He backed away, not wanting Andy to see anything in his expression. But in his mind Lisa represented his mother and his concern skyrocketed.

Jacob waited in the front foyer for the woman to emerge from the back. She said goodbye to Hannah then approached him. He wrenched open the door and stepped to the side to allow Andy's mother to go first. When he glanced toward Hannah, her look communicated a plea for understanding, as though she could read the war going on inside of him.

After asking for Lisa's address, Jacob fell silent on the drive into town. Memories of his own mother assailed him. He'd known he would be reminded of his childhood when he chose to work with children in the foster-care system. He'd thought he was prepared and usually he was. But not this time. His grip on the steering wheel tightened.

Jacob pulled to the curb in an area of town that had seen better days. Trash littered the streets and even with the windows rolled up, a decaying smell seeped into the car. "You live around here?"

Lisa grasped the door handle. "No, but I can catch a bus on the corner."

He scanned the area and wondered who or what lurked in the darkness between the buildings. "I said I'd drive you home, and I meant all the way."

"But—"

His gaze fixed on a broken-out storefront window. A movement inside the abandoned building made him press his foot on the accelerator. "I can't leave you here. It's too dangerous. Where are you staying?"

Silence.

Jacob slid a glance toward Lisa who stared at her hands in her lap. "You were staying back there?"

She nodded.

"Where?"

"In one of the buildings."

"You're homeless."

"It was my boyfriend's place Andy and I was staying at. He came back last night and kicked me out."

"So now you don't have anywhere to live?"

"No."

When Jacob turned onto a well-lit street, he sighed with relief. "How did you get to the zoo?"

"By bus."

Jacob made another turn, heading into the heart of the city. "I'm taking you to a shelter that's run by a couple from my church. They're good people. You'll be safe there." Again he looked toward Lisa and caught the tears streaking down her cheeks. "Okay?"

"Yeah," she mumbled, and dropped her head.

Something deep in his heart cracked open when he glimpsed Lisa's hurt. "I'll let Hannah know where you're staying so she can come there to pick you up tomorrow."

Her sobs sounded in the quiet, and another fissure opened up in his heart. Conflicting emotions concerning Lisa and her situation swirled through him.

"Why are ya being so nice? Ya don't like me," Lisa finally said between sniffles.

"For Andy." Jacob pulled into a parking space at the side of the shelter in downtown Cimarron City near his church.

Lisa lifted her head. "I love my son."

"Enough to stop taking drugs?"

She blinked, loosening several more tears. "Yeah."

"I'll be praying you do." Jacob opened his door, realizing as he slid out of the car that he meant every word. He would pray for Lisa's recovery. In the past he'd always thought of the child, never the parent in the situation. He was finding out there were two sides to a story.

Inside the shelter connected to his church, Jacob greeted Herb and Vickie Braun. "Lisa needs a place to stay for the night."

"We've got a bed. I'll show you the way." Vickie gestured toward a hallway that led to the sleeping area.

As the two women left the large hall where the residents ate their meals, Herb slapped Jacob on the back. "I wondered when we'd see you again. We've missed you down here."

"I've been so busy with Stone's Refuge and my practice."

"Eighteen children can keep you hopping. What you, Peter and Noah have done is great and definitely needed."

"We've appreciated you keeping an eye out for any children in need of a safe place to stay." Jacob walked toward the front door. "In a few months the third house will be finished."

"We'll take care of Lisa. She'll have a place to stay for as long as she needs it."

Back in his car Jacob rested his forehead on the steering wheel. He hadn't wanted to tell Herb the reason he didn't volunteer at the shelter, as many did from the church, was that it hit too close to home. There had been many times he had stayed in a shelter with his mother, but none were as safe and nice as this one. He'd comforted himself with financially supporting the place, but he knew now he should do something more. He needed to face his past and deal with it. He'd been running for a long time.

He started his car and drove toward his apartment near his practice. Emotionally exhausted, he plodded into the building and punched the elevator for his floor. Five minutes later, he plunked down on his bed and lay back, still fully dressed. He needed to get up and check his messages, then finish making some notes on a case, but a bone-weary tiredness held him pinned to the mattress. His eyes slid closed . . .

Darkness loomed before Jacob, rushing toward him.

"Let's go faster," Kevin said, turning the radio up louder, the music pulsating in the air.

"I can't see well." Jacob squinted his eyes as if that would improve his vision so he could see out the windshield better.

His friend shifted toward him until he spied the dashboard. "You're only going forty. What's the point taking Dad's car if we don't do something fun?"

"You're the one who wanted to come out here." Jacob's gaze swept the road in front of him, then the sides he could barely make out. Piles of snow still lined the highway.

"Yeah, so we could put the pedal to the metal. If you don't want to, I'll drive again."

To keep his friend quiet, Jacob increased the speed to forty-five but looked for a place to pull over so Kevin could drive. Suddenly he lost control of the car, the darkness spiraling around him. Screams pierced the quiet, sounds of glass breaking. . . .

Jacob shot up in bed, sweat drenching him. His

whole body shook from the nightmare that had plagued him for years—one of his punishments for surviving the wreck that killed Kevin.

Chapter Six

Hannah stared at the shelves full of medical books with titles that made her head spin. Why was she standing in the middle of Jacob's office waiting for him? She rotated around to grab her purse on the chair and leave before he came into the room. As she gripped the leather handle, the door opened, and she knew she was stuck.

"I was surprised to hear you were here." Jacob's smile wiped the weariness from his face. "I'm assuming everything is all right at the refuge or Teresa would have said something about it to me."

"Everything's fine. I just dropped Lisa off at the rehab center and wanted to stop by and thank you for finding a place for her to stay last night." Hannah released her strap and straightened. "I didn't realize she was living on the street. She didn't say anything to me about that."

"It was nothing. At this time of year Herb and Vickie always have a spare bed at the shelter. Now, if it had been winter, it might have been different."

"I should have figured something like that had happened to her when she mentioned she wasn't working.

I'm learning." She attempted a smile that quivered. "At least she has a place to stay for the next few weeks."

"If she stays there." Jacob dropped a file on his desk, releasing a long sigh.

Exhaustion, etching tiny lines into his face, sparked her compassion. "Long day?"

"Nonstop since I arrived this morning. The beginning of the flu season."

"Don't mention that word to me. I have eighteen children to keep healthy. I know you gave them a flu shot, but that's not the only illness they can get."

"As I well know. You've got your work cut out for you." He leaned back against his desk and folded his arms over his chest.

"I think you're right."

His eyebrows shot up. "You're admitting I might be right. Hold it right there while I get my recorder and you can repeat it for the microphone."

"Funny. I could say the same thing about you. You think I'm naive and idealistic."

"You are, but the world needs all kinds of people."

"So they don't all have to be cynical and realistic?"

He thrust away from the desk. "I hope not or we are in big trouble. Are you hungry?"

"Why?"

"Now, that question sounds cynical." He grinned. "Because I am hungry, and I'd like to take you to Noah's restaurant for dinner."

"According to all the kids that's their favorite place to eat."

"According to Noah it's the best in the whole Southwest."

"Will your friend be there?"

"If he's not out on a date, he's usually there. He's worse than me about working all the time. The one on Columbia Street was his first restaurant so he has a soft spot for it." Jacob snatched his jacket from the peg on the back of the door and slipped it on.

"I know he's a board member of the Henderson Foundation, but I haven't met him yet." Hannah exited the office first, into the dim light of the hallway.

Jacob came up behind her. "I guess everyone skedaddled out of here the first chance they got. Did I tell you it has been a long, crazy day?"

"I believe you mentioned that fact." She was very aware they were probably the only two people left in his suite of offices.

His chuckle peppered the air, making Hannah even more conscious of the fact they were alone. She'd come by to thank him for helping Lisa, and now she was going to dinner with him. How had that happened? For a moment in his office she'd forgotten who Jacob was. She needed to remember it at all times.

Hannah hurried her step toward the outer door. When she emerged from the building, she headed for her vehicle. "I'll follow you. I'm not sure where the restaurant is."

"Fine." Jacob unlocked his car door and climbed inside.

While she dug her keys out of her pocket, Hannah listened to him try to start his engine. A cranking sound that grated down her spine cut into the silence, then nothing. Dead. She peered over her shoulder as he tried again. Frustration marked his expression as he exited his vehicle.

He strode to her. "I knew it was only a matter of

time before she died. I was hoping to get a few more months out of her."

"Maybe you can get it fixed."

"That baby was my first car, and I need to say good-bye to her. Can I hitch a ride with you?"

"Sure." Why hadn't she brought the van? She stared at her very small car that practically forced people to sit on top of each other. "Do you still want to go to dinner?"

"A guy's got to eat, and if you could see my refrigerator, you'd take pity on me. I don't live too far from the restaurant or here. In fact, it'll be on your way to the refuge. If you need to get back, we can skip dinner and grab a quick bite at some fast-food joint."

A way out. She pushed the button to unlock her doors. "I don't have to be back at the refuge for a while. Laura relieves me on Monday to give me some time off."

"That's great." He walked around the back of her vehicle and slipped into the passenger seat. "After rushing around all day, it would be nice to kick back and have a relaxing dinner."

Oh, good. She blew her one chance to end the evening early. She didn't understand what was going on with her. A week ago she would have avoided any time spent in Jacob's company. But that was before she had gotten to know him better. Nothing was ever black-and-white and the gray areas were tripping her up.

Her car purred to life, and she pulled out of the parking lot onto the still-busy street. In the small confines she smelled his distinctive male scent, laced with a hint of the forest. Too cozy for her peace of mind.

"Turn right at the next corner and go three blocks. The restaurant is on the left side of the road."

His deep, baritone voice, edged with exhaustion, shivered through her. "Do you eat at your friend's a lot?"

"Probably once a week. Sometimes I bring the kids from the refuge."

"You do?" She was constantly discovering he was more involved in the children's lives than she had ever thought possible. "All of them?"

"Not usually. I rotate six different ones each time. I don't want to play favorites and cause any problems."

"Do you have a favorite?"

"I try not to. They all need love and understanding. But…"

His voice faded into the quiet.

"What? Fess up. Which one has stolen your heart?"

"It's hard for me not to be drawn to Andy."

Although she thought she knew the answer, she asked, "Why?" She pulled into a parking space next to the restaurant and looked at him, the light from the building washing over his face.

"Because he reminds me of myself when I was his age."

"And that's why you're being so hard on Lisa." Knowing how he felt about Andy's mother, she should be surprised he had taken the time to help her the evening before, but she wasn't, because the more she got acquainted with Jacob the more she realized that would be exactly what he would do.

"No, I'm skeptical of her motives because I've seen that kind of situation before and it didn't turn out well."

"I'm sorry about your mother, but Lisa isn't her."

"It's not just my mother I'm talking about. I've seen a lot over the years as a foster child and a doctor."

"Were there any situations where a parent was able to stay off drugs and take care of her child?"

He thought for a moment and answered, "One of my friends was lucky."

She placed her hand on the handle. "Then maybe Andy and Lisa will be like that one." She opened the door and left her car before they got into a heated discussion as they had in the past when they'd talked about the little boy's situation.

Inside the restaurant wonderful smells of spices, tomato and meats caused Hannah's mouth to water. "I didn't realize how hungry I was until now."

After they ordered at the counter, Jacob found them a table in the back in a less-crowded section and pulled out her chair as if they were on a date. She stared at it for a few seconds before she sat and let him scoot it forward. His hand brushed her shoulder as he came around to his side, and she nearly jumped at the casual touch.

Get a grip. This is not a date. It is simply two people who are acquainted sharing a meal. It could never be anything more than that.

"They're usually pretty fast here, so it shouldn't be long before they bring us our pizzas. And this is my treat."

"You don't have to," she immediately said, not liking how that made this sound more like a date.

"Yes, I do. You're helping me out, and I always pay my debts."

"Is that why you have a car that should have seen the inside of a salvage yard a long time ago?"

For a couple of heartbeats his jaw tightened, a veil falling over his expression. Then it was gone and he grinned. "Contrary to how a lot of men feel about their cars, I don't care what I drive. I wanted to pay off my educational loans before I took on any more debt."

"When will you be finished?"

"In a few months." He looked beyond her and his smile grew. "I wondered if you were here. Hannah, this is Noah, the guy who is responsible for adding at least five pounds to my waist."

A tall man with long brown hair pulled back with a leather strap paused at the table. "I must admit this isn't something I see often. I had to come out and meet the woman who could make my friend stop long enough to go out on a date."

Hannah shook Noah's hand. "Oh, this isn't a date. We're just…" How did she describe what they were?

"We're friends enjoying some pizza," Jacob finished for her.

"Sure. Sorry about the mistake." Noah's gaze danced with merriment as it lit upon first Jacob then Hannah.

"Hannah is the new manager at Stone's Refuge. Why she was interested in meeting you, I don't know."

Noah laughed. "She probably heard of my charming personality."

"No doubt," Jacob grumbled good-naturedly. "Are you leaving?"

Noah's laughter increased. "I can take a hint. You don't have to wound me."

"I couldn't wound you. Your hide is too thick."

The restaurant owner shifted his attention to Hannah. "Don't listen to a thing he says. He doesn't know how to have fun. He's too busy working all the time." He took her hand. "It was nice meeting you. I'm sure I'll see you around the farm."

As Noah strolled away, Hannah turned to Jacob. "Did you tell me y'all are friends?"

"Afraid so. Actually Noah and Peter are like brothers to me."

"Then that accounts for your ribbing."

"You sound like someone who has siblings. A brother or sister?"

The reminder of Kevin struck her low. She struggled to keep herself composed while she sat across from the man who caused her brother's death. Trembling, she clutched the sides of the chair.

"Excuse me." She bolted to her feet and searched for the restrooms.

Seeing the sign across the room, she quickly fled the table. Inside she locked the door and collapsed back against it. When she lifted her gaze to the mirror over the sink, she saw two large eyes, full of sorrow, staring back at her. She covered her cheeks, the heat beneath her fingertips searing them. His question had taken her by surprise and dumped her past in her lap.

She crossed to the sink and splashed cold water on her face, then examined her reflection in the mirror for any telltale signs of her grief. Blue eyes filled her vision, pain lurking just beneath the surface. She stamped it down.

She needed to get through dinner. Thinking about Kevin—the fact she had never been able to say goodbye to him because her parents wouldn't let her go to the funeral—was something she couldn't afford to do right now.

"You can do this." She blew out a breath of air, lifting her bangs from her forehead, and left the restroom.

Jacob stood when she approached. Worry knitted his forehead. "Are you all right?"

She took her chair, noticing that the pizzas had been delivered while she was gone. "I'm fine."

"Did I say something wrong?"

"I did have an older brother. He's dead. Your question took me by surprise. That's all."

He covered her hand on the table. "I'm so sorry about your brother."

Somehow she managed not to jerk back. She forced a smile to her lips and said, "I'm hungry. Let's dig in."

As Hannah took her first bite of the Canadian bacon slice, she knew what she had to do soon. She needed to go out to her brother's grave site. She needed to say goodbye.

The next afternoon at the cemetery, Hannah's steps slowed as she neared where her brother lay at rest. A vase of brightly colored flowers drew her immediate attention. Where had those come from? She had no relatives living in Cimarron City.

Hannah put her mum plant next to the vase, then moved back. The bright sunlight bathed her in warmth she desperately needed. Hugging her arms to her, she wished she had worn a heavier sweater. The north wind cut through her, and she positioned herself behind the large oak that shaded the area, its trunk blocking the worst of the chill.

"Kevin, I'm sorry I told on you that last day. If you hadn't gotten in trouble with Dad, you might not have gone out joyriding that night. If I had only known..." The lump in her throat prevented her from saying the rest aloud. But for years she had wondered: if she hadn't tattled on her brother, would that have changed the outcome of that night? That was something she would never know the answer to.

Lord, I need Your help in forgiving Jacob. I can see he is a good man. I don't want to carry this anger anymore. Please help me.

The evening before hadn't been torture. She wouldn't have thought that possible until recently. But she had seen a side of Jacob—even if they didn't agree about Andy and Lisa—which she liked. He cared about the children at the refuge. He cared about his patients. He cared about his friends.

If Jacob could move past Kevin's death, then so could she. She would find a way because she wanted to continue working at the refuge and that meant being involved with him.

"We need to stop meeting like this," Jacob said several weeks later as he closed the door to the exam room.

Hannah held Nancy in her lap, the child's head lying on her shoulder. "Just as soon as they come up with a cure for the common cold and a few other illnesses."

He knelt next to Hannah. "What's wrong, Nancy?"

"I don't feel good."

He leaned closer to hear the weak answer. "Let's take your temperature first."

While he rose, Nancy's eyes grew round. "I don't want a shot."

Hannah cradled the child against her. "I gave her something for her fever last night, but she didn't sleep well. She ended up in my bed. She complained her throat hurts."

"Nancy, can you hop up here and let me take a look?" Jacob patted the exam table.

The little girl nodded, then slipped off Hannah's lap. Jacob helped her up, then placed a digital thermometer into her ear.

Hannah stood next to Nancy. "What is it now?"

"Hundred and four. When was the last time you gave her something for her fever?"

Hannah checked her watch. "Four hours ago."

When the nurse came into the room, Jacob examined the child, then took a swab of her throat. "Strep is going around. We should know something in a few minutes."

He handed the sample to Teresa, who left, then shook out two children's pain relievers and gave them to Nancy. After chewing them, she sipped the cup of water Jacob filled for her.

"If it's strep, you'll need to keep her away from the other children. It can be very contagious. I often see it make the rounds in a family." Jacob jotted something on the girl's chart.

"I'll have her stay in my room, but she ate dinner and breakfast with the whole crew."

"I'll give you a maintenance dose of antibiotics. I don't want you getting sick, too."

The door opened as Nancy leaned against Hannah as if the child didn't have the strength to keep herself upright. Teresa entered and handed Jacob a slip of paper.

He frowned. "It's strep." He scribbled on a prescription pad, then ripped it off and handed it to Hannah. "Get her started on that right away. I'll come by this evening to check the rest of the kids, as well, and see how Nancy is doing after she's had a dose of antibiotics and lots of rest. I'll bring maintenance doses for the children to take when they get home from school." He smoothed the child's hair from her face. "You'll rest for me, Nancy?"

She nodded and buried herself even more against Hannah.

"Great. I bet Teresa has a toy for you from the box. Do you want one?" Jacob sent his nurse a silent message.

Nancy's dull gaze slid from Jacob to the nurse. "Yes, please."

"What would you like?" Teresa took the child's hand and assisted her down from the exam table. "We've got some coloring books. Do you like to color?"

"Uh-huh."

"Then you can pick from several different ones." Teresa left the room with Nancy in tow.

The second they were gone, Hannah rounded on Jacob. "What didn't you say in front of Nancy?"

"This could be serious. Both Terry and Susie get strep throat easily. Last time Terry was very sick from it. I'll be there not long after they get home from school. Has Nancy been around them much, other than at dinner and breakfast?"

"Susie read to her last night. She's the one who came and told me Nancy wasn't feeling well and was hot." Hannah pictured the children all in bed with sore throats and fevers. "So do you think I'd better dust off my tennis shoes and get ready to run between bedrooms?"

He chuckled. "That's a possibility, but I'll help as much as I can."

The barrier around her heart crumpled a little as she

looked into his eyes. Since he'd come into her life, he was doing that a lot—helping her out.

Hannah collapsed onto the couch in the living area and rested her head on the back cushion. "Thankfully Terry doesn't have strep yet, but I'm worried about Susie."

"I've got her on an antibiotic. We caught it early this time so she should be all right in a few days." Jacob settled across from her in a lounge chair.

"Are you as tired as I am?"

"I could fall asleep sitting up in this chair."

"Are you going to be all right driving home?"

One corner of his mouth lifted. "Sure, if I can persuade you to fix me a cup of coffee."

"Won't that keep you up after you get home?"

"I'm just hoping it will keep me up *until* I get home."

"If you think there'll be a problem, you are welcome to stay here and sleep on this couch." She patted the black leather cushion.

"No. My new car practically drives itself."

Summoning her last bit of energy, Hannah pushed to her feet. "One cup of java coming up then."

In the kitchen she quickly brewed some coffee, amazed that she actually invited him to stay over. It wasn't as though they would be alone, not with eight children in the house—six of them sick and probably up and down the whole night until the antibiotic really took effect.

But a picture of his tired face popped into her mind as she stared at the dark liquid dripping into the pot. It was after one, and he'd spent over nine hours here, helping her with the children—and that was after working a full day at his office. With Meg off, she'd needed the help, and she hadn't wanted to expose anyone else to strep.

Thank You, Lord, for sending him to us.

The aroma of coffee permeated the kitchen, tempting her to drink a cup herself. But she needed to get what rest she could so she only filled a mug for Jacob, then walked back into the living room to find him sound asleep. Even in relaxation he appeared exhausted, his pale features highlighting the dark circles under his eyes.

After placing his coffee on the table beside his chair, she grabbed the coverlet from the couch and threw it over him, pausing for a long moment to stare at him. Until she realized what she was doing. Quickly she dimmed the lights and tiptoed out of the living area. On her way to her bedroom, she checked on the children. The sick kids were separated from the two who were still healthy and she hoped stayed that way.

All seemed well as she headed for her room and bed. She was so tired she didn't even bother removing her clothes. She plopped down on the bedspread and fell back onto the pillow. The softness cocooned her in luxury that her weary body craved.

A thought seeped into her mind. She needed to get up and take her maintenance dose. She'd forgotten earlier. She would…soon….

The next thing Hannah knew someone was shaking her arm. She popped one eye open to find Nancy by her bed, her thumb in her mouth, her face flushed. "Baby, what's wrong?" She pushed herself up on her elbows.

"I can't sleep," she mumbled with her thumb still in her mouth.

Hannah touched her forehead, then cupped her cheek. Fever radiated beneath her palm. She slid her glance to the clock. Four. She'd slept almost three hours. "Let me give you some more pain reliever."

Hannah hurried into the bathroom off her room and retrieved the medicine and a paper cup full of water. When she returned, she found Nancy curled on her bed, still sucking her thumb. "Here, chew these first then drink some water."

Nancy did, then lay back down, her movements lethargic.

"I'll carry you to your room."

"Not mine. It's Susie's. Can I stay here?"

Hannah pulled a chair near the bed and sat. "Okay. This time. I'll take you..."

The child's eyes drifted closed. She'd wait until Nancy was asleep then take her back to the bedroom she shared with the two other girls. Fifteen minutes later she scooped up Nancy into her arms and strode out into the hallway and nearly collided with Jacob, who held Andy against him.

"What happened?" Hannah stepped back.

"He's sick, too. He woke me up in the living room."

"That makes seven now."

"Put him in my bed. I don't want him going back into the room with Terry."

Jacob passed her and entered her bedroom while she quickly took care of Nancy. She tucked the little girl in and brushed her fingers along her forehead. Her skin was cooler to the touch. Relief flowed through Hannah as she checked on the other two girls then slipped out into the hallway. Hopefully by this evening the children would be much better with no complications from the strep.

When Jacob came out of her room, she asked, "Are you hungry? I'll fix you an early breakfast or a late-night snack, whichever way you want to look at it."

"I never turn down a chance at a meal I don't have to fix. And after the past—" he glanced at his watch "—twelve hours I'm starved."

As she made her way to the kitchen, the hairs on her nape tingled as though Jacob was staring at her. She didn't dare look back to see if he was. Just thinking about it caused her cheeks to flame.

After flipping on the light, she crossed the room, opened the refrigerator and removed ingredients for scrambled eggs. "Frankly I love having breakfast at any time of the day. Mom used to fix pancakes for dinner once a month."

When he didn't say anything, she peered back at him. A shadow dulled his eyes until he saw her staring and a veil descended over his expression.

He moved to her. "Can I help?"

"Someone who professes not to cook? I don't think so. Have a seat. This is the least I can do for all your help with the kids."

"I'm their doctor."

"Who's gone above and beyond the call of duty."

He scooted back a chair from the kitchen table and sank down onto it. His gaze captured hers and for a moment she forgot everything but the charming smile that tilted the corners of his mouth and the gleam that sparkled in his eyes.

She blinked and he looked away. She quickly turned back to the counter, found a mixing bowl and began cracking eggs into it. "What made you become a doctor?"

A good minute passed before he answered, "I wanted to heal."

The anguish that slipped through his words froze Hannah. Heal himself? Or heal others? Suddenly she remembered anew who was sitting a few feet away from her. For a while she'd forgotten that he'd been responsible for her brother's death. Her hand trembled so badly she had to grip the edge of the counter.

"Hannah, are you all right?"

The sound of the chair scraping across the tile floor focused her on the here and now. Jacob had asked a question. She needed to answer him. She cleared her throat and said, "I'm just tired and concerned about the kids."

"They're a tough bunch. I think we caught it early." He stood right behind her.

His presence electrified the air. *Lord, help me to forgive. How did You do it on the cross?*

"Are you sure I can't help?"

Fortifying her defenses, she swung around and took a step back. "Yes, I'm sure. You're my guest. Now, sit and behave." She needed him across the room. She needed some space while she mended her composure, and it was hard to think straight with him so near.

He held up his hands. "Okay. I'm going." After he resettled in the chair, he asked, "Has being a social worker been everything you wanted it to be?"

That was an easy question thankfully. She turned back to finish preparing the scrambled eggs. "Yes, I love kids and wanted to make a difference in their lives, but I couldn't see myself as a teacher." She poured the mixture into the heated skillet. "I like a challenge, and I think social work is definitely challenging."

"That's putting it mildly."

She stirred the eggs. "I would think being a doctor is one, too."

"I guess you and I are alike. I enjoy a good challenge. It keeps life interesting."

The third thing they had in common. At this rate there would be no differences between them. After sticking four pieces of bread into the toaster, she withdrew some dishes from the cabinet and brought them to the table.

Before she went back to the stove to get the food, Jacob caught her hand and held it, drawing her full attention to his handsome face. "Thank you for covering me with a blanket." His voice dropped a level, a huskiness in it.

His hand about hers, warm and strong, robbed her of words. For the life of her, she couldn't look away, as though his eyes lured her into their brown depths. "You're welcome," she managed to say, her mouth parched.

The silence grew until she thought he must hear her heart pounding. All she could remember was his dedication to helping the children the evening before. A connection between them sprang up that staggered Hannah, a connection that went beyond what they had in common.

Finally he released her grasp. A smile dimpled his cheeks. "You'd better get the eggs."

She spun around and hurried to the stove, gripping the wooden spoon and counter to keep her hands from quivering. What just happened? How could she betray her brother's memory like that? It was one thing to forgive—but to forget? No!

While she saved the breakfast from being ruined, she tried to bring her rebellious emotions under control. It was because she was so exhausted, she told herself, that for a moment she looked beyond what Jacob had done in the past to what he was doing in the present.

Chapter Seven

Hannah sat at the kitchen table, trying to drink a cup of warm milk to help her sleep. It curdled her stomach. She pushed it away and buried her face in her hands. Fever singed her palms. Her throat burned. She didn't need a doctor to tell her that after a day and a half taking care of the sick children, she'd caught what they had. Thankfully most of them were on the mend, except Terry who had come down with it earlier today. Jacob didn't think the boy would have it too badly since he'd already taken two doses of the maintenance antibiotic. Up until an hour ago when she began to feel sick, she'd forgotten to take hers. Obviously she was too late to prevent it totally.

The sound of the door opening alerted Hannah she wasn't alone. Dropping her hands onto the table, she straightened as Meg came into the room.

"Everyone's in bed. Anything else you need before I go home?" Meg stopped near her, her eyes narrowing on Hannah. "You've got a rash, Hannah!"

"A rash?"

"All over your face and neck."

Hannah glanced down as though she could see it in the surface of the table.

The older woman touched Hannah's forehead. "You've got a fever. Come on. You're going to bed now." She took her arm to help Hannah rise.

She tried to stand and swayed. The room spun. "But the kids need—"

"I'll take care of the children. Don't you worry." Meg supported most of Hannah's weight as she headed toward the bedroom area.

"But you might get sick, too."

"If I do, then I'll deal with it. Right now you worry about taking care of yourself. I wonder why the maintenance dose didn't work for you. You've been on it for a while."

"I forgot until an hour ago. I was too busy taking care of the others."

Meg flipped back the coverlet and helped Hannah ease down onto her bed. "I'll get you some aspirin."

Hannah slid her eyes closed, listening to Meg move about the room, the sound loud to her sensitive ears. Her face felt on fire. Pain gripped her throat and drummed against her skull.

"Here." Meg slipped her arm underneath Hannah and lifted her up to take the pills and drink some water.

The second Hannah managed to swallow the aspirin she sagged back onto the mattress, shutting her eyes to the swirling room.

As the pain continued to do a tap dance in her head, she embraced the darkness.

* * *

"Why didn't she say anything to me before I left this evening?" Jacob stared at Hannah sleeping fitfully on her bed.

"I don't think she was thinking about herself. She's got a bad rash," Meg said.

The tiny red spots stood out like a neon sign against the otherwise pale skin. He brushed back a strand of hair from her face, feeling the warmth beneath his fingertips. "That can happen sometimes with strep. I'm going to give her a shot." He opened his medicine bag and took out a syringe and a vial of antibiotics. "I hate to wake her up, but she needs this now."

"I'm staying tonight to make sure the children are taken care of. You take care of her." Meg crossed to the door and left.

Gently, he shook Hannah awake. Her eyes blinked, then drifted closed.

"Hannah, I need to know if you're allergic to any medicine."

"Medicine?" she mumbled.

"I want to give you a shot of an antibiotic."

Her eyes popped open and focused on him. "A shot? I hate them."

Jacob pulled a chair close to the bed and sat. "I'm worried about you. Are you allergic to anything?"

"No—you don't need to worry…" Her voice floated into the silence as she surrendered to sleep again.

She flinched when the needle pricked her skin, but her eyes stayed closed. Again he combed the wayward lock back from her forehead, then went to the living room to settle into a chair for the long night ahead. He wouldn't leave until he was sure she would be all right.

* * *

Hannah moaned. Every muscle ached. She tried to turn over onto her side, but someone held her hand. Easing one eye open, she stared at Jacob stretched out in a chair next to her bed, asleep. She tugged herself free at the same time he snapped upright, disoriented. His hair lay at odd angles, making him appear younger.

He chuckled. "I guess you caught me napping on the job."

Her mind still shrouded in a fog, she mumbled, "What job?"

He bent forward, taking her wrist and placing his fingers over her pulse. "Caring for you."

She struggled to sit up. "I don't need you…" She collapsed back onto the pillow.

"What were you saying?"

She inhaled a shallow, raspy breath. "I'll be fine with some rest." She shifted her head until she glimpsed her clock on the bedside table. "I've only been sleeping a few hours…" The light slanting through the slits in the blinds attracted her attention. "What time of day is it?"

"It's eleven in the morning."

"I slept all night?" Again she tried to sit up and managed to prop herself on her elbows. "What about the children?"

"Meg has been here taking care of them. I've looked in on each one, and all of them are recovering nicely. And there were no cases at the other cottage."

"What about your patients?"

His chuckles evolved into laughter. "I know I work a lot, but today is Saturday. I'd planned to spend it here making sure the kids were all right."

"You were? I mean, I don't remember…." She rubbed

her temple, the pounding in her head less but still there. She swallowed several times to coat her dry throat. "Can I have some water?"

"Sure." He rose and settled next to her to hold her up while she sipped some cold liquid. Despite its coolness, it burned going down. "I need you to take these." Jacob produced some pills. "And there's no forgetting this time."

She winced each time one went down. "I guess I forgot to tell you I used to get strep throat every year while growing up."

"No, you left that out."

"It wouldn't have made any difference. I'd still have taken care of the children. They needed me." The sound of her voice grew weak in her ears.

Jacob laid her gently back on the bed and stood. "Somehow I figured that. But now I'm your doctor, and I'm telling you to sleep and not worry about anything."

"You're a pediatrician." Her eyes fluttered closed.

"But I'm free and here. You aren't going to get rid of me."

That last sentence comforted her as sleep descended.

"She's awake, Dr. Jacob! She's awake!"

Nancy's shrieking voice thundered through Hannah's head, threatening to renew the earlier hammering pain.

"Shh." Jacob filled the doorway with several children standing behind him, peeping into the room.

He looked good to her tired eyes. Very good. Slightly worn but handsome as ever with his tousled brown hair and gleaming eyes that held hers. "How long have I been asleep?"

"It's Sunday afternoon and Laura and Peter are here."

"I lost another day."

Nancy appeared in her face. "I was worried about you."

Other than the ashen cast to the little girl's features, she looked all right. The dullness in her eyes was gone and a smile brightened her face. "I'll be as good as new in a day or so."

"Okay, everyone, Laura and Peter have dished up some ice cream for you in the kitchen. You'd better eat it before it melts."

The sound of running footsteps faded down the hall, leaving Jacob alone with her. He moved into the room.

"I have news for you, Hannah. You won't be up and about in a day or so. You had a bad case of strep on top of exhaustion. You need to get a lot of rest if you want to be as good as new by Thanksgiving."

She frowned. "You aren't going to be one of these demanding doctors who insists I follow your instructions."

He stood with his feet slightly apart and his hands on his hips, glaring at her. "Yes, I am." But the merriment in his eyes mocked his fierce stance. "I came close to taking you to the hospital."

"You did?"

The implication threw her. If her aching body was any indication, she realized she had been very sick. But the hospital?

"Oh, you are awake? The kids said you were." Laura walked to the bed and positioned herself on the other side of Jacob. "I brought you some ice cream." She held up the bowl.

"Vanilla?"

Nodding, Laura sat in the chair nearby and scooped a spoonful of it for Hannah. "Peter could use your help,

Jacob. By now all eight children are clamoring for more ice cream."

"Make sure she stays in bed," was his parting remark.

Laura laughed. "He can be so demanding when a patient doesn't follow his instructions."

Hannah scooted up against the headboard and took the bowl from Laura. "This does make me realize I have to find a doctor. I haven't yet."

Laura's laughter increased. "Jacob has a way with children, but I can see his bedside manner might be lacking with an adult. He does mean well, though."

Hannah slid the spoonful of ice cream into her mouth and relished the coldness as she swallowed the treat. "I wouldn't know about his bedside manner. I was pretty out of it. I remember him making me take some pills, though."

Laura's expression sobered. "Yes, I know. Peter and I have been here helping Meg with the children. You should have let us know how bad it was. We could have come sooner."

Hannah stared at her ice cream. "You have four children. I didn't want you to be exposed to strep, so I played it down when we talked."

"And got Meg and Jacob to go along."

"I thought we were handling it. We did. I just got sick."

"Running yourself into the ground. In fact, I tried to get Jacob to go home and take care of himself, but he wouldn't leave your side."

"He didn't?" Warmth, that had nothing to do with a fever, spread through her.

"He told me he wouldn't be able to sleep until he

knew you were out of the woods. For the past day and a half he has stood guard over you." Laura glanced toward the doorway. "Now, I'm gonna insist he go home and get some rest."

Hannah took another scoop of the ice cream. "Do we have any Popsicle treats left?"

"You must be getting better. You have an appetite. I'll see if I can find any. The children have been eating them right and left. I had Peter go get some more." She rose and headed for the hallway.

Hannah finished her treat and placed the bowl on the table, tired from the brief exertion. How was she going to look after eight children? She couldn't even feed herself without getting exhausted.

She tried to concentrate on that dilemma, but she kept thinking about what Laura had told her about Jacob. He hadn't left her side. He'd watched over her. She should be upset by that news, but after the past few days working with him to take care of the sick children, she wasn't. A bond of friendship had formed between them.

Lord, if any good has come out of the illness that took hold of this house, it was that. I don't hate Jacob anymore. I can forgive him for what happened to Kevin. The man I've gotten to know would never have done something like that on purpose. The car wreck was an unfortunate accident that I suspect has left a mark on Jacob, too.

She sank farther into her pillow, propped up against the headboard, and closed her eyes. Total peace blanketed her for the first time in years. *This is why you forgive someone. This is why you let go of your anger.*

I understand now, Jesus, why You forgave them on the cross. Thank You, Lord.

Footsteps announced she wasn't alone. She opened her eyes, expecting to see Laura, but instead Jacob entered with a cherry Popsicle in his grasp.

"I hear you're hungry." He sat in the chair by the bed and gave her the treat.

"I thought Laura was making you go home to sleep."

"She tried."

"And obviously failed."

"I can be a very determined man."

"I appreciate all you've done, but she's right. I don't want you to get sick, too." She nibbled on her Popsicle.

"I'm not going to. I've built up quite a resistance. Remember I deal with sick kids all the time."

"Now I see why the children love having you come. The gifts you brought them to keep them occupied and in bed were great."

"I love those handheld video games."

"You sound like you've played your share of them."

"I'm a kid at heart."

His smile encompassed his whole face and sent her heart beating a shade faster. "I'll have to try one sometime."

"I'll loan you one of mine. A great stress reliever."

"I thought exercise was."

"I'm exercising my mind."

Seeing his well-proportioned body, she knew he also had to exercise physically, too. "I like to ride my bike but haven't had a chance yet."

"There are some great places around here to visit. If the weather stays nice, I could show you one weekend."

"You have a bike?"

He nodded. "A great stress reliever."

"Maybe I could get some bikes for the kids, and we could all go on an excursion one Saturday."

"Let's get you well first, then we can plan something."

"I'll be up in no time." She fluttered her hand in the air, but immediately dropped it into her lap, her arm feeling as though it weighed more than a twenty-pound barbell.

He rose. "I'd better let you get some rest. Besides, I promised Laura I would deliver the Popsicle and leave. I don't want to make a liar out of me."

The second he left, Hannah felt the energy level in the room diminish. He charged the air wherever he was. He had a presence about him that drew a person to him. Why hadn't she noticed that before?

Because I had been too busy trying to avoid him.

It was nice having a friend in Cimarron City.

A friend? a little voice questioned.

Yes, a friend. Anything else would be taking this forgiveness thing too far.

"Dr. Jacob has pulled up," Gabe shouted from the window in the living room.

"Mom's here!" Andy jumped up and down, then raced for the front door.

Hannah laughed. "I think he's excited."

"He's been marking off his calendar until Thanksgiving." Susie followed Andy outside.

Hannah heard the car doors slamming shut. She hurried after the children who flooded out of the house and down the steps. Excitement bubbled up in her. She wished she could attribute it totally to the fact that

Lisa had just finished her drug-rehab program and was going to join them for Thanksgiving dinner today. She couldn't, though. After she was up and about at the end of last week, she hadn't seen much of Jacob other than at church on Sunday. But today he was spending Thanksgiving with them.

Whenever he was at the cottage, it seemed to come alive. His relationship with the children was great.

How about his with you?

She ignored the question and greeted Lisa with a hug. "It's good to see you."

The young woman slung her arm around Andy who was plastered against his mom. "Thanks for the invitation. I've been looking forward to today."

Andy yanked on his mother's arm. "Come inside. I want to show you what Dr. Jacob got me."

"I'll show you my gift, too," Gabe said.

"Talk to you later," Lisa said laughingly as her son dragged her up the steps and into the house.

Hannah turned to Jacob. "I appreciate you picking her up."

"No problem. I was coming this way." He produced a bouquet of fall flowers from behind his back. "These are for you."

"Me?" She took them, her eyes probably as round as the yellow mums she held. The scent of the lilies teased her senses.

"Dr. Jacob, have you heard about the bike trip we're going on this weekend?" Nancy asked, tugging on his arm to get his attention.

He knelt down so that they were eye to eye. "I'm going, too."

"Oh, yeah. I forgot." The little girl hugged her worn pink blanket to her and stuck her thumb into her mouth.

"C'mon, Nancy. You need to help me set the table." Susie clasped the child's hand and mounted the steps.

"Where are the other kids?"

Still stunned by the gesture, Hannah was momentarily speechless. She could not recall anyone ever bringing her flowers—not even her husband.

"Hannah?"

"Oh. At the barn feeding the animals. They'll be here shortly. Roman took several of them over with some of the older kids."

"I bet Terry led the way."

"You know that boy well."

"He has been here the longest. I wish someone would adopt him, but he's nearly twelve, which makes it harder." Jacob held the front door open for Hannah.

"Yeah, everyone wants a baby or a young child when they're looking to adopt."

The aroma of the roasting turkey seeped into every corner of the house. "Ah, the best smell. Did Meg make her cornbread dressing?"

"Yes, and my contribution is dessert. Pecan pie."

"A woman after my heart. That's one of my favorite desserts."

"Meg made her pumpkin pie and a chocolate one, too."

"Stop right there. You're driving a starving man crazy."

"Tell you what. Dinner isn't for another hour. Let me put these flowers into water and check with the kids to see if anyone wants to go to the barn. That oughta take your mind off food."

"Great. If I stayed here, I'd probably be raiding the kitchen, and Meg doesn't take too kindly to snacking before a meal."

She waved her hand toward the living room. "Two are in there. See if they want to go," she said while she walked to the dining room and peered in.

Susie gave Nancy a plate to set on the table.

"Want to come to the barn with Dr. Jacob and me?"

Nancy thrust the dishes she still held at Susie. "Yes!"

The older girl scanned the near-empty table. "I promised Meg I would help her. You all go on without me."

Next Hannah found Gabe and Andy in the boys' bedroom, showing Lisa how to play one of the handheld video games. "We're going to the barn. Want to come?"

Gabe leaped to his feet at the same time Andy did. The boy pulled his mother up.

"I guess that's a yes," Hannah said, and went to the kitchen to let Meg know where they would be and put the flowers in water.

Five minutes later the group passed the unfinished third house and started hiking across the meadow. With just a hint of crispness, the air felt nice. The scent of burning wood lingered on the light breeze that blew a few strands of Hannah's hair across her face. Andy practically hauled Lisa behind him at a fast clip while the other children ran and skipped toward the red barn.

"After the busy week I've had, I don't have that kind of energy." Jacob chuckled when Andy's mother threw them a helpless look.

"Do you think Lisa will be successful this time?"

"Honestly? No, I don't but then my experience hasn't been a good one when it comes to successful stories with drug rehab."

"I'm praying you're wrong."

Jacob paused in the middle of the field and looked long and hard at Hannah. "Truthfully I hope I am, too."

The more she was around Jacob, the more she realized she'd never met a man like him. He was honest, caring, and when he was wrong, admitted it. If she weren't careful, she would forget who he was. Yes, she had forgiven him, but she hadn't forgotten what happened all those years ago. To do so would have been to betray her family.

Peter came out of the barn as the children with Lisa raced by him. "The kids are almost through feeding the animals." He swung his attention from Hannah to Jacob. "Now I know why you turned Laura and me down for Thanksgiving dinner. The kids told me you were joining them today."

"I got an offer I couldn't refuse." Jacob's grin accentuated his two dimples.

"Laura and I will eventually get over it." Peter shifted toward Hannah. "I hope you have enough food. You should have seen him last Thanksgiving."

"Hannah, look." Nancy walked toward her with a puppy cradled against her chest. "I got to pick her up this time."

"Yeah, she's just about ready for a home." Peter started for the interior of the barn.

"I can give her a home," Nancy said, trailing after Peter with the mutt still in her arms. "I'm good with puppies."

"So far I've managed to discourage any pets at the cottage, but I've got my work cut out for me this time." Hannah hurried to follow Nancy.

"Why? I think a pet around the house would be good for the kids."

She stopped in the middle of the cavernous building. "And how do you suppose I should pick the pet? Each child wants a different one."

Jacob scratched the top of his head. "I don't know. I'll have to think on that one."

"Fine. You come up with a fair way and they can have one."

Terry entered through the back door, carrying a lamb. "I found him." He passed the animal to Peter, then waved at Hannah. "I'm finished. Is it time for dinner?"

"About half an hour." Hannah swung her attention back to Nancy and saw the little girl put the white puppy back in its pen with the other ones. The child stooped down and continued to stroke the mutt.

Jacob was right. There needed to be some pets at the cottage, not just down at the barn. She'd never gotten to have one because they had always been moving to a new place. She remembered her yearning and her promise to herself that when she had her own home she would have several to make up for the lack while growing up.

"I've got it." Jacob leaned close, his voice low. "Paul used to have a family meeting every week and everyone had an equal say in what was discussed. That's where we often hashed out problems that came up. When something like having a pet needed to be decided upon, we would talk about it at the meeting, then vote. Majority ruled."

His warm breath tingled along her neck. She stepped a few feet away and tried to slow her suddenly pounding heart. "That might work."

"He set up ground rules. One person at a time spoke.

No one was allowed to cut in until that person was through speaking. Everyone had to be respectful of the others. Our voting was done by secret balloting and no one was to be questioned how they voted."

"He sounds like an amazing man."

"He was. I miss him. Thankfully Alice, his wife, lives with Laura and Peter."

"Alice was your foster mother? I didn't know that." She'd met the older woman while visiting Laura once.

"Yes. Both of them were lifesavers to a lot of kids."

"Including you?"

"Especially me. I was pretty messed up when I went to live with the Hendersons at fifteen."

"Why?"

A frown marred his face and his eyes darkened with storm clouds.

Hannah wished she could snatch the question back. Would he say anything about the wreck? Was that even what he was referring to?

Chapter Eight

For a few seconds the urge to share inundated Jacob. He'd never told anyone but Paul. Jacob stared into her gaze, void of any judgment. The words formed in his mind.

"Jacob?"

He turned away from Hannah in the middle of the barn and strode to the entrance. How could he tell her what he'd done, that he'd been responsible for another person's death? He valued her friendship and didn't want to see disappointment, or something worse, in her eyes. Their rocky start had finally smoothed out. He didn't want to go back to how it had been in the beginning.

Hannah's hand settled on his arm. The touch went straight to his heart. The guilt he'd lived with for twenty-one years whisked the words away. He couldn't tell her, but he had to say something.

He glanced at her slightly behind him and to the side. "Before I came to the Hendersons, I was an angry teen who had even run away from several foster homes."

"Because of your childhood?" Sympathy edged her voice.

"Yes. Paul's the one who taught me about Jesus. He showed me there was another way besides giving in to my anger."

"Anger can consume a person."

"It nearly had me. I never want to go back to that place." He shuddered.

Hannah moved to stand in front of Jacob. Her fingers skimmed down his arm, and she grasped his hand. "I don't see that happening."

"Not as long as the Lord is in my life."

"Hannah, I'm finished. I forgot to eat breakfast," Terry said.

She looked beyond Jacob and grinned. "Gather the others and we'll head back."

In the past few years he'd done a pretty good job of throwing himself totally into his work and putting the past behind him. But lately he hadn't been able to do that. *Why, Lord? Why now?*

Nancy took his hand. "I don't want to leave Abby."

"Abby?" That was Nancy's mother's name.

She pointed toward the pen. "The puppy. I named her Abby. I love that name."

His heart ripped in half, and he had no words for Nancy, having been in her shoes and remembering the pain of rejection he'd suffered as a child. Racking his brain for something to say, Jacob cleared his throat. "I like the name, too."

Nancy tugged him down and whispered in his ear, "Will you talk to Hannah about Abby?"

A lump lodged in his throat. "Sure."

Hannah sat at one end of the long dining-room table with Jacob at the other end. For the past minute silence had ruled because all the children were stuffing bites of pie into their mouths.

Jacob pushed his empty plate away. "That's it. I'm full up to my earlobes. Any more and it will come out the top of my head."

A couple of the children giggled.

"Dr. Jacob, you're funny," Nancy said, shoving her plate away. "I'm full up to my earlobes, too."

"That was the best Thanksgiving dinner I've had, Meg." Jacob wiped his mouth with his napkin.

The older woman blushed. "Oh, it was nothing."

"Who agrees with me?"

Everyone's arm shot up into the air. Meg beamed from ear to ear.

"And to show my appreciation, I'll clean up the dishes. Who's going to help me?" Jacob scanned the children's faces.

Everyone's arm dropped.

Hannah fought to keep her expression serious. "I guess you're stuck doing them by yourself."

"Who's going to take pity on me and help?" Jacob's gaze again flitted from one child to the next.

"I will," Lisa said.

"I can." Andy stood and gathered up his plate.

"Thanks, you two, but you enjoy your time together. I'll help Dr. Jacob." Hannah rose.

Before she had a chance to reach for the dishes in front of her, the children fled the dining room with Lisa and Meg following at a more sedate pace.

"I've never seen them move quite so fast," Jacob said with a chuckle.

"Not cleaning up is quite a motivator."

"Wash or dry?"

"You're the guest. You choose." She stacked the plates and carried them into the kitchen.

Five minutes later with the table cleared, Jacob rolled up his long sleeves and began rinsing the dishes off for the dishwasher. "Noah said something about coming over after eating at Peter and Laura's."

"Speaking of Noah, I've been thinking. Do you think he'll give Lisa a job at one of his restaurants?"

"You'll have to ask him. He's always looking for good help. Why? Did Lisa say something to you?"

"Well, no, but she doesn't have a job. I thought I would help her find something."

"Don't you think you should talk to her first?"

Hannah took the glass that Jacob handed her. "I didn't want to get her hopes up if it wasn't possible. She doesn't have many skills and has only worked in a fast-food restaurant."

"It'll be hard finding a decent job without a high-school diploma. Will she be able to stay at the halfway house?"

"Yes, and they have a program there that assists people in getting their GED."

Jacob shifted to face her. "Hannah, you can't live Lisa's life for her. She has to want it—especially being off drugs—if it's going to work."

She averted her gaze, uncomfortable under the intensity of his. "I know. She loves Andy. I know it. They belong together."

"Then she'll stay off the drugs if that's the way to be involved in his life." Sharpness sliced through his words.

Reestablishing eye contact with him, she glimpsed the pain he experienced as a child who hadn't meant much to his mother—at least not enough to stop taking drugs. "I have to try to help. That's why I went into social work in the first place." She took another dish from him. "In fact, I found Nancy's mother. She's only thirty miles from here in Deerfield."

He arched a brow. "And what do you intend to do with that information?"

"I'm going to see her next Wednesday."

"Do you want some company?"

Surprised, she immediately answered, "Yes," then took a harder look at Jacob and noticed the tightening about his mouth and the inflexibility in his eyes. "Why do you want to come?"

"I don't want you to go alone. I've read Nancy's file. I know the rough characters her mother has hung out with." Censorship sounded in his voice.

Hannah straightened, thrusting back her shoulders. "I have to try. Have you seen how upset Nancy is when she sees Andy with his mother?"

"Yes, I've seen her carrying her blanket and sucking her thumb more and more since Lisa has come into Andy's life."

"She misses her own mother."

"Maybe. But maybe she's just plain scared her mother might come get her."

"I don't think so. She's asked me tons of questions about my mother."

Mouth tightening, Jacob squirted some detergent into the sink and filled it up with hot water. "What time did you want to go? I can rearrange my afternoon appointments if that's okay with you."

"Fine. How about after lunch?"

"How about lunch then we can go?"

"Lunch?"

His chuckle tingled down her spine. "Yes, you've got to eat. I've got to eat. Let's do it together then leave from there."

"Sure."

"Then it's a date."

A date? No, it wasn't a date, she wanted to shout, but realized her panic would be conveyed. Instead she clamped her teeth together and didn't say another thing until they had finished up with the pots and pans.

While she put away the meat platter, Jacob wiped down the counters. "Does Nancy's mother know you're coming?"

Jacob's question in the quiet startled her. She whirled around. "No, I thought I would surprise her."

"I hope you're not the one who is surprised."

She frowned. "I'm not totally naive. I don't expect the woman to welcome me with open arms."

"That's good because she won't."

Tension pulsated between them as he stared at her.

Terry burst into the kitchen. "Noah is here! You've got to come see what he brought us." The boy spun around and disappeared back through the entrance.

"Was that Terry who blew in and out of here?" Hannah asked with a laugh, needing to change the subject.

"Yep."

The huge grin on Jacob's face prompted her to ask, "Do you know what Noah brought?"

He nodded and quickly followed the boy out of the kitchen.

Exasperated at the lack of information, Hannah left, too, and found all the children out front, surrounding a pickup filled with bicycles, many different sizes. She stopped at Jacob's side. "I guess that answers my problem about bikes for a ride. I'd only been able to come up with a few. Peter said he would work on it for me."

"He did. Noah and I were his solution."

"Y'all donated them?"

Jacob's smile grew. "Yep. It should have been done before now. Sometimes I'm so focused on their well-being physically that I forget about their mental health."

He waded his way through the crowd of children to help Noah lift the bikes out of the truck bed. As the two men did, they presented each one to a different kid.

Nancy hung back next to Hannah. The little girl glanced up at her. "I don't know how to ride. I've never had a bike."

Hannah pointed toward one still in the bed of the pickup. "That's why there are training wheels on that one. Before you know it, you'll be riding everywhere."

The child stared at it, doubt in her eyes, a tiny frown on her face. "I guess." She lowered her gaze to the ground at her feet.

"I'll work with you this afternoon since Dr. Jacob and I want to take all of you on a bike ride this Saturday. He said something about there being a small lake near here that we could go to and have a picnic. What do you think?"

"Can I bring Abby?"

Hannah knelt in front of Nancy. "A bike ride probably isn't the best place for a puppy."

Jacob approached the little girl. "Here's yours." He set Nancy's small bike with training wheels on it next to her.

She put her thumb in her mouth and looked up shyly at him, mumbling, "Thanks."

Hannah settled her hand on the child's shoulder. She saw the concern in Jacob's expression and said, "I'm going to teach her how to ride over the next two days. She never has."

Before he could say anything, the children encircled Noah and him, vying for the men's attention with their enthusiasm.

"Andy's always wanted a bike. He used to ride the boy's in the apartment across the hall." Lisa said, while watching her son, happiness plastering a smile on his face. "Who's that with Dr. Hartman?"

"Noah Maxwell. He owns the Pizzeria chain. In fact, I wanted to talk to you about applying for a job. Would you be interested in working at one of his restaurants? I could talk to him for you if you are." Jacob had been right—again. She needed to see if Lisa wanted a job at the Pizzeria before approaching Noah.

"At the halfway house they were going to help me look for something. 'Bout the only experience I have is at a food joint. One of the things I learnt at the rehab center was to ask for help when I need it. Thanks."

"Then I'll talk to Noah."

Andy ran up to his mom. "Dr. Jacob said I could go on a bike ride with them on Saturday because my cast is coming off tomorrow." After his announcement, he twirled around and raced back to the group.

Lisa followed her son, plowing into the middle of the children all getting on their bikes.

"Do you want to start your lesson now?" Hannah asked Nancy, who kept her gaze glued to the ground.

She shook her head. "I don't wanna go on a ride. Can I stay here?"

"Why, honey?" Hannah lifted the child's chin.

Tears pooled in Nancy's eyes, and several coursed down her cheeks. "I just don't. I heard Mommy say bikes are dangerous." The little girl pulled away and stepped back toward the porch. She plopped down on the top stair, sucking her thumb and hugging her blanket.

"Nancy doesn't want to ride?" Jacob stood right behind her.

"No. She thinks they're dangerous." Hannah kept her voice low so no one else heard.

"Having seen my share of bike accidents, I can't totally disagree, but we've also gotten helmets for them."

"I'll see if someone can watch her while we go with the other children. I don't want to force Nancy. Hopefully she'll see the others enjoying it and want to learn to ride."

Dressed in black slacks and a gray pullover sweater, Noah approached. "I think our gift is a big hit."

"Did you have any doubt?" Hannah scanned the smiling kids and wanted to bottle this moment.

"No. But what are we going to do for Christmas? It will be hard to top this."

"You don't have—"

"This is the best way I can spend my money," Noah interrupted Hannah. "These kids' lives have been hard. Giving them some joy is priceless."

She realized Noah had as big a heart as Jacob. Too bad, according to Laura, he didn't want to settle down and have his own family. "I do have a favor to ask."

"If it's to go on the bike ride, I draw the line there."

"No. I'd like you to interview Andy's mother for a job at your restaurant. She needs a job and the only experience she's had is as a waitress."

When she started to say more, Noah held up his hand. "Done. I'll talk to her."

Hannah was at a loss for words. Realizing Jacob's misgivings about Andy's mom wanting to change, she'd practiced her speech to convince Noah to give Lisa a chance.

"I'll give her a ride into town and talk to her tonight. Where's she staying?"

"She's staying at a halfway shelter two blocks from your first restaurant."

"Fine. I know where that is." There must have been something in her expression because he added, "I know she just completed a drug-rehab program. I'm aware of what goes on at the refuge even though I don't get to spend as much time out here as Jacob."

"Thanks. I appreciate you giving her a chance." When Noah joined a couple of the boys by his truck, she said to Jacob, "It's a shame he isn't interested in having a family. Like you, he's good with the kids."

"You think I'm good with them?" A gleam glinted in his gaze.

"We might not always see eye to eye on certain issues, but I can't ignore the fact you have a way with the children. Are you interested in having a family?" The second she asked the question she wanted to retreat. Why in the world had she asked him *that?* As if she might be interested in him and the answer.

"Yes. Paul was a great example of what a father can be."

"Then why don't you have one?" The urge to slap her hand over her mouth swamped her. She was digging a deep hole with her inquisitiveness.

He threw back his head and laughed. "I wish it were that simple. It takes two."

Heat flooded her cheeks. She started to mention he was thirty-five, but this time she managed to keep quiet. "Oh, look at Gabe ride."

On Saturday Hannah came to a stop near the small lake and hopped off her bicycle. Susie pulled up next to her while Jacob flanked her on the other side. "This is beautiful. We'll have to come back in the spring when the trees are flowering. I see quite a few redbuds."

"That's our state tree." Susie put her kickstand down. "We've been studying Oklahoma history in school."

"I can see why it is. They're everywhere."

"Can we walk along the shore? We won't go too far."

"Make sure no one goes too close to the water." Hannah took a swig from her water bottle.

"She told me Thanksgiving that she wanted to be a doctor like me." After removing his ball cap, Jacob wiped his hand across his forehead. "I'd forgotten how much work bicycling is, especially that last hill."

"I thought you went bike riding all the time."

"When I was a child, I used to. I…" A frown carved deep lines into his brow.

"What?"

"My grandma gave me a bike one Christmas. I loved that bike. I would go all over the place. If I was quick enough, it became my way of escaping my mother when she went into a rage."

"What happened to it?"

"During one of my mother's rages, she ran over it with her car. I tried to fix it, but the frame was bent too much for me to do anything. I cried when the garbage man took it away." His gaze zeroed in on her. "That was the only time I cried. Not crying used to make my mom madder. She used to shout I didn't have a heart."

Her stomach knotted as she listened to him talk about his mother so dispassionately as though she were a stranger. But she'd gotten to know him well enough to hear the underlying pain that his words didn't reflect. "My mom and I had moved to a new town and I was desperate to impress the neighborhood kids." Hannah sipped some more cool water. "I performed a few tricks with my bike. They were properly awed until the last one. I fell and broke my wrist. I never got back on it after that. I stopped riding for years until college when I took it up for exercise."

"How did we get on a subject like this?"

"I don't know," she said with a shaky laugh.

"I know how." He shifted toward her. "I find it easy to talk to you. I don't tell others about my childhood. I prefer leaving that in my past."

His words made her feel special. Surprisingly she found it easy to talk to him, too. Less than two months ago she'd thought of him as her enemy. Now she considered him a friend—a very good friend.

He inched closer, taking her hands in his. "I haven't had much time in my life for dating. I made a promise years ago to become a doctor and that's where all my energy has gone."

Children's laughter drifted to her, reminding her they weren't alone. She peered at the group near the lake. Terry was showing Gabe how to skip rocks. Susie was scolding the two youngest boys to stay away from the water.

When she looked back at Jacob, the intensity in his

gaze stole her breath. He bent toward her. Her heart fluttered in anticipation. He released her hands and cupped her face. He lowered his head until their mouths were inches apart. The scent of peppermint spiced the air.

Softly he brushed his lips across hers. "I think we should go out on an official date."

"You do?" she squeaked out, her pulse racing through her body.

"Don't you think we've skirted around this long enough?"

"What's this?"

His mouth grazed hers again. "This attraction between us."

She wanted his kiss. His eyes enticed her to forget who he was, to forget the past and grab hold of the future.

A drumroll blared. Hannah gasped and shot back.

Jacob's eyes widened. He stared at her pocket as another drumroll sounded, loud and demanding.

She dug into her jeans. "That's my cell."

"A drumroll? What kind of ring is that?"

She pulled the phone out. "One I know is mine." She flipped it open. "Hannah here."

"I'm so sorry to bother you."

The alarm in Meg's voice alerted Hannah something was wrong.

"Nancy's missing. I've looked everywhere and I can't find her."

Chapter Nine

Heart pounding, Hannah raced up the steps and into the cottage with Jacob and the children not far behind her. Meg stood in the living room with Peter, Laura, Roman and a police officer. The older woman reeled around when Hannah came in. The anxious look on Meg's face tightened a band about Hannah's chest. She gulped in deep breaths, but she couldn't seem to fill her lungs. Bending over, hands on knees, she inhaled over and over. She'd never ridden so fast before.

Meg touched Hannah's shoulder. "She's been gone for at least an hour. We've looked all over the farm, especially the barn."

"You didn't find her in the pen with the puppies? She's taken a liking to one of them."

Peter moved forward. "No, but now that I think about it, I didn't see all the puppies. At the time I thought one was behind its mama in the back."

"Is anything missing from her room?" Jacob strode in with the children.

Meg shook her head. "I don't think so, but I'm not

that familiar with what she has." She snapped her fingers. "Except I know her blanket is gone. She had it with her while she was watching TV in here."

"I'll check her room. I know what she has." Hannah headed down the hallway, her hands shaking so badly she had to clasp them together.

She opened every drawer and the closet, then inspected under the bed and in Nancy's little toy chest. She finished her survey when Jacob appeared in the doorway.

"Anything?"

"Her doll she'd brought with her when she came to the cottage. I don't think she's been kidnapped. I think she's run away."

"Why? Where would she go?"

Her heartbeat pulsated against her eardrums. The constriction about her chest squeezed even tighter. "I don't know and tonight they are predicting it will drop below freezing with rain or snow."

"Let's hope they're wrong."

"Or we find her before then." Hannah welcomed Jacob's calming presence. She saw apprehension in his expression, but above everything his strength prevailed. He was a man used to emergencies and knew how to handle them.

Back in the living room the police officer tucked his notepad into his front pocket then peered at Hannah. "Anything else missing?"

"Her doll."

"I'll call this in and get things moving. Where's your phone?"

Meg pointed toward the kitchen. "I'll show you."

"We need to search the farm again." Jacob placed

his arm about Hannah's shoulder. "Anywhere she really liked?"

"The barn."

"Well, let's start there and fan out."

"How about us?" Susie came forward with the other children, unusually quiet, standing behind her.

"We'll get Cathy and Roman to organize the children and search both cottages, the unfinished one and the surrounding area. Susie, you can help Cathy with the kids in our house." Seeing terror on a couple of their faces, Hannah added, "Nancy will be found. She'll be all right."

"Let's go next door where Cathy and the others are waiting." Roman led the way with the children following.

"I'll have Alexa and Sean meet us at the barn. They can help us search that area." Laura left with Peter.

Hannah started forward. Jacob's hand on her shoulder stopped her. She glanced back at him, such kindness in his eyes that tears welled up in hers. He drew her to him.

"We will find her and she will be all right."

His whispered words, raw with suppressed emotions, fueled her tears. Forcing them down, she backed away from the comfort of his arms. "I don't have time to cry. We only have a few hours before it gets dark."

Two hours later Hannah paused near the creek that ran through the farm. Thankfully it wasn't deep, the bottom easily seen. She peered at Jacob downstream from her. Fifteen minutes ago he found Nancy's doll by a bush where it appeared the little girl had sat. With that they were now concentrating on this area. Nancy had to be near. Nightfall would be in another hour.

"Nancy," Hannah shouted for the hundredth time, her voice raw. She heard the child's name from the others intermittently.

Hannah forged forward into the thicker underbrush, so glad it was too cold for snakes. But there were other animals that could do harm to a small child. Thinking about that possibility, she again yelled the girl's name and heard the frantic ring in her voice.

Only silence greeted her.

Her shoulders sagged as the minutes ticked away. She pushed farther into the wooded area, sending up another prayer for Nancy's safe return.

In the distance she saw a glimpse of pink. Hannah squinted and picked up her pace, although it was slower than usual because of the dense foliage.

"Nancy."

A sound caused her to stop and listen.

The breeze whistled through the forest. Disappointment cloaked her. *Just the wind.*

She continued toward the pink. The little girl's blanket was that color. "Nancy."

Another noise froze Hannah.

A whimper?

"Nancy, honey, where are you?"

Hannah kept moving forward, straining to hear anything unusual, trying to be as quiet as she could so she could listen.

"Hannah," a faint voice, full of tears, floated to her. From the direction of the pink.

"I'm coming."

Hannah tore through the brush, bare limbs clawing

her. A branch scratched across her cheek. She fumbled for her cell in her pocket to alert the others she'd found Nancy. She hoped.

"Nancy, say something."

"I'm hurt."

The nearer she got to the pink the stronger the voice. She reached the blanket, but Nancy was nowhere to be seen.

"Honey, where are you? I don't see you."

"I'm down here."

Hannah stepped to the side several yards from the discarded blanket and looked down an incline. At the bottom lay Nancy with the puppy cuddled next to her, a ball of white fur.

"I see you. I'll be right there." Hannah flipped open her phone and punched in Jacob's number.

After giving him directions to where she thought she was, she started down the hill, half sliding as it got steeper toward the bottom. With a tearstained face, Nancy struggled to sit up and watched Hannah's descent. Abby began to yelp and prance around in circles.

When she reached the child, Nancy threw herself into Hannah's arms, sobbing. "You're okay now, honey."

She stroked the child's back, whispering she was safe over and over until Nancy finally calmed down and leaned back.

"Abby ran away from me. I went after her and fell down here. My ankle hurts bad." Tears shone in the child's eyes. "I tried to climb up the hill. I couldn't."

Hannah heard her name being called. "Jacob, we're down here. Nancy's hurt."

"I'm coming. I see her blanket."

The most wonderful thing Hannah saw was Jacob's

face peering over the top of the steep incline. "She fell. I think she did something to her ankle."

Jacob descended as gracefully as she did, speed more important than caution. "I called the others. They're coming." He knelt next to them, his gaze tracking down the child's length. "Which ankle hurts?"

Nancy pointed to her left one.

Jacob tenderly took her leg into his hands and probed the area. "I don't think it's broken. Probably a sprain. We'll have to get an X-ray to be sure."

"I don't want a shot. I don't want a shot!" Nancy's voice rose to a hysterical level.

Hannah hugged her to her chest. "Honey, don't worry about that. You need to calm down so we can get you back to the cottage."

Nancy straightened, wiping her eyes. "Where's Abby?" She scanned the surrounding terrain. "She's gone again!"

Jacob reached behind him and picked up the puppy. "She's right here, investigating a twig."

"Oh, good." Nancy sank against Hannah, grasping her as if she were a lifeline.

Hannah's gaze coupled with Jacob's. Everything would be fine now. He would take care of Nancy.

And he could take care of you.

The thought astonished Hannah. She looked away. Her feelings for Jacob were more than friendship.

"You aren't mad at me?" Nancy snuggled under her covers with her doll tucked next to her.

Hannah smoothed the girl's bangs to the side. "No. I think you realize how dangerous it can be to wander off by yourself, especially when no one knows where you are."

"I thought I could take Abby for a walk. I thought if you saw how good I can take care of her, you'd let me keep her."

"That's a decision we'll all make at the family meeting tomorrow night. There's a cat Susie would like, and Gabe wants one of Abby's brothers."

"That's great! Abby won't be alone. She'll have playmates."

"No, it isn't great. We can't have a house full of children *and* pets."

"Why not?"

"Well…" Hannah couldn't come up with a reason Nancy would understand. The little girl wouldn't accept the answer that a lot of animals running around wouldn't work. All of a sudden Hannah wasn't looking forward to the family meeting tomorrow night.

"How's your ankle?"

Nancy plucked at her coverlet. "It still hurts a little."

Hannah leaned down and kissed the child's forehead. "Thankfully it wasn't broken. You should be better in a week or so."

"Yeah, Dr. Jacob told me that. I like him."

So do I. "Good night." Hannah rose, tucked Nancy's roommate in, then quietly made her way to the door.

In the hallway she heard Jacob talking to Andy and Gabe. Earlier he'd rounded up the boys and got them ready for bed while she had taken care of the girls. As though they were a team—a family.

Hannah crossed the large living room to the picture window and stared at the darkness beyond. In the distance she saw the lights of Peter and Laura's house. Life was back to normal.

Who was she kidding?

There was nothing normal about her life at the moment. She'd discovered today she was falling in love with an enemy of her family—the man who was responsible for her brother's death.

Among all the feelings tumbling around in her mind, guilt dominated. What would her mother say if she ever found out? Mom hadn't mentioned Jacob Hartman in years, but Hannah could just imagine what her reaction would be.

Hannah shivered as if the cold weather that had swooped down on Cimarron City in the past few hours had oozed into the cottage, into her bones.

This was one problem she'd never thought she would have. How could they overcome the history between them. They both deserved a family—but together?

A sound of footsteps behind her warned her she wasn't alone. In the pane she glimpsed Jacob approaching. She tensed. Then she caught sight of his smile and melted, all stress flowing from her.

He grasped her upper arms and pulled her back against him. "For the time being all's quiet on the home front."

The use of the word *home* in connection with Jacob sent a yearning through her she hadn't thought possible where he was concerned. He had so much to offer a woman.

But how could she be that woman?

His breath washed over her as he nibbled on the skin right below her ear, undermining all the defenses she was desperately trying to erect against him.

"After the day we had with Nancy's disappearance and our vigorous bike ride, I should be exhausted. But I'm not. I'm wide-awake."

How could this man affect her with that husky appeal in his voice? When had her feelings for him changed? The moment she had forgiven him? Or before?

He rubbed his hands up and down her arms. "Cold?"

The humor in his question told her he knew exactly the effect he was having on her every sense. Goose bumps zipped through her, and if he hadn't been holding her up, she would have collapsed against him. "It's dropped at least twenty degrees in the last hour."

"Outside. Not in here."

He swept her around so she faced him, only inches from her. "I don't think it's going to snow."

Why was he talking about the weather when his mouth was a whisper away from hers? She balled her hands to keep from dragging his lips to hers. "If it does, it won't stick. The ground's too warm." And now she was discussing weather!

"Yes, too warm," he murmured right before settling his lips on hers.

As her arms wound about him, he pressed her close. She soared above the storm, high in the sky. Nothing was important but this man in her embrace.

When he finally drew back slightly, their ragged breaths tangled, the scent of peppermint teasing her. She would never look at a piece of that candy and not remember his kiss.

"I'd better go. It's been a long day, and I have to be at church early tomorrow." His fingers delved into her curls, his gaze penetrating into hers.

"Yes, I'm helping out in the nursery tomorrow, so I need to get everyone moving earlier than usual."

"You want me to come to the family meeting in the evening?"

She nodded, aware of his hands still framing her face as though leaving his imprint on her. "I'm new at the family-meeting stuff so I may need your help to get it right."

"Say that again." His mouth quirked into a lopsided grin.

She playfully punched his arm. "You heard me."

"Yes, but I like hearing you say you might need my help to get it right. I may never hear that again from your lips." The second he said the word *lips* his gaze zeroed in on hers.

She tingled as though his mouth still covered hers. When he lifted his regard to her eyes, a softness entered his that nearly undid her. In that moment she felt so feminine and cherished.

Pulling completely away, Jacob swallowed hard. "Seriously I'll help you anytime you need it. Just ask."

"I know." Bereft without him near, she meant every word. He was a good, kind man who had made a mistake when he was young. She realized that she could forget the past now in addition to forgiving him. Peace blanketed her in an indescribable feeling, underscoring the rightness of what she was doing.

He backed farther away. "I can find my own way out. See you tomorrow."

She watched him stride out of the room. Turning back to the window, she glimpsed him descend the porch steps and make his way to his car.

Tomorrow she needed to go to her brother's grave

and put an end to any lingering guilt. And tonight she needed to call her mother and tell her about Jacob Hartman's involvement in the refuge. She wanted to move on with her life.

Hannah made her way to her room and sat on her bed, reaching for the phone on the table nearby. Her hand quivered as she lifted the receiver and punched in her mother's number. She hadn't really talked to her in over a month. On Thanksgiving, her mother had been working and hadn't stayed on the phone for more than a minute.

"Mom, how's everything going?" Hannah asked when her mother picked up.

"Busy. Busy. You know how this time of year people seem to get sicker. My floor at the hospital has been packed this past week."

"I'm sorry to hear that." Her palms sweaty, Hannah shifted the receiver to the other ear. She didn't know how to tell her mother about Jacob. This was really something she needed to do in person. She thought about ending the conversation quickly and waiting until she could see her.

"It's late, honey. Is something wrong?"

Yes, I'm falling in love with a man you hate. "Since I didn't get to talk to you for long on Thanksgiving, I thought I would check in and see how things were going."

"Hannah, what are you not telling me? Something's wrong. I hear it in your voice."

Chewing on her lip, Hannah wiped one of her palms on her slacks. "Are you coming to see me at Christmas?"

There was a long pause, then her mother answered,

"I don't know. It will depend on when I have to work. Why?"

"Because I want to see you." *Because I'm stalling.* She rubbed the other hand down her thigh. "Jacob Hartman is a doctor who lives in Cimarron City." Before she lost her nerve, she rushed on, "He's the doctor for the refuge, so I've seen him quite a bit."

"Jacob Hartman, the boy who killed Kevin?"

"Yes, Mom. I—"

"I can't believe it. I—" Her mother's voice roughened. "I—I…"

The line went dead. Hannah stared at the receiver for a few seconds, then called her mother back. She let it ring fifteen times before she finally hung up. She hadn't handled it well. She should have waited until she'd seen her mother. This news was the kind that should be given to someone face-to-face, the news that she was falling in love with the enemy.

After quizzing the groundskeeper about who was putting flowers at her brother's grave, Hannah hiked across the cemetery, enjoying the cold, crisp day. Several inches of snow had fallen overnight, but the place looked tranquil, as though the world was at peace. The quiet soothed her, especially after the night spent tossing and turning, going over and over in her head the abrupt conversation she'd had with her mother.

Near her brother's grave site, she saw a car—Jacob's new one. Since the groundskeeper had told her Dr. Hartman came once a week to change the flowers, she wasn't really surprised to see him. She stopped by a large oak and waited for him to leave.

She didn't want him to see her. The night before she had come to a decision. She needed to tell Jacob who she was, but she wanted to pick the right moment. This wasn't it. She hadn't prepared what to say to him. And because it was so important she had to consider carefully how she told him she was Kevin's younger sister, especially after messing up the phone conversation with her mother the night before.

After removing the old flowers, Jacob filled the vase with the new ones, paused for a moment, his head bowed, then pivoted away and sloshed to his car.

She waited until it had disappeared from view before she trudged to her brother's tombstone. The bright red roses, stark against the white blanket of snow, were silk. She stooped to finger the petals.

"Kevin, where do I begin?" She fortified herself with a deep gulp of the chilly air. "For so many years I was mad at Jacob Hartman for taking you away from us. I believed he had gone on with his life as though nothing had happened, living happily and unaffected by the wreck. Now I don't think that."

She reached out and traced her brother's name, chiseled in the cold marble. The dates carved into the stone were a permanent reminder of his death at a young age. She rose.

"The groundskeeper said he comes every week. That isn't the action of a man who has moved on. Occasionally I've caught a vulnerability in him that has stunned me. He's good at hiding it, but it's there. Is it a coincidence he became a doctor? Was it because he wanted to or because that had been your dream?"

Her throat closed around her last word. The cold burrowed into her. She hugged her coat to her. "I think the Lord brought me back to Cimarron City to help Jacob. It was time to let go of my anger and forgive Jacob. I have. For the longest time I'd forgotten what kind of person you were. You would have wanted me to forgive him long ago. Better late than never." She smiled. "You know how stubborn I can be."

Hannah touched the tombstone again, comforted by her visits to Kevin's grave. Was Jacob? She hoped so because after twenty-one years she finally felt she had said her goodbyes to her brother and he didn't blame her for telling on him that last day. Kevin had never held a grudge; she had forgotten that. "I love you. I love him. I will find a way to help him heal, and I will make Mom understand. I know that's what you would want me to do."

"I like your new old car," Hannah said as she took a bite of her pepperoni pizza early Wednesday afternoon. "How come you didn't get a brand-new one? I thought you would after that piece of jun—"

"Hold it right there," Jacob interrupted her. "You're speaking about a vehicle that served me well for years."

"And years."

His chuckles vied with the lunch crowd noise in the restaurant. "Okay. I get the point. It was an old rattle-trap."

"There. That wasn't too hard to admit, was it?"

He snagged her look. "Yes. I thought I was being frugal."

"Is that why you didn't buy a new one?"

"It's hard to break a habit. I've been so used to saving to pay off my loans that I just automatically do it."

"You've got to enjoy some of the fruits of your hard work. Have a little fun."

"Are you telling me I don't know how to have fun?"

"Well, no, not exactly, but what do you do for fun?"

"Bicycling?"

"That's recent."

"Let me see." He peered up at the ceiling and tapped his finger against his chin.

"Just as I suspected. You work too much and play too little."

A twinkle glinted in his dark eyes. "And what do you suggest I do about that?"

"Why, of course, play more. I think you should join us in decorating the cottage for Christmas."

"Sounds like work to me." Jacob finished the last slice of pizza.

"Decorating is fun."

"You're a woman."

"I'm glad you noticed," Hannah said with a laugh.

"It's in your genes."

"The kids wanted me to ask you."

"Oh, in that case I'll be there. What time?"

"Hold it right there. I think I'm offended. You wouldn't come when I asked, but I say something about the children and you're wanting to know what time to be there." She exaggerated a pout.

"I was going to come. I was just playing with you. Didn't you tell me I needed to play more?"

The mischief in his gaze riveted her. "I do believe you might be easy to train—I mean, teach."

His laughter filled the space between them, linking them in a shared moment. All of sudden the noise, the crowd faded from her awareness as she stared at Jacob, relaxed, almost carefree.

"Hannah, Dr. Hartman, it's good to see you two."

Reluctantly, Hannah looked away from Jacob. "It's nice seeing you, Lisa. How's the job?" Lisa had been the reason she had insisted on coming to the Pizzeria to eat before they went to see Nancy's mother.

"It's only my third day, but I like it. I saw ya from the back and wanted to say hi."

Jacob wiped his mouth with the paper napkin. "Noah told me he hired you to fill in where needed."

"Yeah, I'm learnin' all the jobs." She squared her shoulders, standing a little taller. "There's quite a few I hafta learn, but I can do it."

"Great! I was just asking Jacob to come out on Saturday afternoon to help decorate the cottage for Christmas. If you aren't working, I'd love for you to join us, too."

"I hafta be here at five that evening."

"I can bring you back into town in time for your shift." Jacob picked up the check. "And I'll give you a ride to the farm. I can pick you up at one on Saturday."

"I'll be ready." Lisa glanced back at the counter. "I'd better get back to work."

"I know how you feel about Lisa being in Andy's life. That was so sweet of you," Hannah said around the lump in her throat.

"Believe it or not, I would love for this to work out for Lisa and Andy."

"But you still don't think it will?"

"I just don't see it through rose-colored glasses."

"And I do?"

He looked her directly in the eye. "Yes, and I'm afraid you'll be hurt when it doesn't work out."

Hannah rose. "I'm not wrong about Lisa. Did you see her at church on Sunday?"

"She was like a deer caught in headlights."

"I realize it was all new to her. But God has His ways." She could still remember when she'd pledged her heart to the Lord. The transformation, a work in progress, was life altering.

Jacob removed his wallet and laid some money on the table. "Only time will tell." At the door he held it open for her. "C'mon, let's get this over with."

"I know Nancy's mother is a long shot, but I've got to try."

"Are you going to do this with every situation?"

She slid into the passenger seat in his car. "I will examine and evaluate every one to see if there's a way."

He gave her a skeptical look as he started the engine. "I hope you don't end up with your heart broken."

She was beginning to realize he was the only one who could do that. "Don't worry about me."

"But I do."

"That's sweet, but I'm tough."

"Yeah, right. You're like Nancy. You wear your heart on your sleeve."

She shifted, sitting up straight. "There's nothing wrong with that."

"As long as things work out."

"Like at the family meeting Sunday night?"

"Exactly." Jacob turned onto the highway that led to Deerfield. "You're blessed with the fact the kids in the cottage care about each other."

Hannah remembered the happiness on Nancy's face

when the children voted for Abby to be their pet. "Like a family."

"Not any family I've been in."

The vulnerability, always below the surface, trickled into his words and pricked her heart.

Chapter Ten

Jacob pulled onto the dirt road. "I don't like the looks of this."

Hannah scanned the yard of the address she had for Nancy's mother. Trash littered the porch and literally poured out of a refrigerator without its door. Two old cars in various stages of rusting decomposition flanked the detached garage. The structure leaned to the side, threatening to crash down on the vehicle minus its engine.

"I'm glad you came with me." Hannah pushed her purse under the seat.

"Are you sure you want to do this? We can always leave." Jacob parked in front but left the engine running.

She studied the dirty windows facing them and thought she saw someone looking out. The curtain fell back in place. "No, we came this far. I need to finish this."

"No, you don't."

"Haven't you noticed how reserved and hesitant Nancy is when Andy's mother is visiting? When I try to talk to her, she won't say anything. She sucks her thumb and holds her blanket."

"As much as you'd love to fix every relationship between the children at the refuge and their parents, you won't be able to. Not every mother has maternal instincts."

"Like yours?"

"Exactly." A nerve ticked in his jaw. "I'm glad no one tried."

"You need to forgive your mother," she said, knowing firsthand how important it was to do that if you wanted to move on.

His hard gaze drilled into her, his hands gripping the steering wheel so tight his knuckles were white. "Why would I want to do that?"

"Because she's still affecting your life and will until you let go of the anger."

"I don't think I can. The things she did…"

"The Lord said in Matthew, 'For if ye forgive men their trespasses, your heavenly Father will also forgive you.'"

"I can't. I…" His voice came to a shaky halt. He drew in a breath and stared at the small house. "Someone's opening the door. Let's get this over with."

The finality in his tone ended the conversation. Hannah climbed from the car at the same time Jacob did, his expression totally void of any emotion. But waves of underlying tension came off him as he approached the house.

A woman in her midtwenties, dressed in torn, ragged jeans and a sweatshirt pushed the screen open and stepped out onto the porch. "We don't want any. Git off my land."

A medium-sized man with a beard appeared in the entrance. Hannah's gaze fixed upon the shotgun cradled in his arms, then bounced to his face, set in a scowl that chilled her.

"Ya heard her. Git. Now." The man gestured with a nod toward the road behind Jacob and Hannah.

Jacob edged to her side and grasped her hand. "Let's do as they say."

Hannah started to move back toward the passenger door when she remembered finding Nancy crying last weekend for her mama. The sight had wrenched her heart. She halted. "Are you Abby Simons?"

The woman stiffened, still between them and the man behind her. "Who's askin'?"

A stench—a myriad of odors she couldn't even begin to identify—accosted Hannah's nostrils. "I'm Hannah Smith. I run the place that Nancy is at."

"So? What's she gone and done wrong now?" Abby planted one hand on her hip, her eyes pinpoints.

"Nothing. She's a delight to have at the house."

Abby snorted. "That's your opinion. I have nothin' to say to ya." She turned to go back inside.

"You don't want to see her?" Her stomach roiled. Hannah resisted the urge to cover her mouth and nose to block the smells coming from the house and the couple.

A curse exploded from the woman's lips. "I say good riddance. All she did was whine." She shoved past the man with the weapon.

He glared at Jacob and Hannah. "What's keepin' ya?" He adjusted the gun in the crook of his arms.

Jacob squeezed her hand and tugged her back. "We're going." He jerked open the passenger door and gently pushed Hannah into the car, then rounded the back and climbed in behind the wheel, his gaze never leaving the man holding the weapon.

Fifteen seconds later dust billowed behind his car as he raced toward the highway. He threw her a look of relief. "We could have been killed. I think they're running a meth lab."

"You do?"

"You didn't smell it?"

"I don't know how one smells."

"When we get back to Stone's Refuge, I'm calling the sheriff, although I doubt there will be any evidence left when he arrives." Jacob pressed his foot on the accelerator.

Hannah waited for him to tell her he had told her so, but he didn't. Quiet reigned as the landscape flew past them.

She'd gone into social work to help others. But perhaps Jacob was right. She was too naive. She had a lot to learn. Even if Nancy was never adopted, she was better off where she was than with her mother.

"I was wrong," Hannah finally murmured in the silence.

"About Nancy, yes. The verdict on Andy's situation is still out."

"You think there's a chance it will work?" At the moment she needed validation she wasn't totally off-the-wall about trying to reunite children with their parents, if possible.

He slanted a quick look toward her, warmth in his eyes. "His mother completed her drug-rehab program. That's a start. As well as getting a job. She's living at the halfway house for the time being, and they're wonderful support for people who are trying to get back on their feet." His gaze found hers again. "Yes, I think there's a chance."

His words made her beam from ear to ear. She felt as though she were shining like a thousand-watt bulb.

"Time will tell and don't be surprised if Lisa backslides. I remember when I quit smoking. I must have tried four or five times before I finally managed to."

"You smoked?"

"Yeah. I started when I was thirteen. I finally stopped when I was eighteen. But it was one of the hardest things I ever did. And staying off drugs will be the hardest thing Lisa does."

"Did you have help?"

He nodded. "Alice and Paul Henderson."

"I'll be there for Lisa."

"*We'll* be there for her."

Like a team. More and more she felt they were.

"I'm glad Peter suggested we cut down one of the pines on his property to use as a tree this year. Until he married Laura, I didn't do much at Christmas other than participate in some of the church functions." Jacob led one of the horses across the snow-covered meadow.

"So you don't mind doing this?" Carrying the ax, Hannah checked around her to make sure the children were keeping up with them.

"Mind? No. It's a good reason to leave work a little early this afternoon."

"This from a man who works all the time!"

"It was a little slow with the snow last night and this morning. Not too many people wanted to get out unless it was an emergency. I noticed the snow fort and snow figures out in front of the cottages. You all were busy today."

She laughed. "We had to do something with the kids home from school. I had a hard time keeping them away from the unfinished house."

"I imagine the kids are intrigued with it."

"You can say that again. I'm glad you don't mind driving in this weather. I haven't had much practice in snow."

At the edge of a grove of pines Jacob stopped and surveyed the prospective Christmas trees. "Okay, guys, which one do you want me to cut down?"

Every child with Jacob and Hannah pointed at a different one. Nancy selected a pine that was at least fifteen feet tall.

Hannah set her hands on the little girl's shoulders. "I like your vision, but that one won't fit into the living room." Then to the whole group she added, "We need a tree that is about six or seven feet tall."

"How about this?" Susie pointed to one near her.

"No, this is better." Andy went to stand by a pine off to the side.

While Terry started toward another, Hannah quickly said, "Hold it. Let's take a vote on these three. They're the only ones the right size." She waved her hand toward Susie's and two others.

Andy spun toward his. "What's wrong with mine?"

"It needs to grow a few more years." Jacob took the ax from Hannah and gave her the reins of the horse.

"Who wants Susie's?" Hannah called out, the wind beginning to pick up.

All the children raised their hands with Andy reluctantly the last one.

"Well, let's get the show on the road." Jacob approached the chosen one and began to chop it down.

The sound of the ax striking the wood echoed through the grove. The smell of snow hung in the air as clouds rolled in.

Terry bent down and scooped up a handful of the white stuff and packed it into a ball, then lobbed it toward Susie. That was the beginning of a small war held at the edge of the grove.

Hannah scurried toward Jacob to avoid being hit. "Do you want a break?"

He glanced up at the sky. "Nope. Not much time. I think it'll start snowing again soon. When that happens, I'd rather be back at the cottage sipping hot chocolate in front of the fireplace."

"We don't have one."

He paused and stared at her with a look that went straight to her heart. "Then we'll just have to use our imaginations. You do have hot chocolate?"

"Of course, with eight children in the house that's a necessity."

"We have marshmallows, too." Nancy came up to stand next to Hannah while Jacob went back to work on the seven-foot tree.

"Mmm. I love marshmallows. I guess I'd better hurry if I want a cup."

A snowball whizzed by Hannah's head. She pivoted in the direction it came. Suddenly she noticed the quiet and the reason for it. All the children were lined up a few feet from her with ammunition in their hands.

"Duck," Hannah shouted, and pulled Nancy with her behind a tree.

Jacob, in midswing, couldn't react fast enough. A

barrage of snowballs pelted him from all angles. When he turned toward the crowd of kids, he was covered in white from head to toe. He shook off some of the powder, gave the ax to Hannah, then patiently walked a couple of feet toward the children with a huge grin on his face. The kids stood like frozen statues, not sure what to do.

Suddenly Jacob swooped down, made a ball and threw it before the first child could run. Another snowball ensued then several more after it. Kids scattered in all directions. Jacob shot to his feet and raced after the nearest boy, tackling Terry. As they playfully rolled on the ground, several boys joined them and it became a free-for-all.

Hannah, with Nancy beside her, watched by their chosen tree. The sound of laughter resonated through the meadow with the girls cheering on the boys in their endeavor to overpower Jacob. Although outnumbered, the good doctor was having the time of his life if the expression of joy on his face was any clue. She knew he wanted a family. He should be a father.

And you want a family. You want to be a mother. What are you doing about that?

When a snowflake fell, followed by several more, Hannah peered up at the sky. Another hit her cheek and instantly melted. She put two fingers into her mouth and let out a loud, shrill whistle that immediately called a halt to the melee on the ground.

"In case you don't know, it's snowing again. We need to cut down our tree and get back to the cottage. Playtime is over, boys."

Amidst a few grumbles Jacob pushed to his feet, drenched from his tumble in the snow. He shoved his

wet hair out of his eyes and strode to the ax Hannah
held out for him.

In five minutes he yelled, "Timber," and the tree
toppled to the ground. "I always wanted to do that."

Having tied the horse's reins to one of the branches
of a nearby pine, Hannah moved toward it, calling to
the children. "Help Dr. Jacob with our Christmas tree."

After quickly securing the pine with some rope,
Jacob guided the horse toward the cottage with their
tree gliding over the snow behind the animal. Snow
came down faster as they reached the porch.

"I'll take the horse back to the barn," Terry said when
Jacob untied the pine.

"Come right back. It'll be getting dark soon." Hannah helped Jacob drag the tree up the steps and placed
it to the side of the front door. "Who's up for hot chocolate?"

Hands flew into the air.

"While I'm fixing it, change out of those wet clothes
then come into the kitchen." Hannah opened the door
and went into the house.

Footsteps pounded down the hallway toward the various bedrooms.

"That'll give us a few minutes of quiet." Hannah's
gaze moved down Jacob's length. "I wish I had something for you to change into. Your jeans are soaking
wet."

He started to remove his coat, but stopped. "I've got
some sweats in my trunk. Can I use your bedroom to
change in?"

Her step faltered. "Sure," she answered, trying not
to imagine him in her room.

As he jogged to his car, she waved her hand in front

of her face and thought about turning down the heater. Memories of his kiss swamped her. She wanted him to kiss her again. Oh, my. She was in deep.

As she prepared the hot chocolate and a plate of cookies under the disapproving eye of Meg, the children flooded the kitchen. They snatched a mug and one cookie then fled the room, nearly knocking Jacob down in their haste.

"Whoa. What was that?" He entered as the last boy zipped past him.

"Those cookies are gonna spoil their dinner," Meg grumbled while she stirred a large pot on the stove.

"Mmm. Is that your stew?" Jacob took the last mug sitting on the counter.

Still frowning, Meg nodded.

"Then you don't have a worry. The kids love it. There won't be a drop left at the end of the meal, especially if a wonderful cook invites a certain doctor to dinner." Jacob winked at Hannah right before he took a sip of his drink.

"Not my call." The beginnings of a grin tempered Meg's unyielding expression as she swung her gaze from Jacob to Hannah.

He turned a pleading look on Hannah. "I worked up quite an appetite chopping down *your* tree."

She took a cookie off the plate. "Here. This ought to tide you over until you can eat."

His fingers grazed hers as he grasped the treat. "The important question is where will I be eating dinner?"

"Meg, we might as well make a permanent place for Jacob at our table as often as he's been here for dinner." The image of him at one end of the table and her at the other darted through her mind. Like a family—with eight children! She should be fleeing from the kitchen as quickly as the kids did moments before. What was she doing thinking of them as a family?

"I heartily agree. Meg's cooking is much better than mine."

Meg barked a laugh. "Your cooking is nonexistent."

"Not from lack of trying."

Meg swept around with one hand on her waist and a wooden spoon in the other. "When? You work way too hard. I'm glad to see you spending more time with the children."

"I think that's our cue to leave the chef alone to create her masterpiece." Jacob grabbed the last cookie, held the door for Hannah and accompanied her from the room with Meg muttering something about him eating everything on his plate or else.

"She's a treasure. You'd better not run her off," Hannah said in mock sternness.

"I want to know what 'or else' means." He headed toward the sound of children talking in the living room.

"You're a brave soul if you dare to leave anything uneaten."

Jacob blocked her path into the room. "I enjoyed this afternoon. Thank you for inviting me. Other than the birth of Christ, the holidays have never held much appeal to me."

"I have to admit Christmas has never been my favorite time of year." After Kevin died during December, she and her mother hadn't done much in the way of enjoying themselves during the holidays. In fact, they had ignored it until they had become Christians.

"Shh. Don't let the kids hear you say that."

"That's why we'll be going all-out this Christmas here at the house and at church."

"I'd love to help you with your activities." His gaze captured hers.

Her pulse rate spiked. "I'm glad you volunteered. Next weekend we're going to the nursing home to perform the Nativity scene. Roman can't come because of a prior commitment, but we're taking some of the animals to make the play more authentic and I could use an extra pair of hands beside Peter."

"How many animals?"

"Two lambs for the shepherds. A couple of dogs. Maybe a rabbit or two."

"I don't remember there being any dogs or rabbits in the manger."

"We thought we would dress up two of the big dogs as though they're donkeys."

Jacob tossed back his head and laughed. "I'm sure they'll love that. This production could be priceless."

"Hey, just for that, you can help with the rehearsals, too. Every night after dinner this week. We aren't nearly ready."

He wiped tears from the corner of his eyes. "Definitely priceless."

"Be careful. That box has all the ornaments in it." Hannah hurried over to help Susie carry the oversized one to the living room where Jacob and Terry were setting up the Christmas tree in its stand on Saturday afternoon.

The scent of popcorn wafted through the large cottage. Meg came out of the kitchen with two big bowls of the snack. She placed both of them on the game table. "One is for stringing. The other for eating."

A couple of the kids dived into the one for consumption, in their haste causing some of the popped kernels to fall onto the floor. Abby pounced on it.

Hannah scooped the puppy up and gave her to Nancy. "There's enough for everyone." Hannah moved the one for stringing over to the coffee table where some of the younger children sat. "Nancy, you might put Abby in the utility room until we're done."

Meg settled on the couch behind the kids working with the popcorn to assist them while Hannah opened the box with strands of twinkling white lights.

She pulled the tangled mess out and held it up, "What happened here?"

"Peter. Last year he took them down and made a mess out of them." Meg gave Nancy who had returned without Abby a needle with a long string attached.

"Remind me not to accept his help this year with taking down the tree." Hannah sat cross-legged on the floor and searched for one end of the strand. "How many are here?"

"Four." Meg scooted over for Nancy to sit next to her while she worked on the popcorn garland.

"Maybe I should just go to town and buy new ones." Jacob squatted next to her.

"No. No, I'll figure this out. No sense in wasting money."

Fifteen minutes later Hannah finally untangled one strand completely and was on her way to freeing another.

Jacob bent down and whispered in her ear, "Ready to call uncle."

"No way. Here's one. By the time you've got it up, I should have the second string ready."

The doubtful look Jacob sent her as he rose fueled Hannah's determination, but the puppy's yelps from the utility room rubbed her nerves raw, pulling her full attention away from her task. "Nancy, please check on Abby."

Hannah had almost finished with the second strand when Abby came barreling into the room and raced toward her. The white puppy leaped into her lap, licking her face, her body wiggling so much it threw Hannah off balance.

"Nancy!" Hannah fell back with Abby on her chest now, one hand caught in the snarl of lights.

The little girl charged into the room. "Sorry. She got away from me." She pulled the puppy off Hannah.

Jacob offered her his hand, a gleam glittering in his eyes. When she clasped it, he tugged her up. "Okay?"

"Sure. Abby just gets a little enthusiastic. Laura's teenage son is going to help us with her." Hannah glanced down at the lights and groaned. The second string was twisted in with the other two.

"Uncle?"

She picked up the snarl. "Uncle."

"Let me see what I can do before ya head into town." Lisa sat next to Hannah. "I'm good at stuff like this."

Ten minutes later the lights were ready to go. Hannah purposely ignored the merriment dancing in Jacob's eyes. She corralled the remaining children who weren't working on the popcorn garlands.

"Let's get the ornaments out, so when the lights are up, we'll be ready to put them on the tree."

Three kids fought to open the box. With two fingers

in her mouth, Hannah whistled, startling them. They shot up with arms straight at their sides.

She waved her hand. "Shoo. I'll unpack them and give them to y'all. Lisa, want to help me?"

Andy's mother nodded.

"There. We're done with our part." Jacob stood back from the pine and gave Terry a signal to plug the lights in.

Nancy leaped to her feet, clapping her hands. "It's beautiful."

"Yes, it is. Just wait until the ornaments are on it. It'll be even better." Hannah peered toward Jacob who plopped into the lounge chair nearby. "And don't think your job is done. Look at this huge box of decorations."

Jacob shoved himself up. "Kids, remind me to find out what my duties are before volunteering next time."

A couple of the children giggled, setting the mood for the next two hours while everyone worked, first decorating the tree, then the rest of the house. Andy rode with Jacob to take Lisa to work. When they returned, Jacob brought large pizzas for dinner.

By the time the cottage quieted with the kids tucked into bed, exhaustion clung to Hannah, her muscles protesting her every move. "Getting ready for Christmas is tiring work." She collapsed on the couch in the living room.

"I know you may be shocked, but I have to agree with you." Jacob gestured around him at the myriad of decorations in every conceivable place. "Where did all this come from?"

"From what Laura told me, most of it was donated."

He picked up a two-foot-high flamingo with a Santa

hat on its head and a wreath around its neck. "What's a flamingo have to do with Christmas?"

She shrugged. "Beats me, but it's kinda cute. Nancy sure liked it."

"She liked everything. We couldn't put it out fast enough for her."

"She's never had Christmas before. She told me her mother didn't believe in the Lord."

"Now, why doesn't that surprise me." Jacob eased down next to Hannah on the couch, grimacing as he leaned back. "After yesterday and today, I think I'll rest tomorrow."

"I think Terry said something about needing your help to build the manger Sunday afternoon."

Jacob's forehead furrowed. "And when were you going to tell me that?"

"Tomorrow when you came to help with the rehearsal."

His mouth twisted into a grim line that his sparkling eyes negated. He tried glaring at Hannah, but laughter welled up in him. He lay his head on the back cushion. "I haven't enjoyed myself like that in…" He slanted his gaze toward her. "Actually today has been great. Thank you again for including me."

The wistfulness in his voice produced an ache in her throat. "It was fun."

"It's what I think of a family doing during the holidays. The only time I had anything similar was when I lived with Paul and Alice. For three years I was part of something good." A faraway look appeared in his eyes as he averted his head and stared up at the ceiling.

Hannah dug her fingernails into her palms to keep from smoothing the lines from his forehead. She felt as though he had journeyed back in time to a past that held bad memories.

"That first Christmas with the Hendersons I was determined to stay in my room and have nothing to do with any celebration."

"Why?"

"Because in December the year before, I had killed a friend."

Chapter Eleven

Hearing Jacob say he'd killed her brother out loud tore open the healing wound. A band about Hannah's chest squeezed tight, whooshing the air from her lungs. Her mind raced back twenty-one years to the day she'd been told Kevin died in a car wreck. She heard her mother's screams then her cries all over again.

"I've shocked you, Hannah. I'm sorry. I shouldn't have said anything but…" He looked away, his jaw locked in a hard line.

His apology pulled her back to the present. She managed to shut down all memories and focus on Jacob next to her on the couch. "But what?" There was no force behind the words, and for a few seconds she wondered if he even was aware she had spoken.

When his gaze swept back to hers, the anguish in his was palpable, as if it were a physical thing she could touch. "Over the past month we've been getting closer. We've spent a lot of time together." His eyelids slid halfway closed, shielding some of his turmoil from her. "I'm not sure where this…relationship is going, but I felt you needed to know."

"What happened?" She knew one side of the story, if she could even call it that. She needed to hear his side.

"It happened twenty-one years ago, but I'll never forget that day. Ever." He reestablished eye contact with her, a bleakness in his expression now. "Kevin borrowed his parents' car one night, and we went riding. We were bored, and he wanted to practice driving. Because we were fourteen, we drove in the country so no one would catch us. After he drove for a while, he let me get behind the wheel and try my hand. Everything was going along fine until…" Jacob pressed his lips together and closed his eyes.

"Until?" Hannah covered his hand with hers, his cold fingers mirroring hers.

Sucking in a deep breath, he looked directly at her and said, "Until I lost control of the car when it hit a patch of black ice. My friend didn't put on his seat belt when we changed places, and he was thrown from the car."

Her own pain jammed her throat like a fist. It was an effort even to swallow. "What happened to you?" She'd known little about what injuries he had sustained in the wreck.

"I had a concussion, some cuts and bruises, but otherwise I was okay—physically. But after that night, nothing was the same for me. At the time I didn't believe in the Lord and had nowhere to turn." Leaning forward, he propped his elbows on his knees and buried his face in his palms.

Her heartbeat roared in her ears. She reached out to lay a quivering hand on his hunched back, stopped midway there and withdrew it. Words evaded her because she was trying to imagine dealing with something like that alone, without the Lord. He'd only been fourteen. A maelstrom of emotions must have overwhelmed him.

"How long before you went to the Hendersons to live?"

He scrubbed his hands down his face. "Too long. A year."

All the agony of that year was wrapped up in his reply. This time she touched him.

"I still have nightmares about the accident."

Her heart plummeted. All these years she had thought she and her family had been the only ones who had suffered. She'd been wrong—very wrong. "It was an *accident,* Jacob."

"Do you know one of the reasons I wanted to be a doctor? Kevin did. That's all he'd talked about."

Beneath her palm she felt him quake.

"I became a doctor. I tried to make up for my mistake, but there's always a part of me that remembers I took a life." Another tremor passed through his body. "I'll never forget Kevin's mother at the hospital. If I could have traded places with him, I would have."

Tell him who you are, Hannah thought. *No! I can't add to his pain. Not now.*

"I'm so sorry, Jacob. So sorry."

He shoved to his feet. "I'm not the one to feel sorry for. I survived."

His rising tone didn't match the despair on his face. "Yes, you survived. I thank God that at least one of you did. Your death would have deprived these children of a wonderful, caring doctor."

"You don't understand." Jacob flexed his hands at his sides. "These past few weeks with you I've been truly happy for the first time in my life. I don't deserve to be."

She rose. "Why not? How will you living a miserable life change the outcome of the wreck?"

He started to say something but snapped his mouth closed and stared off into space.

"Why are you telling me this now?"

"I thought we could date, get to know each other better, but I don't think we should now."

"Because you are happy with me?"

"Yes! These past two days getting the cottage ready for the holidays has shown me what Christmas can be like, what it would be like to have a family."

"How long do you have to suffer before it's enough?"

He plowed his hand through his hair, the tic in his jaw twitching.

"When will it be enough?"

"I don't know," Jacob shouted, then spun around on his heel and stalked to the front door. She sank down on the couch, her whole body shaking with the storm of emotions that had swept through the room. She couldn't forget that Jacob had opened his heart to her. She had to do the same. She would pray for guidance and tell him tomorrow after church.

Hannah stood at the window, watching Jacob help Terry, Gabe and Andy build a manger for the play. The sound of laughter and hammering pounded at her resolve to find some time to be alone with Jacob and tell him who she was. He'd avoided her after church, and by the time she'd gathered all the children together, he was gone. Even when he'd come an hour ago, he'd spent little time with her, as if he'd regretted sharing something so personal with her the night before.

He lived in a self-made prison, and she was determined to free him. This was why the Lord had brought her to Cimarron City, to Stone's Refuge—to heal Jacob, a good man who had made a mistake when he was a teen.

His eyes crinkling in laughter, Jacob tousled Andy's hair. The boy giggled then launched himself at Jacob, throwing his arms around his middle. The scene brought tears to Hannah. The only time today she'd seen him relax and let down his guard was with the children.

Hannah pivoted away from the window and froze when she saw Nancy in the middle of the room, watching her with her thumb in her mouth and her doll cradled against her chest. Hannah quickly swiped away her tears. "Hi, Nancy. Have you got your costume finished for the play?"

The little girl shook her head, plucking her thumb from her mouth. "Susie said she heard you talking to Meg about visiting my mother. Susie thinks you want to get me together with her like you did Andy and his mother." Terror inched into the child's expression. "Is Mommy coming to get me?"

"No, honey."

Nancy heaved a sigh. "Good. She isn't nice like ya and Andy's mother." The little girl held up her doll. "Can we use Annie for baby Jesus?"

"Yes," Hannah murmured, relieved to see the child's terror gone from her eyes.

The child beamed. "I told Annie she could be. No one will know she's a girl."

"We'll wrap Annie in swaddling and all that will show is her face. She'll fit perfectly in the manger." Hannah gestured toward the boys in the court finishing up with the cradle.

"I'm gonna try Annie in it." Nancy raced toward the sliding-glass door that led outside.

"Hannah!"

Out of the corner of her eye she noticed Nancy carefully lay her doll into the manger. At the sound of her name being shouted again, she turned from the window as Susie came into the living room.

"I can't get this to work." The girl dropped her arms and the white sheet slid off one shoulder. "Can you help me with my costume?"

"Sure. This won't be hard to fix." Whereas she wasn't sure about her relationship with Jacob.

"Jacob, you aren't going to stay for dinner?" Hannah moved out onto the porch that evening and closed the front door behind her so the children couldn't listen.

He stopped on the top step and faced her. "It's been a long day. I have a busy week ahead of me."

He'd made sure they hadn't had a minute alone to talk. She wasn't going to let him flee, not after working up her courage to tell him everything so there were no secrets between them. "I need to talk to you."

He stiffened. "Can we another time?"

"No."

He glanced around him as though searching for a way to escape. When he directed his gaze back to her, resignation registered on his face but he remained silent.

She pointed toward the porch swing. "Let's sit down."

He strode to it and settled at one end. Hannah sank down next to him. He tensed.

"This is about what I told you last night."

The monotone inflection of his voice chilled her.

She hugged her arms to her and shored up her determination. "Yes."

She tried to remember what she had planned to say, but suddenly there was nothing in her mind except a panicky feeling she was wrong, that she should remain quiet. That she would only add to his pain.

"I understand if you don't want to see me."

"Is that why you told me?" She twisted toward him so she could look into his eyes. With night quickly approaching it was becoming harder to read his expression.

"I—I'm not sure what you mean."

"It's simple. Did you tell me about your past to drive me away?"

"You have a right to know."

"Why?" A long moment of silence eroded her resolve.

She started to say he didn't have to answer her when he said, "Because I'm falling in love with you and…"

His declaration sent her heartbeat galloping. "And?"

"Isn't that enough?" He bolted to his feet and took a step forward.

She grabbed his hand and held him still. "Don't leave after telling me that."

He whirled around, shaking loose her hold. "Don't you see, Hannah? I carry a lot of baggage. That's why I don't think it's a good idea for us to become involved."

She tried to look into his eyes, but the shadows shaded them. "We all do. Please sit."

"I can't ask someone to share that."

"Why not? It's in the past. Over twenty years ago."

"I've tried to forget. I can't. I'll never be able to."

"Forget or forgive?" She stood, cutting the space between them.

"Both! My carelessness led to another's death. That may be easy for someone else to dismiss, but not me."

She desperately wanted to take him into her arms and hold him until she could erase all memories of that night twenty-one years ago—from both their memories. But the tension flowing off him was as effective as a high, foot-thick wall—insurmountable and impregnable.

"Earlier you said you're falling in love with me. That's how I feel about you."

"How —"

She placed her fingers over his mouth to still his words. "No, let me finish."

The tension continued to vibrate between them, but he nodded.

She lowered her hand and took hold of his. There was no easy way to say this to him. "I need to tell you who I am. Before I married, my maiden name was Collins. I was Kevin's little sister."

Several heartbeats hammered against her chest before Jacob reacted to her news. He yanked his hand from hers and scrambled back, shaking his head. "You can't be."

"I am. I was eight when Kevin died in the car wreck. My parents split not long after the accident and Mom and I moved away. Actually we spent many years running away."

"What kind of game are you playing?"

"I'm not playing a game."

"I killed your brother! Why are you even talking to me?"

The fierce sound of the whispered words blasted her

as if he had shouted them. "I'm not going to kid you. For many years I blamed you for taking my big brother away from me. I hated you."

His harsh laugh echoed through the quiet. "And now you don't hate me." Disbelief resonated through his voice.

"No, I don't. I didn't lie when I told you I was falling in love with you."

"Please don't. I don't want to be responsible for you betraying your family on top of everything else."

"I'm not betraying them."

"I'll never be able to forget your mother yelling at me that I had destroyed her life. I dream about that."

"This isn't about my mother. This is about you and me."

"There is no you and me. I…" He took another step back until he bumped into the railing post.

She quickly covered the short distance, planting herself so he couldn't easily leave. "If that's how you feel, so be it. But I wanted you to realize how I feel."

"I know. Now I need to go." He started to push past her.

She moved into his path. "No, you don't know it all. And the least you can do for me is to listen until I'm through."

He inhaled a deep breath.

She felt the glare of his eyes boring into her although darkness now cloaked the porch totally. "When I came back to Cimarron City, I discovered you were still living here and a doctor. At first I didn't realize you were the pediatrician for Stone's Refuge, but when I discovered that, I considered leaving. I didn't see how I could work with the man who killed my brother."

"It does seem unbelievable." Sarcasm inched into his voice as he tried to distance himself as much as she allowed.

"Have you forgotten what Christ has taught us? To forgive those who trespass against us?"

"Yeah, but—"

"But, nothing." She gripped his arms. "I have forgiven you for what happened to Kevin. It was an *accident*."

His muscles beneath her palms bunched.

"You're a good man who deserves to really live his life. You've paid dearly over the years for the wreck. Don't you think it's time you stop beating yourself up over it?"

"Because you say so?"

She thrust her face close to his. "Yes!"

For a long moment tension continued to pour off him, then as if he had shut down his emotions, he closed himself off. "Is that all?"

All! She nodded, her heart climbing up into her throat.

"May I leave now?"

"Yes." She backed away from him.

It didn't matter to him that she had forgiven him. He couldn't forgive himself.

The sound of his footfalls crossing the porch bombarded her. This was the end.

She couldn't let him walk away without trying one more time to make him understand. "Jacob."

He kept walking toward his vehicle.

"Jacob, stop!"

He halted, his hand about to open the car door. The stiff barrier of his stance proclaimed it was useless for her to say anything. He wouldn't really hear.

She had to try anyway.

Hannah hurried toward him, praying he didn't change his mind and leave. She positioned herself next to him, hoping he would look at her.

He stared over the roof of the car into the distance. The lamplight that illuminated the sidewalk to the house cast a golden glow over them. She could make out the firm set to his jaw and the hard line of his mouth slashing downward.

"When I realized I'd finally forgiven you for what had happened to Kevin, I was free for the first time in twenty-one years. That's what forgiveness can do for you. Let it go."

He cocked his head to the side. "And just when did you decide to forgive me?"

"It wasn't a sudden revelation. But I knew when you took care of me and the children during the strep outbreak."

"And all the time before that?"

"I was fighting my growing feelings for you."

"And you lost."

"I don't look at it as losing. I want to see where our relationship can lead."

"Nowhere, Hannah. Nowhere. So why waste our time?" He wrenched open the door and climbed inside his car.

A few seconds later the engine roared to life, and Jacob sped away. As the taillights disappeared from view, she vowed she wouldn't give up on him.

Hannah leaned against the wall in the back of the rec room at the nursing home as the children began their play about the birth of Jesus. She scanned the crowd one more time, hoping she had overlooked Jacob, but he was nowhere in the audience. Her gaze fell upon Lisa in the front row with Cathy and she was glad that at least Andy had his mother at the play. But no Jacob, although he had promised the kids he would be at their production, via a phone call to Terry. Jacob hadn't been at the house in a week. He was avoiding her. She didn't need it written in the sky to know what Jacob was doing. She'd even thought briefly—very briefly—that maybe one of the children would get sick and she would have to take them to see Dr. Jacob.

Not having dated much, she wasn't sure what to do now. She missed him terribly. She hadn't realized how much until day three and she had reached for the phone at least ten times to call him. She hadn't, but the desire to had been so strong she had shaken with it.

Laura slid into place next to her and whispered, "He'll be here. He doesn't break a promise to the kids."

"There's always a first time." Hannah checked her watch for the hundredth time. "He has one minute before Susie and Terry appear as Mary and Joseph."

No sooner had she said Joseph than Jacob slipped into the room and eased into a chair in the back row at the other end of the room from where she was. Hannah straightened, folding her arms across her body.

Laura turned her head slightly toward her and cupped her hand over her mouth. "I told you he would be here."

"Shh. The play is about to start. I don't want to miss a word of it."

"Who are you kidding? You've heard the lines until I'm sure you can recite every one of them."

Hannah really tried to follow the children as they reenacted the story of the birth of Christ, but she continually found herself drawn back to Jacob, his strong profile a lure she couldn't resist. She came out of her trance when one of the lambs escaped and charged down the aisle toward the door by Jacob, baaing the whole way. The play stopped, and everyone twisted around in his seat to follow the animal's flight. Dressed in a gray suit, Jacob sprang to his feet and blocked its path to freedom, tackling it to the floor, its loud bleating echoing through the room.

"Got her." Jacob struggled to stand with the squirming animal fighting the cage of his arms.

As though the first lamb had signaled a mass bolt for all the animals, the other one broke free, probably because the young boy holding him had let go. Then the two dogs, portraying donkeys, up until this point perfectly content to sit by their handlers, chased after the second sheep. Kids scattered in pursuit of their fleeing pets.

Shocked at how quickly everything had fallen apart, Hannah watched the pandemonium unfold, rooted to her spot in the back along the wall. Then out of the corner of her eye, she saw a dog dart past her. She dived toward the mixed breed and captured it. Thankfully the mutt was more cooperative than Jacob's lamb. Taking the large dog by his collar, she led it back to the front where Peter was trying to bring some kind of order to the chaos.

Sprinkles of laughter erupted from the audience until all the elders joined in. One woman with fuzzy gray hair in the front row laughed so hard tears were running down her rouged cheeks, streaking her makeup.

"I think the show is over," Hannah said, clipping a leash on the dog she had.

"At least they were near the end." Jacob put his lamb down but held the rope tightly. "I'm not tackling this one again."

Hannah gave Jacob the leash then held up her hands to try and quiet the audience while Peter, Laura and Meg gathered the rest of the animals and the kids. Several times she attempted to say, "If everyone will quiet down," but that was as far as she got because no one was listening.

"Remember laughter is the best medicine." Jacob struggled to keep the lamb next to him.

Five minutes later only after Hannah whistled, the last strains of laughter died but whispering among the residents and children began to build. She quickly said, "There are refreshments in the lobby The children made them."

The word *refreshments* sparked the interest of several elders in the front, and they started moving toward the exit.

Slowly the rec room emptied with Laura and Meg taking the children who were serving the food.

Peter took one of the lambs and headed for the door. "I'll be back for the others."

That left Hannah and Jacob trying not to look at each other. Unsuccessful, she finally stepped into his line of vision. "We should talk."

He swung his gaze to her. "I'm not ready. I don't know if I'll ever be ready now that I know who you are."

"You make it sound like I've changed somehow. That I'm a different person. I'm still Hannah Smith. That's my legal name now. Not Hannah Collins."

"And every time I look at you I see Kevin. I should

have seen the resemblance. You have the same hair and eyes."

"Like millions of others."

He started to say something when Peter reentered the room. "I can help you with your animals." Jacob lifted the lamb into his arms, then tugging on the dog leash, walked toward his friend.

"Me, too." Hannah led her mutt along behind Jacob.

"I'll get the props," Peter called out.

Hannah barely heard the man, she was so intent on catching up with Jacob. She reached him in the parking lot at Peter's truck. He hoisted the lamb into its crate, then the dog. After taking care of the animals, Jacob stepped around Hannah and started to make his way back inside. She stopped him with a hand on his arm.

"Jacob—"

"Why did you tell me you were Kevin's sister?" His question cut her off.

And knocked the breath from her. The streetlight accentuated the harsh planes of his face, but distress rang in his voice. "Because I didn't want any secrets between us. You had shared yours. I had to."

"I feel like I'm reliving that night all over again."

She squeezed his arm as though to impart her support. "I didn't tell you to put you through that."

"What did you think I was going to do?"

"I don't know. But it was the right thing to do."

"For you."

She peered toward the building and saw Peter emerge. Through the floor-to-ceiling windows Hannah glimpsed the children playing host to the residents, serving them the refreshments and talking with them.

"The kids missed you this week. They've gotten used

to you coming to see them a lot. Please don't stay away because of me."

Jacob shifted away from her. "I've been especially busy. It's flu season."

"They wanted me to ask you to Sunday dinner tomorrow."

Jacob closed his eyes for a few seconds. "I can't." He strode away, not toward the nursing home but toward his car.

Her legs weak, Hannah leaned back against Peter's truck as the man came up with a box full of props.

"What's wrong with Jacob?" Peter slid the items into the bed of his pickup.

"I think I've ruined everything."

Chapter Twelve

"Dr. Jacob, you came!" Andy launched himself at Jacob and hugged him. "We've missed you."

"Where's Hannah? How's she feeling?" Jacob walked into the cottage, the scent of a roast spicing the air. His stomach rumbled its hunger.

"She's in her office," Susie said, looking too cheerful for someone who was concerned about Hannah's health.

"Office?" The way the twelve-year-old had described it on the phone to him half an hour ago, Hannah was dragging herself around the house, refusing to go to a doctor but desperately needing to see one. Reluctantly, he had agreed to come see what he could do.

Susie shrugged. "You know Hannah. She doesn't stop working for anything."

Knowing the way, Jacob headed back to Hannah's office. Before rapping on the door, he peered back at the end of the hallway and met several pairs of eyes watching him. The kids ducked back around the corner.

He knocked and waited for Hannah to invite him in. When half a minute passed and there wasn't a reply, he tapped his knuckles against the wood harder. Concerned, he decided to give her a couple more seconds before he went in without an invitation.

"Come in," a sleepy voice murmured from inside the room.

He inched the door open and peeped around it to find Hannah with her legs propped up in the lounger and only one dim lamp to illuminate the office. She blinked several times, as though disorientated, and straightened the chair to its upright position.

"Jacob, why are you here?" Drowsiness coated each word.

He slipped inside, aware of the children's whispering voices down the hall.

"Susie called and told me you weren't feeling well and wouldn't go see a doctor. She sounded very concerned, so I reassured her you would be all right. She wouldn't believe me until I agreed to come check you out." He crossed the room, pulling behind him a latticeback chair to sit in. "What's wrong?"

She scrunched up her forehead, then rubbed her fingers across it. "Just a headache. Nothing serious and Susie knew that. I took some pills and came in here to close my eyes until they started working. I must have fallen asleep."

"Then you're okay? No fatal disease?"

She chuckled. "Not that I know of."

"I think Susie should take up acting lessons. She had me convinced you were at death's door."

"I appreciate the concern, but I'm fine. Well, except the headache isn't totally gone. Nothing I can't handle, though." She sent him a smile that went straight to his heart and pierced through the armor he had around it.

"Then if you're all right, I'll be heading home." He started to stand.

"What time is it?"

Weary from many sleepless nights and long days at work, he sank back down and looked at his watch. "Six."

"Stay for dinner. I think what's really behind this little incident is that the kids miss you and want to see you more." Her gaze bored into him. "And so do I."

"To tell you the truth I've missed…coming here." He'd missed seeing the children but most of all Hannah. Yet how could he be with her, knowing who she really was? This woman had haunted his dreams lately. It was hard to look at her and not remember Kevin.

"I'm not going away. You need to learn to deal with my presence. Don't let the children suffer because of the past. When I first came to Stone's Refuge, I had to do the same thing. And I did."

He released a slow breath. "You play hardball."

She scooted to the edge of the lounger. "On occasion. When it's important."

"And this is important?"

"Yes."

He agreed—not just because of the children but because of the woman whose smile played havoc with his heart. Although there was no way he could now see a future with Hannah, maybe he could find a compromise and be her friend, especially if there were always kids around them.

He rose at the same time she did and nearly collided with her. Backing away quickly, he offered her a grin, hoping he appeared nonchalant when he didn't feel in the least that way. "Then I'll stay for dinner."

"No doubt Andy will want you to read him a bedtime story. He has a lot to tell you about him and his mother. She comes out here when she's not working and helps around the cottage."

"Noah's told me she's doing a good job at the restaurant."

"She's hoping to move out of the halfway house soon."

"What's the next step for her and Andy?" Jacob strode to the door but didn't open it yet.

"Once Lisa gets her own place, Andy will stay with her overnight, and we'll see how that goes."

"I hope for his sake that you're right about Lisa, but be careful. It doesn't take much for a drug addict to backslide." He hurriedly pushed away the memories of his own mother's downward spiral. Hopefully Lisa and his mother were different.

"Mom, let me help you with your bags." Masking her surprise behind a smile, Hannah opened the front door wider and scooped up one of the pieces of luggage. "Why didn't you tell me you were coming?" *Why didn't you return my calls?* was the question she really wanted to ask but not in the foyer where someone could overhear their conversation.

"I wasn't sure until a few days ago, and then I just decided to surprise you."

"How long are you staying?"

Karen Collins chuckled. "You know me. I never travel lightly. The weather in Oklahoma can be so unpredictable. It could snow one day and be warm and sunny the next." Her mother came into the cottage. "Hon, once when I lived here I can remember the weather dropping forty degrees in half a day. So where do I stay?"

"In my bedroom. I'll show you, then I'll introduce you to the kids. They're in the kitchen helping Meg with the Christmas cookies for the birthday party for Jesus tonight at the church."

"All eight of them?"

"Yes, it's a big kitchen." Hannah walked down the hall to her bedroom door and pushed it open to allow her mother to go inside first.

"And this is a nice-sized room, too."

"My bathroom is through there." Hannah pointed toward the entrance on the other side of the large bed. "I also have an office off the kitchen."

"And you like living here with eight children?"

"I love it." For the first time in years Hannah felt as if she had put down roots. To her the cottage was her home.

Her mother lifted her bag onto the king-size bed and opened it. "Where do I put my things?" When Hannah glanced from one piece of luggage to the other, Karen hurriedly added, "I'll only unpack part of my clothes."

"Well, in that case I have enough space in my closet, and I can clear out a drawer for you in the dresser."

"I know how much you've wanted kids in your life. Any prospects of a husband?" Hannah's mom hung up a dress and started back toward the bed.

As though they hadn't talked about Jacob at all, her mother as usual was avoiding the real issue and probably why she was here in the first place. "Yes, there is a man I'm interested in." Dread encased Hannah in a cold sweat.

Karen peered up at her as she shook out a shirt. "You are? That's wonderful. Who?"

The air in Hannah's lungs seemed to evaporate with that last question. She'd tried to tell her mother over the phone, but her mom had ignored all of her follow-up calls after the disastrous conversation. "Jacob Hartman."

Karen dropped the shirt. "I thought he was just the doctor here. Nothing more."

"Mom, I know this is a shock, but you wouldn't talk to me." Hannah rushed forward and drew her mother to the sitting area across the room. "Please don't say anything until you hear me out."

Karen pressed her lips together, surprise still registering on her face.

"I didn't realize Jacob was involved with Stone's Refuge until after I accepted the job here. I couldn't walk away. This is the perfect job for me." Hannah's heartbeat pounded like a kettledrum in a solemn procession. "Jacob is wonderful with the children. He's kind, caring and is trying desperately to make up for what happened all those years ago."

"You've forgiven him for what he did to your brother?"

The drumming beat of Hannah's heart increased. "It's the Christian thing to do, Mom. I know how you feel, but please give him a chance."

Karen shook her head slowly. "I don't know if I can. I never imagined you were dating the man." Again she shook her head. "Working with him is one thing, but getting involved romantically…"

"Get to know him like I did, and you'll see what a good man he is."

"Until you called a few weeks ago, I hadn't thought

about him in a long time. He consumed so much of my life for years that once I gave myself to Christ I just pushed memories of him away. I know how the Lord feels about forgiveness, but..." Tears shone in her mother's eyes. "It's so hard. Kevin is dead because of him."

"It was an accident, Mom."

"But he walked away from the wreck with few injuries."

"He may not have been injured much physically, but he was emotionally. His scars run deep."

"Will he be here tonight?"

"Yes."

"When is he coming?"

With a glance at her watch, Hannah rose. "He should be here within the hour. He promised the kids he would bring pizza tonight when he goes to pick up Andy's mother at the restaurant. She's going with us to church later."

"Is that the woman you've been helping?"

"Yes. I need to get back to the kitchen to help with the cookies." Hannah put her hand on the door. "Are you coming?"

Her mother pushed to her feet. "I'm really tired, honey. I'm going to rest for a while. You go on without me and don't worry about me."

Out in the corridor Hannah stared at the closed bedroom door, her stomach in snarls. She was all her mother had in the way of family, and she was afraid her mom wouldn't come out whenever Jacob was at the cottage.

Lord, please help Mom forgive Jacob as You helped me. I love both of them.

* * *

Hannah opened the back door to admit Jacob, who brought their dinner. "The kids were wondering where you were."

"Just the kids?" He waded his way through the mob of children, all wanting one of the pizza boxes.

"Me, too. I'm starved." She took several containers from him and began opening them. "Everyone, act civil. There's plenty to go around."

Jacob stepped away as soon as he lifted the lids and brushed some snowflakes from his coat and hair. "What have you all been doing? They've worked up quite an appetite."

"Is it snowing bad?" Hannah glanced at the window, but the curtains were drawn.

"No, not too much." Jacob removed his overcoat and slung it over the back of a chair.

While all the children were filling their plates with pizza, Andy stood off to the side, his gaze glued to the back door. "Where's Mom?"

Jacob looked around. "She isn't here?"

"No." Alarm pricked Hannah. "She was supposed to ride out here with you."

"The guy behind the counter said she left earlier. I thought she hitched a ride here with someone else." Jacob headed for the wall phone and punched in some numbers.

Concern creased Andy's forehead. "Where is she?"

"She's probably running late. Go on and get something to eat before there's nothing left." Hannah hoped she concealed her rising fear that all wasn't right with Lisa. She didn't want Andy to worry needlessly.

Coming up next to Jacob, she heard him say, "Give us a call if she arrives there."

When he hung up, she motioned with a nod for them to go into the hallway where Andy wouldn't overhear what they said. "Did you call the halfway house?"

"Yes, and they haven't seen her since she left for work this morning."

"What should we do?"

"Nothing."

"Nothing? We need to do something."

Jacob frowned. "What do you suggest?"

"I don't know. Go look for her."

"Where?"

Hannah shrugged, helplessness seizing her.

Andy poked his head around the kitchen door. "Something's wrong with Mom, isn't it?"

Hannah knelt in front of the boy and clasped his arms. "We don't know, hon."

Tears crowded his eyes. "Please find her."

Hannah glanced over her shoulder at Jacob, who nodded once. "Do you know anywhere she liked to go? A favorite place?"

Sniffling, Andy studied the floor by his feet. Finally he shook his head. "When she was gone, I never knew where she went."

Hannah rose. "I think Jacob and I have time to go to the halfway house and check with them before we go to church."

Andy's eyes brightened. "Maybe she went back to the old neighborhood."

"We'll go there, too." Jacob came forward. "Now, will you do me a favor, Andy?"

"Yes."

"Go eat some dinner and make sure everyone is ready to go to church on time."

"Sure." Andy straightened his slumped shoulders.

After the boy disappeared into the kitchen, Hannah asked, "Do you think she went back to her boyfriend?"

"Possibly. We've got a couple of hours to find her. Let's go."

"Will you tell Meg where we're going and if we aren't back in time to get Peter and Laura to take the children to church? I'll need to get my purse. Meet you back here in a few minutes."

Without waiting for an answer, Hannah hurried toward her bedroom. This wasn't the time for her mother to come out in case she had changed her mind. She needed to tell Jacob about her mom's surprise visit. In the quiet of his car would be the best place.

In her bedroom, she put a blanket over her mother who slept on top of her coverlet, then grabbed her purse and quickly left. Two minutes later she sat next to Jacob as he pulled away from the cottage.

"Everything okay in the kitchen?" Hannah fidgeted with the leather handle of her purse.

"Yeah. There's not much pizza left. I should have bought another one. You won't have anything to eat when we get back."

She pressed her hand over her constricted stomach. "I couldn't eat even if pizza was my favorite food."

"It isn't?" Mock outrage sounded in his voice. "Don't tell Noah."

"It'll be our secret." She paused. "Speaking of secrets. Well, this isn't exactly a secret. More of a surprise."

He slid a look toward her as he turned onto the highway. "What?"

"My mother came to visit this afternoon for a few days. She wanted to spend Christmas with me, and her employer gave her the time off at the last minute."

His harsh intake of air was followed by silence.

"This is just like Mom. When the mood strikes, she gets up and goes somewhere. She doesn't like staying still for long in any one place. There were many times while I was growing up that I left my things in boxes rather than unpack. It was easier that way." She heard her nervous chattering and wished she could see Jacob's face but the dark hid it.

"Does she know about me being involved in Stone's Refuge?"

"Yes."

"Before or after she came."

"Before."

"I'm sure that made her day. Why is she really here?"

"That's a good question. One I don't have an answer to."

Silence ate into her composure. She rubbed her thumb into her palm and tried to think of a way to make everything all right. *Lord, what do I do? How do I fix this?*

"Hannah, I'm sorry you had to tell your mother. I imagine that wasn't a nice reunion for you two."

"I told my mother that I had forgiven you for what happened with Kevin, that I cared about you." *That I want to be more than friends with you,* she wanted to add but realized at the moment Jacob wouldn't want to hear that.

His derisive laugh taunted her words. "She was thrilled, no doubt."

"I love my mother, but we don't always see eye to eye on things. This will just be another item added to the bottom of a long list."

"Don't you mean, added to the top?"

Before she could answer him, her cell phone blared with a drumroll. She fumbled for it in her purse and flipped it open. "Hello."

"Hannah?" A voice, barely audible, came through.

"Yes, who is this?"

"I'm in trouble."

Hannah sat up straight. "Lisa, where are you?"

"I'm near my old apartment. He's so angry."

"Who?"

"My ex-boyfriend," Lisa said in a raspy whisper.

"Jacob and I are on our way. We'll be—" The connection went dead.

Hannah snapped her cell closed. "Please hurry. Lisa's near her boyfriend's apartment. Something's wrong. She sounds…" She searched for a word to describe what she heard in the woman's voice beside fear.

"High?"

"Likely."

Jacob pressed down on the accelerator. He remembered the times he found his mother stoned. The memories, one after another, left him chilled in the car's heated air. That last night before the state took him away from her, the paramedics had said she'd been a few minutes away from death. If he hadn't come home… He shuddered and increased his speed even more.

Chapter Thirteen

"Oh, great! It's snowing even harder now. Normally I love to see it on Christmas Eve. Not this year." Hannah gripped the door handle, prepared to jump from the car the second Jacob parked.

"Why did she go with her ex?"

"Some women have a hard time breaking ties with men who've been in their life, even ones who have abused them."

Jacob took a corner too fast, and the car fishtailed on a slick area. The color leached from his face as he struggled to control his vehicle.

She gasped. For a few seconds her brother's wreck flittered across Hannah's mind as a telephone pole loomed ahead.

Steering into the skid, he slowed his speed. Finally he managed to right the car, missing the curb and pole by a couple of feet. "Sorry," he bit out between clenched teeth, his white-knuckle grasp on the wheel tightening.

"It's okay. We need to get to Lisa before her boy-friend finds her."

"It's not okay!" Although the words came out in a

harsh whisper, the power behind them hung in the air, reinforcing the barrier that he had erected between them. "I could have…"

His unfinished sentence lingered. She touched his arm.

He swallowed hard. "I know better. I couldn't live with myself if I caused something to happen to you, too." He retreated into stony silence as he negotiated the city streets.

"I forgave you, Jacob. There were no strings attached to that forgiveness."

"How could you?"

She felt as though she was fighting for the most important thing in her life. "Because I love you. Love yourself."

He shook off her arm, his jaw set in a grim line. His scowl told of the war of emotions raging inside him. She wanted so much to comfort him but knew he would reject it—reject her. All she could do now was pray and turn it over to the Lord.

When the apartment building came into view, Hannah bent forward, scouring the area around it for any sign of Lisa. Jacob brought the car to a stop in front. Hannah leaped from the vehicle and raced toward the entrance.

Jacob halted her progress. "What do you think you're doing?" His hand immediately fell away as if touching her was distasteful.

Snowflakes caught on her eyelashes. She blinked and looked up into his fierce expression. "Going inside to see if Lisa is with him."

"Let's check outside first. That's where she was when she called."

"Okay, I'll look down this side. You go over there." She waved toward the area across the street.

"No, we go together in case the boyfriend is looking for her, too."

"But it will go faster if—"

"I don't want you meeting up with him alone." His determination, a tangible force, brooked no argument.

"Fine. Then let's get moving. We're wasting time." Frustrated, worried, she stalked down the street.

Passing an alley, Hannah walked down its length, inspecting every place someone could hide. Nothing. Back out on the sidewalk, she continued, stopping at the quick market on the corner, the only place open on Christmas Eve.

"Let's check inside. Maybe she's hiding in here since it's cold and snowing," she said as she entered the store.

While she went up and down the aisles, Jacob questioned the clerk at the counter. When she finished her search, she came back to his side.

"If she comes back in, tell her Jacob and Hannah are looking for her and to wait here." Jacob took her elbow and led the way to the door. "She was here about fifteen minutes ago, using the phone in the back. When a man came in that fits the description of her boyfriend, she must have fled. The clerk didn't see her leave, but he thinks she went out the back way."

"Then he may not have found her."

"The clerk told the man she was on the phone in the back."

"No! How could he?"

"He was scared. He knows who Carl is and doesn't want to have any trouble with him."

"Did he call the police?"

"No."

Lord, please put Your protective shield around Lisa.

"We've got to find her first." Hannah rounded the corner of the store, making her way to the back where Lisa would have come out.

Footsteps in the continually falling snow led away from the door, heading toward an alley nearby. Another set had joined the first.

"She's running." Jacob pointed at the long stride between each print.

"He isn't, as if he's stalking her and knows he'll catch her."

"With this snow, it'll be hard for her to hide from him."

"But we can track her, too." Hannah hurried her pace.

The darkness of the alley obscured part of the footprints, but the occasional light from a window showed them the way—as well as Carl. At one place Lisa must have tried to go into a building, but the door was locked.

Jacob slowed, putting his arm out to halt Hannah. "Call 9-1-1."

She squinted into the dimness and glimpsed what he'd seen. A still body curled into a ball in the snow, a fine layer of the white stuff covering the person. She dug into her pocket and pulled out her cell, making the call while Jacob stooped and brushed the snow off the body, revealing Lisa.

After talking to the 9-1-1 operator, Hannah knelt next to Jacob. "Is she alive?"

"Yes." Removing a penlight from his pocket, he began to check out Lisa's injuries. "She's got a lump on the back of her head."

A snow-covered pipe lay a few feet away, a stream of light from the building illuminating it.

A moan escaped Lisa's lips. "No, don't." She raised her arm as though she were fending off a blow. Her eyes bolted open. She saw Jacob, and her arm fell to the pavement. "I'm sorry. I'm sorry." Tears streamed down her cheeks and blended with the melted snow on her face.

Hannah leaned close. "Lisa, I'm going to wait for the police and ambulance at the end of the alley. You're going to be all right. Jacob will take care of you."

Jacob paced the waiting room, wearing a path in front of Hannah's chair. "We should have heard something by now."

"Carl beat her up pretty badly. Thankfully Lisa was conscious enough to tell us what drug she took before she passed out again."

Jacob paused before her. "Let's hope the police have brought him in by now."

"One less drug dealer on the streets."

"But for how long?"

"Do you think Lisa will testify against him?"

"No." He pivoted and started pacing again. "She's afraid of him and rightly so."

"We've got to be there for her. Maybe then she will."

"Maybe." But skepticism drenched his voice.

An emergency-room doctor appeared in the doorway. "Jacob, I heard you found the woman. Does she have any kin?"

"A son staying at Stone's Refuge. Otherwise, I don't think so. How is she?"

"A concussion, two cracked ribs and some cuts and

bruises. I think the man had a ring on that left his mark as he was pounding on her."

Chilled, Hannah stood and clasped her arms, running her hands up and down to warm herself. "May we see her now?"

"They're taking her upstairs to a room. Give them fifteen minutes to get her settled in, then you can see her. I want to keep her overnight for observation. If she does okay, she can go home tomorrow."

After the doctor left, Hannah sighed. "We need to get Andy. I promised him we would."

Jacob glanced at his watch. "He should be at the church with the others right now. I'll go pick him up and bring him back to see his mother while you go talk to her."

"She'll want to see you and thank you, Jacob."

"I don't know if that would be a good idea."

"Because she had a relapse?"

"Some things never change."

"Lisa is human. She made a mistake. We all do. God forgives us thankfully, so the least we can do is try to do the same."

His gaze sliced through Hannah. "I'll be back later with Andy." Jacob strode from the waiting room before he said something he would regret. He'd heard the censure in her voice. But Hannah hadn't lived with a drug addict. He had. His mother had ruined her life and had been well on the way to doing the same with his.

No, you did a good job of that yourself that night you killed Kevin. What she started, you finished.

His guilt that was always there swelled to the foreground, threatening to swamp him. Up until the appearance of Hannah in his life he'd managed to cope with what he had done. Now he didn't know if he could continue to work with the children at Stone's Refuge and see her. He'd thought he could, but he wanted more. He wanted a wife and a family—with Hannah. But how could they ever be really happy with what happened always hanging between them? How could she have really forgiven him?

Jacob found a parking space in the nearly full lot at the church and walked toward the entrance. The snow had stopped and a white blanket muffled the sounds, making it serenely quiet. Christmas music wafted from the sanctuary, reminding him how special this time of year was. He entered the place of worship and stood in the back, searching for the large group from the refuge. He caught Peter's gaze, and his friend leaned around Laura to let Meg know Jacob was there.

Andy exited the pew and started for him. Following close behind the boy was a woman whose image was burned into his memory. For a few seconds the remembrance whisked him back to the hospital corridor where Hannah's mother had accused him of ruining her life, that he might as well have killed her, too. Emotions so strong he staggered back a couple of steps inundated him as his gaze locked with Kevin's mother's.

Around him the congregation sang "O Holy Night" while Jacob desperately tried to compose himself enough to deal with her and Andy. He knew one thing as the distance disappeared between—that he didn't want the parishioners to witness the scene. Fumbling for the handle, he wrenched open the door to the sanctuary and escaped out into the empty lobby.

Why now, Lord?

No answer came as Andy and Karen Collins halted

in front of him. His attention remained glued to the older woman, who was slightly heavier and with strands of gray hair, but otherwise the same as twenty-one years before.

"Dr. Jacob, is my mother all right? Did you find her?"

Andy's voice drew his gaze to the boy standing half a foot away, his head upturned, his eyes large with fear and worry in their depths.

Jacob forced a smile of reassurance. "She's going to be fine."

"Where is she?"

"At the hospital."

Panic widened the boy's eyes even more. "She's hurt!"

"Hannah is there with her. I've come to take you to see her." Jacob settled his hands on the boy's shoulders, compelling the child's full attention. "She has a lump on her head and some cuts and bruises, but she'll mend just fine. She's going to need you to be strong. Can you do that for her?"

Andy drew himself up tall. "Yes."

"Where's your coat?"

The boy pointed toward the hallway that led to the classrooms. "Back there."

"Go get it, then we'll leave."

The second the child disappeared down the corridor Jacob's gaze fastened on Kevin's mother. So many things he wanted to say swirled in his mind, but none formed a coherent sentence.

"Hannah said you were wonderful with the children. She's right."

Her words, spoken with no anger, confounded Jacob. He stared at her, speechless.

"When Hannah first told me today you two were more than associates, that you were…friends, I didn't know what to say to her. After she left to go with you, I had a long talk with God. I wanted to tell you that I've forgiven you for what happened, too. As my daughter pointed out to me, it was an accident that ended tragically for my son. What I said to you in the hospital that day was grief talking, but it took me years to realize that. It took finding the Lord and my daughter's example to see what I needed to do. I'm sorry for what I said."

Jacob heard her, but the words wouldn't register. "How can you say that?"

She smiled. "Stop blaming yourself for something that was out of your control."

Out of the corner of his eye, Jacob glimpsed Andy coming back. He rushed to the boy and clasped his hand. "We need to get to the hospital," was all he could think to say.

A few minutes later he headed his car away from the church, still grappling with what Hannah's mother had said.

"You aren't kidding me, are you? Mom is okay?"

"I promise. I'd never kid you about something like that. She's staying overnight at the hospital and hopefully will go home tomorrow."

"I won't get to see her on Christmas?"

"I'll make sure you do. I'll pick her up and bring her to the cottage to spend some time with you if the doctor says it's okay."

Andy heaved a long sigh. "Good. I don't want her being alone on Christmas. She needs me."

Shouldn't it be the other way around? "You aren't mad at her for all that's happened?" The question slipped out before Jacob could snatch it back.

"No."

"Why not?"

"I love her."

Is love the key? If you love someone enough, you forgive them?

God loved us so much that he gave His only son for our salvation. Hannah had said Christ has taught us to forgive, that she had learned from the Master Himself.

Could he? Can the Lord forgive him for taking another's life? Could he forgive himself for surviving the car wreck? Could he forgive his mother for his childhood?

If he wanted any kind of life, he needed to figure that out.

"Where's Dr. Jacob?" Hannah asked as Andy came into the hospital room.

"He needed to go see someone. He told me Peter will come and take us home." The boy walked to his mother's bed and took her hand.

Lisa's eyes fluttered open. "Andy," she said groggily.

"How are you?" The child's voice thickened with tears.

"Hey, baby. Don't cry. I'm gonna be fine thanks to Hannah and Jacob." She closed her eyes for a few seconds. "I love ya."

Andy lay his head near his mother's. "I love ya, Mom. Dr. Jacob said ya could come to the cottage tomorrow if the doctor says so."

"That's…great. I can't…" Sleep stole Lisa's next words.

"Let's go home and let your mother rest. You'll see her tomorrow morning. We'll come up here early."

"Are ya sure?"

"Yep. It won't really be Christmas without your mother there." Hannah draped her arm over Andy's shoulder and led the way into the hallway.

At the elevator the doors swished opened, and Peter stepped off.

"We were coming downstairs to wait for you." Hannah let the elevator close behind her employer. "Church is over already?"

"No, but I thought I would come right away. It's been a long day for you all."

"Yes, and it's not over yet." She needed to find Jacob.

"My car is in the front parking lot." Peter punched the down button.

"Peter, can you do me a favor?" Hannah got on the elevator when it arrived.

"Sure."

"I need to pay a visit to someone. Can you drop me off then take Andy to the cottage?"

"Yes."

Andy glanced back at Hannah. "Hey, are ya gonna visit the same person as Dr. Jacob?"

"I might be," she said while Peter shot her a speculative look.

In Peter's car Hannah started to tell him to take her to Jacob's apartment. Then suddenly she realized that wasn't where he had gone. She knew where he was and told Peter.

At the cemetery Hannah saw Jacob's car parked close to where her brother was buried. "Right here. I'll have Jacob bring me home."

Peter looked out the windshield. Although night-time, the snow brightened the surrounding area. "Are you sure about this?"

"I'm very sure." Hannah glanced in the backseat at Andy, who had fallen asleep. "I need to make Jacob understand what it means to really forgive someone."

"Forgive?"

"I'll explain later." Hannah slid out of the car, and without peering back, walked toward the man she loved.

The next few minutes would determine the rest of her life. She firmed her resolve when Jacob lifted his head and glanced toward her. His eyes widened.

"How did you know I would be here?"

"You come every Sunday afternoon and put flow-ers on my brother's grave. I've known for some time."

"But this isn't Sunday afternoon."

"True. But I figured you might be here. I had Peter drop me off, so I'll need a ride home. Will you give me one?"

Nonplussed, he blinked. "Sure," he said slowly, rak-ing his hand through his hair.

A snowflake fell, then another one.

"This is the season for hope, for new beginnings. When I came to Cimarron City, I never thought I would come face-to-face with my past, but I did. The Lord gave me a chance to right a wrong by coming here. It's not right for you to stop living because of what hap-pened. Kevin would be the first person to tell you that. I lo—"

Jacob pressed his index finger against her lips to hush her words. "I need to say something first, Han-nah. Then you can. Please?"

She nodded.

The snow increased, causing Hannah to step nearer his body's warmth. He encircled her in a loose embrace, tilting her chin up so she looked into his eyes.

"Over the years this has become the place that I come to think, to work through my problems. I feel as if I've continued my friendship with Kevin. That was important for me to believe. It kept the pain to a dull ache. Then you came into my life and made me really feel for the first time since the accident. I wanted it all—a wife, children, my life back. I just didn't know how to go about getting it."

Hope flared in her. "And you do now?"

"You were right. I have to start by forgiving myself and asking the Lord for forgiveness. That's what I've been doing."

"It's not just yourself you need to forgive but your mother, too. What happened to you as a child has ruled your life too long. Don't let it govern your future, too."

One corner of his mouth lifted. "I'm working on that. Being around Lisa has helped me see another side to the situation. An addiction isn't easy to break. People with them need support and help, not condemnation."

She snuggled against him, seeking his warmth and nearness. "Realistic support and help. You have to know when to cut your losses, like with Nancy's mother."

"I want to be there for Lisa and Andy. I want it to work for them."

"Then we will be."

He tightened his arms about her. "I like how you use the word *we*. Hannah Collins Smith, I love you and I want to see where this relationship can go."

She chuckled. "Personally I'm hoping it leads to a house full of children, adopted and our own."

He bent his head toward hers. "I love your way of thinking."

Softly his lips grazed across hers, then took possession in a kiss that sealed an unspoken promise to love each other through the best and worst of times.

Epilogue

"This is my bedroom?" Nancy asked, standing in the doorway of a room with white furniture, a pink canopy on the bed and pink lacy curtains. "All by myself?"

Hannah entered and turned to face the seven-year-old. "Yep. Every square inch of it. What do you think?"

The little girl clapped her hands and twirled around. "I love it! I've never had my own room."

Hannah's gaze found her husband's, and a smile spread through her as she basked in the warmth of Jacob's regard. "We have a lot of bedrooms to fill."

Jacob placed his hand over Hannah's rounded stomach. "I don't think we've done too bad in a year's time. Two children and one on the way."

"Just think what we can do with a little more time," Hannah said with a laugh, thoughts of their wedding exactly a year ago producing a contentment in her that she had never thought possible until Jacob.

Terry skidded to a halt outside the bedroom and poked his head in. "Welcome to the family, Nancy."

The little girl beamed from ear to ear. "Thanks."

"Have you checked out the backyard?"

Nancy shook her head.

"C'mon. I'll show you the doghouse Jacob and I built for Abby."

As their new daughter raced after Terry, Jacob pulled Hannah back against him and ringed his arms about her. "We need to start working on the adoption papers for Gabe."

"And Susie."

His breath fanned her neck as he nibbled on her ear. "And then another of our own."

"We're gonna run out of bedrooms at this rate real quickly."

"Then we'll add on. We have the room, thanks to Peter."

Hannah swept around to face him. "Living in our own home on the ranch is the best of both worlds. I'm near my job as manager of the refuge and we have plenty of room for our children."

"Not to mention the pets they will have."

"Peter probably will never have to go out looking for homes for his animals."

"Especially with Terry as our son. With the addition of Abby we now have a cat, rabbit and two dogs."

"Just so long as we never have a snake as a pet. I draw the line at that."

"Sure, Mrs. Hartman," he murmured right before planting a kiss on her mouth. "Of course, you're going to have to tell Gabe he can't bring his garter snake with him when he comes to live with us."

She pulled back. "When did he get one?"

"He found it yesterday when Andy was visiting the refuge."

"Which reminds me, I'd better get downstairs and

start lunch. Lisa and Andy should be here soon for Nancy's party. She's coming early to help me set up."

He draped his arm around her shoulder and started for the hallway. "You still don't trust me in the kitchen?"

"No, but I trust you with my heart."

* * * * *